DOMINATION

Book 2 of the One True Child Series

Between the Lines
PUBLISHING

Liminal Books is an imprint of Between the Lines Publishing. The Liminal Books name and logo are trademarks of Between the Lines Publishing.

Cover design by Cherie Fox

Between the Lines Publishing
9 North River Road, Ste 248
Auburn ME 04210
btwnthelines.com

First Published: 2018
Original ISBN (Paperback) 978-0-9996556-6-5
Original ISBN (eBook) 978-0-9996556-8-9

Second edition:
ISBN: (Paperback) 978-1-950502-78-3
ISBN: (Ebook) 978-1-950502-80-6
ISBN: (Hardcover) 978-1-950502-79-0

Also available from L.C. Conn

Realm of Dragons: Fight for the Crown

The One True Child Series

Sentinels (Book 1)

DOMINATION

Book 2 of the One True Child Series

L.C. Conn

Dedicated to my wonderful husband. Thank you for putting up with my blank stares, mutterings, sudden exclamations and note making.

Chapter One

The thick and hazy mist swirled over the water and crept through the reeds at the side of the still loch as a ghostly white swan emerged from it, gliding silently as it looked for its morning meal. An eerie quiet had descended over the bank, punctuated occasionally by a crack of wood, and quickly followed by a splash, making the little girl hiding in the thick reeds jump at the noise. She shivered. Huddled amongst the reeds on the edge of the loch all night, she was cold, cramped, and tired. The noises that had frightened her during the long night were now gone, but she was still too scared to move. She hugged herself, trying to get warm, while her baby teeth chattered.

Her father had woken her and told her to hide. They had come again—the raiders who had burnt their home the last time—and so she ran. The light from the fire had brightened the dark night, and she sank down as low as she could to stay hidden with her hands over her ears as she watched the shadowy figures. But she could still hear the screams of her mother and the growl and shouts of her father as he tried to defend the family and their home. She also heard the men who attacked them. Their yells and cruel laughter as her baby brother had cried out with ear-piercing screams into the night.

Now it was quiet.

The grumbling of her stomach finally made her move and she stood up and stretched. Her clothing was wet and heavy, clinging to her legs. Walking along the shoreline, she made her way back carefully on quiet, bare feet as the mud sucked at them. The smell of damp ash filled her nostrils before she reached the wooden walkway to her home that sat out over the loch. She could not see it through the thick mist and started to make her way slowly over the little bridge, holding on tightly to the railing. The smell was getting stronger, along with another scent that stung her nose. Pieces of burnt and charred wood floated by her, bobbing on the small waves as she made her way closer.

The white mist parted before her with a burst of the early morning breeze, and the remains of their home lay in shattered and blackened pieces. Lazy coils of blue smoke lifted and shifted in the now moving air as the embers still determinedly consumed the wood. She stared at it. In the wreckage she could see her brother's small cot and beside it lay the charred remains of her mother, her arm resting protectively across the tiny bed. Of her father there was no sign.

A blue tattooed arm reached around her tiny waist and lifted her up, carrying her away from the dreadful sight. It stayed with her as she struggled and fought to be let go. With all her might she bit, and she scratched at that arm, trying to break free. But it held on tightly. She was put down, turned, and when she saw who her captor was, gave a great sob and clung to her uncle. She cried into his large shoulder as she finally realised her family was gone. He held her gently until her grandmother came to take his place. The old woman picked her up and carried the small child farther away from the shore.

"Breena and Carvorst need to be sent off properly. Talorgan, go fetch the druid," the gruff voice of her uncle told someone. "Get the child home, Ma. Bron is waiting for news."

The old woman carried the child for as long as she could beside the loch. The remains of the mist were still swirling and eddied around them, and the tears had long since dried. Her grandmother was telling her stories, trying to keep her calm and quiet. The girl loved the stories and remembered running to see her grandmother to hear them—and getting told off by her mother when she came back.

Grandmother put her down and stopped to rest. She stretched her back a bit and then held onto the child's tiny hand. They walked in silence along the little path, and whenever they heard a noise, she would stop and wait. Threading their way through a group of trees, they came to a clearing and a man stepped out in front of them.

He was tall and had a helmet on his head. A red cloak was gathered around him against the cold and damp, and his legs were bare except for the boots he wore, with their many laces. He held in one hand a spear and long shield in the other. With the surprise of suddenly seeing them appear from the trees, he pointed the spear at the old woman and young child.

In a language she couldn't understand he called out. His voice was loud in the quiet of the morning and the mist that still clung to the shore, and it carried far. She heard other feet come running. The jangling of their armour rang out, announcing their whereabouts. Grandmother tried to get away, her fingers digging into the girl's arm as she began to drag the child along, but they were met by another man standing at their back. The shield was up, and the spearhead was pointed at the chest of the unarmed old woman.

Grandmother picked the little girl up and held her close. Turning all around, she looked for an escape, but there was none. They were surrounded and herded further up the track. The child clung to her grandmother's neck, her blue eyes open wide with fright at the sight of the men and their yelling. Tears spilled down her face, leaving clean marks on the sooty skin of her cheeks.

They were pushed into a clearing and found themselves hemmed in by a group of large men. Most laughed at the bedraggled pair as they moved through their ranks, while others were bored and looked away. Grandmother was led to stand in front of a young man with dark hair and hazel eyes, and she placed the girl onto her own feet but clung tightly to her small hand. The man looked down his large, hooked nose at the pair and spoke. Grandmother was forced to her knees and stripped. The man shook his head and a spear entered Grandmother's back, exiting through her chest as she screamed.

The child stood there in shock.

The blood splattered over her face, and she watched her grandmother topple to the ground when the spear was pulled from her body. She let out a scream of her own as the old woman let go of her hand and lay on the ground, gurgling dark blood in great clots from her mouth. The body was dragged away, leaving a trail of blood over the green grass and leaf litter. The child heard a splash as they threw her beloved grandmother into the loch.

A rough hand landed on her shoulder. It was heavy and hard as it turned and pushed her closer to the man. He looked at her and made a gesture with a few words. Cold water from a skin was splashed on her face to rid it of the mix of blood, soot, and dirt. Her tears coursed down her cheeks with it, dripping unnoticed from her chin. The man reached up and turned her head, first one way and then the other. He opened her mouth and felt her limbs. He made a comment to another, and she was taken away. The soldier held on firmly as another tied her hands tightly, then lifted her easily onto the back of a large grey horse. The soldier stayed with her, his hand on her leg keeping her in place.

The young man with the hazel eyes climbed up behind her. With one arm he held her gently against him, so she did not slip off, while the other grasped the reins. Slowly he kicked the flanks of the large animal and it moved off with their horse in the lead. She did not know what to make of it all. Her family was dead, her grandmother killed in front of her eyes, and now she was being taken from the world she knew. It was all too much for her to take in.

Fresh tears snaked down her face, dripping from her chin, and she sniffed loudly. She felt him lean down and speak in her ear, so close she could feel his breath hot on her cheek. She could not understand the words he spoke, but there was a kindness to his voice. The kindness could not stop the tears, though, and they continued to fall.

For two days she travelled with them. At night he would sit by the fire with her, trying to get her to talk and make her smile. She gathered that his name was Marcus by the way he was pointing to himself. When he would point to her, she would shake her head. The girl fully understood what he wanted but refused to give it to him.

This interaction would start over again. He gestured to himself, telling his name, and then at her again, waiting with a smile of encouragement for her to reply. Her mother had always told her names were important in their family and not to give them away to strangers easily. They were a key of some kind. When the man finally got frustrated enough, he gave her a name.

"Tacita," he said, smiling and pointing to her. The men around her laughed when they heard it and all nodded. She felt it was a joke of some kind and she did not like it. She wished they would stop.

On the afternoon of the second day, she saw a wall emerge between the flicking ears of the horse she was riding. It was a large wooden structure, bigger than she had ever seen before. It was surrounded by an earth bank in front of it, with a ditch that was deep and full of sharpened stakes. An enormous gate made of heavy planks and strengthened with great beams was standing open, and they passed through. Marcus stopped to speak to the man who was standing on guard, and he laughed at the guard's reply, then followed the marching soldiers. The rest of the men peeled off and headed down another road while Marcus stayed on the road they were on. An imposing house made of stone and wood loomed before them in the center of the camp.

Marcus climbed down and lifted her gently off the horse, and a soldier led it away. He placed her on her feet and was talking to her as he gently untied her hands. The marks of the rope were red on her wrists as she rubbed at them, until Marcus took her small hand in his. It felt rough, calloused, and hot as he led her inside. The only word she recognised while he talked was "Tacita."

They climbed the stairs and entered the building, with his laced boots clicking on the small tiles laid into the floor. The girl stared at the patterns and pictures, watching as they swirled and curled back on themselves, surrounding pictures of animals she had never seen before. The walls were also decorated with vines and foliage, framing pictures of women and men in brightly coloured clothing, both sitting and standing. They were the most amazing pictures she had ever seen, and she wondered about the stories that went with them. She did not have time to see them properly as Marcus pulled her along when she slowed.

They came to a large door, and Marcus stood for a moment before he knocked on the stained timber. A deep voice called out from within, and he opened it, tugging her on as they entered. Inside, a man was leaning on a table, looking at something that lay there. While Marcus stood and waited until he was acknowledged, the girl studied the man as he concentrated on the paper before him. He was old—older than her uncle—but not as old as her grandmother. He was lean and muscular and was dressed in a short tunic with soft sandals on his feet. Around his middle was a large belt with a knife hanging from it.

"Marcus, my son, welcome back. I trust you have had some success?" The man pushed himself away from the table and came to stand in front of the young man, extending an arm for him to take. Marcus gripped his father's forearm tightly in greeting.

"Yes, my commander. The chief was killed, and his house burnt to the ground—or water, in this case—just as you ordered," Marcus replied with a curt nod.

"Good. That is one less who can rebel against us. Were there any casualties on our side?"

"There were none, my commander."

"Excellent." The older man turned and sat down in a seat, picked up a richly decorated cup, and drank deeply from it. "Come sit."

"Thank you, Father." Still holding the child's hand, he moved to the opposite stool and sat down, leaving the girl to stand.

"Who is this? Not been getting some camp whore pregnant, I hope?" The older man chuckled.

"Not me, Father. This is the daughter of the chief we have just dealt with. We found her the next day in the company of an old woman who was too old to be of any service, so I had her killed. But this young one may become useful."

"Forward planning; well done. Come here, child." The old man beckoned to her, but the girl did not understand and stared at him.

"Tacita," Marcus called to her, and she turned her head toward him. He motioned her to go over to his father.

"Tacita? An uncommon name for a Pict," the commander said with raised eyebrows.

"I named her. She hasn't spoken a word since she was found. God knows I have tried to get her to talk."

"An apt one, then, meaning mute." Again, the older man called her over.

The child walked hesitantly to him, and he looked her over, checking her teeth and her eyes as if she were a horse. His rough hands checked her limbs and he nodded to his son as she stepped back as soon as he had let her go.

"Very sound. Diana is looking for a new handmaiden, so I think she will do nicely. We have a few of her kind as slaves here at the house, so they can teach her how to speak properly. I am sure you are right. When the time comes, she may become a very useful tool, and a pretty one with that golden hair."

Without any warning the door opened, allowing the entrance of a very striking and tall woman. Her dark hair was piled up on her head and held there with ribbons laced through it. Her dress was long and was the most beautiful shade of blue the child had ever seen. She stared openly at the newcomer. Marcus stood up when he saw her, and his face reddened a little.

"I told you that Marcus would be home again today, Diana." The old man laughed and then motioned to the child. "He has even brought you a gift."

The woman glanced at the dirty, bedraggled girl, and dismissed her almost immediately before turning her hard eyes back to the two men.

"Welcome back, Marcus. We had hoped you would be back yesterday. Marinus has been lonely without his favourite son to carouse with." She sat down beside her husband.

"Are you not going to even look at the prize he brought home for you? She even has an apt name, for apparently, she does not speak," Marinus said with a smile.

"You could have washed and dressed it appropriately first, Marcus. Is it a boy or girl?" Diana asked, as she studied the child a little more closely.

"A girl, Stepmother, and I have been calling her Tacita," Marcus supplied.

"I will look at her once she is clean. Who is she, then?" Although Diana asked the question, she did not seem to be really interested.

"The daughter of a meddlesome chief we have been having problems with. He and the rest of his family were killed, and their hovel of sticks burnt to the ground. The child must have been hiding somewhere," Marcus replied.

"Take her away and put her in the care of my woman Brietta," Diana ordered him. "She can clean her up."

"I've been on the road too long and need the baths myself. I'll take her now to Brietta and see you both later for the evening meal." Marcus stood and moved over to the girl. He took her hand gently and started to lead her out.

"We will be having guests tonight, Marcus, in celebration of your victory. A few of the merchants' daughters will be there. I hope you make a favourable impression," Marinus said with an evil smile. The look on Diana's face was stone.

The door shut behind them with a bang, and the girl jumped. She had not understood a single word they were saying, and she did not like the look of the woman at all. She got the impression that the lady was not easily pleased. They headed further into the house, and Marcus opened another door. Inside a woman was sitting sewing. She looked up quickly at the disturbance and stood immediately when she saw who had entered.

The pair chatted for a moment while they were looking at her, and then Marcus knelt beside her. He was speaking again while his hands held her arms. His hazel eyes were kind and concerned, but the girl was uncertain and worried. He stood and left her there with the woman.

"Let's have a look at you," the woman said kindly with words the child could understand, and she sat down again. "What is your name, child?"

The girl shook her head. The woman had bright blue eyes and pale ginger hair, and she smiled at her.

"Are you one of the clans or of The People?" she asked gently.

These were words she knew. Her mother had been trying to teach her the family history and the difference between the clans and The People. If this woman knew of them, then she may be trusted.

"Ma said I was both," she finally said quietly.

"Which is which? Was your father a clansman, then, or was it your mother?"

"Da was clan and Ma People."

"I am of The People, too. Do you know your sigil?"

The girl nodded. "Boar."

"Ah, a mighty group. I am of the Serpent," she said giving the girl a small sad-looking smile. "What is your name, child?"

"Carling."

"It is nice to meet you, Carling. I am Brietta. You have been placed in my care to get you clean and teach you how to speak their tongue."

"You sounded just like them," Carling told her.

"I am lucky. Did your mother talk to you about the abilities?"

"Yes."

"Well, I have the ability to understand other languages. But it is probably best that you don't mention them here. These Romans don't know about them," Brietta warned her.

"I won't," Carling replied, shaking her head.

"Right. Well, let's get you sorted then. There are some old clothes from the commander's young daughter that should fit you. I want you to stay right here. I will be back in a moment," Brietta told her.

She was soon back with some tunics in her hands, and she held them up against the child. The soft fabric flowed down past Carling's legs and puddled on the floor at her feet. They were a bit long, but Brietta seemed to be happy with them.

Brietta took her by the hand, and they left the large building to walk through the streets. There was so much to look at as they made their way, her head turned constantly to take it in all the sights and sounds. As they walked, a few men were whistling and calling out to the woman at Carling's side, but Brietta ignored them. Her head was held high, and her eyes were planted ahead at the building they moved towards, and as they entered, the noise of both men and women talking inside increased.

Brietta handed a small, round object to a man in the doorway, and they passed through another. Quickly the woman stripped off their clothing and tossed it to one side, then lifted Carling into a pool of water. It was warm and took the girl by surprise. Her head was dunked under the water and

Brietta started to run her fingers through the tangled blonde hair, pulling at the knots. Lifting her out, she held her hand again and went to another room, this one noticeably hotter. The steam in the air hung and swirled whenever someone walked through it, and she began to sweat. Brietta put her into another pool, and Carling cried out at the heat. It was only a quick dunking this time and she was pulled out.

Brietta picked up a bottle and motioned away a man who was walking toward Carling. She poured the liquid onto her hand and rubbed it over Carling's little body then took up a stick and started to scrape at her skin to take the oil and dirt away. Another dunking in the warm pool, and Brietta dried both off with a cloth and dressed herself before clothing Carling in the tunic they had brought with them.

"How are those ponds hot?" Carling asked as the tunic was pulled over her head. Brietta tied a cord around her waist and hitched the fabric through it to keep the hem off the ground.

"They are very clever, these Romans," Brietta answered. "They heat the water from underneath."

Very carefully, the woman pulled a comb through Carling's blonde hair until it was neat and knot-free. While she was combing, she checked for lice and was pleased to find the child pest-free. She took the girl's hand and made their way to the exit, where their path was barred by two large, hairy men.

To Carling they looked menacing with their dark hair and eyes. Brietta was talking fast and telling them something until there was a shout that made everyone stop talking. The two men looked around and left quickly, revealing Marcus looking after them with an angry stare, his hair still wet and his face flushed from the heat. He looked down and said something to Carling.

"He said you look very pretty and that you look like a proper Roman lady," Brietta translated for her, clearly a little uncomfortable with the way he had talked to Carling.

Marcus spoke again, and the name he had given her was mentioned. Brietta replied to him, and Carling heard the woman give him her real name. He looked down at the girl and shook his head. When he spoke again, he used the two names together.

"He said that you will never be Carling. That to him you will always be Tacita, the mute one," Brietta told her. She did not approve of what he had said and pulled Carling out of the building, walking quickly.

Marcus caught up with them easily and the man continued to talk, while Brietta answered stiffly as they walked back to the house. Carling, not caring what they said, was looking around. There were people everywhere, and their buildings were made partially of stone, so large they made her own little home look small in comparison. The roads were paved with stone as well, and she decided these people must be made of the cold material to love it so much.

After they entered the house, Marcus ruffled Carling's still-damp hair and left them with a smile. Brietta then turned and opened the door to a room. Inside was a large bed and chairs that were big and beautifully carved. Carling's eyes were moving everywhere, taking in the colours and beauty that she saw before her.

The stern lady from earlier was there and looked up from her work. She said something to Brietta, and her carer answered politely. Carling stood up straight while she stared at the lady.

"Go to her, Carling. She wants to check you over," Brietta said, and Carling took a few hesitant steps towards the woman.

She endured the inspection once more; this time her hair, nails, and ears were all inspected as well. The woman looked up and asked a question over the girl's head, and Brietta supplied the answer. Then the woman did something that amazed the child.

"Carling, you will be safe here with us. I am so sorry you had to go through what you did, and I am pleased my stepson treated you so well. You are a brave young lady. I wish there were another way this could have been handled, but unfortunately, it is the men who are in control here. Brietta tells me you are one of the Boar?" Diana asked.

"Yes," Carling said, nodding.

"Who was your mother? Was her name Breena?" The question was asked quietly and came as a surprise to Carling.

Carling could only nod as the word yes stuck in her throat. A tear sprang from her eye and spilled down her cheek. Diana wiped it away gently.

"We are family, Carling. Breena was my cousin, and you look so much like her." Diana gathered the child in her arms and held her. "I am one of The People as well."

Diana held her close while Carling sobbed. She picked the girl up and held her on her knee, rocking and humming a song softly as she comforted Carling. Brietta stood with her back leaning up against the door to prevent anyone coming in, a tear in her own eye for her mistress, who had lost three children in the last four years.

When Diana went to put the child down, she found Carling had fallen asleep on her lap and held her a bit longer. Brietta moved quickly and picked the child up from Diana's arms, careful not to wake her. Her mistress gathered herself together and stood, smoothing her long tunic dress and sniffing.

"Take the child to your room. I am placing her under your care, Brietta. We will both teach her how to speak their tongue and teach her their ways. If she is to survive this place, she is going to need all the help she can get."

"Yes, Mistress." Brietta nodded slightly to her.

"When you have put her to bed, come straight back. I will need you to help me change."

"Yes, Mistress."

Brietta left the room and carried Carling to the back of the house and across to her own little cell. She laid her on the narrow bed and covered her up carefully. Smoothing back her blonde hair, she thought this child could not have come at a worse time for Diana. Her master was a jealous man and was becoming suspicious of his young wife and son. The loss of the children did not help the matter, either. An idea formed in her mind, and she rushed back to her mistress.

Carling woke in a strange room. She sat up and rubbed her eyes. The room was small with only a chest and the bed contained in it. She left the bed and tried to look out the window beside the door, but she was too small. The latch on the door she could only just reach, and she was trying to open it when it pushed open, knocking her down.

"Carling, what were you doing?" Brietta asked quickly, standing in the doorway.

The child moved back away from the strange woman, her face and eyes showing her fear. Brietta closed the door, picked Carling up, and put her on the bed, checking her over to make sure she was uninjured.

"Are you all right?" Brietta asked and Carling only nodded her response. "That is not going to work when you are in the presence of the mistress and master. You must talk properly."

"Yes," Carling said quietly.

"Good. That will do for now. We can start teaching you a few words tomorrow. Tonight, the mistress wants you at her side for the feast."

"If she is from The People, why does she talk funny and dress like that?" Carling's curiosity got the better of her shyness.

"She was an alliance bride. The master took her to make peace with The People of the Serpent. You must not ask anyone these questions, Carling; it could be dangerous for you," Brietta warned her.

"I won't."

"Now we have to go; the mistress wants to dress you herself and wants me to do your hair."

When Diana met her husband before they entered the feast, the child was by her side, a miniature version of herself. She held the small hand in her own, and it felt natural. Two of Marinus's children from his first wife joined them. She deliberately averted her gaze from Marcus and showed Carling off to Athena.

"She is very adorable, Diana," Athena answered when Diana asked what she thought of her. The young woman only gave Carling a cursory gaze before her eyes flicked back to the room beyond and the young officers who had been invited to her brother's victory feast.

They entered the room with great ceremony and Diana took her seat by her husband, reclining on the low couch, and she made sure the child was at her feet. Slaves brought food out and laid it down in front of the master and mistress and the other guests. Goblets were filled with wine, and they gorged themselves. Every now and then Diana would pass a few small morsels to Carling, smiling when the girl enjoyed them.

"Marcus!" Marinus called out over the noise of the crowd. "You have been replaced as favourite. My wife has a new pet." The old man laughed loudly at his own joke. His son looked to the girl and smiled at her.

"I don't mind, Father. Diana's new pet is prettier than I am and more suited to her," Marcus replied then deliberately turned back to his friends.

"We need to get him married. I know," he said suddenly, his eyes going to Carling. "How about we marry your pet to him? A nice alliance with these savages," Marinus suggested to his wife. He laughed again, but there was not much joviality to the sound.

"Shall I go back to using the name I was given at birth, then, Marinus?" Diana asked him as she drank from her cup.

"Some unpronounceable name that would bring shame on me? No. You were renamed Diana when we wed, and you shall remain Diana until the day you die."

"My pet—as you call her—is too young. One of those simpering merchant's daughters would be more suitable to your son than my little child," Diana told him as she stroked the blond head of Carling.

"She is not your child, Diana," Marinus reminded her softly and with some concern, all signs of his harsh suggestion gone.

"I am well aware of that, my husband." Diana did not look his way but sat up and held the child close to her.

The night wore on, and the husband and wife did not talk much after that. Diana sat and played with the girl's hair, talking softly to her in her native tongue. The rest of the feast went on around them becoming louder, but she was happy. She saw her husband talking to a young girl who was only just old enough, and she cringed. *Better he sleep in his own bed than in mine,* she thought to herself.

Brietta's sister was also a slave to the household, and she had the ability of Foresight. Una's visions had told Diana that she would have a child, but her husband would only live for seven years after the child was born. Until that happened, she would have to keep her eyes averted from every male in the legion. The accusation of her having an affair with her stepson was annoying her, and even though her husband took the rumour as a joke, she knew he was beginning to believe it.

Marcus was a very good-looking young man who was only a couple of years younger than her, but he was not her husband. For as much as she hated Marinus, she also loved him. She watched as he flirted with the girl. Diana had become used to his affairs, and she expected him to do what he had always done. She herself had been his concubine while his late wife was still alive.

Beside Diana, Carling started to yawn. Her eyes were drooping, and her head started to nod. Slowly she lay down beside Diana and closed her eyes. With a wave, Diana called Brietta over. Her friend picked the child up and gently carried her back to the small cell they were to share. Brietta quietly left the room, making sure the door was secure behind her, she headed back to her mistress and to the feast.

Entering back into the house, she was stopped by a hand that came out of the shadows and closed on her arm, holding her firm and making Brietta jump.

"Is the child safe, Brietta?" Marcus came out of the doorway he had concealed himself in. He had followed her.

"Yes, Master; she is safe. As safe as anyone in your father's house." She pulled herself away from his grasp and stepped back from him. She could smell the wine on his breath and could see the same glint in his eye that had alarmed her earlier.

"Thank you, Brietta. Go look after my stepmother. I think she is in need of a friend this evening. Father has taken one of the girls to his rooms," Marcus informed her.

"I believe, Master Marcus, that at the moment my mistress is happy about the arrangement."

"I know your people have strange ways about you," he said darkly. "Do your seers ever see what the future may hold for my father?" He was leaning up against the wall, his eyes on the small bedroom cells of the slaves.

"I don't know what you are talking about, Master." Brietta was not happy in answering his question.

Marcus looked around, pushed himself off the wall, and stepped closer. "I have had enough dealings with the clans to realise that some have very strange abilities, Brietta. My stepmother is one, and I believe you have them as well. I remember you coming to us and instantly knowing what we were saying. You hid it well, but occasionally you would give yourself away."

He had pushed his face close to hers as he whispered, and the smell of wine was overpowering. He may be young, but she sensed he was already dangerous.

"Really, Master, I am not aware of what you are talking about." Brietta moved to go back to the feast and her mistress, but Marcus had other ideas.

"Oh, no, you don't," he said as he grabbed her arm again and held it tightly, his fingers digging into her upper arm. "I know you know, Brietta. Does that child also have a power?"

"She is just a child."

"I will be keeping an eye on her—and you." He released her arm and stumbled away to the privies.

Brietta watched him go for a moment, and the report she would be making to Diana was already forming in her mind. Marcus must not find out about the abilities or the ways of The

People. Her ability may only be the understanding of languages, but even she could see that he would cause trouble if he knew about them.

Chapter Two

Carling stepped out of the shadows and rushed down the corridor. She was late again. No matter how hard she tried to be ready on time in the mornings, she always seemed to be delayed by something or other. The door now stood before her and she knocked on it briskly as she took in a deep breath, then waited. From within the room that lay behind the door, a clear female voice called out in reply. By the time the door shut behind her, she had collected herself and calmed her breathing.

Six years had passed since Carling was first brought to the camp by Marcus, the son of the commander, and now she was almost twelve. Diana had kept her close, and the training Brietta had given her had kept her in good stead. She had learned her duties well, but the language was another matter. Although she could now communicate with the Romans who resided in the villa, there were still words that she had trouble with. Most were indulgent and smiled when she made mistakes, but some scorned her ignorance.

In all the time she had been there, Diana had not had one pregnancy. This was due to perfect planning on her part. She had kept her husband from her bed by inviting beautiful women into their house. They were paraded in front of him, and he had his pick. Diana had watched from the side, playing the role of his dutiful wife, while his concubines became pregnant and bore him children. Not once did she display any disappointment or frustration at her own lack of children.

Marcus had been kept busy as well. Despite many offers of marriage from merchants on behalf of their daughters, he still remained unmarried. The rumours that he was in love with his stepmother had gone by the wayside. Marinus had kept him busy out in the wilds dealing with the clans, and his son and wife were hardly together at all. Marcus's suspicions of Brietta, Diana, and Carling had not dissipated, and he would often quiz Brietta about how Carling was developing. His inquiries raised their own suspicions in Brietta about whom he had been talking to while he was away.

Each morning Carling would report to Diana, and depending on her mood, she would either be sent to ask for work in the kitchen or work with Brietta. When the mood would take her, Diana would have her sit and talk. She would tell the young girl stories of her youth and the tales the Recallers would tell at night around the hearths. As Carling grew, it soon became apparent that she could sing. Diana delighted in teaching her the songs she had learnt at her mother's knee and would listen for hours as Carling sang them back to her.

"Good morning, Carling." Diana was sitting in her normal seat waiting for the girl, her morning's work already on her knee.

"Good morning, Mistress." Carling stood with her hands clasped in front of her and her head lowered.

"This morning I think I would like you to learn some new songs. A bard has come to the camp, and I would like you to spend some time with him. I think my husband will be pleased to hear the songs from his youth sung in your beautiful voice. What do you think?"

"As my mistress wishes," Carling replied. She knew better than to give her opinion to this woman. The first time she had, she was chastised. Diana was kind to her, but if she made a misstep, she was punished for it. Brietta had explained that if she appeared to be too close to her, it would not be very good for either of them.

"The bard will be here soon. But for now, I have a sewing job for you over there." Diana indicated with a finger the blue gown that lay on the seat opposite.

Carling sat and picked up the gown. The needle and thread were already laid out for her, and she started her work. The stitches she made were small and neat—just as she had been taught—and she mended the tear.

"Will you give me a song, Carling?" Diana asked as she picked up her own work and started to sew.

The sound of Carling's young, untrained voice floated through the room, and it made Diana smile. The needles were flying, and soon a knock came at the door. With a word from Diana, it opened, and Carling kept singing. She would until her mistress bade her to stop. She looked up and through the doorway walked a thin man, dressed in a long robe, with a harp in his hands. He bowed to Diana and then stood listening to Carling, his eyes critical on her face, his finger pressed to his lips.

"That is enough, Carling; thank you. You may clear your sewing away now," Diana said when the girl had finished.

Carling picked up her work and took it to the box in the corner and tidied it away until later. She turned and waited, hands held before her and head bowed, as she listened in to the conversation.

"Please sit, Cornelius. What do you think of my songbird?" Diana asked the bard.

"Untrained and untried, but such a natural talent." Cornelius sat and put the harp down beside him, his fingers still resting on the wood as he stroked the instrument.

"I believe you come from the same region as my husband."

"I do, Mistress," Cornelius said with a nod.

"I want you to teach Carling some of the old songs—some that my husband would remember from his youth."

"I could sing them to him myself," Cornelius offered. His songs were a closely guarded treasure, and to share them was only done with other performers, not handmaidens.

"You will get to sing for my husband, Cornelius, but this is for something I have been planning especially for him. You will be paid well for the time spent teaching her," Diana informed him.

"Is she a woman yet?" he asked carefully, as he looked at the girl and sized her up.

"No. She is not."

"As we age, our voices change." He picked up his harp and plucked a string. "Can you copy that note, girl?"

Carling raised her head and opened her mouth. The note was perfect. Cornelius tried another, this time higher, and Carling perfected it first time, clear and ringing into the room.

"It seems she has the ear for it. There are a few songs I can teach her. Is she good with languages, Mistress?"

"She learnt the Roman tongue well enough, although she still has some trouble with it," Diana answered honestly.

"Is there somewhere we can go to teach her, somewhere out of the way so the commander does not hear and spoil the surprise?" he asked, his eyes still on the young girl.

"My handmaiden Brietta will show you somewhere you can go and will stay with you throughout the lessons. Carling, go fetch Brietta," Diana ordered the young girl.

"Yes, Mistress." Carling walked from the room with as much grace as she could muster, but as soon as the door was closed behind her she broke out into a run.

Rounding the corner of the corridor, she ran smack into a solid armoured chest. The metal, cold and hard, rang with the collision. Large hands held her gently, steadying her, and then kept her in place. Carling looked up to see who held her and stepped back at the sight of the smiling man. His hazel eyes reflected his amusement.

"Well, if it isn't little Tacita! Should you be running, young one?" Marcus let her go and stood looking down at her, his arms crossed over his chest.

"No, Master Marcus. I should be walking with grace," she answered, not meeting his eyes and keeping her head down, her hands clasped in front.

"That is all right, little Tacita. I won't tell anyone," he said with a laugh. "How is your training coming along? Is my stepmother teaching you well?"

"I hope that I am learning all I need, Master."

"How old are you now, Tacita?"

"I am twelve summers, Master Marcus."

"I don't think Tacita suits you anymore, Carling." He reached up and held a loose lock of her golden hair, twisting it around his finger, pulling her closer to him. "I do believe I will be changing your name to something more appropriate. I will tell you what I have decided when I see you next." Marcus let the hair drop and he stood to one side. As she passed, he gave her a little bow.

"Thank you, Master Marcus," Carling mumbled as she rushed past him and made for Brietta's room.

It had been a strange encounter with him, but one that had occurred before. He would always appear when she least expected it and talk to her for a minute, checking up on her progress and what she had been taught. It was something she had become used to but was still not comfortable with.

Once more, she calmed herself before she knocked on the door. Brietta opened it and waited for Carling to speak.

"The Mistress requests that you join her in her chambers, Brietta." She waited for the older woman to respond as she had been taught.

"I will come to my mistress's side now, Carling." She stepped out of the room and closed the door behind her. "That was beautifully done, but I can still tell that you have been running."

"I got waylaid," Carling said, blushing.

"Whom by this time? Not that houseboy again?" They were walking down the corridor now and passing the point where Marcus had stopped her.

"No, Brietta. It was Master Marcus," she replied quietly.

"And what did Master Marcus want with a slave child?" Brietta looked quickly at her young charge. She was fiercely protective of her, especially remembering the conversation she herself had with Marcus.

"He told me that *Tacita* did not suit me anymore and that he would have to think of another name for me."

"Did he say anything else or do anything?" Brietta asked.

"He touched my hair, and he said I shouldn't be running." Carling blushed at being caught.

"You should really stay away from him, Carling. As much as possible." She stopped and turned the girl to face her. "Promise me you will."

"If that is what you want, Brietta, I will. I promise."

Brietta let her go and they continued, her words confusing Carling. Entering the room together, they both stood in front of Diana.

"Can you take Cornelius and Carling to the place we discussed, Brietta? You are to stay with them at all times," Diana instructed her friend.

"I understand, Mistress," Brietta said, bowing slightly.

"You may go." Diana dismissed them and they all walked out, leaving her alone.

The tuition of Carling lasted for seven days. By then the bard Cornelius declared there was nothing else to teach her. She learned the songs easily, and she had grasped at the knowledge and the tunes, especially when Carling discovered she could play his harp. The music from the harp and the notes from her voice as she sang were so close, it was hard to distinguish one from the other. She, in turn, had taught him songs from her people that Diana had taught her. At first, she did not trust him, but when he showed her that all he was interested in was music, she grew to like him.

After Cornelius had reported back to Diana that Carling was ready, she organized a special dinner for her husband. The dishes she had ordered were all his favourites and some from his childhood. The meal was just for the two of them, and she was pleased his son and daughter were both away from the villa.

Carling was standing outside the room waiting to be called in. Cornelius was already in there, playing and singing. His tenor voice reached her ears, and she closed her eyes as she listened. The beauty of it washed over her, and she fell into the strains of notes and the words that were sung. When the music stopped, the doors opened, and he came out to fetch her.

"Remember all that I taught you, child," he said quietly to her as he stepped aside, letting her enter.

Carling walked in and stood before her master and mistress. Marinus looked her over and then at his wife. "So now she is a performing pet, Diana?" There was a hint of anger in his voice.

"Cornelius has been working with her, Marinus. Let her sing and you will find how good she is," Diana told him.

"Fine. Sing, girl." Marinus gestured to her and picked up his goblet.

Cornelius took a seat on the floor as she stood beside him. Carling was looking pale, and her stomach started to hurt, but she opened her mouth and let out the first note. She sang the first song the bard had taught her and did not look at her audience, but up at the paintings on the wall behind them. Loud and clear she sang out, ignoring the pain of the cramps that gripped her.

The song finished, and Marinus was staring at her before he launched into an applause that was loud and abrasive. "More," he called to her. "More."

Cornelius stood and handed his harp to Carling to play. She sank to the floor and her hands plucked the strings in a testing manner before launching into a mournful tune. She closed her eyes for this one, as her tutor had told her the meaning behind the sad-sounding song and it made her miss her family all the more. The song was sung with feeling, and a tear ran down her cheek. When she came to the end, she looked to her master for his reaction.

"So beautiful. Such a hidden gem. You have done well with her, my wife. She has brought my home to me." He was looking at Diana again as he reached over for her hand. She gave it to him readily with a small smile, and he led her out of the room.

On the floor, Carling held out the precious harp to Cornelius, and as she stood, she felt a wetness running down her legs. She looked and saw red blood streaks as it trickled down. Looking up in shock, she saw that Cornelius had seen it as well and she felt worried about what was causing it.

"Today you have taken my music and become a woman in the process. You need to go find Brietta at once, Carling. She is as much a mother to you as your own could have been. She will explain it all." Cornelius smiled at her gently and with pride at her accomplishment.

Brietta was careful and kind while explaining what was happening. She gave Carling the rags she would need and showed her what to do. In the morning, Brietta went to Diana and told her of the new development with Carling. The mistress, already in a good mood, gave Carling leave to stay away from her duties for the day.

There was one more subject to do with Carling that Brietta wanted to talk to her mistress about, and she raised it with some trepidation. Even though the women had grown up together in the same village, their statuses now were far apart.

"I am concerned about Carling, Mistress. I was hoping you could do something to protect her more," Brietta said slowly.

"Protect her? Is she not safe? Has someone tried to harm her?" Diana looked up, her good mood gone, replaced with concern of the girl's welfare.

"No, not as of yet, Mistress. There have been clumsy attempts by boys, but she has kept them away. I am afraid that Carling has once more come under the scrutiny of Master Marcus."

"Are you afraid that he has designs on the child? I have never known him to have those types of inclinations," Diana said, her brow furrowing.

"No, I do not think it is that. But I do feel he has an attachment to her that is not healthy for either of them." Brietta stood firm and clasped her hands together.

"I will see what I can do, Brietta. I may have a bit more sway over my husband now. If your sister is correct, then Marinus will be happier than he has been for a while," Diana said with a smile.

"You are with child?" Brietta moved to her side and sat, friends, and equals for a moment.

"I hope so, my friend. I am hoping that last night was the turning point." Diana placed a hand on her stomach and looked up at her countrywoman with a beaming smile. "I will see what I can do, Brietta."

"Thank you, Mistress. And I pray to the Ancestors that it is a healthy baby," Brietta said, placing a hand over her mistress's.

Carling woke one morning to the murmur of many people talking at once. It sounded so close, like they were in the room with her. She opened her eyes and looked about, but she was alone. The voices faded, and she rubbed the sleep from her eyes. The conversation had seemed disjointed to her, and it hadn't made any sense, like the people who were talking were speaking of different things and trying to outdo each other to be heard.

She rose and made ready for the day, dressing quickly, and pulling a comb through her blonde hair, then stepped outside. The day had not even begun. The sun was still well below the horizon and the stars were shining brightly above in the dark night sky. Carling looked around in confusion. Slowly she turned back to her room and returned to bed. She lay there and wondered what had woken her. Slowly her eyes drooped again, and she slept.

The dream was a confusion of people. Her Mistress, Brietta, the master, and Athena, who was crying. Others she had seen around the villa, slaves and freemen alike. She wandered around them, but they paid her no attention. They did not look at her or even acknowledge that she was there. She tried to talk to Brietta, who stopped what she was doing and looked around but then went back to her actions. The last she saw was Marcus. He seemed to be looking directly at her, but when she neared him, he looked away.

Carling didn't know what to make of it; it was confusing and worrying her. Each person seemed to be wrapped up in their own stories. They moved about and spoke, but she could not understand them. Several faded away when she heard a cockerel crow out the coming dawn. Soon there was only the family left. Even Brietta had gone. Through them all Marcus came striding towards her, his hazel eyes boring into her blue ones and a smile spreading over his features.

Letting out a great gasp, she sat up in bed and struggled to catch her breath. She had not seen him much in the last few years and had only been in his presence a couple of times, always with someone else since their last encounter when she was twelve. Now sixteen, she had seen his eyes on her at their previous meeting and felt uncomfortable under his gaze.

Marinus had kept Marcus busy, sending him out further and further into the wilds, trying to bring the clans under the control of Rome. He had had some success, but more often than not they were chased from the highlands and glens that the clans still controlled. His results had not pleased his father, and it drove him on to more dangerous raids on those who resisted the rule.

Carling entered her mistress's chambers and found her inside with her son. A healthy boy had been born, and Cato was now nearly four years of age. He had the dark hair of his father and the bright blue eyes of his mother. A sweet-natured and charming child, he never failed to bring a smile to those around him.

Cato ran to Carling and launched himself into her arms. She picked the little boy up and held him close, depositing a kiss on his cheek. After she put him back down, Cato went back to his mother. Carling stood with her hands clasped in front and her head slightly bowed, awaiting Diana's greeting.

"Good morning, Carling."

"Good morning, my mistress," Carling responded.

"My little boy has expressed a great interest in learning to ride a horse this morning. I have sent for the stable master, so your duties today will be light. You are to go with them, and when Cato is finished, bring him back so I can hear all about his adventures." Diana smiled indulgently at her son.

"Yes, Mistress," Carling responded as Cato quickly crossed the room again and took her hand in his small one.

"I want to go now, Carling!" he said, pulling her hand.

"Cato, I have not dismissed Carling yet, and the stable master has not arrived to receive his instructions. You will have to be patient, my son," Diana told him calmly.

"Mother, I want to go now," he pleaded.

"Cato. Patience is a strong virtue, one that you are going to have to learn. Do you speak to your father this way—or even your brother?" Diana asked him.

"No, Mother," Cato replied sullenly.

"Then I would appreciate the same courtesy." She smiled at her son, and he returned it with one full of as much sunshine as hers.

The stable master arrived and spoke briefly with the mistress before he was soon leading both Carling and Cato out to the stables. He was not a man of many words, but Carling could see the look he was giving her and was becoming very self-conscious of that particular stare. It was not the first time a man had looked at her like that, and she knew it would not be the last. They reached the long stable building, and the nickering of the horses in their stalls filled the air.

From around the corner of the building, dressed in full armour and looking decidedly dirty from the road, came Marcus. His helmet was under his arm and his hair was sweaty and stuck to his head with the exertion of a quick ride back to the fort. The way he looked up at her and was moving towards them reminded Carling of the dream she had had, and she blushed at the thought of it and turned from his gaze.

"Good morning, little brother," Marcus greeted Cato.

"Good morning, big brother," Cato responded politely.

"What are you doing here?" He crouched down in front of the little boy, who still clung to Carling's hand.

"The stable master is going to teach me to ride today, Marcus," Cato told him excitedly.

"Is he? I can do that; you will learn a lot more from me than him. He is stuck here all day looking after them while I ride every day." Marcus looked at the stable master and winked. The jest was kindly meant, and the stable master was not offended. He only bowed and took his leave after one last leering look at Carling.

When the man was out of earshot, Marcus stood and greeted her. "Are you well, Carling?"

"Very well, Master Marcus." She bent her head and tried not to look up at him.

"Good. Shall we go find a horse, then, Cato?" He took the boy's hand and they walked together. Carling felt very awkward, as Cato would not let go of her hand and she was forced to walk at the same level as Marcus.

Carling's discomfort was soon relieved, as Cato dropped her hand when a little pony was brought out, fully saddled and ready for the child. Carling stepped out of the way and watched as Marcus lifted the little boy up and deposited him on the back of the horse. He gripped the reins and showed the boy how to hold them. As he was being led around the parade grounds, she watched how attentive Marcus was to his younger brother.

A group of soldiers was moving back to their barracks and passed close to her. One stopped and looked her up and down.

"I've not seen you about before. Where have you been hiding, then, my sweet?" He moved closer to her.

"I work for the commander's wife," she said, feeling uncomfortable.

"I have heard about you, the one with the beautiful gold hair. So why are you here? Looking for a real man? Those soft houseboys not doing it for you anymore?" He reached around her waist and pulled her close. His breath stank, and he had a foul body odour coming from under his armour.

"Release her now!" A shout come from behind, and the man let her go and turned, ready to tell whoever it was to mind their own business.

Marcus was hurrying towards them, leading the trotting pony with Cato clinging desperately to the saddle. When the men saw who was coming, they quickly formed up. Carling moved away from them and went to steady the boy as Marcus dropped the lead rope.

"Who is your lieutenant?" Marcus demanded of the one who had held Carling.

"Lieutenant Atticus," the man responded quickly.

"I will be having words with him about the way you conduct yourself. She is no common camp follower; she is under the personal protection of the commander and his wife. If I hear that one more man has laid a hand on her, he will lose that hand. Do I make myself clear?" His voice was raised, and others were now looking their way.

"Yes, sir," the man responded.

"Get back to what it was you were supposed to be doing." He dismissed them and turned back to the pony. He took the lead from Carling's hands. "Are you all right?" he asked, concerned.

"I'm fine. It was nothing that many others haven't tried, Master," she told him and moved away from them again.

"Why do men do that?" Cato asked his brother.

"Some men cannot help themselves when they see a beautiful woman, Cato. It will be something you learn as you grow. Now shall we get back to your lesson?" He was still watching Carling.

"Yes, please. Can you let go of the lead, so I can ride by myself?" he asked Marcus eagerly.

"Not yet. Your mother would kill me if you fell and got hurt," Marcus told him with a chuckle at his enthusiasm.

All morning they worked with the horse—not just riding but grooming and looking after it. Marcus insisted that Cato learn everything about caring for a horse, telling him that the animal could one day save his life in battle. The little boy took his words seriously and went about each task with diligence and care. Carling smiled as the little boy chatted away to the pony.

After a hard morning's work, he was tired, and Carling picked him up to carry him back to the house. Marcus was walking at her side, and she became aware of the stares that were being thrown their way. She should be a few paces behind him, and she tried to do just that, walking slower and slipping back. Marcus stopped and turned.

"It makes it very hard to talk to you if you are always behind me, Carling." Marcus laughed.

"It is my place, Master," she told him, blushing, still trying to stay behind him.

"Not while you are holding my brother. I remember a little girl who used to run around the corridors of the villa—Tacita." He smiled as he used the old name he had given her. "But I was going to change that, wasn't I? Give you a new, more appropriate name."

They walked on in silence. Carling had not responded and hoped he would soon make his way to his own quarters in the camp and leave her to the duties she still had to do. She juggled the child onto her other hip so that Cato was between them. She felt the need for the barrier and hugged the boy tighter to her.

"Here; he must be getting heavy for you," Marcus said, taking Cato from her. As he settled him, he looked at her, "I have it! Flora. Like a beautiful flower you are blossoming."

"Please, Master Marcus, do not say such things," she said quietly, looking at the ground.

"Why not? It is true. Your hair shines bright in the sunshine, just like some of the petals of the wildflowers. It suits you. I shall request that your name is formally changed when I see my father this afternoon."

From somewhere inside, an anger welled, and she fought with it until it finally burst out. "You took my family, now you wish to take my name. Is there anything else you wish to strip me of?" Her voice was quiet and hard.

Marcus reached out and touched her face tenderly. "No, that was never my intention, Carling. I am sorry. It was a silly jest."

Carling reached out and took Cato back from him. She walked away from him as quickly as she could, a tear running down her cheek with the hurt she still felt. A life she had here in the enemy's camp, but it was not the life she was meant for. She should have grown with her brother, been taught all the ways of The People by her mother, not strangers.

Reaching her mistress's door, she opened it and walked in, forgetting that the boy was still in her arms. Diana looked up from her work and immediately began to worry something had happened.

"No, Mistress; he is unharmed. Just very tired. I think that working with a horse was a lot harder than he thought it would be." Carling put the boy on the ground, and he walked slowly to his mother as she tried to collect herself.

"Marcus helped me, Mother. He showed me how to groom and feed the pony and how to ride." The smile he had was just as big as it had been earlier in the morning with his anticipation.

"Marcus did? I thought you were being taught by the stable master?" Diana looked up quickly to Carling.

"He was going to, Mistress. But Master Marcus was there and offered to teach young Master Cato," Carling told her.

"Did he speak to you?" Diana pulled the child onto her lap and held him close to her, and his eyes drooped.

"Yes, Mistress, he did."

"He shouted at some man who was holding Carling," Cato said sleepily.

"What man, Carling?" There was alarm in her voice.

"Only a soldier, Mistress. He was nothing that I could not have handled. Master Marcus spoke to him and his friends."

"You look tired yourself, Carling. You are dismissed for the rest of the day. Go get some rest and I will see you this evening for dressing," Diana told her gently.

"Yes, Mistress. Won't Brietta be dressing you?"

"Not tonight; she will be looking after Athena. There has been a proposal issued for her hand."

"Very good, Mistress."

Carling left Diana with her son and headed to her own rooms. Coming out of the dim of the corridor, she almost ran into Marcus coming the other way.

"Carling, I was hoping to see you alone again. I want to apologize for my words earlier. They were thoughtless and harsh," he said quickly.

"They were just words, Master Marcus. And there is no need to apologize to me. I am just a slave." She went to move around him, and he stopped her.

"I have never thought of you as a slave, Carling. You are growing into such a beautiful woman," he told her, his voice hushed and low.

"But a slave I am, Master."

This time she did manage to get past him. His words were still in her mind, and she could feel them wash over and confuse her. This was the man who led the soldiers to kill her father and mother, who had burned her brother alive. This was the man who had her grandmother killed before her eyes and taken her far from family who loved her.

That night at dinner, Carling stood behind her mistress, waiting for her to give her an order. Her hands were clasped in front of her, and her head was slightly bowed. But she felt his eyes on her. Diligently she kept her eyes down and almost missed the request from her mistress.

"Carling, would you give us one of your songs?" Diana said without looking at her.

"Yes, Mistress." She bent down and picked up the harp that had been made for her, sat, and began to sing.

The chatter went on over the top of the song, but she continued. No one could see her from where she was sitting, and for that she was grateful. There were no hazel eyes boring into her, making her uncomfortable. When the song finished, she stood again and found Marinus looking her way.

"Sing one from home, girl," he ordered her. "And this time out here where we can see you."

Carling moved to the centre of the room and sat on the floor. Gathering the harp to her, she started to pluck the strings and then sing. It was a happy tune that did not suit her mood, but it was one of Marinus's favourites. He clapped and sang along with her, his deep baritone voice a counterpoint to her own alto, and she smiled as she sang. When it came to the end, her master was the loudest to applaud.

"Our little songbird is in fine form tonight, Wife. Another. Sing, songbird," he egged her on.

The guests were enjoying themselves; the family was happy and together, and she sang for their enjoyment and pleasure. She felt like a songbird, singing her heart out in a gilded cage. Trapped and alone. Dependent solely on their goodwill and generosity. She sang because it pleased them to hear her.

The next song was the sad one she liked the most. Everyone stopped talking and watched as her emotions welled up with the words, giving them life and meaning. The tune was slow and full of wanting, heartbreak, and sorrow. The tear that escaped her eye glistened in the light of the oil burners. It tracked down her cheek and off her chin, to be followed quickly after by another.

When she was finished, she hung her head, ashamed that her voice had shown her feelings. They were quiet for a while, and she thought that Marinus was angry with her until she looked up.

"We must do something for this child," Marinus said with awe to his wife. "Where did she come from again?"

"I found her. Remember, Father? She was a chief's daughter. We thought she might become useful for bargaining with them," Marcus offered before Diana could speak.

"And why haven't we?" his father asked him.

"The clan she comes from has already made its peace with us. It is an uneasy one, but it is one that is stable for now." Marcus looked her way, and Carling dropped her head once more.

"Well, there comes a dilemma. Do we give her freedom or hold on to her in case she is ever needed?" Marinus pondered.

"How about we wait until morning with clearer heads, Father? The decision does not need to be made tonight." Marcus was watching Carling, still seated on the floor.

"I think that will be all for tonight, Carling," Diana said softly as she watched her stepson. "Tell Brietta to go to my chambers and wait for me. You are dismissed for the night."

"Thank you, Mistress." She stood and left the room. Her hopes had flared when Marinus started talking about freedom, but she did not trust that it would come about. The romans would say one thing one day and change their minds the next.

Chapter Three

The question of Carling's freedom did not come up again, as she had expected, and she continued with her work. Now eighteen, she was a striking figure in the household. Cato was devoted to her and would spend hours trailing behind as she got on with her work, when he wasn't at his studies.

Marcus had risen further in the ranks and was now second after his father. He spent more time at home than he had when he was out on patrol, and Carling would keep out of his way as much as possible. He persisted in calling her Flora to tease her, but she had learned to ignore it. Diana had managed to keep her safe so far and this had garnered a lot of attention, not only from those in the household but also further afield in the fort.

At feasts, she was brought out to sing for the guests and family, and then sent away quickly before anyone could approach her. Diana always made sure there were plenty of other young women around for those who were feeling amorous, including her husband and stepson.

The time from the vision of Brietta's sister was fast approaching, and Diana was intent on indulging Marinus's every whim and taste. As a result, he had grown quite large. He was no longer the lean man she had married and was often quite drunk. There were nights where he would stay up with his men drinking heavily and demanding women for their pleasure. One of these nights, he called for Carling to entertain them.

She stepped into the room expecting her mistress to be present but found only men. Marinus saw her enter and beckoned her over.

"Our little songbird is not so little anymore. Come and sing for us, songbird. Come sing me the songs of my home and happy ones, not the sad ones that make you cry." He was already drunk, and his words were slurred.

She sat on the floor and started to play. The music was happy, and she had them all singing along. She did not notice Marcus arriving and leaning on the doorway to watch her with a smile. It was only at the end of the second song that she saw him and averted her eyes. Marinus saw her blush and looked around to find his son smiling at the girl.

"You will be in trouble with your stepmother if you touch her, boy," he called out. "Come join us; we are having a celebration."

"What are we celebrating, Father?" Marcus asked as he entered and sat near Marinus, pouring himself a cup of wine.

"I don't know. What are we celebrating again?" Marinus looked around the room at men who were gathered there.

"Victory and peace," someone shouted out.

"Victory and peace. Long may it stay away so we may still have something to do," Marinus replied, laughing, holding up his goblet and spilling most of the contents. "You have been working too hard, my son. Enjoy yourself, have a cup of something, and there are some very nice girls around here somewhere. Why have you stopped singing, girl? You are the songbird. You should be singing!" he called to Carling.

Strumming the harp again, she sang some more of the songs he liked and then she changed the tone. This one was one of her own devising, and she sang it in her native tongue.

The tune was happy and carefree, tripping up and down the scales. The words sounded like they were for a cheeky love song, and she hoped that none of them could understand what she was singing.

The song Carling had written was one of hate and revenge. It was a song that spoke of anger and loss. She sang it to the end, and they all cheered, except for Marcus. He looked at her with a new appreciation. Under her beautiful exterior sat the heart of a raging lioness, and she had just expressed how she wanted to rip all their hearts out slowly and leave them to die.

It was a long night of carousing for the men, and at length her throat began to tire. Marinus excused her when she began to sound more husky than sweet, and she left in a hurry. Walking back to her room quickly, she was intercepted by the man she most wanted to avoid.

"That was an interesting song you sang for my father, my beautiful Flora. If he spoke a word of your tongue, he would have killed you in there," he told her.

"I did not realise that you spoke the clan's tongue, Master Marcus," she said to him defiantly, standing firm.

"You hide it well, the anger you have inside. I am surprised we have not all had our throats cut in the middle of the night." Marcus stepped closer to her.

"Excuse me, Master; I must get to bed. I have to be up at first light to serve my mistress." She tried to pass him, but he moved to block her.

"I know about The People, Carling. I am not the monster you think I am. I only wish peace between our peoples."

"Peace at the end of a sword, Master? That is not peace. If you had of approached the clans with respect in the first place, there would have been no need for any bloodshed," she said with a little heat in her words.

"You have such bold opinions for a slave, Flora." He smiled. "Who have you been talking to?"

"No one, Master." Carling stood her ground against him.

"A thinking slave—what a novel idea. I knew there was something special about you when I first saw you as a child. You have found your voice now. Such a pretty voice." He stepped closer to her, his finger now tracing her hairline and moving down her throat.

"Marcus, leave the girl alone," Marinus called out, weaving up from behind Carling. "I am in need of some assistance, I think, my little songbird."

"I can help you, Father," Marcus offered, stepping in front of Carling as he recognised the look in his father's eye.

"No. I want my songbird, not my son. I want her to serenade me to sleep, a soft song that my mother would sing. The one that makes you cry so much, girl." He pushed his son aside and draped an arm over Carling, leaning on her heavily and breathing wine-soaked fumes, making Carling turn her head.

"Yes, Master Marinus," she said, struggling to keep him upright while she helped him to his rooms.

Carling had never been in Marinus's bedchamber before in all the years she had lived with them. It was a manly place, the opposite of his wife's rooms. His armour was on a stand in the corner, now so small it no longer fit his girth. There were weapons on the walls, and the frescos that had been painted were of a sexual nature. Carling averted her eyes from those. Marinus caught her blushes and saw her look away. He grinned at the girl and held onto her tighter.

"I think Diana has kept you locked away from me too long, Carling," he said as she helped him to the bed. He fell onto it, keeping a tight grip and pulling her down with him. His arms were wrapped around her, and she struggled to get free.

"A songbird must be able to use its wings once in a while. Especially when it is a beautiful one such as yourself. I have watched you grow from a scrap of a thing and now you have blossomed. Marcus has dubbed you right, Flora." His mouth was on her face and his hand roughly groped its way into her dress.

Carling's own hands came up to push him away, and they connected with his head. A flash in her mind startled her, and she opened her eyes to find herself in a completely different place. It was dim and hazy. There were hints of order but mess everywhere. She could feel her own body still fighting to be free of the large man. She felt his touch on her skin and her own mind rebelled against it.

She screamed in this place, a high-pitched, loud scream that rent the air. She could feel the pain it was causing him as he pulled away, and she screamed again. Suddenly Carling found herself on the floor next to the large bed, and there was a voice calling—not to her, but to Marinus.

"Father, can you hear me?" Marcus called as he leaned over the large, panting form of his father.

Carling hauled herself up and backed away from the bed. She had no idea what had happened and did not want to stay to find out. Marcus turned his head her way, almost as if he had heard her thoughts.

"Stay there, Carling. Stay," he ordered, then raced out of the room and was joined by Diana shortly after. She took one look at the state of undress of Carling and then at her husband on the bed.

"What did you do, Carling?" she asked quietly.

"I did nothing. He attacked me, and I pushed him away. I swear I did nothing, Mistress Diana." She was still in shock and was breathing heavily.

"Cover yourself, girl. Marcus, close the doors," Diana ordered, and he did as he was told.

Carling gripped the front of her dress that had been ripped away; she had no idea how it had happened. She went to sit down and stumbled, falling to the floor. Marcus began to move towards her, but Diana called him away.

"Stay by your father, Marcus. Keep calling to him—softly, though. We don't want the whole garrison knowing something has happened." Diana then left her husband's side and knelt beside Carling. "What happened, child? Tell me." Her words were soft and calm.

"I don't know, Mistress. One minute he had me on the bed and I was fighting him, then it all went dark. I don't know what happened," Carling told her, shaking her head vigorously.

"Did you lay your hands on his head?" she asked carefully.

"I think so. I was trying to push him away. I am sorry if it hurt him, Mistress, but he was hurting me," Carling stammered.

"I know, Carling; I know." She smoothed the escaped hair from Carling's face and held her in a comforting embrace. From the bed there came a groan. Diana let Carling go and pulled the girl to her feet. "You had better go before he wakes. Go straight to your room and do not open the door for anyone except Brietta or myself. Do you understand?"

"Yes, Mistress." Carling sniffed and ran to the door, not stopping until she was safely inside her little cell.

She barred the door behind her and leaned against it. Tears started filling her eyes as she slid down to the floor. She sobbed into her hands at the thought she had hurt Marinus somehow and the consequences she was going to have to face. A rap at the door sounded loud in the small confines of the room, and she wiped her eyes.

"Who is it?" she called softly.

"Brietta, open up quickly."

Carling stood and unbarred the door, opening it. The cool night air came spilling in along with the light from the lantern in Brietta's hands. She entered and shut the door behind her.

"Are you hurt?" she asked, putting the lantern down on the small chest by the bed.

"He was on me, Brietta. I couldn't get up. I couldn't move." A new wave of sobs hit her and Brietta was there, smoothing her hair and holding her gently.

"The mistress will be here soon. Let's put on another gown, shall we? This one is a little ripped." She moved Carling to the bed and then rummaged around the chest for a new dress for her to change into.

With the old one replaced, Brietta sat on the bed with her, waiting to hear her fate. Marcus had only told her that his father had been hurt by the girl somehow and nothing else. He had instructed her to go to Carling and wait for Diana there, to comfort her as best she could. The fact that his actions and thoughts were more on the welfare of the girl than his father were plain to see. And she had given him a piece of advice.

"Leave the girl alone. Forget her, Master Marcus. She is not meant for you. She has a higher purpose in life."

"I can't. I love her, Brietta. I love her too much to let her go." The anguish that had shown at the idea of doing so had overcome him before he turned and left her to go back to his father.

Carling was sniffing and wiping tears from her face when there was another knock. Brietta opened the door a crack and then wider to let Diana in. Diana went straight to Carling and sat where Brietta had just been.

"He is awake, Carling. There is no harm done. He can't remember what happened. I told him that he had only become too drunk and had fallen. I promise there will be no repercussion for you," Diana told her quickly.

"Thank you, Mistress."

"When you put your hands on his head, what happened, Carling?" Diana asked.

Carling took a deep breath and tried to remember. "I was somewhere else, but I could still feel what was going on. I remember greyness, darkness, and there was mess everywhere, but behind it all, order. I don't know where I was and then I screamed. I was so frightened. I opened my eyes again and I was on the floor. Marcus was there, calling to his father, and I didn't know what was going on."

"That's fine." Diana looked at Brietta. "Has she talked about voices, about anything unusual?"

"No, Mistress, not to me."

"Here in this room, at this moment, I am Keelie of The People."

"You think she used an ability of some sort?" Brietta asked, concerned, and coming to sit on the other side of Carling.

"Yes. I think she has, and I think it might be Mind Touch."

Carling was looking at the two women who had featured so much in her life, who had cared and looked out for her. They no longer sounded like mistress and slave, but friends. She had always suspected it was there, but it was the first time she had ever seen it.

"I thought we might see something when she started to bleed, but there was nothing. She is old to have her ability surface," Brietta said.

"I have an ability?" Carling asked them both.

"I think so. But no more for tonight. Carling, you need sleep and I need to get back to Marinus."

"We have another problem, Keelie. Marcus has his suspicions about what happened tonight. And there is something else." Brietta looked quickly at Carling. "He has told me that he has feelings for her. That he loves her too much to let her go."

"That is a problem. The time to decide her future is now." Diana stood and smoothed her dress. "This is going to take a lot of diplomacy. I want you both to act as normal as possible in the morning. Nothing happened tonight."

They both nodded and agreed.

Carling was up with the first rays of the sun and headed to the kitchen to get something to eat. The lack of sleep had left rings under her eyes. It hadn't helped that she had been plagued by strange dreams of people, and again Marcus had been there. This time he was staring at her, watching with leering eyes wherever she went. It had unnerved her, especially with the news that she had heard the previous night.

Heading out of the kitchen, she watched to see who was around as she headed to her mistress's rooms. Marcus was waiting for her. He was leaning up against the wall beside the door and stood up straight while she walked towards him. Concern was written on his face, and a small smile of guilt curled on his lips at her finding him there.

"Good morning, Carling. I was worried about you last night. Are you all right? Did he hurt you?" he asked her as he came to meet her.

"Master Marcus; good morning. I am fine, thank you."

"Are you sure you are all right? I can't believe she has you working today." He was walking towards her, his hands already reaching to comfort her.

"There is no reason I can see for not serving my mistress." Carling stopped in her tracks.

"But last night…"

"Last night I sang and then I went to my room, Master," Carling said cutting him off.

"But…"

Carling was shaking her head, and Marcus stopped talking. He stared at her for a moment and took another step towards her. Carling dropped her head and refused to look at him as she passed, heading straight for Diana's door.

"Carling, please…" he started with a desperate sounding whisper.

Opening the door after being bid to enter, Carling disappeared behind the it, leaving Marcus looking after her. Inside she felt her stomach unclench, and she wavered for a moment as she stood in front of Diana.

"Sit, Carling, before you fall. I take it Marcus has spoken to you?" Diana asked.

"Yes; just now, Mistress." She sat on the chair opposite.

"I asked him not to, but to leave you alone. He can't understand that you were never meant for him." Diana sighed and looked uncomfortable. "Carling, I cannot have you here anymore. It is just too dangerous for you, and I fear that I am unable to keep you safe like I promised."

"What is to become of me, Mistress Diana?" Carling's heart dropped at Diana's words

"I have arranged for you to meet someone who can give you the training you need for your ability. Because you were a gift to me, it is in my power to grant your freedom and I will be doing that this morning. There will be no objections from anyone in the house, as Marinus is in no state to make any. Brietta is already gathering your things and a list of bits that I have drawn up for you to take with you."

"But where shall I go, Mistress?" Carling could feel the panic starting to rise. Although she was being given a great gift by Diana, the unknown world outside the gates was vast and lonely to her.

"That has all been arranged. Brietta and her sister Una will take you. Now we must go. The family have all been called and they are waiting for us. I have enjoyed the time you have spent with us, Carling, and watching you grow into a beautiful woman your mother would have been proud of. I hope Brietta and I have taught you all you need to know to survive."

It was the first time Diana had mentioned Carling's mother since she arrived, and it startled her. The woman who had held her life in her hands was also a kinswoman, her mother's cousin.

Diana stood and came to Carling. She reached down and took her hands in her own. Pulling her up, she embraced the young woman.

"I wish you well, Carling—a long life and more happiness than you have had so far. Until we meet again."

They broke apart, and Diana led her to the entrance of the villa. The gathered family stood, including Athena and her husband, who was looking bored. Cato was the only person absent, and Carling was sad about that. She would have liked to say goodbye to him properly. Marinus was there, looking a little hungover, and when he looked at her, he winced involuntarily. The pain she had caused him lingered still, and she felt guilty for it.

Standing in front of everyone was Marcus. He looked confused as to what was going on. Brietta came through the house carrying a bundle with her. She was dressed for travel, and she stayed within the shadows of the interior.

Leading her to the centre of the portico, Diana stood facing the villa with her back to the road outside. A houseboy came running and handed her a cylinder sealed and tied with ribbons. Slowly Diana raised it, touching it to Carling's forehead, and then handed it to her.

"This is your manumissio, your papers of freedom. You are free to go from the house and live your life as you wish. If there is any time you need help, please come and see us. We will welcome you back with open arms as a friend to the family," Diana said in a strong voice that Carling could see her struggling with as tears formed in her Mistress' eyes.

Despite wishing for this moment for years, tears still sprang to Carling's eyes. They blurred her vision for a moment until she dashed them away.

"Thank you, Mistress. It has been an honour to serve you and the family, and I shall miss you very much." She clasped the roll to her and saw the face of Marcus. The look of confusion was gone, and now one of hope took its place; now she was a free woman.

Brietta was walking towards her. She stopped in front of her mistress and waited, a large bundle in her hands.

"Look after her, Brietta. Make sure she makes it to her destination safely, then come back straight away."

"Yes, Mistress." Brietta moved to Carling's side.

"I can escort them if you would like, Stepmother." Marcus was at her side, his eyes still on Carling.

"I believe you are needed here, Marcus. Your father is in need of you. An escort has already been organized for both of them." Diana placed a hand on Marcus's shoulder and drew his eyes to hers. She nodded, and he turned and headed back inside with one last look at Carling.

"Come, Mistress," Brietta said softly, and it took Carling a moment to realise that the older woman was talking to her.

They turned, left the portico, and headed out onto the street. A cart was waiting for them, and they climbed onto the back. It was driven by an older man Carling had seen delivering food to the kitchen. The road was bumpy, and she watched the villa fall behind them as they headed towards the gates.

They were passed through by the soldiers on guard, and they continued down a well-worn road. It was the first time since she had been brought to the fort that she had left the walls. Carling breathed deeply of the air, and it smelled sweet after the stench of the camp.

"You might as well get comfortable; we are going to be a while, Mistress," Brietta said.

"Do you have to call me that? You have been like a mother to me, Brietta." She took the woman's hand and held it.

Night was falling by the time they reached their destination. A small house stood in a large enclosure, and Carling could make out a vegetable garden around it. The door opened, and a woman stood in the dim light that spilled out, sending a long shadow. Brietta walked towards the house and then started to run. They embraced, and Carling realised that the woman was her sister.

"Carling, please come and meet Una, my sister." Brietta beckoned her in, and she walked towards her hesitantly.

"Welcome, Mistress Carling," Una said, bowing her head.

"Just, Carling, please. I am no Roman." She felt embarrassed to have been addressed that way.

"I have been waiting to meet you, Carling. There have been many visions of you recently, not just from myself." She ushered them in, and they sat. "You will stay the night here, and then you will be collected tomorrow and taken on to someone who can teach you your ability."

"I really don't know what is going on," Carling said, bemused. "I still don't understand why I have been given my freedom."

"It doesn't matter why, Carling. You are free," Brietta told her with a smile.

Walking down the road early the next morning was an old woman. Her cloak was pulled tightly around her, and her greying hair hung down her back in a long braid. Her steps were still hearty and strong, and she made her way to the door of the house. It opened before she reached it; Una stepped out, along with Brietta, and they greeted her warmly.

"Carling, this is our mother, Sima. She will be teaching you your ability," Brietta introduced them.

Carling stood when Sima entered, and the old woman looked her up and down. Her cloak was cast aside, and she wore the traditional dress of The People, leggings and a long tunic. Sima stepped closer to her and placed a hand on the side of Carling's head. For a moment, the world wavered in front Carling's eyes and her thoughts became fuzzy.

"There is a strength there that is true, but it will take some time to bring it out. She should have had her training by now," Sima said disapprovingly.

"We had no idea that she had an ability, Ma," Brietta said. "If she had shown it sooner, Keelie would have done something, but she didn't. There has been nothing."

"Tell me, girl, have you heard voices, seen other things when you have touched someone?" the old woman asked, looking into Carling's eyes.

"No."

"Have you experienced anything odd, unusual, or strange?" Sima's dark eyes bored into Carling's.

"I do have strange dreams. I woke up from it the first time and then I went back to it. There were people I knew, and they were all talking, but not to each other. They couldn't see me or hear me."

"A Dream Walker." Sima reached up and laid her palm on Carling's forehead, closing her own eyes.

The pressure of her touch was light, but Carling's mind became heavy, and the room darkened around her. She looked about, and Sima was standing beside her.

"Where are we?" Carling asked, confused.

"We are in your mind, child. You have developed parts of your talent without training. There is so much more that you should know before you develop Dream Walking. We will come to that when we start. It had better be soon if what Una tells me is correct, and she has never been wrong so far. This place is so vast, your talent will be great."

"What has Una said?" Carling asked, confused.

"Neither of my daughters have told you the visions?" Sima asked with some confusion.

"No. I didn't even know that there were any until last night."

"It is best that you learn them from Una herself." Sima took her hand off Carling's head and they came back to the small house.

Carling staggered at the broken connection and sat down heavily on the small stool by the fire. She looked up at the gathered women, seeing the family resemblance between them.

"Tell her what she needs to hear, Una. You should not have kept it from her; they are her visions, not yours," Sima chided her daughter.

"Yes, Ma," Una said and went to Carling's side. "The visions I have had all show you as the mother of a great line. It also shows you as the conqueror of the Romans through your actions."

"How can I conquer the Romans?" she asked, looking around them.

"That part is unclear to me and others as well."

"Others? There are more seers here?" Carling asked.

"We have our ways of communicating, Carling. But many have had visions of you. They all tell me that you are important, and your line must be protected."

"And a man? I presume there is a man somewhere along the way," Carling asked with a little laugh, finding it hard to accept what was being told to her.

"Again, it is unclear. This vision only shows a double-edged sword as a representation of him—two faces, both hard and keenly honed. It is confusing to decipher. I am hoping in time it will become clearer," Una told her kindly.

"If we are to get started, we need to go now," Sima said, gathering her cloak.

"At least stay for a meal before you go, Ma," Una said, standing to face her mother.

"No. Drest sent me a message of danger. We have to leave now and get hidden before it happens. Brietta, you need to get back to the fort. Keelie needs your help."

"Yes, Ma. I miss you so much." Brietta kissed her mother's cheek and hugged her.

"I miss both of you too. Tell Keelie her mother is unwell. I don't think she will last through the winter," Sima told her.

"I will. Safe journey, until we meet again."

"Safe journey, until we meet again," Sima echoed the farewell.

Una passed Carling her things, and they both saw them to the door. Carling stopped dnd looked at Brietta, throwing her arms around the older woman.

"I hope we meet again, Carling. Look after yourself and do as Ma tells you. Safe journey, until we meet again," Brietta said, clinging to the girl.

"I will, Brietta. Safe journey, until we meet again." Carling released Brietta and started down the road after Sima. She had to hurry, as the old woman was faster than she thought. She kept looking back at the woman who had become as close to her as a mother.

Chapter Four

They travelled for the whole of the day, taking the small tracks up into the hills through the forests that grew there. The ancient trees creaked in the cool winds, and the brambles underneath them were dense and tall. Amongst the maze of trails, they came to a large stone with carvings on it. Unerringly, Sima turned and headed further up the hill while Carling stared at the pictures there. Her hand reached up and traced one of them, a coiled snake.

"What was that stone?" Carling called after the old woman as she hurried to catch up. They had not talked much the whole day.

"It is a marker. It tells The People who is around, what their abilities are, and where to find them," Sima replied.

"Will you teach me the symbols as well?"

"That will be part of your education, Carling. Keep your breath for the walk, it gets steeper from here." Sima carried on up the hill without missing a step or looking like she was in any way tired.

Sima was right. The track climbed higher up the hills and it became rocky and hard to walk on. The soft sandals that Carling was wearing began to slip on the loose rocks, and she stumbled several times. Her bundle was getting heavy in her arms, so she stopped and refashioned it to sling it over her shoulders. Looking up she saw Sima, sure-footed, far ahead of her, and she carried on.

Jutting out high on the side of the tallest hill was a small plateau where Carling finally caught up to Sima. The sun was setting opposite them behind the lower hills, sending a golden light washing over them. Sima watched Carling as she stood beside her.

"I now see why Drest calls you the golden one. In this light, your hair is the same colour as the sacred metal." Sima was smiling at her.

"Others have likened it to flowers," Carling told her.

"Yes, those that you are not meant for. Drest will tell you more tomorrow. Come, my cave is just a short walk away." She turned and headed around the rocks.

When Carling followed, she found a cloth covering an entrance to a small cave hanging in front of her. Sima pulled it aside for her, and she entered the dimly lit opening.

"Hold this open and I will get a fire going before it gets too dark," she told Carling.

Carling took her place and watched as she gathered fuel for the fire and deftly struck two stones together. Sparks flew, and Sima gently blew on the ember to encourage a flame. Carefully she placed it in the wood on the hearth and fed it more tinder until it caught.

The curtain was dropped, and the flames grew, sending flickering shadows on the walls of the cave. Carling put her bundle down on the pallet bed that Sima indicated and then sat.

Sima busied herself putting a pot on the flames and putting bits and pieces inside to cook. She picked up another pot and handed it to Carling. "Outside to the right you will come to a stream. Fill this and bring it back."

Carling stood and did as she was bid. The last rays of light were just fading, and she made her way gingerly along the unknown track. The noise came first, the tumbling of water hitting stones as it made its way down the hillside. The white of the water glowed in the soft moonlight that was now shining down. Carefully she held the pot under the flow until it was almost full, and then she headed back. The air was cooling quickly, and a strong wind began to blow. The thin fabric of her tunic was not enough to keep her from shivering.

Ducking around the curtain, she entered the cave. The smell of the food cooking was making her hungry, and the small space was already feeling warm. She placed the pot down by the fire where Sima indicated and went to her bundle. Opening it, she found a warm cloak and wrapped it around her shoulders.

"It does get cold up here. Keelie was wise to give you warmer clothes. She knew the day would come when she would have to send you to me."

"You knew her as a child?"

"I did. She is your kinswoman, I believe; a cousin?"

"That is what she told me," Carling responded, staring into the flames.

That night her dreams were invaded again. This time there were fewer people. Diana and Brietta were there, acting out their own dreams, and off to one side was Sima. She was still and concentrating on what was going on around them. Walking towards Carling came Marcus, his eyes fully on her, reaching out with his hand. His mouth was moving, but there was no sound coming from it.

Within moments she was shaken awake. Her eyes flew open, and she sat up, fighting off the hands that held her.

"Wake up, child!" Sima said, holding on to Carling.

"What's happened? Why did you wake me?" she enquired, finally calming down.

"You were about to do a dangerous thing. What are your feelings for that man?" Sima demanded from her.

"What man?"

"The one in your dream; the one who was calling to you."

"Marcus?"

"If that is his name, then, yes, him."

"He killed my family. I only have anger for him—hatred," Carling told her.

"He does not feel the same way. There is a drive about him. He wants you," Sima said, sitting back on her heels and releasing Carling's arms.

"How did you know about him?" Carling asked, a little fear creeping into her voice.

"I was there, looking out for you, child."

"Will people stop calling me that? I am not a child."

"You may bleed like a woman, but you are still an untrained and untried child in the eyes of The People. A Clansman or Roman would consider you a woman, but you are not with them anymore." Sima was staring off into space, and when she came back, she asked a question Carling was not expecting. "What I want to know is how he can see you in your dream, how he can try to communicate with you. Who are his parents?"

"The commander of the fort—and I don't know who his mother was. Diana is his stepmother."

"Keelie! Her name is Keelie. It does not matter what name they gave her. I am going to have to find out who she was. If he is one of The People, then someone has trained him. He could be dangerous to us," Sima said almost to herself.

"He told me once that he wasn't the monster that I thought he was."

"Carling, you cannot trust him. He is a Roman, was raised to think like a Roman. Go back to sleep, child. I will stand guard again to make sure you are safe."

Carling lay back down while Sima went to her own bed. She sat cross-legged and closed her eyes.

There were no more dreams for Carling that night. She woke in the morning to the sound of Sima moving around and she sat up. Pulling the blanket from her legs and draping it around her shoulders, she stood and moved to the fire.

"Good morning," Sima greeted her as she continued to work.

"Good morning, Sima. What would you like me to do today?" Carling asked, out of habit.

"You are not in their camp anymore, child. Drest will be here later this morning, and he likes my little cakes. While I am making them, we can start your training. There is some food over there for you; once you have eaten, then we will begin."

"Yes, Sima," Carling said deferentially.

"I will say one thing for the Romans: at least they have taught you manners," Sima said with a smile as she watched Carling eat.

The next few hours they spent making small cakes, setting them out on rocks to cook by the fire while Sima set Carling tasks with her mind. The exercises were meant to extend the mind and make it ready for the ability to grow and take root in the subconscious. Carling found them easy and quick to master and was looking for more of a challenge.

Sima laughed and gave in to her wishes, setting her harder goals. This time Carling struggled with them, and by the time the cakes were done she was sweating with the effort it took to master them. She worked through them and concentrated on doing what her teacher was asking of her. Putting the cakes aside, the older woman waited for Carling to be at her most vulnerable. When she picked the moment, she entered the girl's mind.

Making a lot of noise, she felt her flinch and search for what had caused it. Finding Sima, she pulled back from the older woman and retreated further into her mind. Waiting patiently for the girl to become comfortable with her being there, Sima inspected her progress and was pleased with what she found.

While the space that was in a normal mind was large, Carling's was vast. It was no wonder that she was finding some of the tasks easy. There were also hints of other things going on. Other abilities that were lying dormant and on the precipice of developing, and it worried her. She looked up, and Carling was walking towards her shyly.

"You are not shy out in the world, so you shouldn't be in your own mind, child," Sima told her.

"It is a strange sensation having you here, where you can see my thoughts and memories," Carling said to her as she came to stand in front of the old woman.

"I have not looked at either of those things and nor would I ever without your permission. I entered without your knowledge to show you how easy it is, that you should have some defenses in place to stop it. But we will get there. First you need to anchor your ability into your subconscious, and I think you have mastered enough to do that now."

"How do I do that, Mistress?"

"Please never call me that again. You need to forget that term, Carling," Sima told her gently.

"I am sorry; it is a force of habit, Sima."

"Better. I can show you how. Watch." Sima lifted her hand, and a small ball of light appeared. She released it into the air, and it flew to Carling. "Take it, child."

Carling took the light in her own hand and stared into the depths as it glittered and shimmered away. "What do I do now?" she asked, still mesmerized by the ball.

"Place it to your forehead and gently push it in. The information will be transferred to you."

Taking the light, she did as she was told. She felt the pressure build and expand through her mind, filling her with a single note that rang through it. Opening her eyes and looking around, she walked away from Sima and straight to her subconscious. Before stepping in, she turned to her mentor.

"I know what to do now, Sima. But will she come if I call her?" Carling asked with some uncertainty.

"You won't know that until you do what you need to do." Sima gestured for her to enter, and without being invited, she stepped in after her.

Carling moved to the centre of the space; it was dark and hazy, and it reminded her of the place she had seen when Marinus attacked her. She told herself to remember to ask Sima about it. There was a task at hand, and she now understood how important it was for it to be performed properly.

Taking a deep breath, she sent out a single thought. It seemed weak at first, and she pushed some of the energy that was around her into it. The message became stronger, and it raced from her. Carling could feel it searching for the one she was calling. The time it took seemed to stretch on forever until it found her. The message called, and she answered.

Coming out from the darkness that surrounded them was the figure of Brietta. She was dressed as one of The People and not in the normal Roman dress Carling was used to seeing her in. Her hair was down and caught in a loose plait that hung down her front. Brietta was smiling as she neared and stood apart from them. Carling went to embrace her friend, but Sima stopped her with the force of her word.

"No." Sima waited for Carling to turn. "That is forbidden in this place. You are bonded by your love for each other already. You need not form an unbreakable one in here. It is important that you heed me on this, Carling. Never take a hand or so much as touch anyone even by accident in this space. You will force upon them the bond that will forever link you. It is a bond that means you can invade their mind and speak to them without their permission. That is the only restriction on our ability. It is for the Ancestors alone to use."

"Yes, Sima." She stood with her hands clasped in front of her and her head bowed.

"Take charge of your life, child. Stop being subservient to everyone. You are the daughter of a great man, a man who fought and died for your clan and for The People of the Boar. The fate of The People is in your hands—not just in your lifetime, but in those that are to come."

"I will remember that," Carling said formally.

"Good. Now visit for a moment with Brietta; she is busy and needs to get back." Sima turned and moved away from them to give them privacy.

"Is everything all right back at the villa?" Carling asked.

"As well as can be expected, Carling. Cato is missing you terribly. He was most upset when he heard what had happened. Marinus has had the odd turn and he has aged a great deal in the last couple of days. I met Marcus on the road when I was heading back. He asked where you were, and I told him that you had gone from where I left you. Be careful he doesn't find you. I fear he doesn't really have your best interests at heart," Brietta told her with some concern.

"I will remember, Brietta. What of..." She paused for a moment to remember Sima's words. "What of Keelie?"

"She misses you, dear one. You became a daughter to her when she most needed it. I am surprised that you called me and not Keelie."

"She is my kin, but you are the mother of my heart," Carling told her, feeling a little bashful admitting it.

"You honour me, Carling. If I had a daughter, my wish would be that she be just like you. If you need me, you only have to call me. As Ma said, we have a bond of love already."

"Thank you, Brietta. I will let you go back to your duties. Tell Keelie that I miss her, too, as I miss you."

"Farewell and safe journey, Carling, until we meet again."

"Farewell, Brietta, until we meet again." With her words, Brietta faded from sight and Carling felt her loss all over again.

Around her, the space began to change. It became the room of Diana, where she had spent so much of her time in the company of the two women. There was sewing draped over one of the chairs and all the brushes and combs were laid out on the table. Beautiful flowers were gathered in vases, and the perfume of the oils the mistress had liked hung in the air. A tear escaped her eye as she missed the ones she had known for so long.

"You will miss them, child," Sima said at her elbow. "But life is about change. We cannot stay in one place for too long, otherwise we will stagnate. It is time we were back at the hearth. Drest will be here soon."

Carling nodded and watched as Sima left. She looked around her once more and then took a deep breath and exhaled, letting it all slip away and back to the real world where Sima was kneeling in front of her and smiling.

"You have done well, child, for the first part of your training. We will do more tomorrow."

"Thank you, Sima."

Drest was late arriving, and Sima was getting worried. She moved from the cave to the path outside her door, searching for him with great regularity. Carling did not know if this was usual behaviour and felt unsure whether she should ask her. Soon she heard Sima call out, and Carling pulled the curtain aside and left the cave to stand at her side.

"Where have you been, you old man? I have been worried sick about you," Sima called to the figure that was using a large staff to climb the hill. His shaggy, dark ginger beard was tinged with grey, as was his long hair that curled around his shoulders. His leggings were strapped with the lacings of his boots, and his tunic was cinched at the waist with a large belt, from which hung bags and knives.

"Stop your gums flapping, old woman. It's a long, hard climb up to your hovel. Why do you have to live up here?" Drest asked with a twinkle in his eye.

"To stop unwanted guests from visiting." She spoke softer now that he was near, an equal spark in her smile as she greeted him.

"Ah, yes; your guest. What a beautiful child she is, Sima. I have been looking forward to meeting you, Carling," he said speaking to her now.

"Show-off! You have talked to Una and found her name from our daughter."

"Caught out again. I can't put one past you, can I, Sima?" He was chuckling as he embarrassed the small woman.

Their banter made more sense to Carling as she discovered the news that they had a child together. She watched as they moved into the cave and headed in after them. She moved to her bed and watched the pair as they settled down and Sima served him a drink and the cakes they had made that morning. They caught up on their news, and then Drest said something that caught her interest.

"Una had a visitor yesterday while I was there—a Roman. He was looking for the girl," he said, biting into the cake and brushing the crumbs from his beard.

"A Roman? Tall, with hazel eyes?" Sima asked quickly.

"Yes. He was very insistent to know where she had gone."

"What did Una say?"

"She told him she didn't know where Carling was. That she had been picked up yesterday and left to go back to her family." Drest reached out and took another of the cakes Sima was offering.

"Good. We will keep her up here for a while. The Boar People don't need to know she is still with us just yet. I have heard rumours there may be a bit of infighting about to begin inside the clan, and they are too closely tied up with them," Sima told him darkly.

"One day the clans and The People will be one, Sima. It is inevitable. It has happened in the past."

"Yes, it will. I know it will. If the visions are correct, The People will spread wide and far but will be kept secret. Their abilities are feared." Sima looked over at Carling for a brief moment. "And this child is the start of it."

"Visions, yes. That is why I am here. Others have had similar messages, Sima. They say that the change is coming soon, but who knows what that means. It could be in the next few days, or it could be many moons from now. The vagueness of our ability sometimes rankles me," the old man said with a wrinkled brow.

"We all wish our abilities were better, that they were not limited in some form or another. We know that the Ancestors had many more and were limitless, but as we breed with those who have no abilities, our children will gradually have fewer. I fear that the vision is not true, that the two to come will be so limited that they will not be able to carry out their destiny."

"You have to have faith in the Ancestors, Sima. I am sure that they are watching and will not let them fail," Drest told her adamantly.

"What is this vision you are speaking of?" Carling asked, her curiosity now overflowing. "And who are the Ancestors?"

"The Ancestors are the guardians of this land. They were the first in the world and were very great in their abilities. They wielded absolute power over the land, carving out the great valleys and filling the lochs. They moved the land and shaped it to their liking. They are the ones who planted the sacred stones deep into the earth so that they will never fall and the mighty trees that we hold so blessed," Drest told her calmly.

"What happened to them?"

"The originals returned to the earth and are still with us, watching and caring for us. Their descendants are us, The People. We are the product of the joining with the migratory people who came after. It was the will of the Ancestors that we join with them, and we have done so as others have arrived. Always our abilities have bred through."

"We find that if the mother is one of The People, then the ability will be passed to the children, but it is less likely if the father is." Sima looked at the man who had sired her children. "It is true; you know it is. Your male ego is getting in the way."

"Yes. It is the way of man to believe the world revolves around him. Our son is unfortunately of that thinking," Drest said with a little sadness.

"Where is Onnist now?" Sima asked him.

"I heard that he is on his way back. He decided he needed to go to the sacred stones to try to communicate with the Ancestors. I am eager to hear whether he succeeded. Not many now are blessed with their presence. It is almost as if they are pulling away from the world," Drest told her.

"We can catch up on our news later. Carling wants to know more information on the visions," Sima chided gently, getting back to Drest's original thought.

"You must remember that visions are not specific, Carling," Drest answered her. "They are vague pictures and words that come to us. Some get them in dreams and for others it is thrust upon them while they are awake. These visions are very much open to interpretation by the individual. But the ones about you, child, are clearer than most."

"Stop beating around the bush, Drest, and tell the girl what she wants to know," Sima interrupted him.

"All right, old woman. I will as soon as you give me a chance." Drest sighed and cleared his throat before turning back to Carling. "It has been told that you will have two children from whose lines will come two who will rid the world of an evil. It is an evil that was here when the Ancestors arrived. It resisted them and fought them. They managed to contain it, but it will come again. That is the first vision of you. The second is the riddance of the Romans from the land. This one is less clear. It is uncertain how you will manage to do this, and because of this, we are at a loss as to how to advise or even prepare you for it to happen."

"When Una told me of them, I thought they were just fancies," Carling told them.

"It has been a trying few days for you, child. It will take time to accept it all and train. And you will receive training from more than just myself as well. There will be one other, who is more adept at Dream Walking than I am. We will take you to him in the next few weeks," Sima told her.

"Una said that the vision of the father of these children was unclear for her. What about you, Drest? Can you see the man I am supposed to give myself to?" Carling asked.

"No. It is the same for me. A double-edged sword is all I see. I cannot understand what it means, child. It will become evident in time. I have not seen whether you are happy with this man, or even if he loves you. I am sorry we cannot help you more," he told her, and she could see that he meant it.

The training was intensive for Carling. She would spend the days with Sima learning all she could about her ability. While she learned, Drest would do the chores, making sure they were both fed and rested well to continue. Some days Carling was in tears at the pressure in her mind. The aches would pierce her head and leave her shivering and sweating.

Other days it was like she was floating on the breeze. Her mind would wander, and her dreams were precise and clear. The visions she had of Diana and Brietta were so clear; she wished she could talk to them. She missed the villa and the life she had there.

Two weeks after she had arrived at the cave, Sima declared she was ready for her next teacher. They packed up their meagre belongings, and in the company of the elderly couple she headed out into the unknown. The trek over the mountains to the north was hard and cold. On one, the largest of them all, there was still snow on the ground, even though it was early summer.

Their destination was nearby, and Sima started to tell Carling who they were to meet. The man's name was Talorc, and his wife was Nessa. They had many children, and they lived in the forest down on the valley floor. It had been quite a few years since Sima had seen them, and she was hoping for a good welcome to their fireside.

They entered the forest as they descended the slopes of the mountain and the gloom underneath the canopy invaded Carling's mind. She was tired and weary from their travel, and she was ready for a rest. Sima sent Drest on ahead to announce their arrival, and the two women made their way at a slower pace.

"What if they don't want to help me, Sima?" Carling gave voice to her worries.

"It is out of their hands. It is the obligation to The People to help and to teach those who come after. Even if Talorc didn't want to, he still has to help you," Sima told her, taking Carling's arm.

"The more you teach me of The People, the more I am amazed. Our abilities are many, so why haven't the clans used them to rid the lands of the Romans?" Carling asked.

"Because The People do not use them to hurt others. We will fight if we have to, to defend our homes and our loved ones. But to actively seek out those who wrong us and cut them down is something we cannot do. We are of the land, and as such, we respect what blood we spill. We only spill blood to feed and clothe ourselves and give thanks for the life that provided those things."

"Meanwhile, our people are being killed—slaughtered in their beds, women and children." Carling stopped in her tracks as she recalled the image of her mother and little brother. The breath caught in her throat, and she fell to her knees.

"What is it, Carling? What's wrong?" Sima was at her side, kneeling and holding on to her.

"I remember them, how they looked, their bodies burned. My mother, her arm across my brother's cot." She gasped at the vision before her eyes.

"Come back to me, child." Sima took Carling's face in her hands and pushed into her thoughts.

It was a storm of emotions swirling around the memory in the center. Carefully Sima caught the memory up and held it.

Immediately she was battered by the feelings of loss and hatred. Standing firm, she carefully hid the memory deep inside Carling, pushing it down and away from where the girl could access it for now. It would have to be dealt with at some point, and not without help from Talorc.

Carling was staring at her when she returned and took her hands away. She sat heavily on the ground, her own hands shaking at the effort it had taken her to achieve what she did.

"What did you do?" Carling asked her.

"You were in pain. I pushed the pain away. It is still there, but cannot be found—not without help," Sima said between gasps of air.

"I can't remember why I was in pain."

"I took the source away, Carling. We will deal with it after we have talked with Talorc. You should have gone to him straight away; I was a fool to think I could teach you at all."

"But you have, Sima. You have taught me so much. I would still be blind and hurting people without you." Carling stood and helped Sima to her feet.

"That is a nice thing to say to an old woman. Come, we must go, otherwise it will be dark when we arrive." They walked arm in arm in a companionable silence for the rest of the way.

The clearing in the trees came upon them unawares, apart from the yelling of children. They stepped from the darkness and into the fading light of the day. A round house stood in the centre, and around it was a garden, bursting with crops. Tethered well away from the garden were a few animals. Leaping through them were a number of children of varied ages. Their hair was light and straggly, their clothing worn and well used. Their feet were bare and covered in dirt, but they were happy. There were squeals of delight amongst the laughter.

Spotting the newcomers, they raced over to them and waited to be acknowledged. Sima smiled at them all.

"Good afternoon, children; did an old man make his way here?" she asked them.

"Yes, he's in the house with Da and Ma," the eldest of the group said. "We are to take you there straight away."

"Lead on, then, child," Sima said, and they followed the boy to the house.

"Da, Ma, they are here!" the boy called out before entering through the low door.

Carling bent over to pass through the entrance, and as she stood up, she looked around the inside. It brought back memories of her own home on the water, and she pushed the feelings down. It was not the time.

A hearth sat in the middle of the floor, and the large single room was divided into smaller areas. On one side lay the pallets and bedding for sleeping, and another side was for working. Various tools and skins lay ready to be used. The middle was for cooking, and a storage area with large pots was off to one side.

Around the fire sat Drest, a cup in his hand, and three other people. The older, Carling presumed, was Talorc and the woman his wife Nessa. The third looked up at her and stared openly. He was younger, about her age. His eyes were a light blue.

"Welcome, Sima. It has been too long since we last saw you," Talorc said.

"Thank you, Talorc, and you too, Nessa. Have you been well?" Sima asked the woman.

"I'm not with child, if that is what you were enquiring." Nessa laughed and stood to help them with their bundles.

"This is my charge, Carling. The child who has been spoken about." Sima introduced them.

"Welcome to our home, Carling," Nessa said, looking at the girl. "Since the message came, we have been looking forward to meeting you."

"Thank you," Carling said quietly.

"Sima, do you remember our eldest, Veda? He has just come home from visiting my brother," Talorc said proudly.

"You have grown, Veda. The last time I saw you, I think you were about the same size as one of the children out there."

"It has been many moons since you last visited us. Many people worry about you up in that cave of yours," Nessa said as she guided them to seats by the fire and handed them cups.

"I'm fine. I am like an old sheep. I can still wander the hills as sure-footed as ever."

"But Drest here is a regular visitor to our hearth. You can't seem to keep away from my wife's cooking," Talorc joked with the old man.

"That is my weakness. Good food and good company."

"Is that why we have never lived together for very long, old man?" Sima teased him.

"Probably, Sima. The only thing you cook well are those little cakes, and as for your company…" He laughed.

Carling smiled. She had grown used to their ways over the last few weeks. Taking a sip of the bitter ale that her cup contained, she looked up and found Veda still staring. She averted her gaze and tried to pick up the thread of the conversation once more.

"So, you are to stay with us for a while?" Talorc was asking Drest.

"Yes, if you will have us. We have brought some provisions to add to yours. Sima and I would rather keep an eye on Carling at the moment. There are other eyes looking for her," Drest said darkly.

"There is no threat to our home, is there?" Nessa asked, concerned about her children.

"No, not here, Nessa. We are too far north for the Romans to worry about," Talorc eased her fears. "Of course, you are welcome, all of you."

"Thank you, Talorc. I have given her all the training I can, but she needs your help in Dream Walking and defending against those who also can do it. There is one in particular that we need to worry about, but we can get to that later. It is just nice to sit and talk for a change." Sima smiled.

"Veda, go round up your brothers and sisters and tell them to get on with their work. Night is fast approaching, and I want those animals in and secure." Talorc placed a hand on his son's shoulder, breaking his stare. Veda started when his father touched him, and Carling noticed a look on Nessa's face when she glanced between her and her eldest son.

"Yes, Da." He got up, and Carling was surprised how tall he was. Long and lanky, he had to duck his head under the beams of the house and bend over nearly double to get outside.

"He is a good boy, but it is time he had a wife," Talorc said to everyone.

"Do you have someone in mind — or more to the point, does he?" Drest asked with a chuckle, helping himself to more ale.

"He has not mentioned anyone at all. I had hoped he would come back with a wife in tow," Nessa said sadly.

"He is still young yet."

"He is nineteen summers, Drest. Already a man."

"Nineteen is nothing, Nessa; I didn't meet Sima here until I was in my twenties."

"How old are you, Carling?" Nessa asked, leaning forward. "You look too old to be going through your training."

"I am eighteen summers," she replied quietly.

"Carling came late to her abilities. There were no proper rituals to see what her ability was," Sima said. "She grew up as a slave in the fort of the Romans after her family was killed. Our daughter Brietta cared for her."

"That would explain it," Talorc said, looking at his wife.

The conversation shifted, and Carling's ability was not brought up again. The night was a noisy affair, and at one point one of the smaller girls climbed onto her free lap and claimed it. She missed Cato and the cuddles he gave her, and she found herself singing softly to the little girl as she held her. The family group quieted when they heard and listened to the floating notes of her voice. Noticing the lack of activity around her and the child who was asleep on her lap, Carling stopped and blushed at having been noticed again.

"That is a beautiful voice you have, Carling. Would you favour us with a song while the young ones go to bed?" Nessa asked as she took the little girl from Carling's arms.

"I only know a few songs from my childhood. Most I know are theirs," Carling replied in the midst of a deep blush.

"Anything will do, child. None of us are musical in any sense," Talorc said.

One that her mother used to sing to her little brother came to her, and she began the simple tune. The children were all on their beds, wrapped up together like a litter of puppies under the blankets. They watched with their sparkling eyes as she sang to them, one by one falling asleep to the soft tune.

"Oh, I wish you could stay with us. I could use help every night to get them down," Nessa said, smiling sweetly at her.

"If the looks Veda is giving her are anything to go by, she may just stay," Drest teased.

Carling blushed and looked down at her hands. She didn't know what to say or do with the comments. Veda seemed like a nice man, but there was nothing there when she looked at him. Brietta had always said that when a woman met a man she liked there would be an attraction, a wanting to be with him. It was not the way she was feeling with Veda.

Still an early riser, Carling was sitting outside in the cool morning air by herself, listening to the birds calling in the predawn light. A blanket was wrapped around her shoulders and her harp rested on her knee. The strings she was plucking slowly and gently, trying not make too much noise and disturb those still sleeping inside.

The notes she was creating echoed those of the birds in the trees. A songbird now free from her gilded cage, Carling was unsure how to sing anymore, or of the music she wanted to make. Her fingers wandered and played without notice or understanding.

"That is beautiful," a low voice said behind her, and she jumped at the intrusion. Veda walked to her side and sat down beside her. "I'm sorry to make you jump."

Carling could not find her voice to say anything and just kept her head down. The tune changed and was discordant. She stilled her hand and rested it on the strings, quietening their ringing.

"Please don't stop; I thought the fairies had come to take some of my brothers and sisters away." He beamed at her, but she still said not a word in reply.

A rooster let out an ear-splitting crow nearby and they both looked at it. Veda turned back to her with a friendly face. "I guess the family will be up soon. Will you play and sing for us tonight?"

Carling nodded slightly. He stayed with her, and the gulf between them was palpable. She felt every second she could see him out of the corner of her eye. He was no longer watching her but was now looking up into the tops of the trees.

Watching them bend slightly with the morning breeze and seeing the birds that moved between the great limbs.

Music sounded as her fingers wandered again, the melody mysterious and strange. It picked up the tune of a bird and repeated itself, becoming unsure and questioning. Having never really been allowed to sit in a man's company alone like this before, Carling was unsure what to feel or even how to act. Diana had protected her well.

"Put the harp away now, Carling, and come get something to eat," Sima said from behind her. Standing, she left Veda sitting there and headed inside.

Nessa was at the hearth, already preparing the morning meal, and Talorc was busy with the children. Carling tucked her harp away again in her bundle and knelt beside her hostess.

"It was a beautiful way to wake up, Carling. Thank you," Nessa told her. Carling looked at her sideways, unsure whether she was unhappy, and only found a woman who was working away at the dough for the cakes.

"I'm sorry if I woke you. I will try not to do it again," Carling said softly.

"I was awake already when you got up, child. There is nothing to be sorry for." She looked up when she saw Veda enter with the water she had sent him out for.

"You took your time, Son. Did you get waylaid by the fairies?" Talorc called out to him.

"No, Da." He blushed, and Carling kept her eyes down on the dough she was now shaping for the cakes, placing them by the fire to cook.

"I'm sure I heard them out there. You children had better watch how you do your jobs and play today; they may come during the night and spirit you away." He scared the children into shrieks of laughter, sending them scattering away outside the round house.

"It is a beautiful sound, to hear the laughter of an innocent child. Just as beautiful as your playing this morning, Carling," Sima said, coming to sit with the women.

"Thank you, Sima."

"In the camp, were they kind to you?" Nessa asked.

"For the most part, yes. My mistress…sorry, Keelie was very kind. She protected me a great deal. Brietta was like a mother to me, and between them both they cared for and took charge of my education." Her voice was low as she talked about the fort, conscious that they were all listening in.

"And what about the men of the house?" Nessa asked.

"Nessa, enough of the questions," Talorc said.

"I cared for Keelie's son, Cato. He is a beautiful boy. Marinus left me alone, except at feasts when he would have me sing." She reached out and turned the cakes to cook on the other side.

"And his son, Marcus?" Sima asked. Carling had not spoken of him to her in the weeks they had been together, and the dream still worried Sima.

"When he first captured me, he was kind. I would not speak to him, so he called me Tacita, which means *mute*. As I grew, he would always ask if I was being treated well and once came to my rescue when a soldier…" She trailed away for a moment. "After that, he started to call me Flora, or flower."

"Did he ever try anything?" Sima asked, forgetting who else was in the room with them.

"No. Never. I would have killed him." Her voice turned steely and hard at the thought. She remembered the way he had talked to her the night his father had attacked her. How he had looked at her. She closed her eyes against it. She could never love him, could never give herself to that man after he had killed her family.

There were no more questions after that. Carling was left in peace until the morning meal was over and the day's chores were to be done. It was mid-morning when Talorc decided it was time to start her training with him. They sat outside in the sunshine, and he investigated her mind, working out what Sima had taught her already and the exercises she had done.

"Sima has done well. There is not much more for me to teach you, child. Dream Walking, I think, we should focus on first. Everything else is just adding a few bits and pieces to what you already know and can do."

"Dream Walking scares me," Carling admitted.

"As it should. It can be a dangerous place to be if you are untrained. Sima has told me of the dreams she has been there for. Are they always the same?" he asked.

"Yes, they are. Just figures playing out their own dreams."

"In your memory is a special place for dream recollection. May I enter so I can see what these dreams are like for myself?" Talorc asked carefully.

"If you think it will help, then yes, you may enter." She nodded as she gave him her permission.

Talorc placed his hands on her head, the palms cupping her ears, and she closed her eyes. She felt him searching and went to find him. Her memories were like the frescos on the walls of the villa, only smaller. They played across large boards, reliving moments in her life. Talorc moved past them all, not looking at any of them, and headed deeper into her memory space.

Finding the dream memories, he pulled one out, held it in his hands, and studied it. She watched again as the figures moved to their own dreams, their mouths working silently, and then Marcus moving swiftly and directly towards her before she woke.

"He is determined, that one. Definitely one of The People, as Sima suggests. I will teach you how to protect yourself from his watching, Carling. I will also teach you how to communicate with those in your dreams. It is a very useful tool to have, to be able to talk to those far away, to pass messages on." He put the dream carefully back in its place. Placed the dream carefully on the shelf, alongside many others and it became still as soon as his hands let go. "Is there anything you want to know from me?" Talorc asked her gently as they left the memories behind.

"Not about the ability. But I do want to know one thing," she said hesitantly.

"Speak, child. I can't tell you unless you ask the question. That is why, after all, you were brought to us."

"Can you tell me why Veda stares at me?" Her head was down, and she was uncertain how he would take the question.

"Is that all you want to know? Well, I can tell you that one easily, child. He finds you attractive and wants to drink in your beauty," Talorc chuckled as he replied, then stopped and turned to her. "You have not had much experience with boys, Carling; I think Brietta and Keelie protected you too much. It is not a bad thing that a man likes you. Not all men are like that Marcus, who thinks a woman is a possession. You could do worse than my son."

"What if I don't feel the same as he does?" she asked, still nervous with the conversation.

"These are questions for womenfolk. But if you don't, then it is best he learns straight away. A heartache mends a lot quicker if the heart hasn't had time to be fully given." Seeing her confused look, he shook his head. "Do you want me to talk to him for you?"

"Yes, please. I don't want to hurt anyone, least of all you and your family," Carling said quickly.

"Sometimes love comes on immediately. You see a person and you know that they are the one for you. Other times it comes on slowly, gradually. I will ask Veda to stop the staring, but how about we take it slowly? You may find yourself in love with him yet." He grinned at her.

Carling nodded and they carried on, knowing that it would not be as he said. Once back out into the bright sunshine, Talorc kissed her forehead as if she were his own daughter and let her go. "Now, shall we get down to work?" he asked her.

That night, she saw Talorc pull his son outside and walk around the enclosure talking. Nessa came to her side and put an arm around her. "It feels like you have been here with us for a long time, Carling. You have fitted into our family so easily."

"Thank you, Nessa." She still had her eyes on the men outside.

"If you were to join us permanently, we would welcome you with open arms. Veda, I think, has already decided on you." There was a satisfied smile on her face as she watched her husband and son.

"He is very nice," Carling said carefully, and Nessa turned to look at her.

"But you don't feel the same way," Nessa said, a little disappointed.

"No, I don't." She did not meet her eyes and felt a little worried she had changed this woman's opinion of her.

"We cannot help who we fall for, Carling. Is that what Talorc is talking about with him at the moment?"

"I think so." Her words were quiet.

Nessa gave her a squeeze. "You are still welcome here for as long as you like. I had hoped, I must admit, that you and he would perhaps join, but if it is not to be, then it is not. But then again, it has only been a few days in each other's company."

"That is what Talorc said this afternoon."

"My husband giving love advice?" Nessa laughed gently. "You will know when you love someone, Carling. It will be like they take your breath away, and it is not just when you meet them for the first time. It is every time they look at you. It is when you can sit and talk for hours and have no idea what you are saying to each other. It is the ache you feel when you are away from them, like your heart has been cleaved in two. It will come for you, I am certain."

"How can you be so certain?"

"The visions, for one. If the children the world is waiting for indeed come from you, then they need to be born of love. A pure and strong love, one that cannot be broken. Because in the end, that is what will save us all. Love." She turned to look out the doorway again and saw her husband and son returning. "Come away now, Carling. Best he does not see you watching them."

Nessa drew her away from the doorway and back to the fireside. The two men entered, and Veda went to his blankets and picked them up. Without a word or a look her way, he headed back outside with them.

"He will be all right," Talorc said to his wife when she looked up, worried. "Give him time."

"Carling, can you give us a song?" Drest asked.

She fetched her harp and began to play. The children gathered around her and listened to the simple words of a child's song she had translated from the Roman tongue. They clapped along, and the next time she sang it they tried to sing along with her. The last song she played that night was again the one she had sung the previous night.

Sitting on her bed, Carling played while everyone settled. Their forms were huddled under blankets, the dying fire sending the shadows to deepen in the house. She finished the song and tucked her harp away, then lay down watching the embers. A figure moved in the doorway, and Veda entered the house. She watched him as he found his spot around the fire and covered himself. His face was clear in the firelight, and she saw him look her way. He had been crying.

Chapter Five

Night after night was spent with Talorc in her mind as Carling dealt with the dreams. She pushed through to Brietta one night and felt such elation at the progress—until Marcus was there again. Hearing her name called, she turned and saw him running towards her. He was reaching out, desperate to contact. She could see the determination in his eyes.

"No!" she shouted and sat bolt upright. Sima was at her side in a moment to comfort.

"He's gone." Sima crooned, smoothing the hair from Carling's face. "He is not there anymore."

Carling looked around and found she had woken them all. They were lying down again, covering themselves up and still watching her. Sima kept her arm around her.

"Set your defenses. Just as you were shown. Go through the steps and set them," Sima told her quietly. Carling nodded and tried again.

The process of working through them calmed her, giving her focus, and the fear began to recede. Why was he so desperate? Brietta had not told her of any problems with the family, but she had not asked either.

She settled down and closed her eyes. The space between wakefulness and dream was dark and empty. She worked on the defenses, funneling energy into them and making sure that they would hold tight. Then slowly she dropped down into the dream world.

Her body was moving, almost like she was flying, and she was directing herself to find Brietta again. She wanted to talk to her. Off in the distance she found her spark of life and steered her course towards it. Just before she reached it, another spark flared on the horizon, burning large and bright. It was not the same colour as Brietta's green, instead it was bright blue. Carling moved toward it, drawn by the sheer size of the beacon.

Nearing it, she recognised the loch that was passing underneath her. She was sure her old home was not that far off, and she lowered herself to the shore. The beacon was on the opposite shore, and she stood looking at it. It was flaring up and dancing, the colour reflecting in the stillness of the loch. Carling knew this was just a dream. Rising back into the air, she crossed over the water and landed near the beacon, watching the waves of light that came from it, seeing the definitive figure inside.

Gradually Carling moved closer. It was dazzling to the eye, the display before her, and became brighter as she stepped carefully towards it. She prayed that the person did not have the ability to see her. The light was now moving away from her, and she quickened her pace. It stopped and turned back towards her.

Carling stepped behind a tree and waited. The light passed her, and she watched the form as it moved. It was definitely a man. She could see his outline now and the way he was dressed. He was stripped to the waist, and his back became clear in the shifting light. Stretched down the length of his torso were strips of scarred flesh. Carling gasped at the sight, and the man turned at the sound.

For a moment—only the briefest of seconds—she saw his face, and Carling gasped again. His eyes were looking directly at her, and they seared into her soul. Her heart felt like it skipped a beat. He moved towards her, a question on his face. The way he moved reminded her of Marcus, and she got scared for the second time that night. She forced herself to wake up.

Carling's eyes flew open, and she sat up. The room was dark, and the embers were still burning dimly. Very carefully she left her bed, taking the blanket with her. The night was clear, and the moon hung full and heavy in the sky, illuminating the enclosure with a silvery light. Moving out into the open, she draped the blanket around her shoulders to keep out the cool air. The vision had shaken her, even more than the rushing Marcus.

She heard a step behind her and turned. Veda was there with his hands up, slowly walking towards her.

"I mean you no harm, Carling. I saw you get up and was worried, especially from earlier," he whispered quickly.

"Thank you for your concern, but I am fine," she said and turned back to face the forest. Looking up at the stars far above them, she still felt unsettled and shaken by the blue eyes.

"Da talked to me. He told me that I was making you feel uncomfortable. I am sorry if I did." He was beside her now.

"I hope I can count you as a friend, Veda. I don't have many of those at the moment—or family," Carling said sadly.

"I think my parents have already adopted you anyway. So, if we cannot be in love, then counting you as a sister will have to do," he told her, and she could hear the sad note to his tone.

"Just what you need, another sister." Carling gave a small laugh, trying to dispel his mood.

"Yes, but I would be honoured to have you as a sister. And you never know, maybe one day…" he trailed off, unable to speak what he really wanted to say.

The man from her dream came back into her mind, and she knew that there never would be a "one day" for Veda and herself. "I don't think so, Veda. I'm sorry."

"Never hurts to dream." They were quiet for a while longer.

Under the trees, something was moving. Carling could hear the brambles rustling, and it sounded quite near. She tensed up and tried to see what it was that was making all the noise, but she only saw a fleeting movement and then it was gone.

"Don't worry, it's only the wolf," Veda said in a calm voice.

"A wolf! Shouldn't we wake up Talorc and the others?" she said hastily, looking out into the darkness. She was instantly fearful of the large creature that was out there, stalking the small enclosure.

"Don't worry, she won't hurt anyone here. She grew up in this forest. I can tell her to go away if you are uncomfortable with her being here." There was amusement in his voice, a lightness that had not been there just moments before.

"You can talk to animals?" She turned to him, her eyes still wide.

"Of course I can, that is my ability. I am a Whisperer."

"When did you discover you could do that?" She turned back to the woods, trying to see the creature that was making the noise.

"The animals told me. They came to me at first. Coming face-to-face with a she-wolf was interesting for the first time, but nothing like meeting a bear." He was now laughing at her reaction to the news.

"A bear? You have communicated with a bear?"

"I have. He is up in the mountains waiting for me," Veda explained. "She was supposed to wait with him."

"Does she have a name?" Carling asked, still peering into the darkness of the forest.

"They don't have names like we do. She is just 'She' or 'Wolf'."

"And the Bear? I suppose he's just called 'Him'?" Carling asked.

"Yes." He paused for a moment before continuing. "That first morning when you were playing out here, the birds were very surprised you could echo back their tones. They said it wasn't words, but the sounds were similar."

"They said that?" Carling asked, turning to him with some surprise.

"They like you," Veda said. "Birds are flighty and shy, squirrels are jittery, wolves are stealthy, and bears are whatever bears want to be. The birds are about to wake. Do you want to sing to them again?" He asked, the corners of his mouth twitching slightly.

"You are teasing me now, Veda."

"I am, Carling." He smiled broadly at her. "She would like to get to know you." This time there was no jest.

Carling's eyebrows shot up quickly. "A wild wolf wants to meet me?"

"Yes."

"How can you tell? She is out there, and we are here."

"I can see her, and our communication is more in the mind than physical," Veda told her. "A bit like Mind Touch, only I brush the minds of animals."

"I would be honoured to meet her," Carling said with a little nervousness.

"We will need to go see her. We cannot let her in, as the cow will stop giving milk in fright—and trying to convince a cow to give milk is not a conversation I want to have to do again."

"Do you tease all your brothers and sisters in this way?" Carling asked.

"The ones I like most, yes." He gave a crooked smile and headed towards the gate. Opening it carefully, they both slipped through and headed into the trees.

Coming towards them on soft padded feet was a large grey wolf with her tongue hanging out as she stopped in front of Veda. He reached out and scratched her ears, and she leaned into his touch. She sat on her haunches, and Veda beckoned Carling on to meet the massive wolf.

"Hold your hand out for her to sniff your scent," he told her quietly.

Nerves gripped Carling as she reached out with her hand. The nose of the wolf was wet and cool as She nudged her hand to smell.

Veda smiled and nodded, "She said that you smell like wildflowers and are very special. She also asked if you were my mate." Even in the darkness, Carling could sense his blush.

"What did you say back?"

"That you were not. She said that was good, as it would not do to be with a littermate."

"See, even She believes that we are not meant to be." Carling smiled. The wolf moved closer to Carling and nudged her hand again. She reached up and rubbed the furry ears, feeling how soft they were. Veda had his head cocked to one side as he listened to the wolf.

"She says that there is someone camping in the forest nearby. I will have to inform Da about it when he wakes. We need to keep a watch on anyone who passes through our forest these days. There are many who are of the clans but are sympathetic to the Romans."

A bird called from the treetops, a lonely sound on its own. The wolf turned her head to look further into the trees and then gave Carling a lick of the hand. Softly the wolf left them and was soon hidden by the bracken.

"Come; we had best be going back in." He led the way and held the gate for her.

More birds were now singing to the dawn that was coming. The darkness was turning to grey, and the horizon to the east was becoming lighter. Carling stood once more in the center of the enclosure and listened to the song that was swelling in the air.

Wings flapped, and a tiny bird landed on a post near her and twittered while turning its head to see her clearer.

"He wants you to play and sing." Veda laughed.

"I can't, it would wake the family," Carling said, worried.

"They will wait. Let's get the fire going inside."

"I'll start the morning meal. It is the least I could do for your mother. She has looked after us so well."

They walked slowly back to the round house, still talking softly. Veda stopped and listened to something far off. He held her back for a moment, and she waited for him to speak.

"She said that the man is on his way here. He is moving quickly and quietly, but she can smell him."

"Who do you think it might be?" Carling looked around the enclosure.

"I don't know, but he is heading straight here. Go inside and wake Da and Drest," Veda instructed her quietly.

Carling sensed he was worried and hastily headed inside. The sleeping forms inside were dark shapes in the dim light of the house and were making the soft sounds of deep slumber. She made her way to Talorc first and shook his shoulder. He came awake immediately, and she placed a finger over her mouth to tell him to be quiet. She found Drest with his arm over Sima, and she carefully woke him. They both followed her from the house and met with Veda, who filled them in.

As the sky started to turn from an inky black into the first blue of morning, a figure stepped from the shadows of the trees. He wore a cloak with a hood, which was pulled up over his head, with only his bright ginger beard poking out. He carried a staff in one hand and a bag over his shoulder. He stopped at the gate and pulled the hood off.

"Is a cousin not welcome then, kin?" the man called out loudly enough to wake everyone.

"Onnist?" Drest called out.

"What are you doing here, old man? I thought you would be in your house slowly going senile." Onnist opened the gate and entered the enclosure. His father rushed to meet him and pulled him into an embrace.

"Why didn't you send word you were coming?"

"This is only a stopping point for me. I am heading south and east to the Bull lands."

"Your Ma will be happy to see you. She has been worried about you, Son." Drest's arm was draped around his son's shoulders as they walked towards the others. He looked up and saw Carling ducking back into the house.

"Welcome, Onnist," Talorc said, extending an arm for the newcomer to clasp.

"Thank you, Talorc. It is good to be here."

"Why didn't you come find us last night?" Talorc asked him.

"There was a wolf trailing me. I spent the night up a tree, which was not very comfortable. This morning when I heard it leave, I took my chance." He was looking around the enclosure.

"She wouldn't have hurt you. I have asked her not to hurt humans in the forest," Veda told him.

"Good to see you again, Cousin." Onnist took Veda's hand and shook it.

"Come inside and get some breakfast." Talorc held the door aside for everyone to enter.

Carling was stirring the fire back to life when they entered, and she looked up shyly from where she was working. Nessa was stirring in her blankets and looked over at the men.

"Could you have made any more noise, you lot?" she whispered at them, then turning to see if any of the children had been woken.

"Look who has come visiting, my love," Talorc said, indicating the newcomer.

Nessa sat and peered through the gloom, and then the fire caught and flared. She gasped a little when she saw the flames sending an evil cast on Onnist's face and then regained her composure.

"Onnist, welcome. It has been a long time since you visited us." She stood, disentangling the blankets from her legs and moving towards the young man. She embraced him and led him over to the fire. "Drest, wake Sima. She will be mad if she wakes to find him here and we had not woken her."

Drest moved over to his wife and gently woke her. Sima turned in her bed and looked at the gathering before her. Her eyes then rested on Onnist. They widened, and she flew out of bed, embracing her youngest child.

"How have you fared, my son? Was your journey worth it?" she asked, checking him over.

"Ma, stop it. I am fine. I have no injuries, I was not attacked, and we will talk about the journey later," he said with a smile, knowing her actions were meant with love.

Carling was not watching the interaction of the little family as she started to prepare the morning meal. Concentrating on making the small berry-filled cakes right, she did not see them sit down on the opposite side of the fire, but she did listen to their conversation. She looked up and saw a pair of bright eyes contemplating her and looked away again.

Sima caught where his gaze had landed. "Onnist, this is Carling. She is training with Talorc and me."

"It is nice to meet you, Carling," he said as he nodded his head to her.

From her side of the fire, she looked at the man and nodded back. Her voice had been taken from her again. Nessa joined her and helped to finish the meal. She was grateful for the steadfastness and sure hands of the woman at her side. There was something about this newcomer that did not sit comfortably with her. The way he looked her over made her feel like she was back at the fort and under the scrutiny of the soldiers and officers.

After the adults had eaten, the children began to rise. Carling helped to feed the youngest child and then held her while Nessa tidied up. The children were all sent out of the house to do their morning work while the adults talked. Sima called Carling over to sit with them, and she brought the baby with her.

"A beautiful child—is it yours?" Onnist asked her as she sat.

"No, Onnist, this is Nessa and Talorc's youngest." Sima laughed and answered for Carling. "Now tell us of your journey. Was it as you had hoped?"

"Yes, it was. The travel there was long, slow, and uneventful, if you don't count a few blisters along the way and the odd encounter with a wolf." He smiled at Veda for a moment, proud of his own jest. "I made it to the house with part of autumn still in the air. Rowena welcomed me, and so did Galen, who was there as well."

"As is right. He should look after his mother. Has he returned there permanently?" Drest asked.

"No. He stayed for the winter. I believe he does so each year. He remained there with her and me until the spring, so he could repair the damage done during the winter. He said he would go back before the summer ends to make sure that she has enough stocks for the coming cold. He was as quiet as ever. I could not get him to talk much at all, only to say a few words."

"But what of the Ancestors? Did you get to speak with them? Did they give you any instruction?" Drest interrupted his telling.

"Yes, Da, let me get to it." Onnist laughed at his father's eagerness. "I did go up to the stones several times, but there was nothing. Then one night I was called in a dream. Only one met me that night. He wore a great cloak that covered him all over. He met me at the entrance of the stones and spoke so softly to me."

"And..." Drest prompted.

"I was told to seek out someone, a person who has lived apart from The People and needs to be brought into the fold," he told them proudly.

Drest and Sima both looked at Carling briefly. "Who is this person, Son?" Sima asked him.

"A man. He lives in the south."

"What do they want with him?" Drest asked while Sima seemed to relax a little.

"I am to give him instruction and a message and I cannot tell you what those are. The Ancestor insisted that it should only be given to him." Onnist's chest seemed to swell in self-pride at the importance of this mission and that the Ancestors had chosen him to carry out their wishes.

"We wish you well, then, for your quest," Talorc said. "But rest here for a while — or is it an urgent mission you are on?"

"Thank you, I can stay for a day or two," Onnist replied, looked Carling's way as she moved the child on her knee as it began to fuss.

Carling was playing with the children through the forest, chasing them and being chased in return. Their laughter echoed off the large trees and bounding among them was the she-wolf. Her tongue lolled out as she chased after the little ones, who would turn and shriek. Veda was amongst them, keeping an eye on the wolf all the time, making sure she did not play too roughly with the little ones.

Hiding behind one of the large trees, Carling was breathing hard from running, waiting for one of the children to run past so she could leap out. To play like this, innocent and free, was a novelty to Carling after the regime of being a slave. Her eyes were bright and there was colour in her cheeks. She was enjoying herself a great deal.

She heard soft sneaking footsteps coming and leaped out from her hiding spot. Rather than the child she expected to see, she came face-to-face with a man's chest. Hands reached out and caught her as she stumbled back and looked up at the face of Onnist, who was smiling at her.

"I am not what you expected?" He laughed, seeing the look of shock on her face.

"I thought you were one of the children." She stepped back, and he released her.

"You are a ways out in the forest, Carling. Aren't you worried about getting lost?"

"I know the way." She started to move back to the house, and he walked with her. He had positioned himself very close to her, adding to her nervousness.

"Ma and Da have told me your story. A child of The People enslaved and then returned. Was it a hard life with the Romans?" he asked her.

"I was one of the lucky ones. My mistress was very kind," Carling replied quickly.

"Yes, that would be Keelie. I was very young when she was sent to the commander of the camp along with my sister."

"Brietta is very special to me," Carling told him.

"Ma told me she looked after you. Tell me, in your time at the camp, did you come across others from The People?" Onnist asked her with a curious tone.

"Only Keelie and Brietta. Why? Is that where the man you are after is from?" A thought flickered through her mind, but she dismissed it as being silly. Why would the Ancestors want him?

"I cannot tell you, child." His tone was condescending. She was not much younger than him, and for him to call her *child* made her feel angry. Carling tried to suppress it.

Not watching where she was going, she stumbled over a root that jutted from the ground. Onnist was there helping her back upright, and he kept his hands on her. She tried to shake him off, but he held on.

"I know something of what goes on in the camps of the Romans. Tell me, are you experienced in that particular area, Carling? Or did my sister and her friend keep you chaste and pure?" he asked her. His voice was low and was full of suggestion.

Finally freeing herself, she turned and walked away from him. Her cheeks were flushed red with the words he had asked her.

"That is none of your business, Onnist," she blurted when she could bring herself to speak.

"Seeing you yesterday cooking at the fire and a child in your arms was a very pleasing thing. It suits you. I was just wondering; that is all."

Before Carling could reply to him, a grey flash sped out of the undergrowth and slammed straight into Onnist. He fell to the ground, his arms going up to protect his head, screaming at the sudden appearance of the she-wolf. The wolf was bounding away as fast as she had arrived. For a moment Carling was able to keep the laughter at bay, but it spilled out when she saw Veda ducking behind a tree.

"It is not funny," Onnist growled angrily, getting back up and brushing himself off. Leaves and twigs were stuck all over his back and in his hair.

"I'm sorry, but it was very funny." Carling was moving off and hoping to leave him behind her, but he followed, still talking.

"Veda needs to keep better control of that animal." He hurried to catch up with her.

"I don't think he has that much control over the wolf. He makes requests and it is up to the wolf to decide what she will do," Carling said, remembering a conversation she had with Veda about his ability.

"That is ridiculous. What is the point of the ability of a Whisperer if they cannot have control over the animals?" he barked back.

"It is not about power, Onnist. It is the same with all the abilities."

"That is a very innocent way of thinking, Carling. The abilities are ours to use as we will. The world is changing, and we are going to need to change with it. The Romans are here to stay, and the faster The People accept that, the better the assimilation will go," he told her with some heat.

"You cannot mean that." Carling stopped and rounded on him. "I may have been protected, but I knew what was happening for those who were not so lucky to have a protector. I know slaves were raped—not just girls, but boys as well. You have no idea what they are capable of. The Romans are a brutal people. They killed my father for not agreeing with them. They killed my mother and baby brother. They kill when they do not get their way. And they kill when someone is of no use to them, like my grandmother."

"I understand you have a personal grievance against them, but they are here, just as the Celts and the clans, and all those who came before. They are another race we need to breed with, to accept into the land," he told her sharply.

With her mouth hanging open and disbelief on her face, she turned and stalked away from him. The Romans to her were conquerors. Even when there was no resistance against them, they took what they wanted with force. Now to hear them being defended by someone like Onnist made her so mad.

"Carling! Please wait," he called and ran after her.

"No. I will never," she shouted back to him. By now she had reached the gate to the enclosure, and she ran through it. Sima was sitting by the door grinding the grain. She lifted her head when she heard Carling yell out, then watched as her son came chasing after her.

"What is going on?" Sima said, standing as Carling came closer.

"Ask him," Carling retorted, heading into the house. She paced up and down the dim room. When that didn't calm her, she tidied her belongings. She could hear them outside talking. Drest was there now, his deep voice a calming murmur under the others. Soon it was only his voice that was talking.

"Your views are not shared by many, Onnist, especially Carling. She has the advantage over you of actually seeing these people up close, how they think and act. Can you blame her for being so anti-Roman?"

"No, Da. But they are just another people," Onnist argued.

"You are young yet still, Son. Your views will change again. We are all working towards this vision, helping Carling prepare for what may lie ahead."

"I have my own instructions. The Ancestors have revealed to me what I must do also. I can only assume it is to do with the merging of our peoples."

"What is this mission they have sent you on?" Sima asked him. "You have not told us."

"You would not understand, Ma. You are just a woman." His tone was of exasperation and condescension.

"That is no way to talk to your mother, Onnist. That is not the way of The People; you know this! We did not raise you this way," Drest said, clearly losing patience with his son.

"And yet you are defending her. If women were as strong as us, she would be defending herself."

"Oh, believe me, Son, I can defend myself. A man is only as good as the woman he is with. If you start a union with the belief that you are better than your wife, then that union will be unfulfilled and unhappy. I don't understand where you got these notions that men are better than women," Sima exclaimed disappointedly.

"Maybe from the fact that my mother abandoned me at the age of seven into the care of my father. You were not together," Onnist threw at her.

"That was a mutual agreement between us and had nothing to do with you, Son. We still love each other, still care for each other," Drest told him.

"This has nothing to do with what we were talking about. The Romans are here to stay; they do not give up territory easily," Onnist insisted with frustration.

"No, they don't. But it has been seen that they do leave our lands," Drest retorted.

"I have heard the vision. That child in there is supposed to drive them out. How? Does anyone know?"

"It is still unclear," Drest confirmed for him.

"Well, my mission is clear. I must do what I have to do. That child—"

"She has a name, Onnist. Carling. Use it," Sima demanded.

"Carling is only a child still. They are many. The man I am supposed to meet is one of us. He does not appreciate what he can do in this mess, what he will bring to The People." Onnist was sounding exasperated at having to explain again.

"She is not a child anymore." Talorc's voice cut through the argument and Carling gasped from the other side of the doorway. "Carling has finished her training. There is no more that I or anyone else can teach her. And you are wrong, Onnist. If there is anyone in our lands who can send those dogs running, it will be Carling. Her mind has a vast capacity, and Sima and I both have seen what else lies dormant within her. Carling still has not reached her full potential, and I pity the man or woman who stands in her way."

"She is only one person, Talorc. With this man we can have more of a hope to succeed in bringing the two peoples together. The Ancestors—"

"And what of the clans? Do they not get a say in this reorganization that you are hoping for? Have they not lived with us together in peace for many years? Are we supposed to abandon them now, leave them to the mercy of the Romans?" Talorc asked, cutting over the top of him.

"It is either that or have them join with us. With The People whispering in their ears, I am sure they can be turned to our way of thinking," Onnist told him.

"Whispering in their ears? Are you inferring we use our abilities to our advantage?" Veda asked.

"Yes, we must. Those who can, must use every ability we have to make them join us," Onnist stated with a matter-of-fact tone, as if it were the most natural thing to do.

"Onnist, no," Sima said, shocked at her son's words.

Carling could stay quiet no longer. She exited the house and stood in front of Onnist. Her eyes were hard and flinty as she faced him.

"Shall we use the same ways to change your mind? Would you like me to enter your mind and make you see what we are talking about? It would be an easy thing, and it would not take long. I can be in and out and you would soon be talking a different way. I just need to reach out my hand—" Carling lifted her hand up and out to him.

"No. You can't." Onnist stepped back from her.

"But that is what you would be asking us to do to others," Carling reasoned. "If you are not willing to have it done to you, then you should not ask it of others to accept. As I have been taught, and I assume you were too, we do not use our ability to harm others."

"But it would not hurt them. It is a matter of changing their minds," he stammered.

"How do you know? Have you used it yourself? Have you gone into someone's mind without their permission?" Carling asked him.

"No, I haven't. I am a Seek. I can't do that," he stammered, stunned that Carling was talking to him this way.

"I have, Onnist. It is not a pleasant experience. Maybe you need to learn of others' abilities before you go talking about things you don't know," she told him quietly.

"Talorc may say you have finished your training, but you still speak and think like a child!" Onnist spat at her.

Her hand was raised and swinging, and her palm connected with his face with a loud slap that echoed around the enclosure. In that briefest of connections, she accidently saw a flash from inside Onnist. His feelings after being visited by the Ancestor had festered in his mind and had become a twisted thing, wound up with his own self-importance. There was something else there that she was sure she was never meant to see. A flash of a face, the hazel eyes and smile of Marcus.

"You little bitch!" Onnist was advancing on her. Veda and his father quickly held him back while Sima steadied Carling, who had stumbled from the vision.

"I think it was time you were on your way, Onnist," Nessa said as she came to stand with Carling. "You are no longer welcome at our hearth."

Drest had already ducked into the house and gathered his son's belongings. He held them out to Onnist with disappointment in his eyes.

"Just go. I hope one day we can agree on something, but I am afraid on this we are just too far apart," he told his son flatly.

"You choose this child over your own flesh and blood? Her over your own son?" Onnist's face was bright red and his eyes wild still.

"We are all of the same blood, Onnist. It is not a choice between you. Go with our blessings and our love. Safe journey, until we meet again," Sima said, leaving Carling in Nessa's care and standing beside her husband.

Onnist snatched his bag from his father and gave them both a look of disgust. "It will be a cold day when we meet again. I fear it is not going to go well for any of you."

He shook off the restraining hands of Veda and Talorc, turned, and walked away from them. Sima was shaking with sobs as she watched him leave. Her youngest child. Drest held her close as they walked away from the small group.

Carling had tears in her eyes at the pain she had caused them. It was not her intention for this to happen; she had not wanted them to be split so drastically. She tried to rise from her seat to go after them to apologize, to try and make things right again, but Nessa held her down with a gentle hand and look.

"No, Carling. Leave them be for a while," Nessa told her as she placed a motherly arm around her.

Chapter Six

Night under the trees was completely dark, and Carling stumbled on the bracken and roots at her feet, tripping often. Reaching out to steady herself as she fell once more, her hand grazed over the rough bark of a large trunk, pressing deep into her skin, and scraping away at it. Her breath was coming in rapid gasps as she pressed on, holding her bundle close to her chest. The cloak she wore snagged on a fallen log and pulled her backwards, and she fell onto the soft leaves underneath her, knocking what little breath she had from her lungs.

She sat for a moment as she tried to catch a breath, leaning against the rotten wood. Carling had waited until she was sure they were all asleep before leaving. It was a decision she had come to while she lay in the dark, thinking of the events of the day. She had smiled throughout the little ceremony Talorc performed around the fire that night, declaring her fully grown. But the smile had faded when she saw the drawn faces of Drest and Sima. She had come to think of them as family, and it hurt her to think she had brought them so much pain by arguing with Onnist.

With eyes closed, she slipped into the state between dreaming and wakefulness and searched out the slumbering mind of Talorc. She waited patiently for him to notice her and respond to her call. Their connection was still strong, and it did not take him long to realise that she was there.

"Carling," he greeted her.

"Talorc. When you wake, I will be gone. Don't rouse yourself now. I am already deep into the forest. I cannot stay and bring more grief to you all. What happened this afternoon should not have, and I am as much to blame as Onnist was. I let my personal emotions and feelings erupt at him instead of listening and discussing the issue. I dishonoured your hearth with my actions and words." She stood before him, her hands clasped in front of her, and her head bowed.

"You don't have to go. You do no such dishonour to us. Please come back. Come back where it is safe, and we can look out for you," Talorc pleaded with her.

"No. I must go on my own. It is time I took charge of my own life, Talorc, to learn to look after myself. All my life I have been looked after and protected. Thank you for all your help, for your teachings. I will remember you and Nessa always. Please give everyone my love, especially Sima and Drest, and tell them I am sorry."

"Running away will not solve anything, Carling. It is never the answer to any situation. They both understand and know that what happened was not your fault. They are not angry with you," he said gently.

"You don't understand. When I slapped Onnist I saw into his mind. I saw the man he seeks, and he is not one to bargain with easily. I know him. He is the one who killed my parents. Onnist will not withstand Marcus's mind and will. He will become his puppet," Carling told him.

"This Marcus is the man from the dreams?"

"Yes. He will use Onnist to find me. If I stay with you, you will all be in danger. I cannot have that happen. I will not be the reason another child is brought up as a slave to them." Her voice shook with the emotions she was feeling.

"If you are certain of your own mind, then that is what you should do, Carling. But please, come back and visit."

"Safe journey, until we meet again, Talorc," she bade him.

Carling pulled away from the connection before he could say another word, and tears fell from her eyes. She hardened her defenses against both Sima and Talorc, shutting them from her mind. The journey would be hard enough without them trying to break through to her every night.

With the message now given, Carling looked out into the darkness that enveloped her surroundings. She sat for a while, pulling her cloak tighter to keep the chill that was creeping in since she had stopped moving. Now that her breathing had slowed from the ragged gasps from her hasty travel, the night noises of the forest began to creep into her hearing. Creatures who inhabited the dark hours moved all around her. She heard rustling in the leaves nearby and the almost silent whooshing of soft feathers overhead. Carling found them strangely comforting. A darker shadow in the night moved before her, and she pulled herself into a tight ball as it came closer.

A furry head and hot breath nudged her cheek, and the she-wolf sat beside her. The warmth from her body was comforting, and Carling leaned against Wolf. With the tears from her eyes skipping over the dense fur, the wolf licked Carling's face with her long tongue, and they curled together in the darkness. Carling slept.

Dreams washed over her, snippets of memory, words spoken in haste. Confusing and incomprehensible. Then he was there. Tall and dark of hair. Eyes hazel and staring. She watched him carefully, trying to move from his sight—but he was just standing, his arms crossed over his chest, a smile playing on his lips.

"I see you, Flora," he finally spoke to her.

"Go away! Get out of my mind!" she yelled to him.

"No, I will not. You have learned much from your teachers. And Talorc is right. Your mind is so vast. I sensed it when you were younger. I had a closer look when you were just twelve."

"What do you want from me?" Carling demanded of Marcus.

"Our destiny. The people who trained me have their own visions. In ours, you and I are together. They told me when I first went for my training. A woman with gold hair, like a summer sun, and as beautiful as a flower. You are that woman. That is why I named you Flora."

"No, I am not. We are not meant to be. My children will never be yours, Marcus."

"Even if I love you? Does that not mean anything?" he said more softly.

"Never. I could never love you, Marcus." Carling stood firm.

"I fell in love with you when you were just a child still, after they showed me the vision you would grow to be. I have waited for you to grow, Flora. I have not forced myself on you and have been patient. I did not use my ability to change your mind, though I was sorely tempted several times, especially after you sang that song. I miss you, Flora. The villa is not the same without your sunny smiles, your laughter, and your beautiful voice," Marcus said, and she could see he meant it.

"You cannot miss what has never been yours, Marcus. The night you killed my parents was the night that I pledged vengeance against you and those who permitted it to happen," Carling told him strongly.

"But that is not the way of The People. A peaceful way, a calm and accepting way is how we are supposed to deal with things," Marcus said.

"I am half clan. Their way is a bit more direct."

Marcus moved towards her quickly and then came to a sudden stop when a low and menacing growl thundered through Carling's mind. The vision of a grey she-wolf stalked in between them and glared at Marcus, her teeth showing in a snarl.

"How is this possible?" he called out slowly, moving away from the wolf.

"You have seen my mind, you tell me," Carling called to him. Gathering all the energy she could, she forced him from her dreams. She worked quickly to keep him out and then sat on the ground. The wolf came to her side.

"Thank you," she said softly to Wolf.

"No need to thank. Protecting the pack is what we must do. And you are pack, no matter what you may think." The voice was like honey in her mind. The golden eyes were kind and friendly, and she sat down in front of Carling.

"How is this possible?" Carling asked, echoing Marcus's question.

"It has always been possible for you. It has been there just as it was for the other. He is worried about you, and he is already on his way. He sent me on ahead to find you, and it did not take long. You leave such a lovely scent in your trail, like sun-warmed flowers."

"He? Do you mean Veda?" Carling asked.

"Yes. Your brother pack-mate is the one I speak of."

"He can't find me. I must do this alone."

"No. It is not the way of the pack. The pack stays together and helps each other. Brother Bear is already on the move. He, too, will join us. A strange pack we all make, but one that will work."

Carling got the sense that the wolf was laughing at her and was confused. The night had taken a very strange turn.

"I am not amused at you, merely amused at the pack we make," Wolf explained after sensing Carling's thoughts.

"How did you know what I was thinking?"

"We use our eyes to watch your movements as well as listening to your words. A gesture can say a lot more than a phrase. Just now there was wonder and curiosity, also a hurt look."

"Will you teach me?" Carling asked carefully.

"I can teach you some, but he will teach you the rest. I have already communicated with him that I have found you," Wolf informed her.

"He will make me go back. I can't go back. I can't protect them against what may come."

"There is more in your mind than you know. If the whole world was in danger, you could protect it. It is all there for you to use." The wolf lay down and laid her head on her paws.

"Is the bear scary?" Carling asked, feeling a little silly.

"He is young still, having just left his mother. Brother Bear is more playful, but harmless. Are you scared of me because I am wild?" The wolf cocked her head to one side with the question.

"No. I am not afraid of you any longer, Wolf. I was when we first met, but now, no."

"There you are, then. It will be the same with Bear," she said in a comforting manner. "Sleep now, our pack mate will be with us soon." The wolf closed her eyes, and Carling sank deeper into her dreams.

The smell of food cooking and wood smoke woke Carling, and her stomach growled loudly. The wolf was already gone from her side when she opened her eyes and sat up from where she slept beside the rotting log.

"Good morning. I thought you were going to sleep all day," Veda said, laughing at her surprise.

"Just resting my eyes. Where is Wolf?" Carling asked groggily.

"Off hunting and going to fetch Bear. He gets distracted easily, especially when he can sniff honey. Come and get some breakfast," he called her over, and she went.

Sitting by the warm fire and eating the food he had prepared for her, she began to feel stupid. Again, she was being cared for, looked after, and protected. She stood and gathered her things to her.

"Thank you for the meal and the company of Wolf overnight, but I think I should head out." She slung the bundle over her shoulder and turned to leave.

"What do you think you are doing?" he asked her from his seat.

"Leaving."

"No. Sit down, Carling." When she didn't do as he asked, he looked at her firmly. "Sit down."

"Veda, I have to look after myself at some stage. It might as well be now," Carling protested.

"Not until I have given you instruction in Whispering. She told me." He watched her and she looked annoyed. "Now sit down and we will talk. Is there a deadline you are working towards?"

"No." She sounded sullen and petulant.

"Good. Then a day where I can teach you the basics and Bear can catch us up will be well used then. We can leave tomorrow."

"Not we, Veda. Just me," she insisted.

"I'm afraid we are pack, so there will be all of us. Was there a specific place you wanted to go?" he asked.

"Yes. Home. Or what's left of it. I have family nearby, and I want to reconnect with them," Carling told him. But there was something else around the loch she wanted to see as well. The blue-coloured beacon shone in her memory, and she could see the man within.

"Then that is where we shall go. Do you know where it is, which way to head?" He was watching her carefully, trying to hide the smile that was creeping up at her obvious confusion.

Carling looked around at the trees that surrounded her, and in the dimness of the wood, she could not pick which way was what. As she turned back to him, he started to laugh.

"Shut up. I would have found my way. I found it in a dream," she told him.

"You and dreams." He was still laughing. "Can you sleepwalk as well, Carling?"

"The wolf was there last night in my dream. She protected me," she told him, scuffing her feet.

"Why was she protecting you?" he asked, concerned.

"He was there again. He broke into my dream." She looked out into the forest and watched a squirrel running up a tree.

"Is this the man who frightened you the other night—when you woke us all up screaming?" Veda asked.

"Yes. He is part of The People. I am not sure which one," Carling told him.

"Why did she have to protect you?"

"He tried to reach out to me, and Wolf stopped him."

"There is more, isn't there?" Veda asked slowly.

"Not for today. I have sorted my defenses and he won't be back," Carling said a bit brighter, trying to cheer herself. "You don't seem surprised that the wolf was there in my dream."

"No. I knew you had it in you that first morning, while you were playing with the birds. They were trying to talk to you. I was just surprised you couldn't hear them."

"You were surprised?" Carling was curious. "She gave me a shock when she spoke to me. She forced the matter, I think. So, can you tell me more? Show me how to communicate with them?" she asked eagerly, sitting down on the other side of the fire.

"I can indeed, Carling. You just need to open your mind to the sounds around you; listen to the small voices. They are there waiting to be heard."

Carling spent the day talking with and learning from Veda. She opened a bit more to him, telling him stories of her growing up and listening to his, and those of his brothers and sisters. In between these stories they would get down to the exercises she needed to do to open herself to the world of animals. A little squirrel, the same she had seen earlier, was the first she tried to talk to. She found its mind was very focused on one thing: food for the coming winter and the trouble he was having with a neighbour, who would sneak in and steal from his hiding spot.

The birds were no different. They were flighty and vain, displaying their feathers and calling to mates, not interested in Carling at all. It was a different matter when she brought out her harp and started to play their songs back to them. One little bird came down from the trees and rested on the log she had slept by. It hopped along the rotted wood and pecked at it for a moment before wrestling a grub from inside. It swallowed it down and then warbled out a song.

Carling plucked the strings and it stopped, looking at her quizzically. It hopped nearer to her, and she played it again. Soon it took to wing and flew to the harp, resting on the top. He sang his song again and she played it back. When he sang again, he hopped down onto her fingers to stop her playing and looked up at her.

In a clear and sweet voice, she returned the call. Veda smiled at her and encouraged her to continue. Again, she vocalized the sounds from the bird, who had flown back to the top of the harp. He called back, and this time she understood what he was saying.

"Chicks are hungry, they need to feed. Must find food for chicks." The sound was sweet, and she tried her own to it. The little bird flew back up into the treetops as she watched.

"Each species of bird is different. It is going to take you a long time to learn all their voices," Veda said, laughing at her.

"They all sound so beautiful. I am just pleased they are here out in the wild and not trapped in a cage."

"Was that what it felt like for you?" Veda asked.

"A songbird in a gilded cage. There for the pleasure of my master and mistress, to be shown off to the guests and dignitaries. To be ogled, leered at, and coveted. I knew what they were thinking, what they wanted. But I was the songbird, and I was put out of reach of them all. Marinus was once offered a lot of gold for me by a dignitary from Rome when he came to visit. Keelie had to do some fast talking to stop him from selling me." She was quiet for a moment as her fingers retraced the song she had written.

"What is that piece of music, Carling?" Veda asked her.

"Something I wrote and performed for them. Only they didn't understand what it was that I was singing." She laughed at the memories.

"Can you play it for me?" he asked her. He stretched out his long legs and placed his hands behind his head.

"I hope you have the stomach for it." With a sly smile, she began the song again.

Carling watched him from the corner of her eye as she sang the words. The words of how her parents died, how she watched as they plunged a spear through her grandmother while she was trying to take her to safety. The meeting with Marcus and being taken as a slave. Of growing up hating him and all Romans for what they did. Finally describing how she had wanted them to die by her ripping their still-beating hearts from their chests and holding them in her hands while their life slowly ebbed away.

Finishing with the last little notes that floated up into the air and away into the trees, she looked at him. He had moved while she was singing. He now sat cross-legged, leaning forward. His face was white at the idea of the gentle woman he thought he knew describing such a grisly death.

"It sounded like such a happy song," Veda said finally.

"That was the point. If it sounded happy, they would have no idea at the meaning of the words. Only one understood."

"Did you get in trouble for it?"

"I wouldn't be sitting here if I had. He did not give me up to his father. It was Marcus," Carling told him as she tucked her harp away into its protective cover.

"You talk about him a lot, Carling. Are you sure you hate him that much?" Veda tried to ask the question as gently as possible and was pleased at how Carling responded.

"Oh, I hate him with a passion. He told me he loved me and that just made it worse. I could never, ever, contemplate loving that man. Every night I would pray to the clan gods and to any other god that might have been listening, to make him fall off his horse. Now that I know he is one of The People, his actions are even worse. He is killing his own kind, enslaving them for his own betterment. There is no true blood in his veins, Veda, and my killing him will help my parents and grandmother rest."

"That is not our way," Veda reminded her with an emphatic shake of his head. "Violence is not the way."

"I don't want to do it with Mind Touch. I experienced some of the mental pain I inflicted on his father when he attacked me, and I don't want that again."

"It is a matter we can speak of another time. I think enough has been said of the subject today. Come, help me collect firewood for the night. Bear and Wolf should be here soon." Veda stood up and offered his hand to her.

Carling placed her harp down on her bundle and took his hand. He pulled her up, and they stood for a moment looking into each other's eyes. Carling looked away first, breaking the feeling that she could sense coming from him. She walked away into the forest and stooped to pick up the deadfall branches off the ground, leaving Veda to watch in his own pain as she went.

Her first encounter with Bear was a strange one. She wandered through the trees looking for wood for the fire, a bundle in her arms. She came to a small clearing, and in the centre sat a large yew tree. It was old and twisted. Gently she placed the bundle of twigs and sticks down and headed under its branches. She could feel the life inside it, watching and waiting.

Placing a hand on its trunk, she marveled at the energy that was contained within and could feel the presence that lived there. It was ancient. Far more ancient than the wood and leaves that now surrounded it. She circled the trunk and felt the tree almost tremble at her touch. When she came back to the spot where she had started, a great figure appeared. They were dressed in a long cloak with the hood pulled up and covering the person's head, hiding the face from view in a dark shadow.

"I was hoping you would find me, Carling," the figure said. The voice was feminine and sweet.

"Who are you?" Carling asked, a little surprised.

"I am what The People have come to call an Ancestor, or as we will become known, a Guardian. The name we have for ourselves and my own personal name I cannot give you, as it would be perilous for me to do so. But I want you to know that you are a child of mine. A descendant specifically created so that the evil will not walk on this land again. Your children's children will play a very big role in the ending of his reign," the Being told her.

"Whose reign? What is this evil?"

"I cannot tell you more here. When you have found what you need where you were born, then come to us at the sacred stones. There is one you will meet who can guide you there. You are so special, my child. The only child of the Ancestors."

The figure stepped closer, and a hand appeared from under the robe. It was pale and bony, and it reached out and rested on Carling's head for a moment.

"Go with my blessings, my child. Go with my love and that of your father's. The Ancestors will watch over you and your children. When the time comes, we will protect them. For now, you must temper your anger; hold it in check. If you let it get the better of you, the evil will take control."

A peace descended over Carling, and she looked up into the dark under the hood.

"Please help me," she begged the figure. "I cannot let it go. He must be made to pay for what he has done."

"Marcus will pay for his transgressions, Carling. His soul will not rest but be bound to his own line. His descendants will carry him with them, and he will be passed along through the generations. He will know neither rest nor peace until the two come, born at the same moment from the same spark of life."

"I still don't understand, but I will do as you wish." She bowed her head to the Ancestor and closed her eyes.

"I must go. There is one here who wishes to get to know you, Carling. He is young yet, but he will be a companion and protector to you. Go now with peace and love. We will meet again, Carling."

When Carling opened her eyes, the figure had gone, but she could still feel the touch on her head. Across the bare expanse of ground and from behind a mighty pine, came a brown bear, not quite fully grown. He stopped and sniffed the air and then came on with a shambling walk.

Standing stock-still, she waited for the bear. There was no fear in her heart since the Ancestor had told her of his coming. The large beast stopped in front of Carling and stood on its hind legs, towering above her. It came back down and sniffed. Carefully and slowly, she reached out her hand. She touched the fur on his head, feeling the coarseness of it. The bear raised his head to meet her hand and she scratched his ears. She searched for him as Veda had taught her. He was there and she could feel his thoughts as they brushed hers.

I sensed an old one, the bear said in her mind.

"There was an Ancestor here," Carling replied, both with the spoken word and mentally, still grappling with this new found ability.

One came to me last night and spoke. She was most insistent that I heed what she said.

"And did you?" Carling asked.

I am here. You are the one I seek. I can smell them on you.

"So, I understand. I am very pleased to meet you. Do you have a name?"

What is a name for one like me? I go where I like, when I like. The world is my home, Bear told her.

The wolf came trotting through into the clearing and came to stand beside Bear. *He would like to know where you are; he thinks you may have become lost.*

"Thank you, Wolf. We should go to him." Carling bent and picked up the bundle of wood, following the wolf from the clearing with one last look at the ancient yew. The bear was still standing under its great spreading limbs, and he turned to follow them.

He will become more sensible as he grows, the wolf said.

"As do most young males, I understand," Carling said with a smile.

Through their trek across the land to the west they encountered no one. Until early one morning, as they were packing up their camp, they heard horses riding towards them. Veda acted fast and sent Wolf and Bear into the scrubby trees while he and Carling hid behind the outcrop of rock they had used as their shelter the night before.

The lead horse neighed and snorted at the smell of the large animals, and the soldier on its back fought to bring it under control. While the horse sidestepped across the road, the soldiers marching behind came to a halt and waited for the order to move. Carling held her breath and waited, hoping that the horse would become calm.

Another horse came galloping up from the rear, sending dust clouds off its hoofs. Carling recognized the amount of plumage on the top of the helmet as belonging to someone quite high up in command.

"What is going on here?" the voice rang out in the valley as he pulled his horse up, and Carling recognized it straight away.

"She got spooked, Commander," the lead man said, his horse now under control.

"We will never make our destination at this rate. Get moving." Marcus turned his horse, and Carling saw his face before quickly ducking back down behind the rock.

"Do we have scouts out for marauders?" Marcus asked suddenly as he looked around them.

"Yes, we do, sir," was the reply.

Carling looked around them, worried about being caught, and quietly whispered the translation to Veda. Carling closed her eyes. The fear of being captured again was overwhelming. She held on to Veda's arm and prayed that they would not be found. From within her a knowledge came, and she grasped it and used it as much as she could.

While the column of soldiers started to move off again, on the other side of rocks the pair remained quiet and still. Hoofbeats came from behind, and Carling sneaked a peek at where they were coming from. Heading straight for their night camp was a Roman. He pulled the horse up and dismounted. Their fire was still smoking slightly from the night before, and Carling whispered softly to Veda to remain still.

The Roman checked the camp over, mounted his horse, and then sped off around the rocks. Carling released her grip on Veda and her energy at the same time. They remained with their backs pressed against rocks, waiting for them to pass.

"How did that man not see us?" Veda asked, his eyes wide.

"I don't know. Well, I'm not sure, that is to say," Carling said. "That man—the one in charge—it was Marcus. They called him commander."

"What does that mean?" Veda whispered back.

"It means his father is dead," she said softly. "I need to contact Brietta tonight."

"That is, if we can find somewhere safe to camp. They can't have been very far away from us last night, and they are heading the same way we want to go," Veda said, looking at the rear of the column as it disappeared down the road.

"It can't be a coincidence that he is here. I'm worried that Onnist has found him," Carling said.

"Onnist?" Veda said as he kicked dirt over the fire.

"Yes. When I slapped him, I saw an image of the man he was to find. It was Marcus."

"Why would the Ancestors send him to find Marcus?" he asked, bending down to make sure it was fully covered and out.

"I don't know. That is why I need to contact Brietta. I need answers before we go on."

"We shouldn't stay here again tonight," Veda said. "There is an easy way to get over the river just up ahead. We'll cross there and go find someone I know who will help us."

"Can this person be trusted?" Carling asked cautiously.

"Let's just say he would defend us to the death, taking as many Romans with him as possible."

Chapter Seven

The river was a bit deeper than Carling had expected. At her side swimming was Bear, and he helped her across. His large build and strong legs cut through the water with ease, and they were soon climbing up the opposite bank. Bear shook himself off, drenching her again, and she laughed at the sight of him looking like a large, shaggy dog.

Veda and Wolf came up the bank after them. He crawled his way to her side and collapsed on his back. The she-wolf shook her grey fur and lay on the ground, rolling around on the grass to dry off. Her legs were up in the air, and she swung herself from side to side. Carling watched her with a smile and then caught Veda watching her.

"You are so pretty when you smile, Carling. And your laugh is music all on its own," he told her with a large grin.

"Veda, don't," she said, looking up to the sky.

"No, I wasn't...I didn't mean...oh, shit." She could hear him breathing next to her, still trying to catch his breath from the crossing. "It was nice to see you smile and laugh, Carling. That is all. We haven't done much of it lately."

"No, we haven't. I'm sorry," she said quietly, feeling like a cloud had passed in front of the sun.

"It's all right." Veda stood and held his hand out to her to help her up.

Carling picked up her bundle and hung it off her shoulder. She smiled up at him from under her wet hair.

"Just as well we crossed the river. You needed a bath," she told him, trying to lighten the mood that had slipped between them.

"I'm not the only one," he exclaimed back. "You were a bit whiffy as well." He laughed and pushed on her shoulder. Carling started to protest, but it soon left her lips, as she could not help but laugh with him.

They headed west again, following the banks of the river. Carling was fully aware that they were on the wrong side to visit the spot where her home used to be. She only hoped that at some stage they could make it to the other shore. They carried on for the rest of the day, and by evening, they came to mouth of the river where the loch emptied out on its way to the sea far behind them.

Keeping the bank to their left, they walked through a wooded area until they found a spot where the hills, which made their way down to the edge of the water, receded and a small plateau with a freshwater brook tumbled down. Carling cleared an area for their fire for the night while Veda went in search of wood.

Bear and Wolf had gone off to forage for themselves, and Carling set the tinder of dry leaves and scrubby bushes into the small pit. Veda brought back the first load and she started the fire, feeding it until the flames licked up on the wood she had started to layer on top. She sat back for a moment and watched the flames as they grew, the orange tongues bobbing and dancing in the gentle wind.

In the quiet under the trees, she heard a splash from the water and went to investigate. In the murky loch, darker shapes moved just under the surface. Not far from where she was crouching, a large fish jumped from the depths and splashed back down, sending out sparkling droplets of water in its wake.

Bear, I have found fish. Can I ask your help to catch some? Carling sent her thought out.

I am coming. The taste of fish is preferable to that of the berries I just found, Bear responded.

Carling waited and watched as the fish swam just out of her reach. She looked up at the opposite shore and caught sight of movement. Squinting, she tried to see what it was when a bright red cloak flashed between the trees. She remained still until they had moved on.

A crack behind her let her know that Bear had arrived. He moved down into the loch, and his eyes watched the water carefully. Suddenly his large front paw swiped, sending a great spray into the air to fall like glistening gems. A large fish landed on the bank, and Carling moved quickly to make sure it didn't make it back to the water. She grabbed a rock and brought it down hard on the head of the fish, killing it with one blow.

Another fish soon followed, and then another. With one more swipe of his large paw, a fourth fish landed beside Carling, and she soon dispatched it. The bear came lumbering up and claimed one of the fish, lying down and starting to eat.

One for Wolf and one for us; the last is for you. Thank you, Bear, for your fishing; tonight, we eat well, she said happily.

We do it for the pack. I am grateful for the two fish, Bear said as he ripped the flesh with his strong and large jaws.

Carling took the two fish back to the fire and found Veda there tending it. He looked up, saw what she was carrying, and smiled.

"Bear did well, then?" he asked.

"Very well." Carling replied, laying them down, and Wolf came out of the underbrush. *Wolf, we have your share here. Be careful of the bones.*

I know how to eat a fish, Wolf said as she picked it up and took it to the edge of the camp.

Veda quickly gutted and cleaned out the remaining fish. He placed a large rock into the fire to heat and then placed the fish on it to cook. While Carling checked on her harp, making sure that the water hadn't worked its way through the wrappings, they chatted quietly about the trip so far while they waited for their share.

"I saw a Roman on the other bank," Carling said, remembering the flash of red.

"I did too. I think they have made camp over there," Veda replied, looking through the trees at the edge of the loch.

"If it is the same ones we saw this morning, then I have a feeling that he came out here looking for me."

"It could just be a routine patrol." Veda turned the fish and licked his fingers.

"If the commander is with the patrol, it is not routine. The commander does not leave the camp unless it is a very important mission," she informed him.

"They are over there, and we are here, about to dine on this beautiful fish. We just need to keep the fire low and stay hidden. They will never know that we are here." Veda sliced off half the fish and handed her a large portion with a grin. "Eat and be satisfied."

With their meal eaten and the mess cleaned away, they sat with the fire between them. Bear and Wolf were already asleep beside each other, and the sun was now down below the hills in the distance. Carefully Veda fed the fire, giving them enough light to see and give them warmth, but not to be seen or noticed.

Carling was strumming her strings, tuning them, and then started a song. It was the one Marinus had liked, the one he said his mother used to sing to him as a child. The revelation that Marcus was now commander meant that Marinus was either dead or incapacitated in some way. Softly she sang the words, keeping it down.

"What does it mean?" Veda asked her when she finished.

"I don't really know. I was never taught that language, only the words to sing. I know it is a lullaby of some sort."

"It sounded sad."

"Would you like me to play a happier tune?" Carling smiled across at him.

"Is there one from your childhood you remember?"

"Yes. One my mother would sing to my little brother." Her fingers were already playing the tune, and her voice joined in. It lifted into the sky along with the smoke from the fire, out onto the loch of her home, and a tear escaped her.

"I think that might be enough for tonight. I seem to have made you sadder," Veda said with concern after she had finished.

"Not really. He was only small. Just newborn. Ma would let me hold him while she cooked or was busy with other things." Carling smiled at the memory. "I remember he smelled sweet and fresh, like a spring morning."

"Ma always says that when she has another."

"I love your Ma. She is sweet and caring," Carling said, the corners of her mouth curling upward.

"She is yours now, too, remember, Sister."

"I think I will get some sleep, Brother. I need to talk to Brietta, and I hope she accepts my invasion of her dream." Carling began to pack away her harp, before placing it carefully beside her bundle.

"Could you invade my dreams? Not in that way, but if you needed to call to me?" Veda asked.

"I'm not sure. I've only talked to your Da, Sima, and Brietta. I could try tonight if you wish."

"It could come in handy. If there was trouble."

"You just have to sleep first." Carling gathered her cloak around her. She lay down with her bundle as a pillow and stared into the fire.

"I'll take first watch, then. Sleep well, Carling." He stirred the fire and watched as her eyes closed.

Carling waited a long time in the dream state until Brietta finally flared into her notice. Her pale green light shone brightly in the distance, and she flew to her surrogate mother.

"Mother of my heart, I have missed you," Carling greeted her warmly.

"I have missed you, too, Daughter of my heart," Brietta replied with an equal smile.

"I take it much has changed there in the villa?" she asked with some hesitancy in broaching the subject.

"Yes, dear one, it has." Brietta's smile slipped away slowly. "Marinus has died. The pains in his head kept getting worse, and he finally fell on his sword."

"Are you and Keelie all right—and Cato?" Carling was suddenly worried for the strange group that she had come to think of as family.

"We are fine. Marcus has been very kind and allowed us to stay. He is really fond of his young brother. His stepmother he tolerates."

"She has her freedom now. Why does she still stay?"

"Because Marcus will not let her take Cato with her. He has changed, Carling. I fear the madness that took his father has a hold on him also."

"What do you mean, 'changed'?" Carling asked quickly.

"He is more driven than he has ever been, and there are secret meetings with strangers dressed in hooded cloaks. The houseboy told me about them. And he has now gone off on some mission."

"I saw him today. He was riding near where I was camped," Carling said, quietly pondering Brietta's words.

"Are you alone? Do you need help?" The concern and worry were written across Brietta's features.

"I am fine, Brietta. I am with Veda, Talorc and Nessa's son."

"Good. I don't like the thought of you out there, with so many dangers." Brietta took an unconscious protective step towards Carling.

"I am well protected. Veda has the wolf and I have the bear."

"You have a bear? What are you talking about, child?" Brietta asked with astonishment.

"I am no longer a child, either. I finished my training with Talorc a week ago. I found that I am also a Whisperer. Wolf protected me against a vision of Marcus." When she saw Brietta's face, she continued, "Marcus is one of The People. He has been trained in Mind Touch. You once said that he had feelings for me and that is because the seers of his People told him of me. He declared his love to me."

"You keep yourself safe, young lady, otherwise I will..."

"You will do nothing." Carling laughed. "In all the years I have known you, Mother, you have never laid a hand on me."

"No, but maybe I should have." Brietta returned a small teasing smirk.

"I must get back for my watch. I'll check on you all again soon."

"We all miss you. Safe journey until we meet again, Daughter of my heart." Brietta bade, and Carling began to reluctantly retreat from her, the return farewell catching in her throat. The image of Brietta began to fade slowly as she saw her returning to her dreams. The actions of the woman who had become her mother had no meaning for Carling, as the image faded to darkness before brightening again, revealing the landscape that lay between them. Heading back mentally to where she and Veda were camped for the night, she once more spotted the bright-blue-coloured beacon, this time near where they were camped. She changed direction and flew towards it, watching it carefully as it moved among the trees near the banks of the loch.

Suddenly a bright red spark rose before her, blocking her sight.

"Where are you going, Flora?" a voice boomed from the centre as it pulsated in front of her, and the figure of Marcus appeared inside it.

"I had hoped to go to my home, but you are already there." Her own golden spark held together high off the ground.

"Come visit me for the night, Flora. It will be more entertaining than the boy you are travelling with." He chuckled at her surprise. "You have not seen, then, the bond between us. The one I have had with you since you were sixteen." Held loosely in his hand was a coil of rope that glowed.

"You created a bond with me without my knowledge?" she demanded angrily.

"It was easy once I was properly trained. Those first couple of nights after we found you, you had nightmares. Do you remember? No, I can see you don't. You drew me into them. It is because of you that I now have these abilities. You awoke them in me, Flora."

"You always had them, Marcus. So, you have enslaved me once more, to be at your disposal," she spat at him.

"Only on this level. In reality you are still free and will always remain so. I only sought the bond because I was falling in love with you. It was easy to invade your dreams and create it. Even your dreams were sweet," he told her softly. Marcus's energy moved closer to her, and she jerkily pulled away.

"No closer, please, Marcus. I do not love you. This bond you created is not good for either of us."

"It is too late now," Marcus said with a shrug of his shoulders. "It is there, and forever it will remain. I have watched with great interest how you have developed. The thoughts that have gone through your mind. Seeing through your eyes. Onnist was a wonderful gift, by the way. When he turned up at camp, I was so pleased."

"You haven't hurt him, have you?" A sudden concern for her friend's son caught her unawares.

"No, I didn't, but he travels with me. He had very interesting words about you, Flora. I didn't have to imagine how you said the things you did, as I had already witnessed it. Your emotions trigger a pull on our bond, and I follow them back. It is almost like being there with you." Marcus was looking about him.

The bright blue light flared once more, and Carling hoped he did not see it. Even though she was sure that he had looked directly at the beacon, he made no mention of it.

"You have talked to me now, Marcus. I have to go." She tried to move past him to enter her own mind fully once more.

"No! Not so fast, Flora. There is only one way this is all going to turn out. You at my side for always. Now, it can be done the sensible way, by you coming to me and giving yourself freely, or I can claim you as an alliance bride, and you will be kept under lock and key again, songbird."

"I am sorry to hear about your father, Marcus. He was always kind to me when I was younger," Carling said, trying to change the subject.

"He thought you were a beautiful pet. It was only a matter of time until he did what he did that night. But you did me a favour. What did you do to him, anyway? I could never figure it out. I even went to the lengths of entering his mind to work out how you had damaged him." His eyes bored into her, burning brightly with the hunger for knowledge and her.

"I did nothing," she shook her head vigorously, both to assure him of her innocence and at the sudden thought that Marcus may have possibly sped up Marinus' madness. "I accidentally entered his mind and screamed, that is all."

"I nearly killed him myself that night, after seeing what he did to you. Diana should have kept you under lock and key. Come to me, Carling. Don't make me come find you." There was a warning hidden behind those words and she caught it.

"You remembered my name, Marcus. No, I won't come to you. And I beg you, do not come for me. We were not meant to be together. I have been told to lessen my anger towards you, but that won't happen if you do not let me be."

"It was not my orders to kill them, Carling. They came from my father," he tried to explain to appease her.

"But you carried them out. My little brother was only a few weeks old. I saw my mother's burnt body, draped over his cot, trying to protect him." The memory that Sima had buried deep was working its way to the surface again. She pulled at it and flung the image at him. "That is what happens when you follow orders, Marcus! Do you give those orders now?" she screamed at him, her anger flaring anew.

"No. I don't. There have been no raids, no acts of revenge since I became commander. And there won't be ever again as long as I am. They are my people as well," he cried back, turning his head from the image of the burnt figures before him.

"Let me go, Marcus. Please," Carling begged him again.

"For now, my flower. I will let you go. But I will be able to find you." His bright red flame moved out of her way, and he bowed to her as she moved past him, wary that it may be a trap.

When Marcus didn't try to stop her, Carling raced down to her own form and re-entered her mind. Her eyes came open and stared at the darkness around her. Across the dying embers Veda stirred and put another piece of wood on the fire. She could hear the slumbering breaths of Wolf and Bear somewhere nearby, and she sat up.

"I was just about to wake you," Veda said softly.

"My dreams were not what I had hoped," she replied shakily. "Go to sleep, Veda. I wish you better dreams than mine."

"The news from Brietta was not what you had thought?" He was lying down and covering himself with his cloak.

"No. They were just as I feared. I drove Marinus mad, and he killed himself. Marcus is now commander as I had suspected."

"If the dream with Brietta was as you thought, then what startled you awake? What other dreams did you have?" Veda yawned loudly in the darkness that was punctuated with the soft flickering light from the fire between them.

"They are not a tale for the nighttime," Carling muttered quietly, remembering Marcus's burning eyes. "We'll talk about it in the morning. I don't want to give you nightmares."

"Will you be visiting in my dreams?" he asked, and she could hear hopefulness in his tired voice.

"Not tonight, Veda. Go to sleep." She stood, stretched, and headed down to the loch.

In the moonlight, the waves sparkled. Across the water she could pinpoint the different fires of the Roman camp. Reaching down, she cupped her hand and drew up the water from the loch, splashing it over her face and the back of her neck.

Carling prepared the meagre rations for their morning meal while Veda still slept. She had not wanted to wake him just yet. Wolf and Bear were already off looking for food, and the clearing was quiet except for her humming a tune. The feelings that were with her during the night were expelled when the sun rose, and the birds sang in the trees. It was something she would deal with when she had found her family once more.

Wolf came trotting back to the fire and sat near Veda. She nudged him with her wet nose, and he pushed her away. Again, she nudged him, and he rolled over. A large paw was raised, and she raked him on his back, then licked the side of his face.

"All right! I am awake!" Veda exclaimed to her. "You are worse than my mother."

It seems to be the role I have taken on—mother of the pack. It is late, and it is time you were up. There are humans nearby, Wolf warned.

Veda sat up immediately and became wary of the surroundings. Carling tried to peer through the trees, but she could see nothing. She sent out a call to Bear. *Where are you?*

No need to shout, Bear responded. There are men behind us, the same as passed us yesterday. I suggest you leave the camp now.

We will. She broke the connection and began collecting their belongings. "Romans coming from behind. Bear said they are the same."

"Let's go," he said, and started to move. Quickly Veda stamped out what was left of the fire and picked up his bag. Wolf ranged ahead, leading them away from the danger.

They ducked and dove through the trees and at one point had to wade through the shallows of the loch to get around a steep part of the surrounding hills. Bear let them know where the soldiers were, and they were leaving them behind. Carling was worried about them attacking him.

They only have sticks, Bear calmed her, but sounded amused.

Those sticks have sharp points on them.

You worry too much. Bear broke the connection again.

Further on, the land began to even out and become less wood, more grass. She stopped at the edge of the trees. So far, they had protected them from sight of those wanting to harm them. Veda came to her side.

"Our destination is only a short way away now. He will hide us," Veda told her in a whisper.

"Who?" Carling was panting and took a drink from her waterskin.

"Galen. A distant cousin of ours. We need to go up on the angle." Veda pointed up the hill and across. "See that patch of trees?"

"Yes."

"That is where we need to go." He led the way out of the trees and headed up the hill. Carling followed him, and Wolf headed back to find Bear.

They reached the trees and moved around the dense brush underneath until a round stone house came into view. The thatch on top was neat and clean, but the stones that made the walls were stacked closely together and looked like they had been in place for a very long time. It jutted out from the side of the hill, and the door was larger than most.

"Galen! Are you there, Galen?" Veda called out. There was no reply from within the house. Veda looked around them and could see no movement.

I hope you are hidden. The men chasing you are about to leave the trees; Wolf's thoughts came to them.

We are hidden. What are they doing? Veda asked.

They are looking around, confused as to where you have gone. They are now heading out further, not up to where you are. Now they are turning back. You are safe for now. The she-wolf said, almost bemused at the stupidity of the soldiers and their inept skills in tracking.

Have you sensed Galen around? Veda asked her.

He is here in the trees, Wolf replied. He has been tracking the men. You passed close to him, and he was amused by it.

"He could have called out," Veda said, a little grumpily both in the mind and out loud. He dumped his bag on the ground by the door and sat down. "You might as well get comfortable, Carling. Galen will chase them down and kill them."

"He is clan, then?" she asked as she settled herself.

"No, he is one of us," Veda assured her.

"But he is killing."

"You don't know his story. I don't even know the full story. He has never spoken of it," he said as he adjusted his position to get more comfortable.

A cloud crept across the sun's face and blocked out the warm light. Carling shivered and pulled her cloak closer to her. More clouds converged on the sky above them, and soon it began to rain. Soft small drops at first, and then harder and more insistent it became.

"We had better go inside," Veda said, getting up then opening the door for Carling to enter.

Inside, it was dark, and the fire pit was burning low. He moved to the store of wood and carefully encouraged the flames to life, brightening the room and warming them along with it.

"I'm coming in," a loud voice called from outside. Carling turned as the door was pulled aside, and a large man with dark, flowing hair bent over and entered.

"Galen." Veda greeted him, and they embraced in welcome.

"Veda. Nice to see you made it here in one piece. Your wolf came to visit yesterday afternoon," Galen told him.

"Cousin, this is Carling," Veda introduced them.

She looked up as a flame flared in the pit beside him. His eyes were bright blue, the same colour as the beacon she had been seeing in her dreams, and she recognised them. But there was a deep sadness to them.

"Welcome, Carling. My hearth is yours to share. Please sit. Have you had something to eat this morning?" he asked.

"Thank you. We were interrupted by the two who were following us," Veda told him. "We have not eaten yet."

"They are not following now," Galen said with a grim tone. "Whose is the bear? Is he new to your pack, Veda?"

"He was; now he follows Carling here." Veda indicated her.

"Another Whisperer. You have chosen well, Veda." He only gave her a glance and then turned from her.

"Carling is not...I mean we aren't together," Veda stammered. "She is an adopted sister only."

"There is nothing *only* about having a sibling, Veda." Galen was moving around the pots stored by the wall. "So where do you come from, then, Carling?"

"I am of the Boar. I was born on the other side of the loch," she said to him.

"I know everyone around the loch. I have not seen you before." It was almost an accusation.

"I have not been here since I was six summers old. My parents died, and I was taken as a slave by the Romans."

"Who were your parents?" He had stopped what he was doing and asked the question quietly, not looking at her.

"Carvorst and Breena. My little brother died that night too." She stared at the flames and did not see him turn his eyes to her.

Veda looked between the pair. The energy in the room was heightened, and he had no idea why.

"You are little Carling?" Galen asked as he came to her side and looked at her face until she stared openly back at him.

"I am. Carling of The Boar."

"I knew your parents. I was with Longus when we found you," he told her softly.

"I only remember the house and being taken away by my grandmother."

"Yes! We had no idea what happened to you. I was sent with my father and brothers to make sure you got there safely, and we found her later that day. We followed the Romans, and they ambushed us. We tried to get you back, Carling." Galen stopped when he realised what he was saying.

Carling remained quiet. She watched as he turned his eyes to the fire, the memories flickering across his face. There was pain there, a deep-seated pain that cut through him still.

"There is nothing left of your home, Carling. It has been destroyed so no one else can build on it," Galen finally said sadly.

"As it should be," she responded. "Is my uncle still alive?"

"Yes. Longus and Bron are both still alive. They live not far from here. I will take you tomorrow. You have many cousins.

Like Nessa, Bron has been busy over the years." Galen went back to the task he was doing and prepared them a meal.

The rain had ceased, and the sun was shining again. Carling stood outside beside the copse of trees and looked out over the loch at the shoreline beyond. It was hard to make out whether anyone was there, and she was trying to remember what the surroundings looked like. She remembered there had been a brook and a waterfall her father had taken her to. He had told her that it was the home of some fairies, and they went looking for them. Carling smiled at the memory of the large man carrying her on his shoulders as they climbed up the hill.

Movement down the hill caught her attention, and she watched as the brown bear came out of the woods with the wolf trotting beside him. They were an unlikely pair but seemed to have formed a very close bond. Bear would need to stay with Wolf and Veda. She could not look after him.

It is not me who needs looking after, Bear's voice sounded loudly in her mind. As I recall, the Ancient One told you that I am bound to you, as your protector. And I mean to keep that bond.

Then it will be as the Ancient One said, Bear, she told him.

"He is a beautiful beast. I would tell him to be careful. There are many here of the clans who would kill him just for his pelt," Galen's soft voice said behind her.

"I will warn him. Thank you." She was still watching the progress of the animals as they made their way up to the house.

"You look like your mother." Galen was beside her now. His hair was loose and blowing in the wind, his sad blue eyes on her face.

"I don't remember their faces, only that Da was a big man, tall and wide, and Ma sang."

"He was, the largest of men. He was also a good chief, a wise man and fair. Your Ma was the prettiest woman around the area. I remember thinking that there was none so sweet as she. She sang and danced, and she played the flute."

"I remember her singing," Carling recalled. "Even when she worked, she was humming a tune. The one I remember most is the lullaby she would sing to my brother." A small, sad smile touched her lips.

"I was there when you were born," Galen told her. "You were just a scrap of a thing, bawling and pink. Your hair was so fair, like your mother's. Your father was so proud and happy to have a daughter like his wife. I was just seven, and my mother had come to help Breena."

"What is your ability?" Carling asked him.

"Stealth. The good it did that night, or the night after. I was thirteen summers and only just starting my training when you were taken."

"I can sense it is a painful memory. Can you tell me what happened?" Carling turned to him, her own pale blue eyes pleading with his.

"I can't, Carling. I still need it to feed the anger, to kill the Romans who did what they did. Why would you want to know such a memory?" Galen asked her.

"Maybe to feed the anger that I know is buried deep inside myself. So that one day I can face the man who killed them and thrust my knife into his heart. So that I can watch his life pour from his body and drip at my feet. To take from him what was taken from me."

"You know the man?" Galen raised his eyebrows.

"Marcus is his name, and he is now commander of the fort. He is the one who killed them, and he is the one who enslaved me."

"So much anger between you. I can almost see it," Veda said, walking towards them. "It happened a long time ago. Can neither of you forget?"

"Veda, you are so sweet. But no, I can't. As long as he draws breath, I cannot forget. I cannot forgive what they did," Carling told him.

"Of the party who went to rescue Carling, I alone came back," Galen said. "My father and brothers all dead, my mother left alone with a dying child."

"But you didn't die, Galen. And you were protected, Carling," Veda told them, trying to reason with their gentler sides.

"Veda, leave it. Let us wallow in our grief a while longer. Let our anger reign over us and consume us," Carling said gently to him.

"It is not healthy for one of The People to do so," Veda went on. "We do not spill blood unnecessarily."

"We know, Veda. It is not the way. We will have to deal with the Ancestors in our own way when the time comes," Galen told him.

Later that night around the fire, Veda was still stewing on the conversation he had heard between them. A blaze burnt in his belly over it, and he was withdrawn from them both. Carling had noticed and offered to sing him the songs he liked, but he refused.

"Why don't you play Galen the one that you wrote? I am sure he would enjoy the message it sends," Veda finally said, getting up and going to his blankets.

Forgive him. He is feeling jealous. Wolf came to her and nudged her arm for comfort.

"I am not, Wolf," Veda said from his spot by the wall.

Carling put an arm around the great grey wolf and laid her head on her soft fur. She felt sad she had upset her friend and was at a loss as to how to mend it.

A silence descended on the house, and Carling found herself falling into the dream world. The blue beacon that was Galen was blinding to her vision. Nearby was the dream form of Veda. He was calling out for someone with tears falling down his face.

Wolf was at her side, and she looked sad. *He loves you still. He had hoped that you would come to love him, but now he sees the other with you. He is jealous, no matter what he says.*

Carling reached out to Veda with her mind; slowly she brought him into the dream space and watched as he finally saw her before him.

"You did it. I thought you didn't want to have a connection with me," Veda told her.

"Of course, I do. You are as a brother to me," Carling said, and she saw him wince at the term.

"A brother. Yes, and you a sister," he said, but she could tell he did not mean the words.

"Veda. I do not feel the same as you. I know you had hoped that I would, but I still don't."

"I know. I understand, Carling." He was quiet a moment. "Is Galen one you could have those feelings for?"

"Why torture yourself with these questions?" Carling asked gently.

"Is he?"

"I have only just met him. I can't tell you that."

"I saw the way you looked at him when I first introduced you. It was almost as if you recognized him, like you had seen him before," he said sadly.

"You know I have never seen him before."

"That doesn't answer the question, Carling. Is he?"

"I don't know, Veda," Carling said quietly.

"Go away, boy, and leave her alone!" a loud voice rang out, and then Marcus was there. He pushed Veda away with a burst of energy and rounded on Carling.

"You cannot do that here!" Carling yelled at him.

"Yes, I can. You belong to me. That little puppy is fooling himself if he thinks that he can win you from me," Marcus exclaimed in a dangerously low voice.

"There is nothing to win. My heart is my own. Marcus, you need to leave." She was backing away from him now.

"Come to me, Carling. I am waiting for you." He reached out and grasped her arm in his large hand. He pulled her to him, claiming her mouth with his own.

With all the energy she could muster, she pushed out at him, and he disappeared. She staggered a little and then forced herself awake.

"Carling!" Veda was there, holding her in his arms. "Carling!"

"I'm awake! I am fine," she said, struggling with him to let her go. She could still feel Marcus's lips on hers and it haunted her.

"What's going on?" Galen said, now beside them.

"A dream and nothing more," Carling told him.

"She is a Mind Touch as well. We made a connection tonight in case she ever needed me. But there was another there." Veda told his cousin quickly.

"It does not matter now. It's gone," she said, waving them both away.

"Who was there?" Galen asked, surprised by this turn of events.

"Marcus, I presume. He looked Roman to me," Veda said.

"That is enough. No more! I don't want to think about it anymore," Carling told them and headed outside for fresh air.

"Marcus was in her head?" Galen asked Veda.

"Yes. I don't know why or how. I just know that he is strong."

"She has two abilities? That is unheard of," Galen said with some surprise.

"The visions about her are all unclear," Veda said. "There is so much about her that is unclear."

"And you love her," Carling heard Galen say quietly.

"Yes. I have tried not to. I have tried to think of her as a sister, but I cannot help the way I feel. There is nothing I can do." Veda sounded defeated.

"There is only one way to deal with this, Veda. Distance," Galen told him in a whisper that carried to her.

Carling felt the wrench at the word, and it hurt to hear.

The morning dawned clear, and Carling had not slept all night. She watched as the light crept into the room, and she heard Veda moving about. She saw his shadow move towards the door and she sat up and followed.

"Veda, wait." She ran after him. "Don't go yet."

"I think I must, Carling." He slung his bag over his shoulder and shrugged it into place.

"But don't leave like this, please. I am losing another person I am close to. Please stay for the morning meal, at least," Carling begged him.

Wolf came bounding up the hill and stood in between them. She licked Carling's hand, and she crouched to hug the large wolf.

"I will miss you." She released the wolf and placed her arms around Veda.

"I will miss you, too." Veda held her close for a moment before letting her go. "Safe journey, Carling, until we meet again."

"Safe journey, my brother, until we meet again," she told him as tears welled up in her eyes.

Veda gave her a nod and Wolf was at his side, nudging her head to his hand. He placed it gently on her head taking comfort from his bonded pack mate. Carling watched until they were both out of sight in the trees. The tears now free, slipped down her cheeks. Bear was at her side, and her hand rested on his neck.

Wolf will miss my fishing, Bear said. I will miss her.

I will miss them both, she told him.

Carling wandered away from the house and down the hill. She stopped at the bank of the loch. Bear had moved away from her and entered the shallow water looking for fish, but so far, he was not having any luck. She meandered along the bank and came to a large rock, which she sat on, staring out over the water.

"He will be all right," Galen said behind her.

"I know. But it just seems to be the way with me. People come into my life and then they go."

"It is the way of the world. We are not stationary things, like that rock you are sitting on. We move and change, just like the loch here. Today it looks peaceful and calm. But tomorrow it could be raging with large waves in a storm. Some of us were meant to be alone, and others surrounded by people."

"I am not so sure," Carling disagreed. "While people have cared for me, I have been mostly on my own."

You are not alone, Bear declared as he came bounding up the bank, splashing water everywhere.

Carling laughed at the antics of the large animal.

"Your laugh hasn't changed," Galen said. "It is like a tinkling bell. And you won't be alone for long. We'll take the boat to your uncle and aunt's crannog later this morning."

"They are on the other side?" She asked reflexively, looking towards the distant shore.

"You really don't remember? Yes, they are on the other side." Galen smiled at her.

"What about the Romans?" she asked with concern.

"They are down that end, and Longus is at the other. Come get something to eat, and then we will go." He held out his hand to help her from the rock.

Carling stood and looked to the other side again for a second or two, turned, took his hand in hers, and stepped off the rock to the bank. He held it for a few seconds longer than necessary before letting it drop and turning to walk back to the house. Carling watched him for a moment before following Galen up the hill. Bear, having caught only one fish, came trundling up beside her.

You are going to have to be careful here, Bear. He said that they would like to take your coat, she warned him.

They can try but thank you for the warning. He is nice, but a bit sad.

Yes. He is taking me to see my other pack. We will be travelling by boat over the water, so you need to stay around here, Carling told him.

He seems to not mind my company. I will do as you ask until we are ready for our other trip.

It is getting late in the summer; I don't think we will be travelling until spring.

Then I need to find a den for the winter. The bear gave a great sigh at the thought of it.

I think that might be wise, Carling told him.

Stepping into the little round coracle, Carling was feeling less sure of herself. She sat on the centre board and Galen stepped in beside her. The small boat rocked violently, and she gripped the side. He pushed off and sat, placing the paddle out in front of him and moving it back and forth with agile sweeping motions. They were soon quite a way from the bank, and Carling could feel it.

"Relax." Galen laughed at her nervousness. His joviality did nothing to ease her state of mind.

Now out in the middle, there was only one way to go and that was forward. She held on to the side of the little round boat and prayed that it would all be over soon. The other side was becoming clearer, and Galen changed course, still working his way towards the bank, but now he battled the current to head up the loch.

Around the bend and from behind the trees that leaned out from the banks, a crannog became clear. It sat on a little island, perched on top of poles made from the trunks of trees, with smoke rising from the vent in the top of the thatched roof. From where she sat, she could see children, both young and older, running around, and crossing the wooden bridge. They moved closer and were soon spotted by them. Some went running, while others stood by the bank waiting for Galen to come closer. Carling suddenly missed Talorc, Nessa and their children.

The little boat nudged the shallow water and Galen stepped out, pulling it further up with the help of the older children. Galen held out his hand to assist Carling onto dry land. The children crowded around him; he was obviously well loved by them. He picked the youngest up and placed him on his shoulders, leading the way to the bridge that took them to the round house on the water.

From the doorway a large man came out. His size made the breath freeze in Carling's lungs as she remembered her father. Behind him came a smaller woman, plump with a round, rosy face.

"Galen, welcome. What brings you…" The large man's words were lost when he saw Carling. He stopped halfway over the small wooden bridge and stared.

"The gods be praised!" the woman exclaimed, seeing what her husband had just seen. "It's Breena!"

"She is not a ghost, Longus and Bron, but your niece, Carling," Galen told them, waiting at the end of the bridge.

Longus moved forward after Bron prodded his back. He reached the shore, his eyes still on the young woman.

"Carling?" he whispered, still not trusting his own eyes.

Bron pushed past him and gathered the girl up in an embrace. She held her at arm's length and studied her face. "You are the image of your ma," she said, collecting her again in a hug.

"How—when?" Longus was still stammering.

"How about we have a sip of Bron's wonderful ale and then Carling can tell you herself?" Galen slapped his friend on his broad shoulder and waited.

"Shift yourself, man, and move!" Bron said, pushing her husband. He moved and headed back to the house.

Carling stopped at the door and stared. The sights, sounds, and smells came flooding back, and she froze for a moment. She was back at the age of six, staring at the burnt remains of her home. She looked around and could see so much that was familiar to her. The little group was watching, waiting for her to enter.

"Carling, come sit." Bron was at her side and gently guided her in. "It must be a bit overwhelming coming back here." She led her to a stool and sat her down, then went and poured the promised ale.

"This is a complete surprise. We thought that she was still with the Romans," Longus said quietly.

"Well, here she is in the flesh. She took me by surprise when Veda brought her to me," Galen told the couple.

"Veda? Talorc of the forest's son?" Bron asked.

"Yes. They arrived yesterday with a couple of Romans on their tail. I took care of them—the Romans, that it is—and took Veda and Carling here in for the night."

"So where is Veda?" Longus asked.

"He left this morning to go back home."

Longus looked over to Carling again, who was sipping from her cup. He shook his head at the likeness and then gulped his own ale. "What is your story? How did you get away from them?" he asked her.

Carling swallowed and tried to find her voice. Bron was now sitting down and looked over at her with an encouraging smile.

"I was given my freedom," she told her uncle in a small voice.

"Just like that? They gave you your freedom?" Longus asked.

"Why don't we start at the beginning, Carling?" Bron urged, giving her husband a baleful look. "What happened after your grandmother took you?"

Carling started her story and relived it all the while she was telling it. She really did not remember much after her grandmother died, but she recounted the first meeting with Keelie and Brietta. She thought it was funny how she had become used to thinking of Keelie by her given name, and not the one the Romans had bestowed on her. She told how she was trained and taught to speak their language. How she was given the gift of music by Keelie. How Marinus had attacked her and how she fought back. Then of Keelie giving her freedom.

"After I left, I travelled to Brietta's sister, and I then stayed with their mother for a while, so she could give me some training, then we travelled to Talorc's enclosure, and Veda brought me here." Carling finished her tale and took another sip of ale to moisten her dry throat.

"I don't understand why this woman would give you your freedom just like that, especially after her husband had attacked you," Longus said.

"I don't think we need to go into all the details right now, Longus," Bron said. "We need to celebrate her coming home to us. It is a blessing from the gods."

"Yes, a feast. You will stay for a while, Galen, and celebrate with us. You have fulfilled your duty at last and brought her home," Longus said loudly and jovially.

"I only rowed her across the loch," Galen responded with a wry smile, draining his cup. "It seems to me that she made her own way back; I cannot claim credit for that."

"Well, the rest of the family needs to be informed that she is back. They will all want to see her. A feast we shall have. Which means we need to go on a hunt. Will you lend your skills for it, Galen?"

"That I will do," he agreed readily, his eyes seeking out Carling once more.

"Children!" Longus's loud voice called out. From the bridge, many running feet could be heard, and the older ones ducked into the house. "Go out to the family and let them know that there will be a feast here tonight. But don't tell them why—just let them know that they need to be here."

"It is going to take some of them a while to get here, Longus," Bron said.

"Be careful if you head east. There is a group of Roman soldiers camped along the shores," Galen warned.

"And you haven't gone after them?" Longus slapped him on the back, laughing.

"No, there are a few more than even I can handle," Galen replied.

"Right. You have your orders; off you go." The children scattered and ran off.

People started to arrive shortly after, bringing food to contribute to the feast. Carling stayed in the house, as Longus wanted to keep her presence there a surprise. Bron could see no need, but she kept her husband's wishes and said not a word to anyone.

The feast was in full swing with music, food, and ale. Longus presided over all, and in the middle, he stopped the proceedings and called for quiet. Standing up from his seat at the fire, he waited for the gathering to give him their full attention.

"You have all asked me the occasion of this feast tonight, and we have a very good reason for it. I am not going to tell you; we will show you. Bron."

Bron stood beside Carling and gave her arm a squeeze. Very slowly, they exited the house and came down the wooden bridge to the gathered throng. As she got closer to the large fire and her features were recognizable, there were gasps and calls from those who had known Breena and Carvorst. The pair stopped at the edge of the circle and stood for all to see.

"Carvorst and Breena have been gone for so long. We all thought little Carling was lost to us, but the gods have brought her home," Longus declared.

A great cheer went up, and many crowded around her to check for themselves, marveling at the likeness to her mother.

Carling became uncomfortable at the scrutiny and blushed. Bron waved everyone away and brought her to a seat. She was waited on by the younger children, and she averted her eyes from everyone's gaze.

The heat from the large fire in the centre was getting to her. The sound of the drum was beating through her head, and the eyes staring at her were making her very uncomfortable. The first moment she could, Carling slipped away from the gathered crowd. Heading away quietly, she found herself down on the shore, and she walked along the bank slowly while listening to the music that swelled into the night behind her. She stopped at the water and watched the reflection of the moon dancing on the waves further out.

You are overtired, Bear's voice sounded in her head. I don't understand the human need to congregate together. It is much more satisfying being by oneself.

That is because you are a bear. Did you have luck today finding a den? Carling asked him.

No. I will try again tomorrow.

I could ask Galen if he could make you something.

We shall see. Get some sleep, Carling.

She heard him yawn and then draw away from her.

"Carling," a voice called out to her. "What are you doing here? They're calling for you."

She turned and saw Galen walking towards her. The sight of him silhouetted against the light of the fire made her gasp. There was strength about him. A vengeful strength that kept him going.

"I became too hot. I thought I would cool off for a bit," she said, trying to excuse her actions.

"The evening has been too much for you, hasn't it?" He was at her side, looking down at her.

"It has been a bit difficult. But there are other things on my mind as well. Winter is on the way and Bear needs a den. I have to go somewhere, and it will have to be delayed until spring. Then there is the question of where am I going to live? How will I survive what is to come? How can I live up to the expectations of everyone?" she said, her thoughts spilling before him.

"That is not much to have on the mind." He chuckled at her wandering thoughts. "As to living, you are to stay here with Bron and Longus. I know a cave where Bear can hole up for the winter. And where is it that you have to go?"

"I have been told to go to the sacred stones. Although I have no idea where that is." She stared out at the water.

"That is easy. I can take you there. It is only a few days' walk from here." He was still watching her, her golden hair now silvery in the moonlight and her skin glowing. The feelings that were welling up in him took him by surprise, and he stepped back.

"Come, they are waiting." He stammered for a moment then cleared his throat. "These are questions for tomorrow. Come celebrate finding your family." He took her elbow and guided her back to the fire and her seat. He moved away to talk to the other men but found his eyes resting on her face.

The music faded for a moment, and the chatter of the people filled the void. Carling moved to the musicians and looked at their instruments. One man saw her interest.

"Do you play, Carling?" His voice was like silk, and she recognized him as the one who had been singing.

"I play a harp and sing." She smiled.

"A harp? I have one with me. It is not usually an instrument that we play. Would you give us a tune?" He had a kind face and an encouraging smile.

"I would like to, very much." The man reached in and pulled out a cloth bag. Inside was a harp fashioned with smooth wood and unadorned.

"It is only a simple one," he said almost apologetically.

Carling strummed the strings and found that the tone was beautiful. She sank to the ground and started to play. The song she sang was one Keelie had taught her from her home. It was a love song, sweet and pure, and her voice soared into the night with the sparks from the fire. She sang fully and heartily, and with the dying of the notes she realised she had stopped several conversations, including that of Galen's. She blushed, and the musician clapped loudly.

"Give us another, Carling," he called out and was soon joined by others.

The harp remained in her hands for the rest of the night. She accompanied them as they played the songs of the lands about them, learning them quickly. The music helped her relax in the company of so many strangers, and she smiled and laughed with great joy.

Carling was home.

Chapter Eight

Carling slipped into the life of the crannog with great ease. She enjoyed the simple tasks of everyday life and was soon an invaluable help to Bron. The season changed, and summer released its tenuous hold on the world to be overtaken by the colourful autumn. The trees about them changed their colours to bright oranges and yellows. The ground at their roots was soon a carpet of changing hues.

The children fell in love with Carling's kind and sweet spirit, and her nightly singing was a joy to all who shared the hearth. She heard many stories about her parents and was grateful to learn more about them. She learned from Bron the many things she should have from her mother, and she blushed at some of the matter-of-fact ways Bron would put things of a delicate nature.

The winter soon descended onto the loch valley, and snow came to cover the mountains that surrounded it. Longus was called away to a meeting of the clan, and while he was gone, the snow fell deeply and harshly around them. The family all slept together around the hearth to protect against the cold. When he finally came back, he was all smiles as he trudged through the built-up snow.

"I have news, but first I need to warm myself. I think my feet are about to fall off." Longus called to them as he stepped onto the wooden bridge. He entered after the children, and they helped him strip off his damp protective clothing. He sat by the fire, warming himself up with a cup of the broth that was hung there to keep warm.

"So, what is this news, then?" Bron asked, coming to sit beside him.

Carling looked up from the sewing she was doing and waited for him to speak. He took a long gulp of the hot liquid and then glanced her way.

"It is to do with Carling. You are to be betrothed in the spring," Longus told her as if it was the greatest news in the world.

"To whom?" Bron asked. She looked as shocked and surprised as Carling.

"He will come and claim her in the middle of spring, and then she shall see who she is to marry. Don't look so frightened, Carling. I would not have agreed to the match if I didn't think it were a good one. And believe me, it is a good one—not only for the clan, but for us as well. With the match, I have the full backing to be chief after Broc dies."

"So, this is all about you and not how she feels. What if there is another who loves her?" Bron asked angrily.

"What other? She has had no suitors since she arrived here. I can't see why you are getting upset, woman!" Longus reacted to his wife's outburst.

"I am getting upset because you are not taking into account her feelings. We married for love, not because we were forced to. And anyway, she has had a suitor. Why do you think we have seen so much of Galen over the winter, and he has delayed going to his mother?"

"Galen? In love with Carling? I think the fairies have been putting notions in your head," he replied with a laugh, and then became serious. "It is all arranged and settled. I cannot go back on my word now."

"But—"

"No. That is the end of the matter," he cut across her with his voice raised. "She will be wed in spring to the one we have chosen. It is already settled with the man. If Galen loved her, then he should have spoken up earlier."

The silence that followed was very heavy. The children were sent out to play in the snow for a while, and Bron ignored her husband. It was the first time Carling had seen them fighting. Normally the words between them were kind and loving. She packed up her sewing and headed out the door.

"Carling. You have not had your say in the matter," Longus said, watching her.

"Is he kind?" she asked as she shut the door back in place.

"Who?"

"This man I am to marry. Is he kind?" Carling asked again, moving slowly back to the fire.

"I don't really know. I have had dealings with him before and found him agreeable," Longus told her, still confused with her question.

"Is he the man the visions have said?"

"I don't know that either. But they are just nonsense and don't come true most of the time," Longus told her, finishing off his second cup of broth.

"Are the other abilities nonsense too?" she asked quietly.

"No, of course not. I know you think I am just a brute who cannot understand The People, but I do know them and what they are capable of, Carling. Your mother was most proficient at hers."

"I do not think you are a brute, Uncle. If this is what you wish, then I will obey," she told him quietly.

"It is not a matter of you obeying. You still have the right to refuse when you meet him. You are not a slave any longer, Carling." Her uncle's tone had changed to a softer one.

"But you said that it was all arranged. That he would come for me in spring."

"For the betrothal. I would not give you away like chattel, as if your feelings do not matter. You can refuse him if you wish. Though I don't think you will. He is handsome and brave. He will be able to look after you like no mere clansman will," he told her gently.

"Who is he?" she asked.

"I cannot tell you. I gave my word to not speak of him until he comes."

They did not speak of the betrothal again for the rest of the winter. But the thought of it did run through her mind often.

The snows soon melted and the first flowers of the spring burst into life. The trees were starting their first blush of green, and the air was warmer. Carling was moving about the reeds, looking for the plants that could be eaten when she heard a voice call.

"Carling, I bring news." Out on the water, the little round coracle was moving towards her, and Galen was waving.

She waited for him to pull the boat up onto the shore and push his hair from his face.

"So, what news do you bring, then, Galen?" She held the basket on her hip, and she watched his blue eyes sparkle.

"Bear is back. I warned him to stay out of sight of humans, but I don't know if he understood me."

"He would have. I have not heard him." She was worried by that fact, and she bit her lip as she sent out a call to him.

I am awake, only just. Spring is such a fickle time. I will eat and sleep some more, Bear told her when she asked if he was all right.

Good. I have missed you over winter.

You only missed the warmth my coat would give you. It was the nearest to a laugh as Bear could get, the great snort he made, and Carling chuckled at it.

When she came back to herself, she saw Galen looking at her, and she explained what Bear had said. Moving off, she was very conscious of how close he was to her as she remembered Bron's words.

Galen walked with her and helped her in her harvest, and they talked very companionably. Until he mentioned something that reminded Carling of her own promises.

"I will be away for a while. I have to go visit my mother," he told her.

"Does she live far?"

"No, only a couple days' journey. She lives near the sacred stones. Normally I would have wintered with her," Galen told her.

"When do you leave?" Carling moved a stray strand of hair from her face and stopped to watch as he bent down and pulled a plant up, cleaning its roots.

"In a few days." He handed the root to her, and she placed it in the basket. "Carling, I have heard of the marriage that Longus has arranged. Please don't agree to it."

"I have no idea what I will do, Galen. I have not met the man," she told him, moving further along the bank as she felt her face redden.

"You have. And what Longus has arranged is not fair to you. The only reason he's keeping his identity a secret, is so you do not run away." Galen caught up to her and took her hand in his and held it tightly.

"Galen, you're frightening me. Who is it?"

"The commander of the Roman fort." He kept hold of her hand as she went as white as a sheet.

"Why would he do that? After hearing my story, why would he give me to that man?"

"It has to do with politics. He wants so desperately to become chief, and with the backing of the Romans he hopes to secure it. I only learned this last night when Talorgan stopped for the night. Your cousin made me promise not to say anything. He is not happy with his father's plan himself, but I had to tell you. To warn you."

"He will be here in four days," she said out loud, voicing the thoughts that ran through her head.

"Come with me. You are supposed to make the journey anyway, remember. Come with me and I can protect you along with Bear." His grip on her hand tightened.

"I can't just leave. What about Bron and the children? What would happen if Marcus discovered I wasn't here?" She asked, looking at him in fright, the images of long ago once more rising.

"That is up to Longus to deal with. It was his decision to make the match," Galen said angrily.

"I'm not sure, Galen. I don't want to leave them, but if I stay it will be a far worse fate for me."

"There are a few more days before you have to decide. Think on it, Carling, but make your choice quickly. Once I am gone, I cannot help you." He told her tenderly, his eyes pleading with her.

"I will. Thank you for the warning." She pulled her hand away and turned from him, heading back to the crannog. "You would have been seen by one of the children. You had better come and say hello. Bron will be mad if you don't." She looked back at him and forced a smile, and he followed.

Within the darkness of the house over the water, Carling lay still on her pallet. Her mind was racing, and her eyes stood wide open. The sound of the water underneath was not soothing as it had come to be, and she could hear each creak and movement the house made. Over on the other side, she could hear Longus snoring. Bron was near her husband, and she was also asleep. The time had come.

Very carefully she gathered her belongings from under the small bed and crept from the room. Gently putting the door back into place, she felt the chill of the air and shivered. On silent and unshod feet, she crossed the bridge, stopping at the end to cover her feet in deer-hide boots that had seen her through the cold months.

Heading west, she followed the bank of the loch, moving quickly and quietly to put as much distance as she could between her and the sleeping forms of her kin. The decision had come the night Galen had told her the news. It was a hard one, but it was one she knew she had to make. She had sung to them that night all the songs they loved to hear and had said good night, trying to imprint their faces on her memory.

Now through the cold spring night, she trudged alone. A dark shadow came out from behind a tree and waited for her to meet him. Bear walked beside her with her hand resting on his back, giving her as much comfort as he could. It was still two days until Marcus arrived, enough time for Longus to find her and drag her back. And she was worried about that.

On they went through the night until they came to the river that fed the loch just as the sun was starting to rise. Across the river was the figure of Galen waiting for them. The gap was not wide to cross, and Carling tossed her bundle to him. Bear crossed first over the raging water of the snow melt as it cascaded over the large boulders in its depths. Carling entered the river carefully, moving through the fast-flowing water.

Suddenly her foot slipped between two stones hidden in the depths and caught. Carling tried to free herself, pulling hard on it, feeling the stones holding it fast. The water was freezing, and she could no longer feel her feet. Slowly the iciness crept into her body, and she started to shiver. With an almighty tug, she managed to free herself but lost her footing with the other. She tumbled into the water and felt the flow carry her away down through the rocks.

It bounced her and threw her up against the obstacles. She heard her name being called just before she went under, spilling over a small waterfall. Cold water closed over her, and she gasped at it, taking in a lungful. Up she came from underneath, breaking the surface and desperately gasping the clean air, coughing up the water she had taken in and feeling like she was choking on it.

"Carling!" Galen called to her.

She tried to reach for a rock to grasp onto, but her frozen hands refused to grip anything. Further down the river she flowed, hearing the rush of another fall coming and tried to brace herself. Tumbling over the edge, she felt herself be pushed towards the rocky bottom of the deep pool. It was quieter under the surface; the rushing water above was only a gentle roar.

Her arms and legs instinctively started to move, pushing her back to the surface and the morning that had just broken. A loud splash nearby caught her attention, and then he was there. Galen's arms, sure and strong, enfolded her to him as he pulled her to the shore. She felt the power of his muscles in his grip and held on to him.

Galen pulled her gently up the bank and lay there with her briefly while he caught his breath. The shivering, which had started in the water, was now overpowering her. Her teeth chattered, and her limbs felt heavy and tense. Galen was not at her side any longer, and she looked to see where he was.

The bare back she saw made her eyes open wide. Long, ropy dark scars were cut across his back. The memory of a dream came back to her, and she accepted that he was the one. With the scars covered in his tunic, he rushed to her side.

"We have to get some dry things on you before you freeze to death." He picked her up and helped her to stand. "You are going to have to help me, Carling."

She nodded, her words stuck behind chattering teeth as she started to undo the clasp at her throat for the wet cloak, her fingers fumbling with the pin. He pulled her hands away and had the cloak off within seconds. He tugged her tunic off and the undershirt; she stood in the cold air stripped to the waist while he rubbed her down and then slipped a dry tunic of his own over her head.

"We have to get moving; they will be following soon," he said gently. He picked up their bags and placed an arm around her, sharing the warmth of his body.

The water was still squelching in her boots, and she could not feel her toes, but she was warming up in the early sun's rays. They trekked on through the morning, and by midday she was warm again. Her bundle was at her back, and she could feel the harp digging into her hip, so she moved it carefully. Stopping for a rest on the side of the mountain they had to cross, she looked out at the loch below.

The water was dark, and she could see the smoke from the hearths in the crannogs along the shore. Turning her back on it, she headed up the slope. Bear was ranging ahead, and Galen looked back at her.

"Not far now," he said, trying to encourage her. But she needed none. Just the thought of going back was enough to keep her moving.

Late afternoon they reached the ridgeline and walked over to the other side. Out before them were rolling hills and rivers.

The mountains in the distance still had their white winter caps on, and they gleamed in the sunshine. They started to descend, and Carling found it harder than the climb.

I have found a place for the night, Bear's voice came to her.

Good, I am ready for a rest. She relayed Bear's message on to Galen, and they spotted the shaggy brown bear further down the slope.

The shelter he had found was a small cave, which became even smaller with him inside as well. Galen started a fire at the entrance and heated some food for their growling bellies. They both sat beside it in the dying light of the day.

Carling pulled her boots off. The skin of her feet was white and wrinkled from the water that was still trapped in the fur lining. Carefully she pulled them inside out and placed them by the fire to dry. The cloak and tunic had already been placed on rocks to finish drying.

"You can share my cloak tonight," Galen said softly when he saw she was looking at them.

"Thank you." She did not meet his eyes, and her stomach did a flip at the thought of her body touching his. Remembering how it felt when he pulled her from the water. She was rubbing her feet and testing the skin.

"Don't rub too hard or you'll take the skin off." He reached down and pulled her hands away. "You will need to be careful tomorrow that the boots don't wear too much as well."

The quiet spread between them, and suddenly Carling didn't know what to say. Her mouth had gone dry, and she felt restless. She watched as he fed a little more wood onto the fire. Under the shirt he wore, she could see the muscles that had held her and kept her safe. He looked up and caught her staring, and she blushed.

"You're very quiet tonight, Carling. You have never been this quiet with me before." There was mischief playing on his lips and in his eyes.

"Maybe I am just tired," she said, pulling the long tunic down over her knees and covering her feet.

"Maybe," he agreed with her. "Or is there something else?" He was watching her from the corner of his eye, seeing the red flush her cheeks once more.

"No, nothing else," she told him, her chin resting on her knees, eyes firmly fixed on the horizon.

The night was fast approaching, and the stars were soon winking into existence. Carling was counting them as they appeared, but soon there were too many to keep up. Her eyes started to droop and finally succumbed to sleep. Galen moved to her side and gently woke her, leading her further into the cave and to the side of the slumbering bear.

He lay down at her side and wrapped his cloak over them both, holding her close in his arms. Her head was resting on his shoulder, and he kissed the top of it. She snuggled in closer, and he smiled.

"I had a dream one night. Not long before you arrived at my door," he said softly to her, thinking she was asleep. "In that dream was a beautiful woman, golden hair, soft blue eyes, fair of face. I couldn't believe that she was real when I saw you."

"I found you by the loch, a beacon of bright blue, the same colour as your eyes," she whispered. "I saw the same scars that I saw today. You turned and looked directly at me."

Galen didn't say anything else. He lay there with the woman in his arms and felt happy. Carling tipped her head to look at him and placed a hand on the side of his face. Slowly she kissed him. At first their lips were just touching, testing, and seeking. Then he pulled her closer, his mouth taking hers hungrily.

With the dawning of the new day, Carling slipped out from Galen's arms and headed outside, just in time to see Bear ambling down the hill to find something to eat. She stretched in the light as it shone from the east. Out in the valley below, a deer moved from the trees, his antlers large and spreading. He stopped and waited, watching the world before moving off into the bare hills.

Carling turned and saw Galen watching her. She smiled and sank to the ground, pulling her boots towards her. She pulled them back into shape and started to strap them onto her feet.

"Good morning," he said, still under the cloak.

"Good morning to you." She still refused to meet his eye, feeling shy and nervous after the night before. She stood and checked her clothing. With her back to him, she quickly pulled off his large tunic and donned her undershirt and own smaller tunic.

Turning back, she discovered he was up and behind her. He took her in his arms and kissed her gently. Her arms moved slowly around his neck and held him.

I hope there is not going to be a repeat of last night's activities, Bear interrupted her thoughts.

Carling pulled away from Galen and laughed. She tried to move away from him, but he pulled her back for one last kiss.

"I guess the betrothal is definitely off then," he said as Carling moved away to start getting their morning meal.

"Definitely," she replied.

With the camp cleared away, they moved off down the slope towards the forest. Galen told her the route they would take to get to their destination, and she tried to imagine it—the woods, rivers, valleys, and hills as he described them in detail. They merged into one long line of travel to her, stretching out for the next couple of days.

Onwards they trekked, and the going was not as bad as she had first thought. They talked and opened up to each other about their lives. And it was as they were making camp on the third night that he told her the story of his scars.

"We were tracking you, although it wasn't hard. The Romans leave a wide trail behind them. I was thirteen and just in my training. My Da and brothers were with me. As we were running up to their rear, we tried to flank them and were caught. My eldest brother was cut down first. It didn't take them long to overpower us. We were taken to a clearing and forced to our knees. A young man—about the same age as my eldest brother—came, and at first, I thought he was just another soldier, but when he talked the others obeyed. I was pulled up and made to stand in front of my family. I watched as they were killed one by one." His voice caught in his throat, and she could hear the anger swelling.

"I was stripped bare. I felt each slice of my back as he cut it. The words I could not understand, but I got the meaning of them. I was to be a warning. He set me free, and I wandered back towards the loch. I stumbled and fell. I don't know who found me. I just know I woke up with my mother beside me, dressing my wounds."

"You said he cut you," she said softly.

"Yes, the one in command. His hazel eyes burned with anger." Galen's hands were clenched in front of him, and she placed her own over them.

"We survived for a reason, Galen," Carling said turning his head towards her.

He looked into her eyes and nodded slowly. "Yes, we did. To find each other, to heal. And to kill him."

That night as she lay in his arms, Carling dreamed. It was not the dream space, but a deep, enclosing dream. She wandered through a forest. The trees were ancient and close together, while the air was heavy with expectation. She came to a clearing very much like the one where she had met the Ancestor and sat beside a well-used trail was a large oak. She reached out and touched the tree, feeling the life force within, and then he was there at her side.

As the other had been, he was tall and covered in a long, dark cloak with the hood pulled all the way over the head. She stood with her hand still on the tree and waited for him to speak.

"Carling. You must hurry here. Those who pursue you are closer than you think. You must leave Galen and come to us now. Bear will guide you—keep your trust in him," the man told her.

"What of Galen? I can't just leave him."

"You must. For the visions we have granted to come true, then you must. Come to us, Carling. Join us at the sacred stones."

"I can't lose another. I can't lose him. I love him," she said desperately, shaking her head and stepping away.

"As was foretold. And you will be reunited. The time is very short. Wake now, Carling. Wake!"

With the force of the word, she woke and found Bear rousing from his rest. She sat and rubbed her eyes, wiping away the tears that had already formed at the thought of leaving him. Galen slept on beside her. She moved the hair from his face and kissed him. He did not stir.

As quietly as they could, they left their little camp, and Bear led her on into the darkness. They came out of the trees and started to climb the hill, moving along a ridgeline until they came to a place where two hills met. A spring sent forth its waters to tumble down the hill and into the darkness below with a tinkling sound. Around an up-thrusting piece of rock she was led by Bear, and she came into sight of a stone circle. The large lichen-covered stones clawed at the sky, and she could feel the energy that was stored there.

Carling's hand came up, and she placed it on the first stone, feeling it vibrate under her touch as it sang to her, such a sweet song. Through the entrance she went and stood in the centre.

"I am here," she called out into the darkness.

From around the rocks came a procession. Seven tall figures in long cloaks walked in single file around the circle until each space between the stones was filled. She turned on the spot to look at each of them as they raised their arms and began to chant. The voices rose and fell until they reached a crescendo, and they stopped. Two left their places and moved towards her, linking hands, and holding them around her. Again, the host began to chant.

This was different and felt harsher, more urgent and hurried. Above them, the wind swirled the clouds and whipped around the circle. Golden sparks of light began to appear over the stones, leaping from one to another. Soon other colours appeared and joined them, shades of blue, green, and purple, yellow, orange, and red. Like a rainbow they became as they moved faster and faster, catching up with the wind and circling her.

The chanting slowed to a murmur, and she looked at each of the figures that now surrounded her. They released their hands, and each placed one on her shoulders.

"Our child, you will need to be strong. The coming seasons will be hard sometimes to bear, but it is necessary. The one you seek to harm will be cursed down through the ages. It has been seen. You must not harm him. It is not our way. We had hoped to temper his evil with love, but we are unsure of the results. We now grant you the rest of your abilities—abilities that were yours from birth. As our only child, it is right that you have them. In your line, shall you pass them down to the two that shall come in the far-off future who will face the evil that threatens our lands," the man to her right said.

"Your line is the great hope for the future. From this line will also come one who will be great and will even surpass you. It is important that the two succeed so that the one be born. This great burden we place on you and your line. We shall protect and care for the line. It was the reason you were created. The only true child to be born from us, the Ancestors," the woman said.

The other figures began to chant once more, their hands raised in benediction over her. They began to slowly walk towards the centre and soon encircled Carling. The words were in a language she at first could not understand, until slowly they made sense. Each word a blessing, as they passed their knowledge on to her. The weight from it became heavy in her mind. Carling fell to her knees. Still, they kept on chanting, filling her head with the abilities she would pass on.

Chapter Nine

Carling woke to the sun rising over the hills to the east. Bear was sitting at the entrance to the circle waiting for her to wake. As she rose from the ground, she felt light-headed and waited for the world to stop moving under her feet. She headed towards Bear, and two figures appeared before her.

"No more. Please," she said, her head hurting.

"Calm, Carling. We just wish to visit with our child," the woman said.

Carling sat down heavily on the ground and Bear entered the circle to be by her side. The pair joined her on the soft grass and waited for her to gather her thoughts together.

"If you have questions, Carling, now is the time to ask them," the man said.

"Can I see your faces?" she asked, trying to see under the hoods.

"No. That is forbidden. What we look like does not matter," he said.

"How am I your child? There are those who remember the day I was born."

"You are born of a long line that reaches back to us. To us you are still our child. The face and the hair are all the same as the original and will remain so. Your spirit is the same," the woman told her gently.

"I was told that I would need to be separated from Galen. Can I return to him now?" Carling asked them.

"Not yet. There are two tasks that need to be completed. Another who was not spoken of last night will also come from your line. This line shall be corrupted by the evil of the land, but the one who must come will be special. It is he who will sire the awaited one. He is a great protector and is necessary for the two," he said.

"This is all very confusing," Carling said, placing her head in her hands.

"Yes, it must be. Your mind will grow under the knowledge that was passed to you last night. And when you are ready, you will see for yourself what the future holds. But for now, those who seek you must find you. To protect those who protect this place, it must not be here or at the little house in the valley. And you must not harm Marcus."

The woman reached out and placed a hand on the side of her head. The touch was warm and caring, but Carling felt the command she had given being reinforced in her.

"I must not harm him," she said with great resignation.

"For all that consumes him, he does love you. That is the love we have instilled in his soul, to combat the evil. We hope that it is enough to keep you safe," she said.

"And what of Galen? Am I supposed to forget him?" Tears sprung from her eyes.

"No, my child. You will be together once two tasks have been completed. Four seasons hence, when spring is at its equinox, you shall be together again," he said.

"Will he want me back after I left him so?" The fear of rejection was building, just as the loss she felt in having to leave him.

"One of our gathering will explain to him when he arrives to see his mother," she said.

"Will it be one of you?"

"No. He is not of our issue, but another's, and as is right, he will talk to Galen and impart the knowledge he needs," she said gently.

"If Galen is of this one's issue, then surely that makes him like me?" Carling was confused.

"No. We joined with the people who came to this land and settled here. Many children were born from those unions. But there has only ever been one who is born from the joining of two of our kind," he said.

"Why were there not more?" Carling asked.

"It was forbidden. Our abilities were meant to trickle down through the lines. Our child was born of necessity to fight the evil one. A true child of the Ancestors is the only way that he will be banished for good," she said.

"Now it is time for you to go. You must not be here when Galen arrives. You must go meet those who follow. Take the ridge down to the river. In the trees you will find a great oak. Rest and wait there until they arrive. And if you see Galen, you must hide from him. It all rests on your actions, Carling. Bear will help you," he said.

They stood and waited for her. Now upright again, they each placed a hand on her head.

"Go with our blessings and our love," she intoned.

"We shall watch over and protect you," he said, and then they were gone.

A peacefulness descended over her as she felt them leave. She walked out of the circle and around the large rocks. Bear followed as Carling headed down the ridge and into the forest that was there. With no missteps he led her to the tree. Standing still on the track, she looked at it and recognised it from the dream. Slowly she walked up to the old oak and placed a hand on the bark. Just as before, she felt the life force inside and felt closer to it, now knowing what resided within.

Bear was already past it and entering the closely growing trees. *Hurry, Carling. We need to be hidden.*

I have a way to keep us hidden, Bear. She sat with her back leaning against the tree. Bear came and lay beside her.

You had better do it quickly, he will be here soon. He rested his head on his paws.

Carling reached out and placed her hand on his head. She concentrated for a moment and felt herself fade out. Opening her eyes, she found Bear invisible to her, although her hand could still feel his warm fur. From the track came the sound of a pair of running feet. She looked up and saw Galen running towards them, his face a mask of determination, fear, and loss. She desperately wanted to stop him, wanted to talk to him. To let him know that it would all be all right, that they would be together once more.

Her hand raised for a moment off Bear's head before the animal lifted it and reconnected. Galen halted in his tracks at the momentary flash and stared at the base of the tree.

You did it now, the bear said to her.

Galen moved closer for a moment, trying to make sense of what he had just seen. Carling willed him forward, wanting him to discover her, but he backed up, shaking his head, and headed up the track again. She let out the breath she had been holding and released Bear from her grasp. Tears trailed down her face, and she dashed them away angrily with the backs of her hands.

Hours later came the sound of horses. The tack jingled, and the sound of the hooves hitting the compacted earth as they stepped along the track reached her. Carling stood and steeled herself for the meeting that was to come.

I will be following you, Carling. They will not take kindly to a bear in their midst. Bear told her as he shambled away deeper into the forest at her back.

Thank you, Bear. It would be best to do so.

If you have a need of me, I will be just a call away. He walked off into the woods and was soon hidden by the ancient trees.

She watched as the horses came into view. At the head, leading them all, sat Onnist, looking uncomfortable astride the horse he was on. Behind came the others, Marcus first, then Longus. Following them came a couple of Roman soldiers.

Carling stepped out onto the track in front of them, then released her hold on the ability that had kept her hidden from Galen. Her sudden appearance caused the horse Onnist was on to sidestep and rear. He slipped off the back and landed on the ground hard, knocking the wind out of him. The horse danced around and reared again, almost stepping on the man. Carling moved backwards out of its way as the front hooves flailed in the air above her.

"Move, man!" Marcus cried out to Onnist. He urged his horse forward and grabbed hold of the lead, calming the horse down. He turned in his saddle and stared at Carling, his mouth open and about to call to her.

"Carling!" Longus yelled as he slipped off his horse and ran to her. He picked her up in his strong arms, and she was taken back once more to the night when her parents were killed. He put her down gently and checked her over. "Are you all right?"

"I am fine, Uncle," she said, disengaging herself from him.

"Where have you been, girl? We have been worried sick about you. Bron is frantic, and the children are convinced you were taken by the fairies."

"I had a task to do, Uncle. I had to do it before anything else happened." Carling stood tall and defiant to him.

"You came out here on your own? Where's Galen?" Longus demanded.

"I am not with Galen. Do you see him here?" Carling's voice was getting louder.

"Don't you talk back to me." Longus raised his hand to slap her.

"Longus!" Marcus shouted. "I will run you through if you lay a hand on her." He had slipped off his horse, given the reins to a shaken Onnist to hold, and strode the short distance between them.

"She is my kin, and I will chastise her as I wish." Longus rounded on the Roman.

Marcus stood toe to toe before the large clansman, each equal in height, build, and strength. Only in colouring and voice did they differ.

"You will not touch her again." Marcus kept his voice low and even as they faced off. "There are others who could be chief, Longus. Maybe I will take Carling with me and find one of them who will be willing to fill the void."

Carling watched the pair of them, both holding her life in their hands. She waited for her uncle to speak. The strong man who had once hoped to protect her was now staring at the man who wanted to possess her. His face was red with anger, and he stepped back. He shook his head and turned his back on them.

Marcus turned towards Carling and took her hand. He held it up to his mouth and kissed it.

"I have missed you, Flora. Diana and Brietta will be happy to see you again," he said, smiling down at her.

She pulled her hand away from him roughly and spat in his face. "I may come to you of my own accord, but you will never have all of me."

"But you did come to me. You have offered yourself up. I was worried that I might have to start killing your kinsmen to get your attention." Marcus said with sly grin, wiping away the spittle that ran down his face.

"More killing and maiming? That seems to be the way you do things, Marcus. Leave more children alone in this world, is that the plan? More slaves for the camp?" she asked heatedly.

"Carling, hold your tongue." Longus said to her, coming back.

"And you, Uncle. Are you happy with yourself? To be backed by the man who killed your brother and his wife. The man who took the life of an innocent child and your mother?" She almost spoke about Galen's scars but heeded his advice.

"I do not forget what he has done, girl. But I do what is best for the clan. If that means I have to deal with a demon, then I will." He turned from her for a moment and faced her again. "We all must do what is best for the survival of the clan." His voice became softer and more controlled.

"That is why I am here, Uncle," she responded standing taller.

"If you two are finished, I think we had best be getting back to camp." Marcus seized Carling's arm and led her to his horse.

"No!" Longus called out. "Carling is not betrothed to you yet, Marcus. She will ride with me," Longus insisted, taking Carling by the hand, and leading her away from Marcus.

He lifted her up into the saddle and then climbed up behind her. He reached around and grasped the reins, then turned the horse and kicked its flanks before the Roman could object further. They rode fast back down the track and waded across the river. She heard the others splashing through the water behind them, and Carling closed her eyes as they moved further and further away from Galen.

"I'm sorry, Carling. We can always race off from him, if that is what you want," Longus said in her ear.

"No, Uncle."

"So where is Galen?"

"Not here," Carling replied sadly.

"You love him, then?"

"Yes. I do."

"Then I will get you away," Longus told her eagerly.

"No. There is something I have to do. The visions were right, but I can only do it from inside the camp. If that means I have to give myself to him, then that is what I must do."

"You do not need to."

"This way, no one else gets hurt. I am being guided by the Ancestors."

"As you wish, then, girl." Longus kicked the horse again and sped up.

When they arrived at the camp, there were many more soldiers than Carling had first thought. Mixed amongst them were men from her clan. Longus pulled the horse up and dismounted. He helped her down and led her away to a fireside. The Romans all formed up when Marcus arrived, and he leapt from his horse and followed them.

"I will take her straight to our camp," Marcus said as he closed in on them.

"No. We will do this the right way, Marcus. The betrothal will take place at our home; the traditions must be observed. Be happy she has agreed," Longus responded.

"I want this over with as soon as possible." Marcus turned and walked back to his soldiers.

"For your own protection, Carling, I am setting a watch on you. I don't trust that man," Longus said, his eyes still on Marcus' back.

"As you wish, Uncle." She sat down on the ground and crossed her legs. Her heart was breaking.

Longus called for two of his most trusted men to stand watch over her. One of them was his oldest son, Talorgan. He came and stood over her, so much like his father in looks and stature, with a smile that was both apologetic and sympathetic.

"You will be safe with us, cousin," he muttered under his breath.

"Only until the betrothal," she replied.

That night Onnist came and sat at her side, a cup of wine in his hands, and already far gone with the drink he had consumed. He stank of not only the alcohol but of an unwashed body and other things she could not name.

"You should have listened to me, Carling," he said as he breathed heavily beside her.

"You should not have sought him," Carling replied.

"I did as the Ancestors asked of me," he retorted.

"As do I. Though I do not do it willingly."

"It is your duty as a woman to respect the wishes of your uncle and Marcus. They will make a great alliance and shall turn the tide of fighting between the clans and Romans."

"At my expense," Carling said quietly.

"You have an effect on men, Carling, that I think you are unaware of." He was looking at her with bleary eyes, leaning back so she would be more in focus. "Your beauty was created for a reason, and I think that reason was for the enjoyment of men. Veda, I saw, was in love with you. Marcus is definitely in love with you. I myself felt some stirrings when we first met. Until I saw the true you, child," he said, placing a heavy emphasis on the last word.

"The true me, Onnist? That is funny. I think you need to go pay the Ancestors another visit and ask them who the true me is. You should not linger long with the Romans. Their ways do not agree with you."

"I like them fine. These Romans know how to live, how to treat a guest," he said, drinking from his cup.

"Marcus only tolerates you. When you stop being useful to him, he will kill you without a second thought. Just as he did with my grandmother when they slipped the spear into her heart in front of my eyes." She waited for the anger that the image had always brought forward, but it was not there anymore. It would not surface, and she felt the loss of it.

"Well, then, if that is the case, then you need to play nicely, child. Because he will probably do the same to you."

"No, he won't. The Ancestors spoke to me last night, Onnist. Do you wish to know what they told me?"

"You have been blessed, then, child." Onnist took another long gulp from his cup as he swayed where he sat.

"They told me that they planted the love he holds for me in him to balance out the evil that had invaded his soul. Do you know of the evil one, Onnist? The one who wishes to destroy this world?" She spoke softly so no one else around could hear what they talked of.

Onnist's eyes opened wide as he looked at her and a spark of red glistened in them. Carling sighed and leaned back from him.

"I see you have. I see it in you, Onnist. That is why you are not acting like one of The People. Did he come to you while you hoped to see the Ancestors? Did you really get your message from them? Or was it him?" she asked.

"That is not for you to know, Carling, the One True Child." Onnist's voice had changed. It was harsh and deep and not as affected by the drink in his hand. She felt her flesh crawl at the sound, and she moved away from him. "My puppets dance to my strings and my wishes. I will defeat your children, and then your soul will be my prize. You shall sit at my side and watch as I destroy this world that was not meant to be, and we shall give birth to a new race of people that will worship only me."

Onnist's eyes rolled back into his head as soon as he finished speaking and fell sideways, landing hard on the ground. Carling gave a small cry of alarm and Talorgan was at her side, pulling her away from him. The other clansmen dragged Onnist's inert form from their fire and left it somewhere between them and the Romans. Carling thought it was fitting. A man of one, wanting to be of the other. Caught between what he had been taught and that which he strived for. Cast out from his own people and caught up with forces that he could never hope to understand or comprehend. Carling felt sorry for him.

Bron ran across the wooden causeway as the horses came into sight and waited for them to arrive. The children were all gathered on the small walkway around the house, watching the procession coming down the path. Longus halted his horse and slipped off, helping Carling down after. The older woman ran to the girl and held her close, and with her other arm pulled her husband into the embrace.

"Whatever possessed you to run away like that, Carling?" she asked kindly.

"We will talk inside, Bron. Take her in, love," Longus said, sending them on their way. He turned and waited for the Romans to arrive.

Carling watched from the doorway as Longus spoke to Marcus, who looked up at her. He kicked his horse into movement again and they filed past. Her uncle walked back towards the house; moving further in, she waited for him to enter.

Ducking under the doorway, he entered and stood. "A fine mess I have made of things," Longus said to no one in particular.

"There are other forces at work here, Uncle," Carling told him. "The Ancestors have a plan and we all must go along with it."

"What is it that you are supposed to do? I have heard tales of these visions since you have come back to us, but they don't tell much." He sat heavily on his stool and Bron brought him a cup of ale.

"That has not been made clear to me. The Ancestors would not tell me specifically what it is that I must do. Only that there are two tasks that must be performed."

"So, the betrothal is going ahead, then?" Bron asked, handing a cup to Carling.

"Yes, she is adamant that it does. What I want to know is, where is Galen in all this?" he asked her again.

"He is where he needs to be right now," Carling said sadly.

Bron turned to her husband, exchanged a look that confirmed her suspicions, and asked, "He helped you run?"

"Yes. He helped me."

"Why won't you tell us where he is now? Has something happened to him?" Bron asked.

"He is with his mother. I saw him hours before you arrived running up the track. By now he will have been told and will not want anything else to do with me." A tear threatened to spill from her lashes, and she dashed it away with some annoyance.

"We don't understand what is going on, Carling. It is hard for us clansmen to get our heads around The People's way of thinking," Longus said.

"I know it must seem so. And I am not the right person to talk to. This has been thrust upon me only since last spring.

The reason I was given my freedom was that my ability finally came out. When Marinus attacked me, I entered his mind. My screams at the unknown drove him mad—so mad he killed himself."

Longus let out a long breath at this news. "Did you know what you were doing at the time?"

"No. I did not even know I had an ability. For one of The People to hurt someone is not allowed. The Ancestors have placed a restriction on my mind so that I cannot attack Marcus." The tears spilled down her cheeks, now unchecked, at the thought her long-awaited revenge was being thwarted by the command.

"The betrothal ceremony will take place tomorrow. Marcus insisted," Longus said as he drained his cup. "I have sent Talorgan to go get the priest Elfin. They will be here by tonight."

That afternoon Talorgan came riding in with a man seated behind him. Longus walked out to greet them both and welcome them to his home. The priest walked stiffly into the house and was again welcomed by Bron. Carling waited to be introduced to him, studying the man as he spoke to the children. He had long white hair and a short beard that matched. Around his neck he wore the token of his office, a large torc of beaten gold, decorated with coils of the same precious metal. In his hand was a staff, richly carved with symbols and decorated with colourful feathers. His tunic was plain and unadorned. She compared him to the priests of the Romans and found she preferred his understated and friendly air to their pomp and ceremony.

Elfin turned his eyes to her now, and they flashed with the smile that was on his face. The lines at the corners of his mouth and eyes deepened, and she found herself smiling back.

"Carling." Elfin bowed to her and then came to stand before her. "As beautiful as your mother. I remember marrying her to your father all those years ago. And now here you stand ready to make your own pledge. I must ask, do you make this betrothal of your own free will?"

"I do, Elfin," she told him simply.

"Good. Will you walk with an old man for a while, Carling? There is a place I think you have not been to since you came back. It is not far."

"I would be honoured to," she told him.

They made their way along the shoreline with a few of the children in tow. There was no talking between them as they walked. Carling was lost in her own thoughts about the coming day.

"I know it is a match you did not want, Carling. That is why I had to ask," Elfin said finally.

"It is still one I do not want. I mean no disrespect to you and your gods, Elfin, but I follow the Ancestors' wishes."

"The old ones. Yes, I know you are of The People. So far, our two ideals have worked well together. I will be asking the same of the man who has been chosen for you, even though he is a Roman and has his own gods."

"It may surprise you to learn that he is actually one of The People also. His mother was an alliance bride," Carling told him.

"I had not heard that." A worry line creased his brow for a moment.

Silence stretched on a while longer between them. Carling was now looking around at the place they had come to. There was something very familiar about the landscape, and she stopped for a moment. She recognised the trees that were in a grove near the hill and the stream that was running down to the loch.

"Our destination is not far, Carling," Elfin said gently.

"Why are we going there?" she asked, a panic rising inside of her.

"To put the spirits of your family to rest. I have heard them calling for the last few months. You are their anchor in this world, and they must be let go to travel to the spirit one," he told her.

They walked further along the path, and he suddenly stopped. Carling looked in the water and could see the remains of the posts for the bridge that had once taken her out to the house. A dark patch, just under the surface of the water further out, was the only evidence that the crannog had been there.

Elfin stood at her side and raised his staff into the air. He started to speak, but the words were lost on Carling. At her side was a presence, and she knew who it was. Calmly she entered into her own mind and found a woman there. She was the mirror image of herself. The woman walked towards her and took her face in her hands.

"My daughter, so grown," she said and kissed her forehead.

"Ma," Carling said simply and burst into tears.

"The Ancestors have told me what has been happening to you, dear one. I lend you my strength and my energy to use as your own."

"Thank you." Carling clung to her as she had when she was a child. "I miss you, Ma, all of you. Where is Da?"

"He will come soon to see you, dear one. He must first get past that rabbiting old man who thinks he has power of the spirit."

"Is the baby with you?"

"No. He has already returned to the world. He was too young to be taken, and the Ancestors have placed him with one known to you already."

Carling thought for a moment and her eyes opened. "Is he Cato?"

"Yes. That is the name he was given, but he shall be known by another—his true name." Breena smiled.

"What of Da? Will you two be separated?"

"Fortunately, no. When we wed the Ancestors accepted him as one of The People. I have seen what is to come, Carling. You will be strong, and Galen will wait for you. He will be there when you call."

"Is he the one, Ma?"

"What one?" Breena asked.

"The one from the visions. The man I am meant to be with."

"That vision is still unclear. It is still showing as a double-edged sword. But you have the ability to look for yourself now. Why are you not using it?"

"I don't want to see. I'm afraid," she said, and Breena put her arms around her.

In the distance Carling could still hear Elfin chanting and wailing. Another voice now was added to it. A frustrated and impatient one. He burst through the noise and walked towards the women.

His large arms enfolded them both and he hugged them close to him. There were no words just yet for his daughter, just the love of that embrace. He held her out and looked at her hard. A tear escaped his eye and disappeared into his bushy ginger beard.

"My daughter," Cavorst said with pride. "You have grown so beautiful. Just like your mother. We are so proud of you, girl."

"Thank you, Da. I have missed you."

"I know, girl. I know. But look at you. My daughter, the True Child." He was beaming from ear to ear. His blue eyes were sparkling and not just from the tears of their reunion. Carling blushed at his words and wondered what it would have been like to grow up with their guidance.

"We don't have long, Carling," her mother told her. "Tomorrow is going to be a trying day for you. We will be watching over you along with the Ancestors."

"My brother is a fool!" Carvorst said bitterly.

"But it is the Ancestors who have arranged this, not Longus. He is only following what they wanted," Breena told him.

"But a Roman! And the one who ripped our family apart," he added.

"Da, it will be all right. I know Marcus. I know how to handle him, and I will have guidance along the way," Carling told him.

"We must go, Carvorst; our time is up," Breena said, linking her arm in his.

"No; I only just got here. I have only had a moment with our child." His face screwed up with frustration and longing.

"Not a child any longer. A woman," Breena said.

Carvorst gathered her again into his arms and held her tightly. "Safe journey, Carling, until we meet again," he said into her hair.

"Safe journey to you, Ma and Da." She switched parents and accepted her mother's embrace for the last time. "Until we meet again."

"Stay safe, my child. Our love and blessings go with you always," Breena said. They turned and started to walk away. Carling watched as they slowly disappeared from her sight, then brought herself back to the present moment.

Elfin had finished his chanting and now was laying a little bundle on the water, pushing it out. It was covered in flowers and leaves, bound up with brightly coloured feathers. It bobbed on the small waves and started to float away. Carling kept her eyes on it, the tears that brimmed on her lashes blurring her vision.

Turning to Carling, he waved the staff over her head for a moment and then was still. Elfin was looking at her expectantly, waiting for her to say something. She smiled a little and nodded.

"Thank you, Elfin. They have gone now and are at peace." She gave him a gentle and thankful smile and nodded. He returned the smile, and for some reason it gladdened her heart to know that he thought he had helped her in some way.

The children were sitting watching the pair, impatient to be back and playing with their siblings. Carling walked over to them and took the girl's hand.

"We have enough time before we have to be back to go see a very special place. Would you like to see where the fairies of this area live?" she asked them.

A chorus of *yes, please* greeted her and she smiled. For one last afternoon she would be free to do what she wanted. She led them on up the path that meandered on the hill. They could hear the water tumbling down the rocks and every now and then spied it through the trees. They scrambled over a large rock and down the other side to a small platform with a cave behind it.

"There, see." She pointed to the white ribbon of water cascading down the other side of the chasm in front of them. "At the bottom is their home. It is a magical place, one full of wonder and danger. You shouldn't get too close, otherwise they will claim you as one of their own."

One of the older boys neared the edge of the platform and Carling grabbed him, making him jump. They squealed with delight at the fright she had given him, and all remained away from the edge but still trying to see the bottom.

Carling looked up and saw a man standing on the other side. He was hidden in the shadows and was watching them carefully. He moved into a patch of sunlight, and Carling could feel the day turn cold as she recognised Marcus.

"Time to go. Your Ma will be worried about you," she said, turning her back on him and gathering them up. She watched them as they climbed back up the rocks and waited for her with Elfin. Soon she was with them, and the priest put a hand on her arm.

"Is that him?" he asked, concerned.

"Yes. We have to get back. We shouldn't have come." She pulled her arm free and led the children back down the hill. Making a game of it, they had little running races to hurry them along. Elfin did his best to keep up, and they would stop and wait for him.

Carling saw the lone horseman in the distance behind them and tried to ignore him. She chased after the children until a blinding flash made her stumble and fall.

"You may run from me today, Carling. But tomorrow you will be mine," his voice called through and echoed in her mind.

"Just give me this one afternoon, Marcus. Just this afternoon and night, then I will be yours," she pleaded, and he faded away.

"Carling, are you all right?" Elfin was at her side, helping her up.

"I tripped over my own feet." She laughed, trying to make it sound convincing. When she looked, she saw Marcus turn his horse and move away from them. She turned back to the

children and started to chase them again, threatening to tickle
them all the way back to the crannog.

Chapter Ten

Clouds billowed white in the sky, moving sluggishly across the bright spring sun. Carling stood in the meadow before the crannog of her uncle and aunt and awaited the one who would claim her. Flowers were laced through her long golden hair and the new tunic her aunt had made for her hung past her knees. At her waist was a new belt with a knife tucked into a decorated scabbard, gifts from both Longus and her cousin Talorgan. It felt heavy on her hip but comforting.

She saw the procession of Roman soldiers exit from the copse of trees, Marcus at the lead with his heavily plumed helmet blowing in the wind. Behind her stood her family, aunts and uncles, cousins, distant kin. All who supported Longus in his bid for chief. Elfin stood at her side with the staff raised in his hand as Marcus dismounted and walked towards them.

Hazel eyes boring into her blue, he looked at no one else. Marcus stopped just steps from her and waited. Elfin moved so that he stood to the side of them both. He lowered his staff and pulled out a ribbon of material, long and blue in colour.

"Your right hand, Carling, and your left, Marcus," he asked. They raised their hands and he linked them together. "With the tying of hands do you, Carling, promise yourself to Marcus?" He placed a loose loop over her hand.

"I promise myself to Marcus," she said.

"With the tying of hands do you, Marcus, promise yourself to Carling?" He made another loop around Marcus's hand.

"I promise myself to Carling," he said.

"Do you both accept this union and any children that may come from it?" Elfin asked.

"I accept," both Marcus and Carling intoned together.

With a quick twist and another loop, the priest pulled the knot between them and laid a hand on the top of theirs.

"With the tying of the knot I call down the blessings of the gods on these two. May their lives together be blessed with many children, be blessed in their regard for each other, and be happy for the years to come."

Elfin removed his hand and stepped back. Carling stood by Marcus's side and faced the family that had gathered. She saw their faces for the first time, and while some were smiling, others were scowling. To some, the union did not sit as well with them as they had thought, now seeing this Roman in their midst.

"They have joined together, and the bond cannot be broken for a year and a day," Elfin called out and the crowd cheered.

Longus and Bron were the first to congratulate the couple, even if it were subdued. Their hands still linked by the blue ribbon, they were guided to their seats for the midday feast. Carling ate little and spoke even less. Marcus was just as quiet.

The feast lasted into the afternoon, until finally, at sunset, Elfin stepped in front of Carling and Marcus. He slipped the knotted ribbon from their wrists and handed it to Carling.

"The time has come for you to depart your family home, Carling. Go now with your chosen partner, and may the gods bless you both," he intoned.

Marcus helped Carling rise from her seat, and she went to Bron.

"Bless you, Carling. Remember our talks." A tear welled up in her eye as she hugged the young woman.

"You know where we are if you need us, Carling," Longus said as he wrapped his arms around her and kissed her forehead.

Carling's words were stuck in her throat, and she only nodded to the pair of them. The children followed the couple to where the soldiers held Marcus's horse. He lifted her onto the saddle and then climbed up behind her, placing a protective arm around her waist. She waved goodbye to them all. Knowing that she would see them in a year still did not make the parting any easier.

Marcus kicked the horse's flanks, and it took off with the Romans following. The tears streamed down Carling's cheeks, and she did nothing to stop them. The ground flew under the horse, and she was soon passing the spot of her childhood home. With a brief glance as they passed, she put it out of her mind. She had made her peace with her parents and wished all the best for her brother.

On they rode, further and further away from those who loved her. As they raced on into the unknown, she felt him behind her and remembered the time from childhood he had held her the same way. For the second time, he was taking her away from her family. This time into a different form of slavery.

They reached the camp on the banks of the loch, and Marcus led her into his tent. The flap was lowered, and he stood looking at her in the flickering light of the oil burner. Slowly he walked towards her and plucked a flower from her hair, handing it to her. She took it and then the others that were soon to follow.

Taking the flowers from her, he smelled them and then put them on the small table that sat to one side. Coming back, he unclasped her belt and pulled the knife from its sheath. He tested the edge and slipped it back in.

"You won't be needing that," he said, his voice husky with desire. He tossed the knife and belt to the table, where it hit and slid to the ground.

"Help me with my armour, Wife," he urged her. It was not a command, but she still did not like him calling her that name. She fumbled with the buckles, and soon he heaved the heavy metal breastplate off and placed it on the stand by the table. The greaves on his legs she knelt for. They were simpler and easier to undo and soon joined the breastplate.

Marcus came to her and gently helped to pull the tunic from her body, pushing her hair off her face. His hand reached around her neck and pulled her in for the kiss he had been waiting for, finally claiming her as his own.

There was nothing gentle in the way he took her. It was hurried and impatient, and he was soon rolling off her. Carling pulled the covers up over her nakedness and clung to them. Marcus was watching her and smiled at her reaction.

"I was in too much of a hurry. I am sorry. Next time I will make sure to make love to you the way you deserve. I have waited a long time, my Flora." He reached up and stroked her face.

"It will be as my husband wishes," she said meekly.

"No, I don't want subservience from you, my Flora. I want to shower you with gifts, show you how much I have loved you for all these years, how much you have occupied my waking thoughts and my dreams. Oh, Carling, my dreams, where you have taunted me." He kissed her again, this time more slowly and gently, his hands moving over her body.

Despite Carling's thoughts of him, despite her feelings, her body betrayed her and responded to his touch.

Carling woke the next morning to the sound of the camp breaking up. She moved under the covers and discovered that Marcus was not with her. Pushing the blankets from her and standing, she dressed quickly, then exited the tent. He was standing in the middle of the camp talking to some of his men with his back to her. One of the soldiers motioned to him that she was there, and he turned. The smile he greeted her with was wide and happy. He walked over to her and led her back inside.

"I had hoped to be but a moment," he told her as he poured some liquid into a goblet and handed it to her. She accepted and took a sip. "I thought we could take a small platoon and ride on ahead, and hopefully make it to the fort before nightfall."

"I remember last time we were on the road for a lot longer than one day," she said, taking another sip.

"Yes, we were. But we had other troubles to deal with that you were not aware of." He came and sat beside her. His hand took up her own, and he held it. "I woke this morning with you beside me and realised I was the happiest man alive."

"Please do not ask me if I am the same, Marcus," she said, dropping her head a little.

"Please look me in the eye when you talk to me. You are not a slave, Carling." He raised her hand and kissed it.

"You must allow me to get used to this, Marcus. I do not love you."

"I know. I am hoping that love will come over the years we will spend together and with the children we shall have." He stood and let her hand drop. Crossing the tent, he bent and picked up the belt with the little knife attached.

"I want you to wear this." He held it in his hands and then passed it to her. "I want you to wear it knowing that I trust you not to use it on me."

"I cannot use it. The will to kill you is not in me anymore. The Ancestors took it away," she said sadly, looking down at the intricate engraving on the sheath.

"Then I am grateful to them. It may help you come to love me as I do you." He helped her stand and then placed the belt around her waist, fastening it. "There, back where it belongs." He bent and kissed her again—a soft kiss. "Can you ride a horse?" he asked her.

"The only times I have been on a horse have been either with my uncle or with you," she told him.

"Then we shall have to teach you how to ride. I wish I had known when I was teaching Cato; I could have given you lessons then as well."

"When do we leave?" Carling asked.

"When you are ready. Do you want something to eat?"

"No, thank you. If I am to ride a horse, then I want nothing in my stomach. Just the thought is making me nervous," she told him.

"My little Tacita, nervous?" He gave her an amused and teasing grin.

"I am not mute anymore, Marcus. You may come to regret that," Carling told him flatly.

He laughed at the statement and kissed her again. "No, you are not a mute. But you are still a flower. Come. If you are ready, then let us leave." He held her hand and pulled her out of the tent and into the morning light.

The journey was slow at first until Carling became used to the horse and its movements. As they went, they became faster and faster, and soon she was racing him along the road. Her hair flew out behind her in golden waves. Her eyes sparkled with delight at the speed and the brute force of the horse underneath her. She laughed at the wind and urged her horse on.

At midday they pulled up alongside the river and let the horses drink. From the packs, fruit and bread were brought to them, and they ate as they sat on the grass. Carling's face was flushed from the exercise, and she lay on her back.

"You enjoyed yourself this morning," Marcus spoke.

"It was the most amazing thing in the world," she said with a smile on her lips.

You better not bond with that creature. Horses are the stupidest animal in the world. Bear's thought came to her, and she sat up and quickly looked around her.

"What is it? What's wrong?" Marcus was at her side in a moment, looking for the unseen danger.

"Nothing. I thought…it was nothing." She tried to relax and brought her knees up to her chin as she gazed across the river.

Nothing? So, I am nothing now? Bear snorted.

Of course not, Bear. You mean a lot to me. But you cannot come where I am going, Carling replied.

I know that. I have guided you to where you needed to go. Now I go back to the pack, Bear responded.

Marcus sat beside her, still not convinced that there was nothing to fear.

Give my greetings to the pack. Tell them my news. He will not be happy but tell him that I wish him happiness.

You are not happy, and he will not understand the decision that you have made. I will tell him of the ancient ones and their wishes. Farewell, Carling, Bear bade her.

Farewell, Bear, my friend. Until we meet again, she said sadly. Across the river a large, shaggy brown bear came into view and raised up on its hind legs. She raised a hand to it, and it dropped back down and moved out of view.

"I think I am missing something here, Carling. You just waved to that bear." Marcus kept his voice low so as not to let the others nearby hear.

"I am a Whisperer," she said softly. "A Foresight, Seek, Stealth, Hide, Mind Touch, Charm, Tongues, and so much more." She was still gazing where Bear had disappeared.

"That is not possible," he said, stunned.

"Anything is possible when the Ancestors wish it. You should know that I am the One True Child of the Ancestors. A true descendant," she told him, still not looking his way.

"But aren't we all?" Marcus asked.

"No. Two Ancestors had one child. That child was born of necessity to combat an evil. The evil has been contained, but one day in the long-distant future, there will be two who come from my line to defeat the evil once and for all."

"Your line? That means my line as well," he said with a grin.

"The reason the abilities run through the female line is to ensure that the two who come will be true children. I have not seen it fully, as I have not dared to even try to see it. But this is the truth."

Suddenly Marcus was looking at her differently than he had just moments before. He leaned back onto his elbow and tried to digest what she had just told him.

"Are you happy you are betrothed to me now?" Carling asked him, looking him dead in the eye to gauge his reaction.

He leaned in and kissed her. "Yes, I am still happy. They will still be from my line as well. They will be our children."

It was late in the afternoon when they came upon the gates to the fort. They halted outside for a moment until the large doors swung open and allowed them entry. The soldiers on duty snapped to attention as Marcus passed them. He led the way to the villa in the centre of the growing camp, now resembling more of a small town. They pulled the horses up outside the portico and dismounted.

Carling looked up at the building she had left a year ago and could not believe that she was back there. It looked just the same. As she followed him into the house, a couple of houseboys came running to their master, and he tossed his cloak to one then turned to the other.

"Go fetch Diana," he ordered. "And Brietta," he yelled after them. He grabbed her hand and led her into the main audience room. From the corridor came running footsteps followed by a young boy bounding in. His dark curly hair was flying wildly, and his eyes were excited.

"Marcus, you're home at last. What have you been up to? Were you in any battles?" The boy stopped dead when he saw Carling.

"Do you not remember her, Cato?" Marcus was laughing at his younger half-brother.

"Carling!" Cato ran into her arms and threw his around her neck. "You came back to us!"

She laughed at his enthusiasm and held him close, remembering he was the spirit of her lost brother. "You have grown so big while I have been away," Carling said as he left her arms.

"Are you back to stay?" he asked.

"Yes, Cato, I am."

"Where is your mother, Cato? Why don't you go fetch her for me? And don't tell her. I want Carling to be a surprise," Marcus told him, smiling indulgently at his younger brother.

"I'll go right away." The boy ran from the room and skidded around the corner.

"He hasn't changed," Carling said, feeling nervous about meeting Keelie again.

"He did when you left. He became quiet and withdrawn. He actually reminded me of you. I spent hours with him, trying to bring him out of the shell he surrounded himself with," Marcus told her.

"I am sorry to hear that."

"He adores you, Carling. You were the one to look after him as a child, you were just as much his mother as Diana is." He came and sat beside her, holding her hand.

Hurried steps came to them once more, along with Cato's voice. "Hurry, Mother; you will love who Marcus has brought with him."

He came into view, pulling on his mother's hand. Keelie entered the room and stopped when she saw Carling sitting there. Carling stood and ran to her. Keelie shook her head.

"You can't be here. You can't be here." Her arms closed around the young woman and held on to her. "How are you here?"

"Where is Brietta?" Marcus asked her. "We will share the news when she gets here."

"I'll go. I know where she will be," Cato offered, and he was off again.

Carling guided Keelie to a seat and sat with her. "I am so happy to see you again, Diana." Carling remembered to use her Roman name as she guided her to a seat and sat with her.

"As am I, but I still don't understand. I set you free, so you could leave and now you have returned to us?" the older woman asked with disbelief.

Cato came skidding into the room with a large grin on his face. "She's coming. I told her it was really important." He ran to Carling again and into her arms.

Keelie was still staring at her when Brietta walked into the room. She was about to open her mouth to ask what Keelie had wanted when she spotted Carling. Her hands flew to her lips.

Carling moved Cato from her lap and ran to the woman who had raised her.

"Mother of my heart," she greeted Brietta.

Brietta placed her hands on either side of Carling's face. "Daughter of my heart." She gathered her up and held her. Tears were streaming down both of their cheeks.

"Now will you tell us what is going on?" Keelie demanded.

Brietta let go of Carling and wiped her face clear of the tears. She stood apart from the family and waited. Marcus went to Carling's side and positioned himself, so he could see their faces.

"Stepmother, Brother, Brietta. Many years ago, I brought home a scrap of a child to become your handmaiden, Diana. Now I bring her back as my wife," he declared, beaming at them, waiting for the jubilant reaction. But he was to be disappointed.

There was stunned silence in the room. Keelie looked between them both while Brietta went white and almost fell to the floor. Carling was at her arm, guiding her to a chair and sitting by her side.

"Is this true, Carling? Have you married this man?" she asked in a barely audible whisper.

"It is, Mother. I agreed to betroth myself to him," Carling said, confirming Brietta's fears.

"Why would you, my daughter, after what he has done?" Brietta asked, forgetting who was in the room with them.

Carling took a quick glance at Marcus to see his face darken slightly. "It was my decision, Mother. I was not forced into it but was guided to it. We will talk more about it later and I will explain." She stood then, and to appease him, she took his hand. "We were betrothed yesterday and came home straight away to share our news with you."

"I always thought that you would fall out of love with her, Marcus. That is why I sent her away," Keelie said, turning to him.

"Stepmother, there is only one way I will stop loving Carling. Your reactions are not what I thought they would be," he admitted with a frown.

"I think it is wonderful!" Cato said brightly.

"Thank you, Brother," Marcus said with a smile.

"I would like to clean up a bit," Carling said, hoping to get Keelie and Brietta alone. "Would you both do me the honour of accompanying me?" she asked the two women. Beside her she felt Marcus about to say something and she squeezed his hand. "I wish to have a moment with them, Husband. We have all the time in the world to be together.

"It shall be as you wish, Flora," he said, kissing her. "I will leave you ladies to your chat. Cato, come and tell me what has been happening here while I have been away." He turned, and Cato followed, already talking.

Once he had left, she sat down between the two women who had come to mean so much to her. "I know you both have questions, and I will try to answer them as much as possible."

"What happened?" Keelie asked simply.

"I have grown a bit since I left. I completed my training with Sima and then with Talorc. I left them and travelled back to my home, and I was taken in by my uncle and aunt, who cared for me. Not long ago, I made a journey to the Ancestors, who gave me knowledge of what must be done. I came back and acted upon it. Marcus is part of the tasks that I have to do," Carling told them, still coming to terms with it herself.

"So, you haven't fallen in love with him?" Brietta asked.

"No. I have not, Mother. And I do not want to kill him anymore either. The Ancestors have forbidden me. Even if I wanted to, I could not." Carling gave a small shrug of her shoulders.

"I knew you distrusted him and even did not like him. But I did not know that your feelings ran that deep," Keelie said with some shock.

"Yes, they do—did," she corrected herself. "Now I would really like to clean up. I smell of horse, and I am finding it is not a pleasant odour."

"I will accompany you, Mistress," Brietta said, standing.

"No, you must never call me that. I am not your mistress, Mother." Carling stood and grasped Brietta's hands to her.

"But Master Marcus will expect it."

"Then I will have to have a talk to him. Now shall we go to the baths? I am going to have to beg a clean tunic."

"We have had a change since you left. We have our own baths here in the villa now. The camp has grown so large, and the camp baths are always crowded with men. Marcus thought that it would be good idea to have one that just the family can use, and you will need to dress in the style of the Romans. I can lend you something to wear and we will start on your wardrobe tomorrow," Keelie told her, coming to her side.

"You have Master Marcus's status to consider, Daughter," Brietta said before Carling could argue.

"I will leave it to your best judgment," she agreed and followed them out.

In the middle of the night Carling was dragged from her deep sleep by a call. It was persistent, and she finally answered it. Before her stood Talorc, agitated and concerned.

"We thought you might have contacted us by now, Carling," he said by way of chastisement.

"I am sorry, Talorc. I should have. It was very remiss of me," she apologised. "How are Nessa and the children?"

"She is worried about you. And the children are growing." He seemed a little at loss as to how to put something. "We have a visitor with us at the moment, Carling. Actually, two visitors."

"Who are they, Talorc?"

"One is the bear. He caused quite a stir, especially with Veda. Bear told him some news he was not happy about."

"I can guess what it is," Carling said sadly. "And the other visitor?"

"Galen. Did you know…um…" Talorc's voice trailed away.

"Talorc. Please, this is hard enough as it is. Why are you contacting me?"

"I wanted to confirm…that is, I need to know…"

"No. Either Veda or Galen wants to know," Carling said, cutting him off

"Yes. They both do. Is it true? Have you tied yourself to that man?" Talorc asked.

"I have." She did not look at him.

Somewhere in her mind she could feel someone else searching for her and could sense who it was. She became frightened and turned to Talorc.

"Please, you need to break the connection. He is looking for me," she told him quickly.

"When you can, talk to them, Carling. You need to clear the air."

"I will. Please, you must go now. Give my love to Nessa and the children. I miss you all."

"Keep in contact, Carling." With his last words he was gone.

Morning found her alone in the room she had shared with Marcus. As she was dressing, Brietta came in and helped her, including doing up her hair. Carling sat and put the twisting and pulling of her hair in the expert hands of her mother. When she was finished, she stood for Brietta's inspection.

"Do you really want to wear that belt and knife?" Brietta asked her, concerned.

"Yes. I do, Mother." Carling responded and then went to her little bundle of things, pulling out the blue ribbon that Elfin had used in the ceremony. Carefully she wound and tied it off onto the small knife, making sure to not undo the original knot.

"Carling! To display it like that, wound around a knife—it will make people talk," Brietta said with astonishment.

"I don't care. I want it there as a reminder to him of the words Elfin said. 'One year and a day.' I may not be able to kill him with my knife, but there are other things I can do."

"You play a dangerous game. Make sure you know what it is you do." Brietta busied herself tidying the table that contained the brushes and pins she had used on Carling's hair.

"I will, Mother of my heart. He may have caged me again, but my heart and my mind are free."

"Your heart?" Brietta stopped her tidying and stared at the young woman. "Have you given your heart to someone, then?"

"What you do not know, Mother, you cannot tell. I will not speak of it again."

"It is best you don't. He is waiting for you in the garden." She walked with Carling from the room and headed down the corridor. "Diana wishes you to come to her when you are able."

"Tell her that I will come." Carling left Brietta and walked through the doors to the colonnaded internal garden.

In the center sat a pond, and around the edges small shrubs grew. Marcus was staring into the water and looked up when he heard her coming. He took in her dress and hair and smiled.

His eyes alighted onto the belt around her waist and the knife that sat there, including the blue ribbon.

"You wear it well, Flora. But I did not think you had such thorns," he said with a smile.

"I have always had thorns, Marcus. I thought you knew that," she replied with a smile of her own.

"At least yours are decorated. I can now see them coming."

"I put it there as a reminder. A year and a day," she said as she stopped in front of him, almost as a challenge.

"It can stay there for always. There will be no sundering of the betrothal. You are tied to me forever, and the knot will remain. I have pledged not only my heart to you, but my soul, Carling. Forever it will remain that way, forever and a day."

A shiver ran up her spine at the pledge, and she hoped that it had not been taken seriously by whatever gods he believed in or the Ancestors. She put it out of her mind and turned back to the present.

"You wanted to see me this morning?" she asked him.

"I did. Is that such a bad thing, a husband wanting to spend time with his wife?" he raised an eyebrow with his question.

"I thought you would be busy today running the camp. You are commander, after all. Is it not your duty to attend to such things?"

"It is my duty, but the people I have in place to run the day-to-day things are so good at their jobs that there really is little for me to do. I do have a few of the merchants coming to make complaints directly to me later this afternoon, but this morning I am all yours."

Marcus took Carling's hand and led her to the seating, where food had been laid out for them. After she had seated herself, he poured a goblet of wine and handed it to her. She sipped it as he poured his own, then came to sat beside her.

"There really is nothing I can think of for us to do together," she told him.

"Isn't there? I could think of a few things." He briefly touched her lips with his own. While his face was so close to hers, he whispered to her. "Who was it you were talking with last night in your dreams?"

"My teacher," Carling answered honestly. She had nothing to hide in that quarter.

"Teacher? What teacher is this?"

"He taught me to control Mind Touch and the ways of Dream Walking." He was still close to her, and he leaned in and kissed her cheek.

"Are you sure it was your teacher and not that boy that I found you with that night?"

"Marcus, I am not lying. He was my teacher only. That boy was also my teacher in Whispering. There was never any romantic involvement between us," she tried to reassure him.

"Maybe not on your part, but I sensed it from him. He was in love with you, Carling. If I ever sense him around you again or see him in person, he will die. I will not tolerate other men lusting after my wife," Marcus told her darkly.

"An innocent man dies because you think he has feelings for me?" She pulled away from him.

"Any man," he told her. The look in his eye made her believe that he meant what he said.

The moment he left her side, Carling sought out Keelie. She entered her rooms and found them empty. There were no brushes laid out, no sewing left on the chair. Nothing was as it used to be. She turned and found a houseboy.

"Where is your mistress?" she asked him.

"You are my mistress," he said, obviously confused.

"Where is Diana?"

"In her room, Mistress," he answered.

"Can you please show me where her room is?" Carling requested.

"Yes, Mistress." He headed back the way he had already come, and Carling followed. He led her to the back of the house, almost to the slaves' quarters, and stopped outside a door. "This is her room, Mistress."

"Thank you. What is your name?"

"Bead, Mistress," he replied, bowing his head to her.

"Thank you, Bead." She watched as he went back to the main house and then knocked on the door.

"Come," Keelie called from the other side, and Carling opened the door.

Keelie was seated by a window with fabric on her lap, threading a needle. She looked up and stood when she saw it was Carling, the fabric falling to the floor in a rustling hiss.

"You never have to stand for me, Keelie," Carling said as she moved further into the small room. "Why are you not in your rooms? Why are you here?"

"This is where I have been put, Carling. This is not my house any longer. As long as I allow Cato to remain here, then this is now my room." Keelie told her with a sigh, looking around the meagre furniture that was little more than one of the slaves would have the use of.

"But the other is empty; it is not being used."

"It soon will be. Those are your rooms, Carling, as they should be as mistress of the house."

"I don't want them," Carling told her, shaking her head.

"Did you think that when you got back here everything would be as it was? Our situation has changed. Marinus is dead, and we only survive on Marcus's kindness to Cato."

"I am so sorry," Carling said, rushing to the woman's side and holding her tight. "It's all my fault."

"How did you come to that conclusion?" Keelie asked, pulling her away.

"What I did to Marinus that night. Marcus told me that he died because of what I did, that it drove him mad and he killed himself."

"He should not have told you that. That was not fair. You did what you had to do in order to defend yourself. You did not send him mad. He was already heading that way. The Marinus I married would never have forced himself on a slave girl, especially one that was the favourite of his wife." Keelie let her go and stooped to pick up the cloth up from the ground, hiding the tears in her eyes.

"I have made you cry."

"I do not need an excuse these days for the tears to spring from my eyes. I miss him—the old Marinus. He was kind and gentle, and very sweet. I was so scared when I was sent to him, but he let me get used to the ways of the villa. He got to know me first and I him. I loved him," Keelie said a little wistfully, taking her seat once more. Carling went and sat beside her, taking the cloth from Keelie's hands, and moving it away.

"My coming has upset everything again."

"Please do not think we are not happy to see you. You are so very welcome. We were all very dull without your songs, without your laughter. Brietta would tell me when you talked, and I felt jealous that you never contacted me. But I understand that she has a larger space in your heart than I do."

"You both cared for me and taught me so much. And I love you just as much as Brietta," Carling told her taking her hand.

"Never mind me." Diana sighed and wiped her eyes. "I am becoming a silly old woman." The chuckle she gave was only half there.

"I need your help, Keelie. I need your guidance. I fear Marcus, of what he is capable of."

"That is why I sent you away, to get out from under his gaze. I don't believe what you did to Marinus was the cause of his death. I think it was Marcus." Keelie glanced at the door as if they were being spied upon. "He has an ability," she whispered softly.

"I know—Mind Touch. He created a bond with me that I was unaware of until he contacted me in my dreams and showed me. He created it when I was sixteen," Carling told her.

"Oh my, girl. What are we going to do?" She reached up and placed a caring hand on the side of Carling's face. "It is too late for you to run. We are just going to have to manage him. We can start placing pretty serving girls around him for a start, to try to distract him from you."

"That may have worked with Marinus, but I do not think it will with Marcus. How many offers of marriage did he turn down?"

"Yes. He has only one focus, and that seems to be you. The Ancestors—can they help? Can you contact them? You said that they have spoken to you before."

"I don't think that they will help. The tasks are all they are focused on."

"For now, we will just have to play it by ear, and you will need to be mindful not to anger him," Keelie told her.

"He told me that he would kill any man who showed even the slightest interest in me. I am afraid that he will." Carling looked down at their still joined hands.

"That means a walk to the market is out. I remember how you used to turn men's heads with your golden hair. So striking and beautiful you are. There wouldn't be a man left alive in the camp if he carried through with that threat," Keelie said with a laugh.

"I am back in my cage, then," Carling said with a resigned smile.

"But we can make you look stunning so that he will forget about other men. Here." She reached across and picked up the fabric once more. "I have started a new gown for you. The fabric has come all the way from Londinium. I believe before that it came from Gaul." Keelie held the soft green material up to the filtered light coming from the small window.

"It is beautiful. But the light in this room is no good for sewing. You shall have your rooms back," Carling declared.

"No, Carling. He will not grant that to you," Keelie protested.

"He will. What is the point of being mistress of this house if I cannot decide who shall sleep where?"

Carling was careful about the first month of her time at the villa. Any decision about the house she ran past Keelie first before presenting it to Marcus. The older woman helped her immensely to learn her role. The rooms that Keelie had been evicted from were soon restored to her, and Carling would join her and Brietta there every afternoon.

Mornings were spent with Marcus. He would take her riding out of the gates and into the countryside, where he would pick wildflowers and place them in her hair. He would make love to her in the meadows as the birds sang around them. He would sit while she sang and present her with gifts of jewellery and cloth. He was attentive and gentle.

It was one of these mornings that they sat in the garden, her harp resting on her knee, and she was playing it while her thoughts wandered. Suddenly a soldier stepped in front of Marcus and saluted.

"I left orders not to be disturbed," he said harshly.

"Commander, sir. A messenger has arrived with grave news," the soldier said.

"What news?"

"There has been an attack. Patrols are being decimated by the clans."

"Since when?" Marcus demanded, instantly on his feet.

"Yesterday. The messenger is waiting in the atrium, sir. I thought it best to bring him to you straight away."

Marcus stood and took the hand that was strumming the strings and kissed it.

"I am sorry about this, Flora. I will be back as soon as I can." He dropped it and left her sitting there.

The news of the attack jolted her back from the thoughts that were flitting through her mind. If Marcus could have heard her thoughts, he would have sent out a search for the man who had caused them. She put the harp down beside her and stood. Slowly she made her way through the house and to the atrium.

"Where?" she heard Marcus ask the man.

"By the lake, sir. At this end. They came out of the trees and attacked us. As soon as I could I came back to bring the news."

Carling crept closer and saw him swaying on the spot, a large gash down his face and his armour covered in blood. The eye was swollen and closed with crusty scabs that still wept.

"You sure by the lake?" Marcus demanded of him.

"Yes, sir."

"Take him away to the healer, then get the lieutenants who are in camp here now," Marcus told the soldier at his side.

Marcus turned away from the man and saw Carling standing in the doorway. For a moment he hesitated and then walked towards her.

"If this is your uncle's doing, then I will not give him quarter," he said to her heavily. Marcus entered his office and went straight to the charts that were open on the table.

"We cannot be certain that it is, though, Marcus. There are other clans in that area," Carling told him as she followed him in.

"War is not the place for a woman. Do not presume to advise me on this, Carling. I do not want you sullied by the mess that comes with it," he said as he looked down at a map that was laid open on the table.

"I am afraid that it is too late for that. Or do you not remember how we first met, Husband? How I first came to be in this room?"

Marcus looked up quickly at her words. His expression changed to one of pain as he walked to her and caught her up in his arms, his forehead pressed against hers.

"Every day I remember. You are my living memory of that night. I wish to the gods and to the Ancestors that it was not me who carried out those orders. I can never ask for your forgiveness, Carling, because I know you will never give it. And I could never accept it. It was the will of the Ancestors that brought you to me and I thank them every day that they did. We cannot change the past, but I hope that the future will be easier on us," he told her tenderly.

Running footsteps through the house came to them, and they broke apart. The declaration of regret and guilt from him had shaken Carling deeply. She moved aside as men began to file into the room, and she left them with one backwards glance at Marcus.

Outside she ran into the houseboy Bead, and she stopped him. "Go to the kitchen and tell them the master requires wine and food for himself and officers."

Bead set off at a run, and she watched him go with an idea forming in her mind. She hurried down the corridor and into the room she shared with Marcus. The bundle she had brought with her from her uncle's house was still under the bed, and she pulled it out.

Chapter Eleven

Carling was shaking out the tunic when Brietta came into the room. She took one look at the crumpled garment and shut the door behind her. Walking quickly, she pulled it out of the young woman's hands and laid it on the bed.

"Whatever you are thinking, rethink it, Carling. Is what is being said between the slaves right? Is the master declaring war on the clans?" Brietta asked quietly.

"I don't know about that, Mother. A patrol was attacked near where my uncle lives, but I don't think it will come to a war," Carling replied.

"Then why are you getting these things out?" She indicated the tunic and bundle that was on the bed.

"If I can get to my uncle and ask him if he was behind the attack, then I can treat between them."

"Or you could be cut down by some overzealous soldier. It is a dangerous place out there, and if they think you are a spy or even pose any sort of threat, they will make an example out of you. You cannot risk yourself this way."

"But what if this is the moment that I am to make the Romans flee? Should I not risk it?" Carling asked her desperately.

"No, you should not. Now pack these things away before Marcus comes in and sees them. He may accuse you of spying on him. Wife or not, it is his duty to deal with all spies."

"I cannot just sit by and sew while the clans are attacking," Carling cried out.

"You can for now until we find out more. Bead has been set in the office to be at Marcus's beck and call. He is a smart boy and will let us know what is going on and being said. Daughter of my heart, you must promise me that you will do nothing," Brietta begged her.

"I promise, Mother." Carling sat on the bed and lay back. Her hair escaped the coils and pins holding it in place.

Brietta began to fold the tunic up and place it back into her bag. She dropped it to the floor and kicked it back under the bed, from where it had come. Sitting down beside Carling, she took up the girl's hand. "I know it is hard, and you want to be doing something, but you just need to be patient."

"I know, Mother," Carling sighed and sat up. "I feel so cooped up. The only time I go out is in the company of Marcus. I want to smell fresh air and be able to just *be* without someone watching me."

"It will come, Carling. The time will come when you will be able to do those things."

The next few days she did not see Marcus much at all. He was there first thing in the morning and again at night for the evening meal. Otherwise, he was in his office or over at the headquarters with his men. Bead was invaluable with the information he was passing to Brietta, who would then pass it on to Carling.

One morning Marcus woke her early with a gentle shake. She opened her eyes and blinked a couple of times.

"I'm going away for a few days. Do not leave the villa unattended, my Flora. Feelings are very high against your people at the moment," he told her gently.

"I won't. So, when did it get decided that you would go?" she asked. Carling sat up and watching as he shrugged on his armour. Bead was there to cinch the buckles.

"Last night. I didn't want to wake you when I got back." Marcus winced as Bead pulled on one of the straps. "There will be guards on the house to protect you while I am gone."

"I don't think it will be necessary, Marcus," she said, pulling a tunic over her head.

"I do. Three women of the clans, two of those of high status. You could be used by those who are against me."

"Is there a faction like that here?" she asked, stopping what she was doing.

"There is always someone who does not agree with what the hierarchy are doing." His greaves were now on, and Bead was standing waiting with his helmet and sword. Carling took the belt and sword off him and placed it around Marcus's waist.

"Is this a peace offering or are you in a hurry to have me leave?" he asked as he held up his arms while she buckled it.

"It is what it is, Marcus." She reached up and kissed him. "Come back safe."

"I intend to. Do you have a message for your uncle?" he asked her, accepting the helmet from Bead.

"Do you intend to deliver it before or after you kill him?" Carling sat back down on the bed.

"Preferably before, and I don't intend to kill him. I want to treat with him first and then we will see." He said, his helmet held under his arm and a strange expression on his face.

"Tell him that I miss them."

"Wait for me outside by my horse, Bead," Marcus said and waited for the boy to leave before walking over to Carling. "There is something I want you to do for me while I am away."

"What is that?" she asked, rising to stand before him.

"I do not want you Dream Walking. I will be checking up on you," he told her as he stared in her eyes. She knew that he would be waiting in her dreams.

"Do you distrust me that much?" she asked, raising an eyebrow with the questions.

"Just wanting to keep what is mine."

"There is no one else, Marcus. There is only you. The one you are thinking of was like a brother and no threat to you — to us," she said, hoping to ease his jealousy.

"Please do as I ask, then there will be no issue to worry about." Marcus bent and kissed her gently.

"I will do as my husband commands," she said tightly.

Marcus closed his eyes for a moment at the words. "I love you, Carling."

"Safe journey, Marcus. Until we meet again," Carling intoned the traditional farewell.

He nodded sadly and left her. She watched him go, following him out of the house, and stood on the threshold while he went under the portico. Marcus climbed on his horse and looked back at her, raising a hand in farewell. Carling waved back and he turned the horse towards the head of the column of troops.

Two soldiers turned and moved to the front of the house and stood on either side of the doorway. Just like that, she felt like a prisoner.

When Marcus returned home four days later, he was looking very happy with himself. Bead was there, skipping around him, trying to undo the straps on his armour while he was telling Carling all about his trip.

"Your uncle is at a loss as to who is behind it. He is not happy that they have been attacking us and bringing our truce into dispute. I have left it up to him to find out who is stirring up all this trouble."

"Do you trust him to do it?" she asked.

"Of course not. I have my men out there looking as well." His armour now off, he dismissed Bead and led her to the bed.

"You could visit the baths first. You smell of horse," she said as he picked her up and placed her on the bed, pulling up her tunic.

"I can't wait. I have missed you so much." He entered her, and within a few strokes it was all over, and he lay on top of her, panting. "Come with me to the baths, Flora."

Marcus pushed himself off her and pulled Carling up with him. His hand reached up and caressed her face. She nodded, and he led her out of the room.

The raids and attacks continued for the next month, keeping Marcus occupied. He had left her one early summer morning to deal with the dispatches that had just come in, and she lay on the bed listening to the villa waking. There was a knock at the door, and Brietta walked in without Carling calling out. She stood at the end of the bed and waited for Carling to speak.

"Good morning, Mother."

"Good morning, Daughter. Are we feeling a little lazy this morning?" Brietta asked without even the hint of a smile.

"Yes. I suppose I am," she replied as she stretched.

Carling sat up and swung her legs out of the bed. Her head swam, and her stomach cramped. She felt cold and hot at the same time, and she began to sweat. Her hand clamped to her mouth as she could feel her stomach lurch. Brietta was there with a pot for her, and she grabbed it and proceeded to lose the contents of her stomach into it. When she had finished, she lay back on the bed and placed her hands over her face.

"I think I ate something bad last night," she said through them.

"I don't think so. When did you bleed last, Carling?" Brietta asked with a grin.

"Bleed? What does my bleeding have to do with throwing up?" she asked, feeling her stomach lurch again.

"It has a lot to do with it. I think you might have a little one on the way, Daughter." Brietta brought her a drink and a wet cloth to wipe her face.

Carling sat up quickly and then regretted it immediately with another wave of nausea. Brietta was there, holding her hair out of the way and rubbing her back. When she had finished, the older woman helped her back onto the bed.

"Stay here. I will fetch Diana." She kissed Carling's forehead and left her.

Carling's head was swimming. A child. Could this be the child that the Ancestors told her about? A child. Thoughts chased each other around her head, trying to figure out what she was going to do. There was still so much that was unsure and unanswered. The tasks to do.

"Calm, my child; calm," a voice spoke to her. She opened her eyes, and before her stood the figure of the woman in the robe. "The first task has been completed. The child is created within you."

"Is this one of the children that has been seen?" she asked.

"Yes, it is. And there are still two more to come to you. From this first child, shall come the father of the one."

"What is the other task?" she asked, pushing herself up.

"The same as the vision, to rid the land of the Romans. They do not belong here. Their gods are too overbearing and dark."

"How do I do that?" Carling asked in frustration.

"It will come to you when the time is right. My child, we are so proud of you. This child must be loved, Carling. He must be cared for," the woman insisted.

"I will love him," she told the Ancestor. "I promise I will love him."

"Good. I will leave you now. Keelie and Brietta will want to fuss over you. I leave you with my blessings and my love, and that of your father."

"Thank you," Carling said and closed her eyes. When she opened them again, the figure was gone.

The two women walked through the door moments later. Carling was resting her head and lifted it up when she heard them come in. Keelie fussed and held her hand, but all Carling wanted to do was sleep.

"I have called for the master," Brietta said.

"Why?" This news alarmed her. She had not wanted to tell Marcus about the child just yet.

"Because he will want to know, Carling," Keelie said. "Do you want us to be here when you tell him?"

"No. I think this is best done in private." Carling swung her legs from the bed and attempted to rise once more. There was no lurching or spinning of the room. She stood and breathed a sigh of relief.

"I will help you dress. I know the perfect tunic for you." Brietta went to the chest and pulled out a tunic of soft green.

Her hair was just being pinned into place when Marcus came stalking through the door. His face was grim, and he looked agitated.

"Why have I been summoned? I have work to do, Carling." He stopped when he saw Keelie and Brietta there.

Carling rose, and the two women left them alone without a word to Marcus. He looked after them with some curiosity and then back at his wife.

"I need to tell you something before you hear it from somewhere else," she said. Her hands were beginning to shake at the thought of telling him, and her voice wavered.

"Tell me what? I am supposed to be in a meeting with the lieutenants at the moment." His agitation had not eased any with the shaking of her voice.

Carling took a step towards him and then stopped. Her courage was leaving her. She knew he would be pleased and happy with the news, but she didn't want to share it with him. Her child.

"We think—that is, Brietta thinks that I am..." She swallowed hard. Her throat had gone dry.

"What does she think?" He looked at Carling finally and took in how white she had gone, how she was shaking like a leaf. Within a few steps he was at her side. "Are you ill? Do you need a healer?"

"No, I am fine. I am still taking the news in myself. Marcus, I am pregnant." She finally spat it out and waited for his reaction, and it was exactly as she thought it would be.

"Pregnant?" he asked as he took her and guided her to the bed, sitting down with her. "A child?"

"Yes," she confirmed.

"You must rest. Diana can help with the running of the house. I don't want you overtaxing yourself." His arm came around her and he held her protectively.

"It is only a pregnancy, Marcus. I am not gravely ill." She gave a little laugh.

"Yes, I know. But I also know how many Diana lost before she had Cato. I don't want that for you." He kissed her gently and continued to hold her.

"Don't you have a meeting to get to?" she asked, wanting to be alone with her thoughts for a while.

"They can wait. We will have a feast tonight to celebrate the news." He was enthusiastic, and the smile had not fallen from his face once since she had told him.

"Maybe not tonight. Let it be just a family meal," she requested softly.

"Yes. Just family." He kissed her once more and then stood. "You have made me so very happy today. A glimmer of good in the nasty business we are dealing with." With one last kiss, he was gone.

Carling sat on the bed and no thoughts came to her. A child. Her child.

Along with the pregnancy came a rushing of emotions. Little things would make her burst into tears or raging mad. One morning Cato came to the garden where she was sitting, with a bunch of wildflowers in his hands. He looked so innocent and sweet as he smiled, his arm extended, offering them to her. Tears sprang from her eyes and poured down her cheeks at the simple gesture, and she pulled him up onto her lap.

"I'm too old to do this now, Carling," he said seriously as he escaped her grasp.

"Never get too old to tell those you care about how you feel, Cato. Time is a fleeting thing, and it goes by so very fast," she said, taking the flowers and sniffing them.

"You have become strange since you got pregnant. Do all women get like that?" he asked her.

"Not all women, but most. Your mother did when she was pregnant with you. But then again, she was not allowed to move until you were born."

"Girls are weird." Cato just shook his head and walked away.

Carling held the flowers to her face once more, drinking in their perfume. She smiled at the boy's words and sighed.

"I don't think girls are weird," Marcus said, coming from behind one of the columns. He crossed the grass and sat by her side. He plucked one of the flowers from the bunch in her hand, trimmed the stem, and carefully placed it in Carling's hair.

"A flower for my beautiful Flora," he said with an adoring smile.

Carling blushed and looked away. From her side she heard Marcus laughing softly. He reached up and turned her head back to him and kissed her.

"I think women are amazing. They are the givers of life. From their own bodies a whole new person is born, as a gift to the world. Men are the weird ones. We take lives." His whole demeanor suddenly changed with those last three words.

"There has been another attack?" Carling asked.

"Yes. Though the casualties are low. The patrol managed to capture one prisoner. Carling tell me, have you heard of a man called Galen?" he asked her gently.

"It is a common name in the clans. I have heard it many times for many men," Carling said quickly, hoping to hide the shock of hearing that name spoken out loud again.

"These raids are all led by one man, this Galen. He comes from around the lake area. I just thought you may have come across such a man," Marcus said.

"As I said, I have met very few. There is not one that I could think of who would be so courageous as to take the Romans on in that area. Besides, they are all loyal to my uncle."

"Good. I had hoped that was the case. You see, apparently this Galen had lost his love to the Romans, and he hopes to get her back." There was a hint of suggestion to his tone as he told her this piece of information.

"There are many girls who have become slaves. You could release them and maybe the attacks will stop," she suggested, hoping to free some of her people even if she couldn't free herself.

"It is an idea to consider. But I think I would rather crush him under my heel," he told her with a hint of venom in his voice.

"All this killing does nothing to help. It only leads to more killing. If you release the girls, then it will show that you are at least trying to make peace with them," Carling suggested.

"I will not be releasing any slaves. These clans have to realise that we are here to stay, and under our rule they must obey Rome and her laws." He stood from her side and went over to the pond, peering into the depths.

"But you are only half Roman yourself. Can your other half not rule your head once in a while?"

"It cannot, Carling. While I am here, I must be fully Roman." He turned and saw her frown. "I think you have been cooped up too long lately. Shall we go for a ride?"

"Brietta and Diana would not like me to. They will say I am endangering the baby." She placed a hand on her now swelling belly and caressed it.

"We don't have to ride. We can go by cart or carriage." He placed his own hand on hers. "I will make sure that it doesn't hit any lumps or bumps that may jar you along the way."

"I would like that," she said, standing. His eyes roamed her body, and he smiled.

Within the hour they were leaving the gates of the camp behind, with two mounted soldiers following. Carling wasn't happy about that, but she knew what Marcus's answer would be if she had voiced her objection. They travelled away from the camp, and she was enjoying the fresh air, breathing it in deeply. Marcus himself was driving the cart, and he looked relaxed and happy at her side.

They stopped at a meadow beside the road, and Carling wandered the long grass picking the flowers she found there. Marcus walked at her side, playing idly with a piece of long grass in his hands. Her hair was down, and the golden locks floated on the breeze. She stooped to pick another flower and stopped.

Carling, I have a message for you, a voice came to her, and she recognised it as Bear.

She picked the flower she was reaching for and then stood, placed it with the others, and raised them to her face to smell. While she did so, she looked around, searching for her large brown shaggy friend.

I am in the woods, and you will not see me.

What is the message, my friend? She pushed her hair from her face.

The pack's friend, the one he left you with, is watching. He is beside me, Bear told her.

Carling's heart skipped a beat at the thought of Galen being so close. *He must leave now; he is in danger. Please tell him that he must go, Bear. I cannot protect him. Marcus knows of him.*

The message that this one wants to let you know, is that he understands that you cannot be with him. He knows and waits for you, Bear told her.

Tell him to stop the raids and attacks. It is not helping, only making Marcus mad. I am trying to get some of our people free.

I will pass the message on through the pack. He is agitated that you are there, and your mate is with you.

Carling closed her eyes a moment. *Tell him I think of him every day.*

Your littermate wanted to let you know that he has a mate now. A whisperer who is partnered with an eagle, Bear told her.

That makes me very happy to hear his news. I wish them both a long life and happiness.

We need to move on before the one beside me decides to lose his head and come and get you.

Look after him for me, Bear. He holds my heart, Carling told him, barely holding onto the sob which threatened to escape her.

I will, Carling.

Carling felt the loss of the connection and made sure that she was facing away from Marcus while she dealt with it. He came up behind her and placed an arm around her waist and held her.

"Were you just talking with someone?" Marcus asked her quietly.

"No. I was just enjoying the freedom of a wide-open space," she lied.

"It felt like you were reaching for someone or something. Was it the bear?" he asked suddenly.

"I have not heard or seen anything of Bear since you brought me here, Marcus. He has gone back to where he came from. If you do not trust me, take the knife from my belt, and slip it into my heart now."

"Why would I do that?" He turned her in his arms and pushed the hair from her face. "I would rather kill those who take your thoughts away from me."

"Again, with the killing, Marcus. Can't you just let things be? I am with you. I do not fight against you. I am carrying your child. Your son," she told him with a smile, hoping those happier thoughts would mollify him.

"A son? How can you be so sure?"

"I have seen. A healthy son who looks like his father," she told him honestly.

"I think it might be time to get back to camp," he said, smiling down at her.

"Do we have to go now? I was enjoying my semi-freedom." Carling broke his hold and moved away from him.

Marcus glanced at the two soldiers who were sitting in the shade on the other side of the cart. Their horses were staked and grazing on the rich, green grass. He made a grab for her hand and pulled her back to him.

"Or we could just stay here for what I had in mind. We haven't done that for a while."

He picked Carling up and knelt with her in his arms, laying her down on the sweet-smelling grass. Her golden hair spread out around her head like a halo, and he joined her, already stripping his garments from him. While he took her, Carling's thoughts were far away on Galen, as they always were when she was with Marcus. She hoped that Bear had gotten him away before he could have seen any of what was happening now.

For the rest of summer there were no more skirmishes between the clans and the Romans. Carling breathed a sigh of relief at that and was still planning a way to get her people free of slavery. Every now and then she would test the waters with Marcus, asking him if there was a possibility of sending some of the slaves home.

Each time she brought the subject up, Marcus would brush her aside. He kept using the same excuse of not wanting to let them go to show the clans who held the power in the land. This would upset Carling, and she would seethe inwardly about it. The subject became a thorn between them until finally Marcus relented.

"You choose out of all the slaves in camp who can go back home. I will let you release ten!" he yelled, his anger getting the better of him.

"You want me to choose?"

"Yes. It is your idea, and you are the one pestering me. Ten and no more. Ten women," he added.

"If you agree to release them, will you allow me to go with them as escort to their homes?"

"No. I will not allow that," he said quickly.

"Then how can I guarantee that they will get back safely, that your soldiers will leave them unmolested?"

"I will send Diana."

"Diana has not left this camp in years," Carling argued.

"Then it is about time she did. She can leave also. I will let her," Marcus declared with an excited smile.

"What about Cato? She will not leave him here," Carling told him.

"My brother is to stay here."

Carling was so angry with his suggestion, she was breathing heavily, and her fists were balled up at her side. "What if I got a delegation of clan and The People to come get them?" she asked hopefully.

"How would you, Flora, organise that?"

"By contacting my teachers." She held her breath for a moment, waiting for him to explode. Carling had felt him at night waiting for her to reach out to someone, and she had not used her ability because of it.

"If you do that then I insist I be with you. We will do it together," he said, finally bringing his anger under control.

His response surprised her, and it took her a moment to comprehend what he was saying before she replied to him.

"Yes, together. It will show them that you are willing to give and not just take," she said brightly, happy that he had agreed to that much. "Thank you, my husband."

"Flora, I don't like fighting with you. We will contact them tonight and organise it, then you can choose whom you wish to be released tomorrow."

"How can I choose?" Carling asked him.

"I will let you figure out how only ten will get to go free, out of so many." He smiled and kissed her forehead, then walked out of the room.

The question played on her mind. She knew some of the women had taken up with the soldiers even though they were not supposed to marry. It was becoming a worry for her, and she did not want to really think about it. That night, she had difficulty getting to the dream state. She tried several times before she entered and found Marcus waiting for her.

Sending out the call to Sima, she worried that the old woman would not answer, and she waited for the response with great nervousness. Eventually it was answered, and the old woman walked through the barrier and greeted Carling with great caution, especially when she saw Marcus at her side.

"Carling, it has been a long time." Sima greeted her with a nod and a quick side glance at Marcus.

"It has, Sima. I am sorry not to have contacted you before. I have been unable to use my abilities for a while now," Carling told her. There was no point in making any other excuse except for the truth.

"This is your husband?" Sima was now staring at him.

"Yes, this is Marcus. Marcus, this is one of my teachers, Sima."

"It is nice to meet one of The People who have cared for Carling," Marcus said with a small bow for the older woman.

"It would be nice to meet you if you would stop killing our people," Sima said.

"Sima, please," Carling begged. "I need your help. Marcus has allowed me to free ten women, so they can return to their homes. I need you to organise a meeting where we can release them to you and others who can help them."

"Only ten? How many have been taken from their parents, their children, and their husbands?"

"It is a start. Please help me," Carling begged her old teacher.

"We will meet you and get them back to their homes." She glanced at Marcus. "There are some who are with me that wish to know how you are. They are concerned that this betrothal had been forced on you by your uncle."

"You can tell them that my uncle did not force me. I went where I was sent. Also, can you let them know that I am expecting a child? I know a few will be happy with the news, and others will not."

"Are you happy, Carling?" Sima asked her with concern.

"As happy as I can be, Sima. My life is not what I thought it would be when I left you all those moons ago. My life is not my own to do with as I will. The Ancestors have seen to that. One day soon I hope to be able to sit down with you and tell you fully what they have told me." A single crystalline teardrop fell from her eye.

"I look forward to that day. We will meet you on the Roman road, at the river near the camp, four days hence," Sima said. "I look forward to seeing you in person, Carling."

"I never said you could go," Marcus spoke quietly. He was standing behind her with his hand on her upper arm.

"Please, Marcus, I must. I need to make sure for myself that they make it and are away without incident." She turned to face him. "This is important to me."

"I know it is. Do you not trust me to carry out your wishes?" he asked her.

"I trust you. But I do not trust your soldiers. You yourself said there is always a faction that does not agree with your commands."

"I will think on it, Carling," he told her.

Carling turned back to Sima. "We will see you in four days, my teacher. Safe journey, until we meet again. Give my love to those that are with you."

"Safe journey, Carling, until we meet again." Sima stopped and looked at Marcus. "Marcus." She inclined her head.

"Sima," he acknowledged her.

The issue of how to choose the women became an easy one with the help of Brietta. With her knowledge of the goings-on in the camp, she had soon selected ten young women, who had all been abused in one way or another. They were brought before Carling, and she gave her approval of the choices.

The day arrived to leave. Keelie and Brietta insisted on coming with them to make sure that Carling did as she was told and not risk the child. The arguments had gone on between Marcus and Carling in the lead-up to leaving. At first, he was going to make the women walk, until she complained and said she would walk with them. He then agreed to have them ride in carts. He had delegated the choosing of the soldiers to one of his lieutenants, until Carling had insisted that they be chosen from the guards from the villa, men she had become used to.

"I will be happy when this is all over and you are back at home, Wife," he said to her once they were on the road and heading towards the river.

"I will be happy when there are no slaves at all, Husband," she retorted.

The going was slow, and they spent one night camped at the side of the road. For that night, Keelie, Brietta, and Carling all joined the women in the same tent. When Marcus found out her plans, he was not happy.

"You are my wife. I want you with me," he said cajolingly.

"Yes, and that is why I am going to be sleeping with the women. If any of the men decide that they are feeling a little friendly, then we will be there to raise the alarm," she explained.

"They would not do that. You chose them yourself for this very reason," he retorted.

"But you can never truly know the heart of a person and what they hide."

"I know your heart, Flora."

"I beg to differ," she said. "You would not like what you would see if you did."

"I know you hide things from me. Your defences are always up and I cannot get past them."

"It is for your own protection, Marcus. I know I must be with you for the moment, and I will be without question. But my heart does not belong to you."

"So, there is another. Is it this Galen that was leading the attacks?" he asked in a hurried and dark voice.

"My heart is still mine to give away. It has not been taken or won. It is not a possession of someone else. I choose to whom I give my affections. You have been kind, gentle, and patient with me, and for that I am grateful. It is the reason I do not fight against this betrothal. Our child will be loved as a result of your actions. But do not seek to try to own me, for I will rebel against it."

"I have never tried to own you, only to grow in your affections. My love for you is so strong that sometimes I think it will last the ages. That when our souls meet again in another life they will recognise each other, and the love will continue to grow between us."

"Do not speak of that kind of love. It frightens me." She buried her head in his chest and he folded his arms around her.

"Have you seen something?" he asked quietly.

"No. Talk like that can change things, affect our other lives to come," she said. "Please do not pledge that kind of love to me."

He kissed her gently and she responded to his touch. "I cannot help the way I feel, my Flora."

"I know you can't, Marcus." She pushed away from his hold and turned. "I must go. I will see you in the morning."

"I will be with you in your dreams, Carling." She smiled sadly at his words, and he watched her go. Marcus stood in the entrance to his tent, and his heart was bursting with love for her.

"I do make that pledge, Carling. With all my heart and soul, I pledge that my love will find you no matter what other lives we have. I will make you love me. You will be mine fully—mind, body, heart, and soul."

The night was a restless one for Carling. Her dreams were mixed, but the constant watching of Marcus over her coloured it all. She woke frequently, and she would turn and find a new position. The talk in the tent had gone on for many hours as the women all told their stories. Some of their tales had played on her mind. She thanked her lucky stars that she had been handed to Keelie and not put with the general slaves.

It was the stories of how some of these women were treated that had made her want to help them. She was still unhappy that she could not help more. Brietta had chosen well. The ones who had been selected were those who had been treated badly by soldiers and officials alike. The news that she was doing this was not welcome by all in the camp, but she would deal with that another time. Carling was already planning for the next release.

The camp was struck early in the morning, and they headed off down the road. The rocking of the cart was gentle and soon lulled Carling to sleep next to Marcus, her head resting on his shoulder. She dreamed she walked through a meadow, and all was calm and peaceful. A grey flash came bounding up to her with tongue hanging out and an almost-smile on the jaw.

It is nice to meet you again, my pack-mate, the she-wolf said as she sat on her haunches.

It is lovely to see you too, pack-mate. Are you well? Carling asked politely.

I am well, as are the other members of the pack. He has a mate and pup on the way, Wolf told her.

I am pleased it has worked out well for him. Is Bear with you still?

Bear is still with us. He misses you a great deal, Wolf told her.

I miss him too. I talked to him a little while ago. Did he pass the messages on? Carling asked.

He did. The one who was with him was not happy. That one nearly got them both killed with his recklessness.

Carling was afraid that it had. Please tell me that he won't be at the meeting at the river?

He will be. But he will be hidden with more men in case there is treachery.

He does not trust that I can keep the Romans in check? Carling asked with some surprise.

He trusts you, dear one. He does not trust the Romans.

Thank you for letting me know, Wolf. Please tell the pack-mates that we are coming. And please pass on to that one that it would be best to remain hidden.

I will pass the message on. He will not like it. I have grown quite fond of him. We also look forward to you returning to the pack. Wolf told her.

So, do I, Wolf. You had best be gone. And stay hidden yourself.

Always. Wolf came and licked her hand and then ran off into the distance.

Carling stirred in her seat and sat up. Looking around, she began to recognise the landscape and a small smile came to her lips.

"Did you have a nice dream?" Marcus asked from beside her.

"Were you listening in?" she turned to face him.

"No. I have not worked out how to do that—be awake and dream at the same time. Have you?" he asked quickly.

"That is something I have actually not tried. We are almost there," Carling told him by way of changing the subject.

"Yes, we are. A little around the bend and the meeting place will come into view. I thought I saw a bear earlier but was mistaken. It was a large wolf."

"How could you mistake a bear with a wolf?" she asked him, laughing a little.

"All I saw was something in the trees. You are not partnered with a wolf as well, are you?"

"No, I am not, Marcus. Bear is the only one."

The horses drew them on and around the bend, the river came into view. On the other bank, a group of people was assembled, and Carling recognised most. Sima was standing beside Drest, his staff in his hand. Talorc was there also, and at his side was Veda.

Marcus pulled the cart up, and Carling was down from her seat in moments and standing on the bank before he could react. She waded through the ford and threw herself into their arms, crying at the reunion with those that held a special place in her heart. Tears of joy streamed along with the smile that stretched across her face.

Sima stood in front of her now, her hand pressed against Carling's belly. Her eyes opened wide with what she felt inside, and she hugged Carling.

"The child is strong, Carling. But there is something there," she whispered in her ear.

"Not here, Grandmother of my heart," she whispered back, shaking her head. "Not now."

Carling stepped back from them and turned to the other side of the river, finding Marcus standing there waiting for her. His soldiers were lining up behind him. She stepped back into the water and crossed over, standing before him.

"Husband, they are here, only them, to welcome the women back. Please release them and give them their freedom once more," she pleaded formally.

"Wife, into your care I give these women for you to set free as you wish. They will not be chased or harassed either by me or by my troops," he told her grimly.

Marcus raised a hand and gestured to his lieutenant. From behind him the women came, still wary of what was going on. Carling went to walk across the water with them, but Marcus held her back.

"No, you stay here. My scouts report that there are men in the woods on the other side."

"Please, they will not attack if you do nothing, Marcus." She felt her stomach drop. Shortly Keelie and Brietta joined them at her side, and she tried to put on a brave face.

"Stepmother, do you not wish to join them?" Marcus asked the older woman.

"No, Stepson, not while my child is still under your care," she said, refusing to look at him. She held her head high and her back straight.

The women were on the other side now, and there were no backwards glances at the group of Romans. Carling raised her hand in farewell and turned from the scene, feeling happy that it had gone off without a hitch.

A noise made her turn back as a horse came thundering down the road towards the women and her friends. The rider's dark hair was flowing behind him, and he leapt from the back of the horse in one fluid motion, coming to Sima's side, speaking to her quickly. Carling's old teacher started to hurry the women away from the river. Galen stood staring at the other side, his eyes on Carling.

"Why are there more troops coming?" he called out over the water. "Do you betray your own people, Carling of the Boar?"

"No. I know nothing of troops," she called back and looked at Marcus. "Do you seek to dishonour me, Husband?"

"I seek to protect you, Wife." His hand clamped around her arm and pulled her away from the water's edge. Keelie followed. Brietta stayed where she was, staring at the dark-haired man for a little longer before turning and catching up.

Carling looked behind her at Galen, who was still watching her. His face was grim and set as he stared. The women were now disappearing into the trees, followed closely behind by

Sima and Drest. Talorc came to Galen's side and placed a hand on his shoulder, drawing him back from the edge.

Marcus lifted Carling up into the seat of the cart and turned the horses around. As they headed back the way they came, a column of mounted men was headed their way.

"Do not send your men after them, Marcus, please. They did not attack."

"Quiet, Carling! I will not send them. Just as they brought men to protect them, so did I. I knew they would." He urged the horse forward with the crack of the reins, and they started at a trot. "So that was the famous Galen. He stared at you only, Wife."

"I have not met him before, Husband. I did not notice him staring only at me."

"He sought only your face from the moment he came around the corner. Is he the man who helped you run from our betrothal? I do not want your words that are meant to appease me, Carling. I only want honesty," Marcus demanded.

Carling shut her eyes. The moment had come to either keep up the pretense or tell him the truth. "I know him, Husband. He was the one who guided me to the sacred stones."

"And is he in love with you?" Marcus was facing forward and not looking at her.

"I don't know. If he is, then I have no knowledge of it. He never showed any signs of loving me." This time she did lie. This was information that Marcus should not know.

"Why did you run that day?"

"I was scared of you, of what I wanted to do to you. I left him on the side of a hill one night and made my own way to the stones by myself. I have not seen him since."

"Have I ever, in all the years we have known each other, given you cause to be frightened of me?" He turned his hurt eyes to her.

"Right now, you are frightening me. You have the power to send your men after those people—my people—and kill them all."

"But I won't. I gave you my word I would let them go. But I was not talking about now. As you were growing, did I frighten you?" he asked her again.

"Yes. Whenever you stopped to talk to me. The way you looked at me made me frightened. My first memory of you, Marcus, is you giving the order to kill my grandmother in front of my eyes. Is that not a reason to be frightened?"

Marcus thought on her words for a moment and nodded slightly. "Yes, it is. It was handled poorly. I was young and in charge for the first time. I wanted to show the men that I could lead and make decisions. It was a moment I have regretted ever since."

Carling sat quietly, holding on to the moving cart. The story Galen had told her about how he had treated him came to mind but asking Marcus why he had done it would only make him mad, and she bit her words down. They travelled on for the rest of the day with no words between them, both stewing on the conversation.

That night she shared his bed in the tent, but there was no affection from him. He did not seek her out under the covers but lay with his back to her. In the night, she got up and headed outside. The cold night air made her shiver, but she did not go back for a cloak to cover herself with.

On silent and ghostlike feet, she stepped out into the darkness and past the sleeping soldiers. The guards posted for the night paid her no mind, as she had hidden herself with a cloak of a different kind until she was clear of them. Out into the open field she walked until she could no longer hear the noise of the camp, and the fires were only twinkling spots. So much sadness washed over her. Seeing Galen at the river had torn at her heart again, but the guilt she felt with being the cause of Marcus's anger surprised Carling greatly.

The ancients have their plan, Carling, Bear said in her mind.

"Bear," she said his name softly out loud. Out of the gloom of the night a shambling form came, and he sat beside her. Her fingers worked, feeling his coat and reaching deep into the fur. *Oh, Bear, why did he have to show himself?*

He was concerned for you.

"He should have stayed hidden," she said out loud sadly.

"But I couldn't," Galen said, stepping nearer to her with silent steps.

Carling's head shot up and searched for him. Her eyes connected with his bright blue ones and her hands itched to touch him. "You shouldn't be here. What if he comes looking for me?"

"Will he?" He stepped closer again, only Bear standing between them.

"I don't know. He might."

"Do you want him to?" Galen asked.

"No," she whispered back.

"You carry his child."

"Yes, I do. But the child shall be mine, not his. There are only a few more seasons before we are parted, and the Romans leave."

"He will fight for his child, Carling."

"He can try, Galen." She said his name softly, testing it out on her lips after so long silent.

"When the Ancestor came and explained everything, I did not want to believe. He had to come twice more to make me believe. He even showed me visions," Galen told her.

"And what did the visions tell you?"

"That you love me."

"And do you love me?" she asked quietly, almost a whisper.

"With my heart and soul, I love you, Carling."

Her breathing deepened, and her grip on Bear's neck tightened. Bear growled, letting her know she was hurting him. Galen placed a hand on hers and lifted it off the bear's body. He guided her around the animal and drew her into his arms.

"Only a year and a day he has you, Carling. On the day that the time is up, I will come for you. I have seen how you defeat the Romans, how you drive them out. I am at your side when you do."

"Can you let me in on the secret, then, and tell me what I am supposed to do?" she asked as she leaned into his chest.

"I wish I could. It will come to you, the One True Child. I am ready for your call. I know you can reach me whenever you wish. It does not have to be in your dreams. I am supposed to tell you to hone your abilities, all of them. Did you know that if you really wanted to, you could stop time?" he said with a chuckle.

"No one can stop time," she told him.

"You can. I was told by the Ancestor. They are in awe of what you can do. Your abilities far surpass even theirs." He placed a finger under her chin and tilted her head back. "I wish you could speed it up, so I can be with you sooner."

He lowered his head to meet her lips. They stood for some time, their mouths locked together and arms holding tight.

Someone comes, Bear warned, and she broke the embrace.

"You must go. You cannot be found, Galen. Please," she begged him.

"I will go for now, Carling. I will be waiting." He kissed her once more and then headed into the darkness with Bear at his side.

Watch his back for me, Bear, and stick close to him, she pleaded with her friend.

I will, Carling, Bear promised as their shadows disappeared into the gloom, and she stood watching them leave. The feel of his arms around her and his lips on hers still burned on her flesh. The night was quiet once more, and she longed to run after them.

"What are you doing out here?" Marcus demanded from behind her.

"I couldn't sleep," she said as she faced him.

"It is not safe out here. Come back to the camp." He did not try to touch her, only stood aside and held out his arm, gesturing to the light of the fires.

"No angry words? No demands?" She stayed standing where she was, her voice threatening to tremble.

"No, Carling. We have said all we are going to say on that matter. I do not wish to fight with you, only protect you."

"Protect me from what? There is nothing to protect me from. They were my people, and I was trying to help them. They would not have done anything to me or you," she said.

"It wasn't the people I was protecting you from, but yourself." He came closer and placed his hands on her hips. "I don't want to lose you, my Flora. I am afraid of losing you to any man."

Carling sighed. She took his hands in her own and looked up into his eyes.

"The only man you need worry about is yourself, Marcus, and the little man I carry under my heart. While I am with you, you are the only man in my life."

"And what about this Galen?"

"No more talk of him. Is he here? Is it his child I have growing inside me? No. Marcus, you are my husband, and I am your wife. That is all that matters now."

He placed a large hand on her belly, and the baby kicked under his touch. He smiled at her and dropped a kiss on her forehead.

"He is going to be strong," Marcus said with pride, as they walked back to the camp side by side.

Chapter Twelve

The baby grew inside her, and she became large and uncomfortable. She would walk from one end of the house to the other and be out of breath at the weight she was carrying. Marcus was attentive as always, but the affections were now stolen kisses and hand holding. The bedroom activities had ceased, and Carling moved to another room to sleep.

He was still watching jealously over her dreams at night, but Carling's days were spent doing as she had been told, honing her abilities. She was surprised when she managed to contact Brietta in her mind while they were both awake for the first time. It was almost like a light had been turned on, and the knowledge was there for the asking.

The weather had gone cold with the turning of the seasons. She spent the autumn as much outside as possible until it became too wet and cold. Once confined to the inner rooms, she would sit by the fire sewing little garments for the baby and searching her own mind to find what abilities she had. There was one that she found intriguing, and she studied it carefully.

A silver bracelet sat on the table by her bed, and she looked at it carefully. Her mind focused on the object and willed it to move. It gave a slight twitch, and she let out the breath she was holding. Again, she tried. Pouring more energy into the action, she told it to move. This time it flew off the table and rolled around the floor. She stood and very carefully bent to pick it up. Holding it in her hands, she thought about what Galen had said that night.

Did you know if you really wanted to, you could stop time? The words sounded loud in her ears, and she immediately knew where he was. The vision that came to her was a camp, the fire dancing merrily in the centre and men huddled around it talking.

Gasping at the sight of Galen sitting there wrapped up with blankets around his shoulders, Carling sat down heavily on the bed. She could not hear what they were saying, but the discussion was heated. Wolf was sitting on the outskirts just behind Veda and she looked up, staring at her. She saw Veda look around him with a puzzled look and then say something to Galen.

Carling moved in her mind to stand beside him. Veda was talking once more. She sat on the log, and Galen turned his face towards her and smiled. He said something, but she could not understand. Looking now at Wolf, Carling shook her head. She reached out to take his hand in hers, but it passed through as if the image was water.

Pulling away, she opened her eyes and came back to the room she was in. He was safe for now, and that was all that mattered. Standing from the bed, she went back to her sewing just as Marcus walked into the room.

"How are you this afternoon, Flora?" he said, coming to her and taking her hand in his own.

"I am well, Marcus. A little tired, but well," she answered as she took her hand back and resumed her stitches. "You don't normally visit me in the afternoons. What has happened?"

"Nothing. The first snow is falling, and the camp is all settled for winter. I am not sure if you are aware, but a fire broke out in the camp outside the walls. My men have been sent to stop it from spreading," he told her.

"And the people whose homes are destroyed—what will happen to them?" she asked, taking her eyes away from her work to look at him.

"I have already anticipated your question. And I hope you will be pleased with the answer. The houses will be rebuilt. It will take time, but it will occupy my men while winter is about, and they cannot go out on patrol as much. I am thinking also of changing the palisade, replacing the wood with stone, make it a proper command centre."

"Leave a permanent mark on the landscape," she said as a flash of fire flared in her mind.

"Something like that. One of the houses was rather close to the ditch and logs; it scorched it some. I thought that if it were rock then it would be a bit safer from fire."

"It will also occupy some in the quarries," she said absentmindedly. Then realising what she said, she looked at him. "Or will that be manned by slaves?"

"Again, with the slaves? Was the exercise with the women not good enough, Carling?" he smiled indulgently at her.

"No, Marcus, it was not. It was only the beginning. But I don't want to argue with you today, Husband. I am too tired to raise my voice." She put the sewing down and ran a weary hand over her eyes. The fatigue overtook her and encompassed her fully as she spoke of it.

"Let me help you to bed, Flora." Solicitously he was at her side, lifting her from her seat. She leant her head into his shoulder as he carried her to the bed and laid her down. "Are you comfortable?"

"Yes, thank you." Her eyes were closing, and she was already drifting off.

What she fell into was no normal dream—she could see that already. It felt different, and the sights and sounds were all strange. She was high up on a mountainside, looking down into a deep valley below. At the bottom stood a small loch, the sun glistening off its waters in a shimmering and dazzling display.

"It will take you time to learn how to use your abilities without feeling tired, Carling." Bear was there beside her, sitting on his haunches and staring out over the land.

"You should have found a den by now, friend. It is getting late in the season," she said, worried.

"I am not your friend Bear, Carling. My true form is not something you would be used to, so I chose the one that would be the most comforting," the voice from Bear said.

"Who are you, then, that takes this form?"

"I am an Ancestor. Not your father nor your mother. I am Galen's ancestor."

"Why have you summoned me?" she asked.

"Because I am concerned for his welfare. While you are here, my son is out there worried about you. Dreaming up more and more reckless ways to get you back."

"I have just seen him in the company of men. I could not hear them," Carling told him.

"It is just as well, for they are not making much sense at the moment. You have already been given the answer to what you seek. The time will come after your child is born, as your mother and father have told you."

"I know—in the spring. A year and a day after the betrothal."

"Marcus is also one of my sons," the Ancestor said sadly through Bear.

"Marcus and Galen both?" she asked.

"Yes. Hence the double-edged sword vision. Two of my descendants, equal in height and strength, both warriors. Equal in their love for you. I fear that the interference of my brother and sister with my sons has made things hard on you. They did not talk to me about their meddling," the Ancestor said darkly.

"Why have you come to me and not them?"

"Because their love of you is too encompassing. They cannot see beyond you and what may happen in the future. It has always been that the evil shall come out in a single line of one of us. Sadly, it is my line, which is why Galen was formed."

"It is Galen's line that has evil?" Carling was shocked.

"No, dear one, you have misheard me. Galen was formed to counteract the evil line. Marcus's line will be the line that is tainted until the father of the Ultimate One is born. There's something else they would not have told you, but your brother will be the spirit which inhabits that form. The ties of family are great, Carling, and he shall be like a brother to the two."

Carling sat down on the hard, cold rock at her feet. This news was too enormous to absorb. Several times, questions formed only to be taken away from her. The comprehension of what lay before her was vast.

"This is all so much to take in," she said quietly.

"There is more. The catalyst for the decimation of the Romans is in your hands—or your mind, rather. There is one talent you have not seen yet. Search for it, and when you find it, you will know what it is for. This is my meddling in my brother and sister's affairs. My gift to you. A revenge that will be suitable to sate the bloodlust of both you and Galen."

"I cannot feel that anymore. They took it away from me," she told him.

"It is still there; I can feel it." Bear turned his face towards her. "It is the only way, Carling. He is my son, but he is just the start. By the time your children face the evil again, the one they come up against will be wholly evil. He will give his soul to the madness that wants to consume this world. The danger he poses to each and every person on this planet is great. He cannot win. I am ashamed to call him son."

"Why could you not do something about him? You are an Ancestor."

"I cannot. Individually and collectively, we cannot stop him. Which is why we came to the decision to create you and your line. It was forbidden for us to mate together for good reason. The power of the abilities would be enhanced and multiplied. You, dear one, hold more power in your hands than we could ever have. We shaped the land and made it as we wished, and we created The People to bear our abilities on. You have the power to snuff out the sun, to turn the world back into the dust it came from. The daughter who comes from you will be just as powerful, and we will be there to guide her."

"Do you tell me this to boost my ego? To make me hold it over the ones I love?" Carling asked confused.

"No. I tell you these things because you need to know. I tell you, so you are prepared for what must come, because it will be bloody and harrowing for you to deal with. I tell you so that you can stand by my son and protect him from the brother he does not know he has."

"Brother?"

"Galen and Marcus are not just my descendants. They are brothers, born of the same mother. Galen was sent to her sister. His mother could not raise him in the house of Marinus. He was not that man's issue."

"But Marcus tortured Galen," Carling whispered horrified.

"Yes, he did, but he did not know Galen was his brother. He was five when Galen was born, and he had already been taken from his mother to start his schooling. I have been keeping an eye on Marcus carefully. There is no doubt that the evil has already been implanted into his soul. So, too, has the love he feels for you. It will haunt the generations to come." The bear sighed. "We created this land, brought it up from the sea. We created the volcanoes that brought forth new rock. Together we worked in shaping it, carving it, and covering it with the animals and plants that pleased us. We stood together and brought life forth onto the land. He could not accept it— accept us. He was not willing to share, and so we fought him."

"Who is he?" she asked quietly.

"He is the one who caused the explosion—a destroyer, Chaos. But from the explosion came our planet, and from the sparks came us, the seven Sentinels. We are The People. We stand together, and he is alone. That is the key to defeating him. You must work together with Galen. For all of our sakes, Carling."

"I will try, Ancestor. Why can't I know your names?"

"As your mother and father have already told you, it is dangerous for our names to be spoken now. You will learn them when you come to us. It is time for you to wake now, dear one. My son is still by your side," the Ancestor said gently.

"He will have sensed I was talking to someone."

"No, he could not. We are in a different time. This is the world before man was created. Now go wake up. My blessings, and as always, my love go with you, Carling."

His words echoed in her mind as he receded from her. It felt like she was coming up for air again after being in the water for a very long time. She gasped and opened her eyes. Marcus was there by her side, holding her hand.

"You were dreaming," he said. "It must have been a very deep dream, as I could not sense you."

"I was so tired. How long have I been asleep?" she asked him.

"Only a little while. It is still afternoon," Marcus told her.

Carling took the Ancestor's advice and concentrated on her abilities. What she found in her mind scared her. She looked at them all, discarding those that she felt were too dangerous, pushing them down to repress them. Then she found it.

Picking it up, Carling searched it and turned it in her hands. It felt heavy, and it was perfect. The ability spread through her mind, and she readily accepted it. She toyed with the effects that it could have on people and the images that could be created with it. Looking down at her feet, she also found something else left for her by the Ancestor.

Her hate.

The emotion seethed in her hands, pulsating with the rawness of the rage that was contained within. Carling found it so tempting to release it and let it overtake her once more, but she tucked it away to be used at another time. She did not want to tempt fate by allowing herself full control of it just yet.

The tiredness that had overwhelmed her was now abating. She could use her abilities with as little drawing on her reserves of energy as possible. One such ability allowed her to appear to and be heard by Galen. The first time she had done so, she had scared him half to death.

Finding him was easy. His bright blue beacon of light was her guide, and she would find time to just watch him as he went about his daily life. Pulling more energy to her, she forced her way at first into hearing what was going on around them, and then what he was saying. But that was not enough to satisfy her. With further study of it and pushing out, she managed to appear in front of him, making him stumble back in fright.

"Carling!" he called out and looked around him to see if anyone else could see her as well.

"Galen." She went to help him up, but her hand moved through him, and all the blood drained from his face.

Scrambling to his feet, he stood ready to face whatever this apparition could say to him.

"I am no ghost. I still have not perfected this," she told him, trying not to laugh.

"But how? How is this possible?"

"Do you remember telling me the last time we spoke that I could stop time if I wanted to?" she asked him.

"Yes, that is what the Ancestor said."

"He was not lying to you, Galen. There is much I can do. He gave me a gift, the Ancestor who appeared to you. And that gift was my anger and hatred back," she told him carefully.

"You can kill him, then?" He was looking at her hopefully.

"I could if I had absorbed it. But I have not and will not yet."

"Why stay with him? He is raiding again. Did he tell you?" Galen said with some heat.

"No, he did not. This is news to me—otherwise I would have let you know."

"Come to me, Carling, and we can face him together."

"We will, Galen. In the spring, when my child is born. A year and a day. We shall have our revenge on him, and he will be sent to the darkest of hells to be tormented for all time."

"It sounds like you have your anger with you already." He smiled at her.

"I must go. I have been trying so hard to make you see me."

"I knew you were. Wolf told Veda. Come back to me, Carling. I love you."

"I love you, too." She faded out from his sight and opened her eyes to the world.

"Did it work?" Brietta said at her side.

"Yes. I could talk to him." Carling gave her friend a broad grin as she told her.

"Good. We can start planning now. It is midwinter, and spring will be here soon along with your child." Brietta started sewing again.

Carling did not confront Marcus about the raids he was sending out. There was an easy truce between them, and she wanted it to stay that way for a while longer. One thing she did manage to do was use another of her abilities to enter the minds and change the thoughts of some of the lieutenants slightly. She did this by suggesting to Marcus that they should come to the house the night before leaving on patrol to have dinner with them.

She played the part of hostess greatly. Carling even sang for them, wishing them well in their journeys, meanwhile slipping into their minds and planting other seeds. Seeds such as doubt in Marcus's plans, self-doubt of their leadership ability, and suspicion of their own men. She released these seeds to grow and flourish inside them slowly, so that by the time she needed them to burst forth and bloom, it would be the exact moment she needed them to crumble and fail.

Another thing she had changed was the introduction of young women to the evening. These were handpicked by her and Brietta. Free women who hoped to better themselves by marrying a man of wealth and standing in the army. They looked after the men, including Marcus, for the evenings while she slipped away early.

"Wife!" Marcus called out to her one evening when she was heading to her room. Carling stopped and waited for him to catch up, turning to face him. "I want an explanation, please."

"For what, Husband?" she asked, trying to sound innocent.

"For these dinners and the women. I found one in my bed last night," he told her.

"Who you wish to take to bed, Marcus, is none of my business," she said and tried to turn. He reached out a hand.

"No, it is your business. Especially when you send someone who is supposed to look like you. I don't want another, Carling. I only want you." He kissed her and pulled her close. "You are to go to my room and wait for me, my Flora. I want you there to see me off properly in the morning."

"I will do as you wish, Marcus," she said softly, disappointed her plan had not worked. If he could only take a concubine, her life would be easier.

"I wish you would want the same, Flora. That you would come willingly to me."

"You had best go back to your guests, Marcus. I will be in your bed waiting for you," she told him, pulling herself away from his grasp and then walked away.

Marcus watched her go, indecision playing on his mind. To do as she had told him or to go after her and be with her only. A call from the room behind him made up his mind, and he turned and walked back to his friends.

It was late when he finally made it to his room. He was drunk and staggering about. He landed on the bed heavily beside her and pulled her roughly to him, pressing his body against her back. Reaching around, Marcus caressed her while giving clumsy kisses on the back of her neck. His breath reeked of wine.

The thought of giving herself to him that night was unthinkable to Carling. She crept into his mind and sent him to sleep, giving him flashes of their lovemaking to make him think she had relented to his wishes. The anger was creeping into her mind and possessing it once more. *Soon*, she kept telling herself, *soon*.

With the morning, she woke Marcus and had no sympathy for the hangover that pounded away at his head. Bead arrived and helped him into his armour, working even harder as Marcus swayed on the spot. Carling rose from the bed and came to stand in front of him. Her hands rested on his chest plate, and she kissed him.

"Come back safe, Husband," she said carefully.

"I will, my wife. Take care of our little one and do not overtax yourself," he said, accepting his helmet from Bead.

She escorted him to the portico, where his horse was waiting. A cool spring wind was blowing in, and she sensed danger on it. This patrol was no ordinary one. Marcus was to see the chiefs of the clans that had pledged loyalty to the Romans to reinforce their rule. One of those was her uncle.

"Can you tell my uncle I miss them?" she asked quietly.

"I will. Take care, Flora," he replied almost automatically.

Marcus left her side and climbed into the saddle. He turned without a backwards glance at her and headed off to the front of the column that was waiting nearby.

With him gone, she was able to relax more and explore the abilities without the fear of being interrupted. She visited Galen more and outlined her plan. He was skeptical at first but agreed to it. They would often just sit and talk, happy to spend time in each other's company.

Five days passed before Marcus came back. Carling was sitting in the garden taking advantage of the weak spring sunshine as she played her harp. The little boy in her belly would move and kick as she sang to him. It made her smile.

She heard him before she saw him. His shouts for her rang through the corridors and his sandals sounded loud on the tiles.

"Where are you, Carling? I have a present for you," he called out.

"I am here, Husband." She stood awkwardly; the bump of her baby now fully extended out. She rested a hand on it while she waited for Marcus to find her.

"There you are. Look, I have brought you a rich gift. I killed it myself," he said, beaming from ear to ear.

Bead came running after with something large in his arms. As he reached, her he laid out the bundle and she stopped and stared at it. Lying on the grass was the grey fur of a wolf. It had not been washed, and dried red stains still covered it.

"The beast attacked me along with some rebels. We fought them off, but not before I plunged my sword into the belly of the thing. The man who was attached to it died as well." He stood looking at her, enjoying the look of horror and shock that played on her face.

Carling staggered back to the seat and landed heavily. She shut her eyes from the thought that Wolf was gone, that Veda was gone. A hand came to rest on her cheek and then gripped her hair tightly.

"I told you, Wife, I will not suffer another man loving you," he said quietly, and she opened her eyes to look at him. The hazel eyes staring back were manic, and she cringed.

"But he did not love me, Marcus. He had a wife and a child on the way. Another child left fatherless in this world of hate and blood you have created. Is that the legacy you wish to leave our son?"

"My son will be a Roman, woman. My son will follow his father's footsteps and carry on the work my father started," he said through clenched teeth.

She stood to face him, her face turning red with the anger as it filled her. "Our son, I hope, will be better in treating with people. Not betraying his heritage by these acts of violence." Her voice rose to match his.

"My son shall know nothing of The People. I have already decided that. He will be brought up in the proper manner of the Romans." Marcus held tightly to her head, pulling it to the side.

"And what of me? I have no say in how he is to be raised? Or are you going to put me in a back room, a hostage held here by my child?"

"No. We will have many more sons, Carling, and you will be always at my side." There was a slightly different note to his voice, and she shuddered inwardly.

Carling was shaking with fury. She could see nothing except for the triumph in his face. The love he had for her now was twisted and not what it had been. He wished to possess her and use her. He had no wish to find out what she wanted or felt. Marcus released her, and she stumbled back, her hands surrounding her belly protectively.

Quickly she stalked away from him, deliberately averting her eyes from the bloodied remains of Wolf. Tears sprang to her eyes as she remembered the beautiful wolf who had opened her ability up to her, had protected and befriended her. Her friend and her brother gone as well—his sweet nature and face gone to the violence he had tried to turn her from. As she walked into the shadows of the corridor, a sudden pain in her back brought her up short and she clung to the wall for support. Carling cried out with it and felt her stomach clench. She slipped to her knees.

"Carling!" Marcus called and came to her side just as her waters broke, spilling over the tiles. "Bead, go get Brietta and Diana."

His hand was at her elbow and his arm around her waist as helped her up and walked her to her room. As carefully as he could, he helped her onto the bed and then went back to the door.

"Someone find Brietta and Diana—now!" he called out to the empty space beyond. Running footsteps came and entered the room.

"Out. You will be no good to Carling here, Marcus," Keelie said, taking charge.

He was pushed through the doorway, then turned as the door was shut in his face. The last view he had of Carling was her in pain on the bed, staring daggers at him. For the first time in his life, he felt scared of a woman.

The labour went on for hours. Drenched in her own sweat, Carling cried out when the contractions hit. Finally, she felt the need to push. She bore down on the feeling. Her only focus was the need to get the baby out from her body.

"Gently does it, Carling." Brietta was there, wiping her face with cool cloth. "Not too hard, you will only cause damage."

"I want him out of me," she cried weakly into Brietta's shoulder. She was tired and drained.

"Pull on your resources, Carling. Use your energy. He won't be long now." Brietta tried to calm her while looking up at Keelie.

"One more big push and he should be here. I can see his head now," Keelie encouraged from between Carling's legs.

Carling could feel the pressure building, could feel the contraction pulling at her muscles and she bore down on it. She pushed and felt the blood rush to her face. She felt the head as it slipped from her body, and she released her effort.

"Gently now. Another push and he will be born," Keelie said softly.

The next contraction came, and she pushed as she was told. Keelie caught the small infant in her hands, carefully placed him on a cloth, before placing him in Carling's arms.

"There will be a little need to push to get the afterbirth out, and then we can get you all cleaned up." Keelie smiled at the new mother and child.

Brietta tied off the cord and snipped it. The expelling of the placenta was nothing to Carling. She was more concerned with the child. He was not crying.

Brietta took him in her arms and rubbed his back. The little face was blue and unresponsive. Keelie gave her handmaiden a worried look while she washed Carling down and cleared away the mess.

With a great audible gasp, the baby began to cry. His lungs finally taking in his much-needed first breath, he let fly with the cry of a newborn and the door banged open against the wall. Marcus was standing in the doorway, his face shocked and pleased. He came to Brietta's side and took the baby from her arms.

"He will need to feed, Master," Brietta said, worried.

"Just a moment. Please. I just want to hold him for a moment," Marcus said in wonder as he uncovered his son from the blanket he had been wrapped in. He looked at the tiny feet and hands and then at the child's face. The dark hair was already thick on his head, and his eyes were already hazel.

Marcus looked up at Carling and smiled. He moved to the side of the bed and gently handed her their son, waiting while he had his first feed. Carling slept with the child at her breast. She was exhausted and drained. In her dream, a figure stood at the end of the bed with a hand raised.

"The traits of the father shall continue on to the son. With your guidance and understanding, he will be taught correctly the ways of The People. I bless you both and claim him as a son of my line," he intoned and then he was gone.

Days were now filled with wonder for Carling as she fell in love with the little boy. She did not mind getting up to feed him in the middle of the night and refused the help of a woman to take care of him during the day. Marcus had insisted that they name him after himself, so little Marcus he became. Carling shortened it to Marc when her husband was not around.

To celebrate the birth, Marcus held a feast, and it was a noisy affair. For three days it stretched until Carling came to him and said that it was enough. Chastised and still in good spirits, he held her in his arms and produced a present. Around her neck on a fine golden chain sat a pendant, a carving of a goddess that was meant to protect her. The moment she was alone, she took the pendant off and laid it by the bed, never to be worn again.

Amongst the revelry, the news of Veda's death and that of Wolf had time to sink in, and she seethed at the fresh and new act of Marcus. When she found the time to be alone with Galen in their private dream space, he confirmed for her that Veda had indeed been killed. Together the couple grieved for both him and Wolf. She gently approached Talorc and waited for him until he responded to her. He took one look at her and crumpled before her.

"I am so, sorry, Talorc; I am so sorry." She crouched beside him, desperate to touch and comfort him.

"You could not have stopped him, Carling. He changed after he came back from guiding you. He was a different man. Then the news that you had given yourself to that man came, and it crushed him. All he could think of was getting you away from him. He took greater and greater risks. My son, my lovely boy."

"I am so sorry. No one was supposed to get hurt. They were not supposed to come after me. I did not seek their rescue."

"We know, Carling, and we do not blame you. It is not your fault. Veda knew what he was doing, knew the risks. He will be survived by his child, and that child shall know what his father did."

"May the Ancestors protect you all. May you know only peace and love from now on. May your children grow strong and healthy and bear many children of their own. May you and Nessa live to be old and wise, and may the Ancestors grant me the privilege to be at your hearth once more." She sent out her blessing to him with tears still in her eyes. She waited until he had collected himself.

"Our blessings on you, too, Carling. May your time with that man be short now, and you can be with the one who truly holds your heart. May your child grow strong and healthy and be protective of the two to come. May you never know the pain of losing a child." He passed on his own blessing.

"My time is short, Talorc. I hope to see you all soon. Please give my love to Nessa and the children."

"Go with our love and support, Carling. We will see you soon." He retreated from her, and she cried once more for his loss.

Carling remained in her dream and allowed her defences to lower slightly. Carefully she crafted an image that lay at her feet, and she averted her gaze from it. As Marcus entered her dream, she began her performance. She ripped and tore at her hair and clothing as she saw him come towards her. Her tears were real and fresh, and one look at the bloody mess at her feet was enough to keep them going.

Falling to her knees, she picked up the limp and lifeless form of Veda she had created and held him close. Her sobs and howls rang out into the space around them. He was at her side, trying to pull her away.

"Carling, let him go. He is not real, this is just a dream," he called to her as he extracted her arms from the dream Veda. "Carling, my wife, my Flora. Please wake. Wake up."

"What for, Marcus? For more of this?" She reached again for the image she had created. "To the news that one more innocent life has been cut short and obliterated from this world? What is there to wake for?"

"Our son. You must wake for our son," he pleaded with her.

Carling stopped and looked up.

"No, Marcus. You mean *my* son. He will never be yours." The tears dried where they stood on her face, and the image of Veda disappeared.

Marcus scrambled away from her and looked confused at the change in her. "What are you talking about, Carling?"

"I am going to show you something that will come to be. It is an image of the future, one that is not that far off in time. I want to sear it into your memory so that it stays with you for the rest of your short life." She made a gesture with her hand, and a picture appeared before him.

The image was of a small family group, the children smiling and the couple with their arms around each other. Carling watched his face as he came to realise what he was seeing. One child was the image of himself, and he was on the shoulders of a man that was not him, but Galen. The other two were both girls, one the image of her mother and the second that of her father.

"What is this? This cannot be true." He was shaking his head.

"It is true. You will not survive what is to come. Your destiny has already been decided by the Ancestors. I wanted you to see what was to come. What is to become of my son. He shall be raised by a kind and just man who will love him as his own. This is what will be," she told him fiercely, enjoying his discomfort and confusion.

"No, you cannot mean that. Why are you doing this?" he demanded.

"Because my hatred and anger for you has almost fully taken over me again. I wanted to enjoy the look on your face, the look of bewilderment and loss. Marc will never be yours. He will know of you. We shall teach him about you and what you did. I will let him know his father. But you do not get to raise him in your image. In this twisted love you have for me," she told him.

"When we wake, Wife, I will take steps against you," he said furiously stepping away from her in a mixture of fright and anger.

"No, you will not. You see, Marcus, you may have joined me in my dream space, but I am already in your mind with my hand around your memory. This memory we are creating together will be crushed as soon as you wake, and it will only appear to be a bad dream that will fade away with the new day." Carling smiled sweetly at him.

He looked uncertain and confused still backing away from her. "How can you do two things at once? That is not possible."

"It is possible," she said proudly. "It is very possible for me. Do you want to see what else I can do?"

Marcus's eyes opened wide. "No! I want to wake, Carling. I want to wake." His steps backwards were now hurried, but he didn't seem to be getting further away.

"You shall wake. Wake up now, Marcus. Wake up," she called to him. Carling was up on an elbow and shaking him.

"I'm awake," he called out and moved away from her. The dream was still fresh with him for a moment and then eased as he looked around.

"You were having a nightmare, Husband. Just a nightmare," she told him tenderly to ease his fears, reaching out and smoothing his hair from his forehead gently.

"A nightmare. Such a strange dream," he agreed as he relaxed under her touch.

"Can you remember it?" she asked with a whisper.

"No, it's gone. I just remember fear, and something being taken from me." He reached out and she gathered him up in her arms.

It's all right now, Marcus, the dream is gone." She said as she soothed his fear and a small smirk played on her lips. "It's all gone."

Chapter Thirteen

The implanted feelings she had placed into the lieutenants and certain soldiers before Marc was born were now starting to take effect. Patrols were coming back, having been chased away by the rebels, and the lieutenants were less inclined to go further afield and risk their men. Amongst the men themselves, there were mutterings and desertions were becoming more frequent.

The small village that had sprung up outside the walled enclosure of the Roman camp was swelling in numbers, as Galen and his men infiltrated it with help of the residents who sympathised with their cause. Carling was keeping contact with Galen all through the planning. It was going to be a close thing.

Carling calculated the days of the betrothal precisely. A year and a day had finally come. The bundle she prepared that morning contained only things she wanted to take with her — small things only. She dressed carefully that morning, not wanting to draw Marcus's attention to what the day was. Once more around her waist she fastened the belt made by her uncle, with the little knife from her cousin hanging off it. The blue ribbon was still tied around the handle.

Carling had warned both Brietta and Keelie the night before of what was going to occur, and Keelie was not happy. She berated both Brietta and Carling for leaving her out of the scheming and fretted for the safety of her own child, Cato. They prepared as best they could, and at the morning meal they let her know they were ready.

Mid-morning, Carling was seated in the garden. She closed her eyes and sought out the two soldiers she had picked to start the mayhem that would be the downfall of the fort. It was easy enough to start the fight. The men were bored and restless with the strange goings-on in the camp. They were seated opposite each other in a small tavern in the marketplace, already drinking heavily from their cups.

Carling set to work.

The two large Roman soldiers suddenly stood toe-to-toe screaming at each other. Their faces deepening into a dark ruddy hue with their belligerent anger, and spit flying from their mouths as they shouted. One shoved the other in the chest, and the fight broke out. Arms were flying as fists connected with flesh, and bone broke under the pressure. They wrestled and fell into market stalls, the merchants crying out in dismay at their damaged and scattered goods. They angrily entered the fray to dole out their own punishment to those they thought were at fault. More stalls were smashed in the process as the fight grew bigger and bigger, attracting a large crowd who were all shouting out their encouragement. A small stall still stood in the way of the fighting men, a food stall that sold cooked meat over a small brazier of hot coals. One of the soldiers was on the receiving end of a large fist and he fell on that stall, knocking the brazier over, sending the coals scattering amongst the debris of wood and cloth.

Small at first, the fire became brighter and larger as it caught at the fabric and wood that surrounded it. Flames licked higher into the sky and leapt from one stall to another, spreading fast in the packed market. Smoke billowed up dark and black as the merchandise caught alite. People started to panic, and screams could be heard now in the quiet confines of the commander's villa.

Brietta was beside Carling with Marc in her arms. The bundle was already slung over her back, and she was nervous. Keelie came with a struggling Cato in hand. He was resisting her, wanting to go look at the fire and fighting. Feet were running now to fetch the commander. Carling heard Marcus leave the villa in a hurry, following the soldier to see for himself what was going on.

In the marketplace, all hell was breaking loose. The camp had become so large that the buildings were crammed together, and the fire was spreading fast into the semi-wooden structures. Screams and yells rent the air and thick black smoke poured into the sky, floating over the camp and bringing with it the choking smells.

Carling opened her eyes and waited.

Marcus appeared, running towards them, his face angry and set. "You must leave now. I have soldiers to protect you. Get out the south gate, it's the only one free at the moment." He was out of breath as he spoke. He gave his wife and son a quick kiss, and he was off.

Carling stood and took her son from Brietta. The soldiers escorted them from the house, and they found themselves hurried towards the only passable gate along with the press of panicked merchants, slaves, and freemen. Soldiers were stopped as they tried to escape and were sent back to help with the fire. Women were crying, some holding children of their own.

Once at the gate, Carling handed Marc back to Brietta and kissed his small head. "Look after him, Brietta. I'll see you when it's all over. Make for the trees, Bear will meet you there.

Do not be frightened of him. He will protect you," Carling told her quickly.

"What about the ones who guard us?" Brietta asked as she settled Marc into his sling.

"Already dealt with," Carling said as the two soldiers left their side to head back into the inferno. "Go and don't stop for anyone or anything. Only when you see Bear." She watched them leave and breathed a sigh of relief, then turned and battled the crowds trying to escape.

Making her way back to the villa, Carling found it on fire already. The sights and sounds of those dying in the fire she blocked from her mind. The smell of their burning flesh strangled her nose and finally brought forth the last piece of the buried memory and anger. This had to be done. The land had to be purged of the Romans. Quickly and carefully, she found a spot to finish her work. Flames erupted from buildings that were nowhere near the fire, trapping the soldiers who went to put them out.

Galen, she found. He had entered the camp now with his men, who were dispatching the soldiers not perishing in the flames. Their swords and daggers were running red with blood. She felt the rush of adrenaline as it passed through his body, as he attacked man after man. She felt him near her even before she could see him and moved to meet him.

They stood together amongst the burning and death. Galen took her in his arms and kissed her roughly. She broke at the sound of her name and turned to see Marcus rushing towards them.

Holding up her hand, she stopped him in his tracks. His feet were planted firmly on the ground, and he could not move. In his hand his sword shook with his frustration. Carling walked towards him, her anger and rage now fully hers again. She stood before him and pulled out her knife.

From around the handle, she untwisted the blue ribbon and held it out for him to see.

"One year and a day it has been, Marcus. I am no longer your betrothed. I sever the ties that bind us." She slipped the knife under the ribbon in her hand and sliced through the knot. The pieces fell from her fingers and down onto the ground at his feet. She lifted her foot and pressed the remains into the dirt, not once taking her eyes off his.

"Carling! No! Please, don't do this," he begged her, his eyes showing the pain her actions caused.

"This is the day that was foretold. You had been warned by the visions as well as by me. I have worn the ribbon every day as a reminder to you that my time with you was short. Every day I was with you was a torture for me, knowing what you did not only to my family but to others. And I was unable to take my revenge on you for ripping my family apart," she told him. Her anger, still tenuously held in check, was starting to show in her voice.

"You cannot mean that, Carling. What about our son? Will you rip his father from him?"

"He will know who and what his father was. Who better than his own mother, the One True Child, to raise him in the way of The People?"

"The People are nothing but ground-grubbing peasants who know no better life!" Marcus yelled at her. His own anger was now taking control as he realised what she was telling him.

"No. We are The People. You are only one," she said and saw the spark of red flare in his eyes that had nothing to do with the raging flames that were surrounding them. The evil that would contaminate the world and the work that The People had created.

"Let me free then, Carling, and face off with me. I will crush you as I will those who follow you." Marcus's voice deepened and became hollow sounding. There was another note there, as if someone else spoke the same words at the same time. It was the same voice that had taken hold of Onnist's the night before her betrothal with Marcus. One she had heard in his own voice once before.

"You cannot harm us. We will not bow down to your wishes and will not falter in our steps to vanquish you." Her own voice took on that of a chorus. From down the ages, her family spoke through her and lent their energy to her efforts.

Beside Carling, Galen now stood. His own blue eyes flashed hard and flinty as he stood before the man who had taken his love from him and more.

"You killed my brothers and my father. You sliced my back and sent me as a warning. I now come and stand before you as a message from our people. We will survive." Galen's voice was dark and heavy with the words he spoke.

"Release me to fight," Marcus demanded of Carling.

Carefully she stood back from him, and Galen followed her lead. Carling released his feet, and he came on, his eyes burning as bright. Carling stood her ground, holding up her hand at his advance. Marcus stopped again, unable to move.

"This is unnecessary, Marcus," she told him. "Just kneel and accept your fate."

"Never to you and your kind," he cried, flailing his arms, trying to set himself free. Carling saw the moment the evil finally took over him, and she released the bindings on his legs.

With his sword raised high, Marcus came rushing at them. A blaze of red sparks sprung from the metal, and he sliced it through the air, aiming to cut Carling down. A flash of blue sprung from beside her as Galen blocked his blow and turned it aside.

"She is mine," Marcus growled at him, stepping away and facing Galen.

"Carling belongs to no one. Her will is her own. Her heart is her own. You cannot possess her," Galen said calmly. He brought his sword back up to face off with Marcus.

Sparks flew from their blows as they connected over and over. The ringing from the metal weapons clanged like great bells. Neither gave quarter nor ground as they faced off. Carling stood still as they fought around her. Her eyes closed as she fed energy and strength into Galen's body, feeling each movement he made and each blow that was rained down on him.

There was only one outcome to this confrontation, and she worked hard to make sure that it transpired. With every ounce of her strength, she lashed out at Marcus. Her own little knife grew before her eyes and glowed golden. She drew it through the air and saw red appear on Marcus's arm as blood dripped from the wound she had inflicted. Again, she swung the sword in her hand and another cut sliced through Marcus.

His screams at the pain only spurred him on in his attack of Galen, fighting now to get to Carling and kill her before she could inflict any more damage to him. Cut after cut appeared on his body as Carling sliced, not once touching him.

Marcus staggered for a moment and fell to his knees, his sword now lying on the ground, the blood from his wounds dripping from his fingers. He looked up at Carling and cried out to her.

"Why?" he called.

"It is as it should be, Marcus," Carling said with a little sadness. "The Ancestors will explain it all when you meet them in your final moments."

"I will never let them have him," the guttural voice cried out from Marcus' lips. "You will be mine eventually, Carling. The One True Child will be in my control. Her mind, body, and spirit shall all bend to me. I will use her to finish what I have started. The Romans could not do what I wanted, but there shall come a day when there will be one who can. He will be my true vessel and you will be his bride."

"She and her sister will see that you do not have that chance. You may take the minds of Marcus's line and corrupt them with your evil. But remember from his line comes the father of the greatest one. I already know whose spirit will inhabit that form. He will be a brother to the two and together they will see that you are gone from this world for good," Carling told the entity that now inhabited the fading body before her.

A great struggle played out on the face of Marcus then. The evil that possessed him was fighting for freedom from the dying flesh that encased it.

"Kill me, Carling. Kill me and stop him," Marcus whispered to her, his eyes pleading.

"I cannot kill you, Marcus. I will not kill the father of my child," she said, stepping back.

"That is my job," Galen said as he stepped around the bloody and hurt body that knelt before Carling. Standing at Marcus' back, Galen raised his blue sparking sword and looked into Carling's eyes. "I do this in the name of The People. I do this to defend my homeland. I do this to defend my love, the One True Child of the Ancestors." His voice rang out into the empty space that surrounded them.

From out of the raging fire and smoke came seven figures. Each was covered in a long, hooded robe, their faces hidden from view. They arranged themselves around the three and each raised a hand.

"In this act you are absolved from the prohibition on killing one of The People. This is a necessary deed by you in defence of yourself and the One True Child. As your father, I grant you permission to kill this man in order to confine the evil for a while longer," one of the figures said with his hand raised.

The blow was swift as it cut through Marcus. His hazel eyes never once stopped looking at the face of his wife and beloved. In his dying breath he told her he loved her before crumpling to the ground. A pool of blood formed around him, and Carling watched the light leave his eyes as she felt the noose of the bond he had created slip away. She felt the constraint of his constant vigil over her lift and disperse with the smoke of the fire that surrounded them.

Carling finally felt free.

At her side stood two of the hooded figures, while the one who had spoken was now with Galen. The world turned dark for a moment, and when the light returned, they were both standing in the sacred stone circle, the Ancestors spread out between the stones. All evidence of the fight and fire was gone from their skins and clothing, and Carling took in a deep breath of the sweet-smelling air.

"Your tasks are now done, Carling, our child," the woman spoke, coming to stand before her. "The day you have waited for is now here."

"Raise your hand, my son, and accept the hand of the One True Child," the man standing in front of Galen instructed.

Galen raised his hand and looked to Carling. She placed her own in his and they clasped their fingers together. Both the hooded figures reached out and forged between them a ribbon of multiple hues crossed over each other, with a band of gold running through it. The ribbon wound its way around their hands and between their wrists.

"This ribbon represents the bond between you. Galen, do you give yourself to Carling until the darkness is gone from this land?" the Being to his right asked.

The enormity of the promise hit Carling. Their spirits and souls were to be bound together for eternity, forever coming together down the generations.

"I do give myself," Galen said. His face somber while agreeing to the huge act.

"Carling, do you also give yourself to Galen until the darkness is gone from this land?" the woman asked her.

"I do give myself," Carling said. Somewhere far off came the sound of a bell, a deep intoning that acknowledged the pledge, and it made her curious.

"With the tying of the knot you are so bound together. Go with our blessings, our love, and our support," the two said together. They backed away from the couple and stood between the stones with the others.

"My child, we are so proud of you. You stood, and you did what you had to do to rid the evil from the land for the moment. Galen, you stood at her side, lending your support, just as she supported you. Your actions today have helped keep him at bay, and for the deaths of his minions you are absolved. The lives of The People will go on. Down through the ages they will descend and spread out around the world as was foretold. We do not look forward to the next coming of evil. But we have already seen the two who shall face him and the one who will support them. It is now in the hands of your ultimate children. Go now and be happy, my child. Go now and be happy, son of my brother." The remaining Being said as he backed away.

The figures faded from view, and they found themselves once more in the dark. It was the smell of the camp burning that first came to Carling as she opened her eyes again. The heat from the flames burned at her skin, and she could feel it becoming hotter. Her hand still grasped Galen's, and she looked up at him.

"We have to leave before we die," she said to him, and he agreed.

No matter which way they turned, they were faced with a wall of flame. They tried to get through to the gates that she had seen Brietta and Keelie through with the children, but that way was blocked. Carling was becoming desperate and alarmed that they would not make it.

"Can you fly?" he asked her, yelling to be heard over the noise of the flames.

"I have never tried," she yelled back.

"Hold on and don't look down." He grinned at her and placed his arms around her waist, holding on tightly. With their eyes locked, he lifted them up out of reach of the flames and above the smoke. He carried her away and landed safely beside the trees. With his arms still around her, he bent and kissed her.

"I thought…you told me…" Carling stumbled.

"My Ancestor thought I might need to know how to fly." He grinned still.

"I am pleased that he meddled, then," she said.

And I am pleased that you made it out alive. Your cub is hungry, Carling. Bear came out of the trees and made his way towards her. Behind came Brietta and Keelie. In Brietta's arms, Marc was complaining, loud and strong.

Thank you for looking after them, Bear. You will always have a home with us when you want it, Carling told him.

I am grateful, Carling. My time with you is still not done. My protection is now over the cubs. This loud one and the two to come. He had reached her now and she buried her face in his coat, wrapping her arms around his neck.

Brietta was there and passed the child to her. His face was bright red and his arms and legs kicking in frustration at the hunger pains that gripped him. Carling sank to the ground and placed him to her breast, and he took it greedily. She looked up at Galen, who was crouching beside her.

"This is my son, Marcus. He shall carry his father's name. I will not change it. For as much as I hated him, he was kind and gentle towards me. His son will know of his deeds and actions, all of them. I call him Marc," Carling introduced them.

"Marc shall be as much my son as yours. I promise to protect him and raise him as my own. I honour his father for his good deeds and shall try to be a good example for the son," Galen said with his hand on the baby's head.

The rest of the afternoon was spent with the small family group. Cato enjoyed the company of the bear and was asleep leaning up against him. Carling smiled at Keelie's son, as she held her own. Galen had gone to see what was left of the small settlement and the men he had brought with him. They were slowly gathering together by the trees, their numbers growing steadily.

The men were a mix of clans and People both, kin and neighbour. They had fought for their lands and their freedom—fought bravely and strong. Carling was pleased they had come together as one and could see that The People were once again merged into another culture. Their abilities would be passed to another generation, all the while diminishing with time.

With the last of the stragglers came Galen, along with a string of horses and a few carts. Beside him strode the large figures of Longus and Talorgan. Longus' ginger beard was singed, and an arm was in a sling. Carling stood and handed the baby to Brietta and then ran to her uncle. He embraced her with tears in his eyes and did not care who saw them fall. She walked between them back to the fire and introduced the child to her family.

Galen came to her side and sat with her, his arms enclosing both her and the child. The fire that night was nothing compared to the inferno from the day, but it was enough to cook meat on and celebrate. As the sun was going down and the golden-orange glow settled on the land, a large white stag came from the forest and stared at the gathered group. It flicked its tail and turned, stepping back into the dark forest.

Galen stood and faced the men he had gathered for the fight. He raised his cup, and all became silent around them.

"We drink tonight to those who fought with us. May their souls be at peace. We drink tonight for those who fought against us. May theirs never find redemption. We drink tonight for those who have survived and shall go on. May our memories be long, and may our fight be remembered. To the children we wish peace." He drank long from his cup, and everyone else did also.

The morning dawned, and smoke was still filtering up from the embers of the fort. People moved about the little fire as they gathered their belongings together, ready to return to their homes. Galen rose from the cloak that covered both Carling and Marc and went to claim a cart for himself and a horse to draw it. The group broke up with promises to get together in the coming months to plan the march on other forts and camps that the Romans had placed on the eastern side of the land.

Longus led them, mounted on a horse beside his eldest son, while Carling sat with Marc in her arms beside Galen on the seat of the cart as he handled the horses. Brietta sat with Cato and Keelie in the back, as comfortable as they could make themselves on the jostling wooden tray, and with Bear ambling along behind. They made their way past the fort, and Carling did not look at it. The memories that the camp held for her were painful to think of. Her hatred was now abating, but the anger was still there, simmering just under the surface.

They bumped along the road and crossed onto a track. The wildflowers were bursting forth their blooms, and the air was sweet with the smell, while the grass grew richly around them. The river that they followed flowed past, clear and deep. When they stopped for the night, Cato helped Bear fish, bringing six great salmon back to the fire.

No one had talked much that day. Carling was lost in her own thoughts and the needs of the baby. Galen was happy he now had her beside him, and the two women were still coming to terms with the loss of the house that had been their home for so long.

The crannog came into view late in the afternoon. The children who were playing outside called out to the little house over the water, and Bron came out to see who was coming. Longus spurred his horse on and leapt from it, straight into the arms of his wife. Their children surrounded their father and mother, all crying out to be noticed.

The cart came on at a more sedate pace, and from out of the doorway came another couple of figures. Sima and Drest moved down the wooden bridge and welcomed back Longus and Talorgan, and then waited for the cart to stop. Galen jumped down and helped Carling with Marc while the women and Cato climbed from the back.

Brietta greeted her parents warmly, and they, in turn, greeted Keelie and Cato, welcoming them into their family. Bron was over by Carling, fussing over the baby while Longus was laughing and telling her no more children.

There were people missing still from their little homecoming. But their greetings would have to wait until they could travel to see them.

Around the hearth that night, Longus told the others the tale as he had seen it, describing the flames and the battle with the soldiers. His younger boys were wide-eyed and drank in every detail while Talorgan rolled his eyes at his father's exaggerations. His daughters were by their mother and the baby.

Carling took the opportunity while Marc was being cared for, and the others were occupied with the story, to slip out and get some air. The night was a warm one, and she wandered down to the bank of the Loch, watching the reflection of the moon and stars play on the flat surface of the water.

"So, what now for the One True Child?" Sima asked, coming up from behind her.

"A life with Galen. Being a wife and mother," Carling replied as she pulled on a reed and played with it.

"Is that going to be enough for you with all the abilities you have now?"

"Grandmother, I think it just might be. I am content. I am happy it is all over and I have my son to look after," Carling told her wistfully.

"You never thought of, you know, finishing the line?" Sima asked carefully.

"Never! How can you say that? If I did that, then the Ultimate One would not be born. It will be a complicated and trying line, but a necessary one. The father of the one will be my brother's spirit. And my daughters will need him at their side."

"I am just checking, Carling. Some would not blame you if you did."

"He is MY son, Sima. He will become Galen's son." Carling became quiet a moment as she returned her thoughts to what was worrying her. "There is something I have not told Galen yet and I am not sure I should. I could use your advice."

"What is it?" Sima asked.

"Marcus and Galen were half-brothers. They shared a mother."

"This I know, and this Galen also knows. Rowena told him while he was still a child."

"Galen knew he was killing his own brother?" Carling asked in a whisper.

"To Galen he was not a brother. The cousins he grew up with were his brothers. Marcus was just a man who hurt him, killed his kin, and took you away from us," Sima said, taking her hand.

They stayed silent for a while as they listened to the night. The waves lapped at the shore with a soft, gentle sound, and an owl pierced the night with its haunting cry.

"Another thing you must know, Carling. The night you were born, Galen was there. His mother had brought him along to carry her bundle. The birth was not a difficult one, and Breena could have managed on her own, if truth be told. But he was there where he was supposed to be that night. He took one look at you and fell in love. You are the reason he lived after Marcus cut his body to ribbons. You are his life," Sima told her quietly, taking her hand and giving it a squeeze.

"Why do I not remember him from before I was taken, then? I remember my family and places around here. But I do not remember him."

"If you did, then you could not have done what you needed to do. You found him easily enough. His love for you burns brightly, if what you have told me is correct."

"It is the same colour as his eyes." She was pleased it was dark, so Sima could not see her blush.

"Yes, his eyes that do not leave your face for one moment, even when you are out in the dark." Sima pointed to the walkway of the crannog and the dark figure that was standing there watching them. "He does not want to lose you again, I think."

Sima left her side and met Galen halfway across the bridge. She gave him a pat on the arm and carried on into the house. Galen came to her side and placed an arm around her.

"Are you all right?" he asked her.

"I am. I am more than all right."

"I'm just concerned that with all that has happened, that at any minute you might break down."

"The One True Child break down? I do not think so." Carling laughed and laid her head on his shoulder.

"You came out here, away from the family and friends you so desperately wanted to get back to."

"I just needed a moment to breathe. I used to hate the time spent alone, and it seems for the last few days that I have not had a moment to myself."

"Shall I leave you, then?" he asked, and she could hear that he did not mean it.

"I did not say that. With you, I can just be." She sighed and thought about the conversation she had had with Sima. "Sima told me you were there when I was born."

"I was. I told you that. I came with my mother."

"She said that you fell in love with me when I was just a baby."

"That might be a bit extreme. It was the dream, actually. I saw this golden woman before me, and I fell in love with her." He kissed her head. "Then when I saw you standing in my house, I was saddened to find that you were with Veda. The revelation that you were little Carling come home was mind-blowing. I felt I could finally fulfil my duty and take you home."

"But I wasn't with Veda. Poor Veda," she said shaking her head.

"He became reckless, Carling. I warned him that he would end up getting himself killed. I found them. The wolf had—" he started.

"I know. Marcus brought it home as a trophy. It is gone now in the flames. He boasted of killing Veda, that he had killed a man who loved me. That was the day Marc was born."

"We don't have to talk about him, Carling," he said gently.

"I know." She stayed quiet for a moment as she leaned against Galen, feeling the comfort he was giving her. Until she heard Marc crying in the house. "I had best go to him." She tried to pull away from Galen, but he held on to her.

"We will go together to look after our son."

Chapter Fourteen

Galen and Carling made the trek around the loch after a couple days of rest at Longus and Bron's house. A call was sent out for a meeting of the clan chiefs to organise the next raid. News had reached them that people were picking through the remains of the fort and moving further away downriver to start a new settlement.

Accompanying Galen and Carling were Sima and Drest, Brietta and Keelie. Cato walked behind the cart with Bear. The two had become inseparable, and Cato was held in awe by Bron and Longus's younger children. Carling looked behind them at the pair. Cato's dark head was bent and concentrating.

"When did Veda begin his ability, Grandmother?" Carling asked Sima.

"At the normal time that abilities develop, why?" the older woman responded.

"I have a feeling about Cato." Carling smiled as she turned back to the front.

"It is just as well, then, that we are out of the Roman world," Keelie said as she looked at her son and smiled.

"Veda's wife still lives with Talorc and Nessa. We can take you there so that you can talk to her if you like," Sima said to her.

"I think that might pay," Keelie replied.

You could ask me, Bear said to Carling, and she smiled.

So, am I correct? she asked her friend.

Yes, you are. I am helping him slowly. He is young still. But the ability is there and strong. I have already seen who he is partnered with, and it will be a great partnership. Although I cannot see what the fuss is with a horse, be it a stallion or not. But you have the sight. You can see what comes for him. What does your vision tell you, Carling? Bear asked.

Carling took another peek behind her at the boy who followed with Bear. She concentrated for a moment, and the vision made her heart leap with pride for the boy she had helped raise, her brother's spirit. She saw an older Cato, his name changed, leading a charge at the final forces of Rome. He sat astride a large black horse, and they moved as one. His arms and chest were covered in the blue tattoos of the clans but not of their design. The symbols that covered him were of The People.

There; you see, I was right. He has always had a thing for horses; the boy told me of his first ride, Bear said with a chuckle.

I remember it. He wanted to so much be off the lead rope and cantering around by himself, Carling told him.

That was the first time he touched minds with a horse. It has stayed with him since.

How is he? Carling asked, concerned about Cato's state of mind after everything that had happened.

He is finding it hard. He wants to know where his brother is. No one has told him. He is afraid that his brother is still lying hurt in the ashes somewhere, Bear said. I have not told him, as it is not my place. He is not my cub."

I will talk to his mother tonight. He needs to be told, and I am afraid of what he will say when he finds out. He idolised his brother. Carling bit her lip with worry about how Cato would cope with the news.

He might surprise you with his understanding. This is not his first time on our lands.

No, I know it is not. Thank you for your insight, Bear. I appreciate your thoughts.

No thanks needed, Carling. The boy is part of the pack." Bear retracted his mind from hers, and she continued to think on the matter.

They arrived at Galen's house that sat on the other side of the loch, after a few more bumps and finding a suitable place to cross the river that fed the loch, further upstream from the falls. The house was soon swept out and a new fire laid. Sima and Brietta took over the cooking and Carling found herself sitting with Keelie.

"Why does Cato not know what happened at the fort?" Carling asked quietly. She had not known how to approach the subject and decided to just jump into it.

"Because it would cause him too much pain," Keelie said.

"He does not know and is worried that Marcus is still alive somewhere, hurt. Do you want me to tell him?" Carling offered.

"What can I tell him? I don't know what happened in there. No one does. You have not told us." Keelie's voice was low and careful.

"Only Galen knows, and he will not speak of it until I am ready."

"As is right. I think it would be best to come from you, Carling," Keelie said. "Don't think I am leaving it to you because I am afraid to give him the news. Only, I think you could answer the questions that he will have."

"I understand, Keelie. I will talk to him." She moved Marc to the other breast and settled him while she thought about the problem.

Later, after a hot meal, Cato went outside to be with Bear. Carling passed Marc over to Galen for him to get to know and laughed at the way he held the child. Seeing his difficulty, Sima came to his rescue.

Outside, the clouds were gathering in the last rays of the sun, and she wandered over to the copse of trees that hid the house from the track down below. Bear had made a nice sleeping area in there, and that is where she found the pair of them. Cato looked up and smiled at her.

"Bear told me that you would come out tonight, Carling," he said as he moved to make room for her.

"He was right, then. You are young to develop your ability, Cato. I understand Bear has been helping you."

"He is nice to talk to, but I miss my horse," the boy said sadly.

"What about the horse here? Is he not good enough?"

"He was busy with his job and did not have time to talk." Cato pulled at a piece of grass beside him, then asked quietly, "Carling, can you tell me something?"

"I will if I can, Cato. What is it that you want to know?"

"I know you can talk to Marcus. He told me. Can you find him?" His little face was very grave, and she took a deep breath before answering.

"I can't, Cato. Marcus is no longer in this world. He did not make it out of the fire." She placed a hand on his shoulder. "He died so that others may live."

"What happened?" he asked.

"What has your mother told you about the Ancestors?" Carling asked him.

"The Ancestors created our world and there was something evil that they were fighting. She said that you were helping them. I didn't understand that part."

"I will tell you the truth, Cato, because I believe you deserve to know it. Marcus was possessed by the evil that the Ancestors were battling. He died while we were fighting. He begged me to kill him so that the evil could not continue." She sat looking at her hands, waiting for him to yell at her and blame her for his brother's death.

Instead, the boy came to her, placed himself on her lap, and pulled her arms around him. She hugged him close, as she had when he was small, and kissed his head.

"Did you kill him?" he asked her quietly.

"No, it was not me."

"Was it Galen?"

"Yes, it was."

"He died a warrior's death, then." Cato nodded. The sound of tears could be heard in his voice, and he sniffed loudly. Carling held on to him as he cried for his brother. She rocked and sang to him softly as she had when he was a baby. Cato fell asleep in her arms, and she held him still.

Lay him by me. I will care for him overnight, Bear said sleepily. He moved so Carling could place the boy next to him.

Thank you, Bear. Protect him for me.

As is right, Carling. The cub is one of the pack.

She stood and left them to the warm summer night, heading back inside to the hearth.

Drest was nodding onto his chest and Sima, Brietta, and Keelie were talking softly. Galen looked up when she came in. Marc was nestled in his arms, fast asleep. She sat beside him and put her head on his shoulder, smiling at the sleeping form of her own child. His dark hair was sticking out and his tiny mouth working away. Marc stirred and opened his eyes, they sought out her face, and his arms started to tense up and move.

Carling took him from Galen and held him close, crooning to him softly. Marc settled once more, and his eyes slowly closed.

"He knows his mother," Galen said.

"He does indeed," she said to him. "And soon he will know his father."

Drest came wide awake with a shout. He stood suddenly and looked about him. Carling and the others all watched as he started to mutter. Sima was soon at his side, helping him back to his seat. His eyes were wide and following something, his mouth forming words the others could not hear.

"Onnist," he said finally and turned his now focused eyes to Sima. "Onnist is going to the Romans. He will tell them the news of Carling and her abilities. They will come for her."

"They can try," Galen said, getting to his feet. "Where is Onnist now? Did you see him?"

"I could not see. I could not see where my son was." Drest was alarmed and dismayed at the actions of his son. "Sima, he will bring great pain to the world if he succeeds."

"We must get Carling to safety, warn the clans that this battle is coming. The chiefs are meeting in a few days, and we can warn them then," Sima said. "It is too late for our son. He must accept whatever fate comes his way."

"I will not run and hide from them while others die protecting me. I will not sacrifice anyone else," Carling said quietly, her anger gathering quickly. "Let them come."

"What are you talking about, Carling? Think of Marc. Think of our own children yet unborn who are so important to the world. You must be protected," Galen told her, crouching down at her side. "And as for the chiefs knowing what she can do and who she is, I say not. It will be dangerous for them to know it, too tempting for them to use her."

"That is what I was born for, Galen. To fight the evil, to send off the Romans and to bear the children to come," Carling said quickly.

"What if something happens to you?" he asked quietly, taking her hand. "I could not stand to lose you again. Twice in one lifetime is too much, but three will send me mad."

"You will not lose me, Galen. We have been bonded together by the Ancestors themselves. They promised that we will be together not only in this life but others as well."

"You will not be going alone, then," Brietta said. "You cannot and will not leave us behind, Carling. For a start, who will look after little Marc?"

"Yes, you need us to support and care for you," Keelie spoke up, standing by her friend.

"You endanger yourselves rashly. I cannot risk you all." Carling looked around at those in the house, all staring back with determination on their faces.

"We risk ourselves, Granddaughter," Sima said, coming to kneel in front of Carling. "For you, we risk ourselves."

A single tear tracked down her cheek. She was not alone anymore.

The meeting of the chiefs was in shambles. Many of those who lived further out into the wilds of the lands did not want to risk their men, helping those in the thick of the Roman occupation. There was much arguing and fighting amongst them. The discussions went on into the night around the large fire, with no headway made.

Carling and Galen, along with their companions, had travelled to the meeting with their knowledge and heavy hearts. Drest's vision was explained to everyone, and they discussed it much.

Nearing midnight, Carling had finally had enough. She stood from the little fire where she sat with the other women and strode into the circle of chiefs. A stunned silence hit them as they watched her circle the fire. Longus looked at his niece, smiled, and nodded to her, encouraging her to speak.

"There are those who know me here at the fire and many who don't. I am Carling, daughter of Carvorst and Breena of the Boar. I am both of The People and clan. I was enslaved by the Romans, brought up at their fireside. Married to one of them. I saw their cruelty every day. Saw how they treated our people. They will not stop at the lands they are now occupying. They will spread their diseased thoughts and ways throughout our lands. They will not stop until they control it all. You all know of The People and our ways. You all know of our abilities and some of you have them yourselves. I am the One True Child of the Ancestors. Born of necessity. The Romans are the creation of the evil one and must be stopped."

Carling took a moment to look each and every chief in the eye. Her voice was not raised, but each heard her clearly and understood her words. Some were nodding, while others still shook their heads.

"Hark, my words, then, my brothers," Longus said as he stood. "My niece speaks the truth. I have seen what she is capable of and the pain it brought her to do it. I believe that we can push these foreigners from our lands and take back what is rightfully ours once more. Also, there should be no more talk of The People and clans as separate. We are one people. We work together, side by side. The bloodlines have been mixed and there is no separating them. I am in favour of chasing the Romans out. Who is with me?"

Many got to their feet, and only a few remained seated. Those were of clans further into the highlands and the deep glens that were hidden there. One of these stood and faced Carling.

"How are we to believe that this girl is telling us the truth? The talk of the One True Child is but myth in my lands. The visions of our seers have not included her," he said gruffly, still standing waiting for a reply.

"Our seers have. All have seen and reported what they saw. It is recorded in the journals, held by the most sacred," Drest said from the edge of the circle. The man who spoke nodded his deference to Drest.

"But the One True Child is still a myth in our lands," he spoke again.

"Are you demanding a demonstration?" Longus asked him darkly, standing to face the man.

"That is not what I am asking. I would never ask that. It is not the way of The People."

"You are still wanting some sort of confirmation, though?" Carling asked him.

"Yes," he said simply. There were mutterings amongst the others at his admission.

Carling bowed her head and sent out a thought. This was no ordinary thing, and she did not even know if it would work. But she hoped that they would answer her call. She felt it spread wide around the world until it found the two that were needed and brought them to her gently.

Exclamations and gasps sounded around the fire as Carling's two Ancestors appeared beside her. The fire died down to a combination of soft blue and yellow flames that licked at the wood in the hearth, and the light dimmed around them. Each hooded figure placed a hand on her shoulder, and together they spoke.

"This is our child. The One True Child of the Ancestors, our beloved daughter. The sum of all our people is within her. The abilities she holds are vast, more than our own. We have charged her with our tasks, and she has performed them well. There is one more that needs to be completed. This task starts with the purging of the Romans from our lands and will continue down the ages until the evil is gone. Her soul will perform this task and be tied to it forevermore. By her side her soul mate shall stand, their bond secure. It has been seen by us, and the work has already been started to support them. This is our wish. This is their fate. We are all one."

The silence was heavy as each person pondered the words of the Ancestors. The one who had spoken the first words of doubt knelt before her, his hand on his heart.

"I pledge my support to the One True Child and her mate," he said, his head bowed to her. Others followed, and soon Carling was standing alone in the circle, the Ancestors also kneeling before her.

Carling looked around her and found only one who was not kneeling. She faced him and smiled. Carling did not expect to see him kneel and was pleased he hadn't. Galen made his way towards her, stepping between the bent figures, and came to her side. He placed an arm around her shoulders and stood with her.

"I will follow you, Carling. I will follow and support you, but I will not bow down to you. We are partners. Equals," Galen said to her.

"I would have it no other way. You are my husband and my right arm. We are equal. Two halves that make the whole," she told him.

The fire flared once more, and the Ancestors were gone. The chiefs around them stood and cheered for both her and Galen. Longus raised his cup and toasted the couple.

The preparations and discussions ceased that night but continued the next morning. Carling rose and found Galen already in a heated talk between three of the chiefs, each one trying to put their point across. He looked up as he was gesturing wildly about his idea when he caught her smile. She turned and headed towards the makeshift kitchen where Sima and Keelie were working.

"If you are looking for Marc, Brietta has taken him again," Keelie said to her as she kneaded the dough for the bread. "She has taken him and Cato to the river to bathe."

"Thank you, Keelie. It is just about time for his feed. I will go find them." She headed off towards the river and Bear came ambling out of the woods to join her.

Your mate will need to stop talking soon. Otherwise, he will not be able to make a noise, Bear said.

They are making plans, Bear, she replied with her hand resting on his back.

A war with other men. We at least only battle over females, he said sadly.

What if another bear were to come into your territory? Carling asked.

The world is our territory. Now, a fishing spot is another matter. We will even fight females over a prized spot. The bear snorted his laughter.

They came to the bank and followed the sound of Cato's laughter to where Brietta was. The baby was lying on a blanket, freshly washed and changed. His little feet and hands waved up in the air. Bear bent his head and sniffed the child, and a little fist came up and grasped his lip. Carling carefully released the little boy's grip and picked him up.

Brietta and Cato came walking up the bank. Cato was still laughing and reached Carling first, hiding behind her as Brietta came after. Her smile was broader than Carling had ever seen it before, and she soon joined in the fun. A whistle by her ear, and the feel of wind whipping past, startled Carling for a moment.

Brietta stood still, the smile dying on her face as an arrow jutted from her right shoulder. The dampness of her gown helped to spread the dark blood. She fell to her knees, and her hands went around the shaft of the arrow. Carling put Marc down on the blanket and rushed to her friend's side, her own hands moving Brietta's away from the wound and wood of the arrow.

"Cato, go get help. Quickly." The boy stood over them white with shock. "Cato! Now!" She held her friend and placed a hand on the shaft. "It has to come out, Brietta," she said calmly and tried to break off the arrow with her hands.

"No, Carling. I am dying," Brietta said, trying to stop her.

"You will not die today, Mother." Carling gathered her strength and energy together and transferred it to her hands. Again, she tried to snap the wooden shaft, and it gave way. "Okay, now to get the shaft out. I am going to push it through and then try to heal you."

"Carling." Her hands came up and grasped the shaft herself. Carling placed her hands over Brietta's, and together they pushed. Brietta screamed as the head of the arrow pushed through the flesh of her back. Blood erupted from the wound, and Carling placed her hands at both ends.

She closed her eyes and felt the wound with her mind. She found the ragged and torn flesh and started to knit it back together while pushing the excess blood and debris from the puncture holes, cleaning as she went. She found where the blood was coming from and stemmed the flow as best as she could. When she removed her hands, the flesh had knitted together, but it was puckered and red.

As she worked on Brietta, Bear had placed himself between the women and the spot that the arrow had come from. He was watching the trees, and he called out to Carling.

Another! Quickly get to cover! Bear cried out as Carling looked up.

The arrow came speeding towards them, and Carling spotted it. Time slowed in her vision as she stood and waited for it to arrive. Lifting up her hand, she reached out as it neared and grasped it around the shaft as it slipped through her hand and stopped at the fletching. The arrowhead grazed her arm as she caught it. She held it out and dropped it to the ground.

Her mind searched out the area and found the man who was behind the bow and several more were behind him. She sent out a wave of pure energy and reduced them to unconsciousness, falling where they stood.

From the camp, men were running with hastily collected weapons. At their lead was Galen.

"In the woods—there!" Carling called to him and pointed. He raced off where she had indicated, and the men behind followed.

Keelie and Cato soon arrived and rushed to Brietta, looking for the wound that had caused all the blood covering her tunic.

"Carling healed me," Brietta gasped, pushing away Keelie's questing hands.

Carling picked Marc up and held him close, his cries piercing the air. She sank to the ground. Bear still stood between her and the danger, waiting until the men came out of the trees again. Carling fed her son and concentrated on him as she felt the fatigue creep through her, from the strain of using so much energy to heal the wound. Her eyes were closing as she held her son, and Keelie saw her start to tumble to her side.

"Carling, stay with us." Keelie held her up and kept an arm around the baby, holding him in place. Brietta was at her other side, and between the women, they laid her down on the blanket, safely keeping Marc at the breast.

Sima was hurrying towards them carrying a bag of healing herbs and bandages. After checking to be sure her daughter was all right and marvelling at Carling's work, she moved to her granddaughter's side. She placed her hands on each side of Carling's head and entered her mind.

Moving around, Sima searched for Carling and finally found her in the depths, far from her conscious or even her subconscious. Carling was sitting with her back up against a wall as she watched a memory play out before her. The vision she was looking at was one when she was small, a child with golden hair and toddling around, being chased by a boy with dark hair and blue eyes.

"Look what I found," Carling said, smiling at Sima as she sat beside her. "I couldn't remember him, but now I can."

"You both look so happy," Sima said.

"I wish I was that happy now." Carling gave a little sigh and a sad smile. "There are more, so many more memories of him and me. Why could I not remember? Why were they hidden away back here?"

"They were of another life, Carling. You probably pushed them away because they reminded you of happier times with your parents and with Galen." Sima smiled at the image that played before them. The child Galen picked the child Carling up and spun her around.

"Why have you come in here, Granddaughter of my heart?" Sima asked quietly as the visions played on.

"I don't know. I was tired and found myself here. The memories were just there, and now I don't want to leave until

I have seen them all. I want to remember, Grandmother. I need to remember him."

"But he is here already. You need to be making new memories with him."

"There is a reason I found them. There must be. Why after all this time would I just stumble on them? Look at us, at him. He was so happy. When I look into his eyes, sometimes I see so much sadness and pain."

"When I look at the pair of you, I see love and caring. You both have been through so much, but you found each other again. There is hope in the world, Carling."

"Those arrows were for me, Sima. They were meant to kill me." She looked at her hands, which were bunched up in the material of her tunic. "Brietta nearly died because of me."

"She *didn't* because of you. You healed her. My daughter will live because of you, my wonderful and special granddaughter. Now it is time that we went back to the world. Marc needs his mother and Galen needs his wife." Sima stood and waited for Carling to move. Slowly Carling put the memories away with a final, regretful sigh, and she joined Sima as she walked out and back into the world.

The sun was shining down on her and she opened her eyes. The blue of the sky was the same colour as the eyes that were looking down on her. Galen held her in his arms and smoothed the hair from her face. The wonder in his eyes caught at her heart, and she reached up and clung to him.

"I remember you," she whispered in his ear. "I remember us as children, Galen." She moved her hand to the side of his face and passed the memories on to him. She saw his eyes widen at the feelings she had rediscovered.

"I had never forgotten, Carling. How could I ever forget you? Your sunny smile, your golden hair, your laughter, and those eyes—such a soft shade of blue. You are the light in my heart, the very breath that I take. I am only happy when I am around you. You make this life worth living, Carling. I loved you then and I will always love you."

They clung together, reconnecting in their memories of each other. Tears streamed from her face as she remembered her childhood. She became aware of everyone standing around them, and she pulled away, wiping her eyes. Once she was composed, Galen helped her stand, and her foot nudged the arrow. She bent and picked it up. Galen took it from her hands and turned it in his.

"This matches the fletching from the archer we captured." Brietta handed him the remains of the one that had pierced her, and he compared them. "How is this one still intact? What stopped it?"

"Carling. She grabbed it out of the air," Brietta supplied and then noticed the blood on Carling's arm.

"It's nothing, Mother, just a scratch," she said, pushing her hands away and then covering it with her own. Within seconds, the bleeding had stopped, and she pulled her hand away. "Do you have them all?" she asked Galen.

"Yes. They were asleep when we got there. It made it very easy, although I think the other men were a bit disappointed not to swing a sword or axe," he said with a small grin. "I am going to lead a group to find out where they came from. They dress like clansmen, but something doesn't ring true with them."

"Do you think they may be Roman? Some of the men who were not at the fort when it was destroyed, perhaps?" Carling asked.

"That is a possibility. You are going to have to be vigilant, Carling. You were lucky this time, but the next could be far worse."

"I will. Let's get back to the camp. I still have not had anything to eat, and I find myself very hungry." She took Marc from Keelie and held him close. The little boy snuggled into his mother and closed his eyes.

Chapter Fifteen

The group set out with Galen at their lead to track where the strange men had come from. The band that had attacked her was tied and guarded by large clansmen, who carried their weapons threateningly in their hands. When the search party was out of sight, Carling wandered over to Talorgan, who had been left in charge of the guard.

"I wouldn't advise getting too close to them, Cousin," he said in his gruff voice that sounded so much like his father's.

"I want to talk to the one who fired the arrows," she said darkly. "I must see who they are."

"We have had no luck in getting them to talk so far." Talorgan was still barring her way.

"I have other ways. Now you can show me who he is, and I can sift through his mind, or you can make it difficult, and I can put you to sleep so you stay out of my way." Her hands were clasped in front of her, and she stared him down.

"As you wish, Cousin. The one by himself is the man you seek." He nodded in the direction and stepped out of her path. Carling followed his gaze.

To one solitary tree, a man was tied by his hands to a limb. His face was bloodied, and his clothing torn. Carling moved closer to him and Talorgan followed.

"Why was he beaten?" she asked curiously.

"When he didn't tell us what we needed to know, a few blows found their way to his face and body." The matter-of-fact way he spoke irked her a little.

"Why can't you men just ask before you go beating people up?"

"Because that is the way we are made—react first, then ask questions. Plus, I am clan and not one of your lot, Carling."

"One of my lot, Cousin dearest?" she turned to him with a sweet smile.

"You know what I mean. One of The People," he said quickly.

"I know what you mean, I'm just teasing you." She crouched down in front of the man and saw the bruising and swelling that had appeared due to the beating they had given him.

"This is not my work either, Carling," Talorgan told her.

"No. I know who did this." She reached out and lifted the man's head up. He groaned and opened his eye. The other was so swollen shut, it was just a slit in the stretched skin. "Do you want me to heal you?" she asked him in the speech of the Romans.

"I want nothing from you, witch!" He spat at her, and a gobbet of phlegm and blood hit her face.

Carling wiped it off and stood as Talorgan was about to kick him. "No, Cousin. That does nothing to help." She placed a hand on his chest.

"But he disrespects you."

"I know he does, but he has been taught to hate. It is not this man's fault that his education was not the one he would have received had he been born of our people." She knelt beside the man once more and placed a hand on his head. "Please don't fight me. I just want to take your pain away and make you a bit more comfortable."

The man tried to jerk his head away, but she held firm. Inside his mind now, she sent out calming thoughts and felt him slowly stop his resistance. She moved through the untrained mind and found it so much different from those who had abilities. It was more enclosed, dark, and grey, and it made her remember Marinus' mind.

Walking through the empty space, she found him cowering in a corner, his hands over his head and shaking like a leaf. Slowly Carling walked to him and sat down in front of him.

"I am not going away. I only want to talk," she told him softly. "Can you tell me your name?"

"No, no, I won't. You are not here with me. Get out of my head." He was rocking back and forth.

"If you won't tell me your name, then I will have to go look for it, and it could cause you more pain. I don't want to hurt you. You should not have been hurt in the first place."

He pulled his hands from his head and stared at her with wide eyes.

"I saw you pluck my arrow from the air like it was a feather falling. You are the witch the lieutenant was talking about. You were the commander's wife," he whimpered.

"I was his wife, yes. But I am no witch. I understand what the term means, and it saddens me that your people do not hold those with abilities in higher regard. Our purpose is not of hate and malicious intent, as some of your stories tell. Ours is one of peace and love. Will you tell me your name?" she asked again.

"They say you killed him, the commander," he stammered on.

"I did not kill him. That was done by another. I do not wish to speak of him. We did what we had to do, and it gave me great pain to do it. Your people are here because you have been used as the tools of an ancient evil. Your time is up, and you must leave. The evil cannot help you anymore. The time of the Romans is done."

"We have a mighty empire at our back. It reaches to all corners of the world. Romans are strong and mighty," he told her defiantly.

"I tell you that I have seen the demise of your lands. The people your countrymen have enslaved and conquered will rise up and defend their homelands, wrestling them back under their own control. Rome will be sacked, and the empire decimated. There will be no more emperors sitting on the throne of Rome," she told him gently.

"That cannot be! We are strong and stable. We will rule all," he told her emphatically.

"What is your name?" Carling asked again gently.

"I am Stanislas. Stanislas Sergius."

"Thank you, Stanislas. Now I can heal you." She closed her eyes for a moment and concentrated. Before her, Stanislas tensed as he felt the pain disappear and the bones that had been broken stitch themselves together.

"Why did you do that?" he panted after it was finished.

"Because I needed to. You were hurt, and I could not let you suffer anymore. You should not have been beaten. I already know that you were part of the fort. How did you find out about me?" she asked and dreaded hearing the confirming answer she already knew.

"I will not give you any information," Stanislas told her.

"Stanislas, I can make you tell me, but that would mean more pain for you. I did not expend my energy healing you for that to happen. The pain will not be physical. There will be no bruises and broken bones. The pain will be inside your mind, and it will linger. Were you at the fort when the previous commander was in charge?" she asked him slowly.

"Marinus, yes. He was a great general."

"He died because of the pain I inadvertently inflicted upon him."

"You killed him also."

"He tried to rape me. I did not know what I was doing to him when I fought back."

"You were a slave. It was his right."

"It is not the right of any man to rape a woman," she said darkly. Her anger rose to the surface, and she tried to push it down.

"We had a running bet on who would bed you first. I was one of the men who found you as a child. What did Marcus call you? Tacita?"

"Tacita and Flora are both dead. They died with Marcus. Now tell me how you came to find out about me." Her voice was flat and dangerous, and he blinked at the change in tone.

"One of your people came to us and told us who was responsible for the fire. He said that you had set it along with the other rebels, including a man named Galen," he said quickly.

"Onnist?"

"Yes, that is his name."

"What else is there? I sense there is more."

"When they go looking for the rest of us, they will be slaughtered. Onnist does not like you one bit, witch."

Carling pulled away from him so fast that she felt dizzy, and he groaned and passed out. Talorgan steadied her and helped her stand.

"What is it? What did he say?" her cousin asked quickly.

"There's a trap," she told him breathlessly. She held on to his arm and concentrated on Galen. She was at his side in a moment and startled him as he crept through a wood.

"Carling, what is it?" he asked worried.

"There is a trap. It was designed to lure you into it. They were to kill me, so you could follow them. Be careful."

"Can you sense where these other Romans are?" he asked her, crouching down behind a bush for a moment to listen to her.

"Yes. Further up the valley they wait for you to pass. There are more to box you in. Come back, my love. Come back so we can organise properly," Carling begged him.

"You have given me all the warning I need. There is nothing to plan out now. We will be back soon. Take care and look after yourself and Marc." He stood and started to advance again.

"Galen, please, come back. Or am I to come to you?"

"No. I could not do what I have to do if you were here. Please, Carling, on this one let me do what is best," Galen whispered to her as he kept walking on.

"Be careful, Galen," she said as she pulled away from him.

"Gods, you have a strong grip, Carling," Talorgan said as he pulled away from her, rubbing his arm.

"Where is a horse?" she asked him.

"What do you need a horse for?"

"Men!" Carling exclaimed and ran from him. He hurried after her as she rushed to where the horses had been picketed. She grabbed up a lead and started to place it on the first horse she came to.

"Carling, where are you going?" he yelled at her. His voice carried over the camp, and others looked their way.

"I have to go and help. There are so many lying in wait." She pulled the horse over to him and stopped. "Help me up."

"No, I won't! You can't just run off."

"I can, now help me up," she demanded.

"No." He was backing up away from her, shaking his head.

"Fine." She pulled her energy and lifted herself up. The horse skittered about and away from where she was hovering. *I can't convince you and keep like this, Horse. Please just stay still.*

Finally, Carling was on its back, and she dug her heels into its flanks. The horse bolted away, and she crouched low over its neck. *Thank you, Horse,* she sent the message to the animal.

We are in a hurry, yes? I like to run. I run fast like the wind. The other herd members don't run as fast as me, the horse spoke back to her. He was very young, and he put on another burst of speed.

Carling focused on Galen and found where he and the other men were. They were climbing a hill to outflank the Romans that were hiding. She showed the direction to the horse, and he turned slightly. The ground below them was flashing by so fast. She transferred more energy into the creature who was carrying her closer and closer to Galen, her heart beating in her chest as fast as the hooves were hitting the ground.

She saw them descending into the valley, flanking the enemy. The horse ran on, eating up the distance. They were moving towards the Romans on silent feet, each readying themselves for the battle that was to come.

Carling urged the horse on.

Cresting the hill, she looked down at the valley below. The wood covered half of the floor below, so thick and dense she could not see through it. A flash of red cloak caught her eye, and she spurred the horse down the hill towards it. The man was running fast on his feet, going for help. Sounds of battle came from the trees as she passed them and gave chase to the one who had broken the ranks.

He looked behind him at the sound of hoofbeats, and his eyes widened. He sped up, trying to outrun the horse on his sandaled feet.

I am sorry to ask this of you, Horse, but we need to run him down, Carling called out.

It will be as you wish. The horse kept up his pace and soon caught up to the man. He screamed as the horse knocked him down, and he tumbled under the hoofs. The bloodied body rolled like a rag doll and came to rest on his stomach.

Horse turned at her command, and they raced their way into the woods. He slowed as they entered under the low branches and leapt effortlessly over fallen logs. Carling held on tightly to him as he weaved his way towards the sounds of the battle and then pulled him up when she saw the first men fighting.

Feeling each individual person in the woods, Carling called for a stop—not with her voice, but with her mind. Clan and Roman alike froze mid-strike. Their war cries stuck in their throats and the woods went silent. Very carefully they picked their way through the stationary men until she found Galen. She climbed off the horse and went to his side. He was on the ground, about to roll out of the way of a sword that was poised to strike him down.

Carefully she made him aware, and he continued his movement, coming to his feet. His axe in hand, he turned to face her with it raised. Pulling himself up for a moment, he stared around him at the frozen figures.

"What are you doing here, Carling?" Galen roared at her. "You could have gotten yourself killed."

"I seem to remember you saying that we would stand together. This is not together, Galen," she yelled back at him.

"War is not a pleasant thing. I was protecting you like I should."

"I do not need protecting. I can protect myself. Remember, I am the One True Child, who can stop the world if she wanted."

"I do not want you killing anyone. Let me be your sword arm."

"Too late for that," she said, her voice lowering. "I have already run down a messenger."

Galen dropped his axe to the ground and closed his eyes at the thought of her going against the Ancestors' wishes. "What are we to do, then? Keep arguing while these men are in mid-battle?"

"No. I do not want to argue, Galen. There has to be another way we can deal with these men."

"Then what do you suggest, oh great One True Child?" he asked sarcastically.

"Don't do that again, Galen," she warned him. "I will allow you one time only to throw it in my face."

"I am sorry, Carling." He came to her and placed a hand to her face. "What is it you wish to do with them?"

"I could place a suggestion and let them walk away, far away from the lands of the Ancestors. Or I could stop their hearts now and let them fall where they stand."

"I think the first option would be better. But you had better do it before you wake our men up. They will not take kindly to the enemy just turning and leaving. They will want to chase them down and kill each one. The attack on you they saw as an attack on their honour in keeping you safe," he told her gently.

"I will do it now so that they have time to get away." While he still held her, she closed her eyes and sent out the message. She touched each individual mind of the Romans around them and planted the deep need to turn and walk away and to keep walking. She added for them to abandon their Roman ways and live in the forests and meadows of the world, well beyond the borders of the Ancestors lands.

With a wave of her hand, they started to move again. Some were already stripping off the armour that encased them as they walked away from the battle. Carling and Galen watched them leave and waited a good while before awakening the men who had followed him. To them, Carling suggested that they had won a great victory, and it was time to head back to camp. The men clapped each other on the back and congratulated themselves as they gathered together to head back to camp.

Carling sought out Horse and called him to her. He came trotting through the forest and she rose up onto his back. She turned the horse the opposite way from the men, and Galen held the reins before she could move off.

"Where do you think you are going now?" he asked her, knowing exactly what she was going to do.

"Do you want to come with me?" Carling asked with a grin.

"Of course, I do. I will not let you go alone. For a start, you need to know how to track properly," Galen told her as he hauled himself up behind her and wrapped an arm around her waist.

"I already know how, but if you wish to guide us, I will not object." Carling smiled as she leaned back against him, feeling weary from her efforts.

"You already know where they are, Carling. Lead us on." He kicked the horse's flanks, and he moved off. By the time they had broken out of the trees, they were already passing the once Roman soldiers who were now looking for a better life.

With great ease, the horse carried the pair and unerringly led them to the other platoon of soldiers. From a safe distance she performed the same command, and they watched them leave and then turned back to head to camp.

They moved slower now, enjoying the time together without the demands of anyone else around them or the baby crying. Horse took no direction from them, but he knew the way home.

When we get back, Horse, there is someone I would like you to meet, Carling told the young stallion.

I have already met him. He and I are of the same mind, and he has already ridden on my back, the horse said happily.

I have seen great things for the pair of you.

The foretelling of the future does not interest me, True Child. Only that he and I will be one. The horse lifted his head and neighed. They were close to camp now, and from behind a tree Cato came running.

With the immediate danger past, Carling relaxed that night in the company of her family and friends. She leaned against Galen, his arm draped around her and Marc asleep in her arms. Happy and healthy the three were, and she thanked her Ancestors for that. Across the fire she watched as one of the chiefs was paying particular attention to Brietta, and Carling smiled as she indulged in a little foresight.

There was no more discussion that night, just celebration at the victory. The Romans in their area had been defeated, but there were still more in the lands. It would be some time before they left for good, and that was a fight to be left up to Cato. She turned her attention to the young boy and noticed how much he had grown. The Roman traits she used to see all the time in him, were fast changing as he spent more time with the men of clans and People.

Keelie was another matter. She looked lost and afraid, adrift now from the life she had grown used to and had spent most of her life in. Carling became worried for her. Her former mistress turned her head and saw her staring and smiled. A flash of insight came to Carling, and she saw her with a man who cared deeply for her and who would adopt Cato as his own. That man was not at the fire, but she felt him close by.

Sima and Drest were sitting together, their heads close, talking quietly. It was as if the rest of the world did not exist except for them alone. She knew that their son's actions had hurt them deeply and there was no way of her making it right for them. Her mind wandered a moment until she found where he was.

Alone on a dark road, Onnist was huddled beside a small fire. His clothing was in rags, and he was unwell. He shivered with a high fever and started to fit. Carling called out to him and tried to help, but she was held back by the sudden appearance of an Ancestor.

"You cannot help him, my child," the woman spoke.

"But he is ill. I can cure him," she begged.

"No, you can't. The evil has left him, and this is the result of that. It is his time to pass over to us. He will face his actions at the sacred circle when his soul comes to pass."

"Please be gentle with him."

"That is for us to decide, my child. But your empathy for him does you credit."

"Can I stay with him until he does pass? Can I bring his mother to him?" Carling asked.

"Yes, you may. We will allow that to happen. He is not long for this world, Carling, and you will meet in another." The figure evaporated into the air, and Carling brought herself back to the fireside. She stood and passed the sleeping child to Galen and then went to Sima's side.

"Grandmother, there is something very important we must do, and it must be done now," she said to the old woman.

"What is it?" Sima was alarmed at the urgency of her voice.

"I will explain, but we must go away from the fire to do this. Please, we don't have much time."

"I will come." Sima stood and followed Carling away from the fire, out into the dark meadow beyond. Carling stood in front of Sima and took her hands.

"I have seen Onnist, and he is sick. The Ancestor told me he is not going to make it. I asked if I could help take you to him. Would you like to go to your son?"

"Carling, if that is possible, then yes. Is he far?"

"We do not need to travel by foot to see him. He is in need of his mother's kind words." Carling closed her eyes and prepared herself.

The world shifted for the pair, and soon they were standing on the side of the fire opposite Onnist. It was dying down to embers, and Carling made it flare again to keep the man warm. She moved to his side and gestured for Sima to do the same.

Sima knelt by her son and reached out to touch him but stopped halfway there. Carling nodded, and she grasped his hand, feeling his fevered flesh in her own. His eyes opened at the touch, and he smiled when he saw his mother.

"I must be dreaming. Ma, you are here," Onnist said in a weak whisper.

"I am, my son. I am here. Shush now, it is all going to be all right." She smoothed the damp hair from his forehead and pulled him into her arms. "Ma is here to help her sweet boy."

Carling sat beside her and Onnist looked her way.

"I am sorry, Carling. I was turned the wrong way. You are so much more than just a beautiful woman, and I was so mad when you rejected me. I have loved you since I saw you." He struggled to speak, his voice low and shaky.

"Don't talk of such things, Onnist. They are in the past. We all love and care about you, and you are forgiven. There was another force who turned your head and made you believe what you did. He was to blame, not you. I understand that, and your parents will too," Carling told him.

"We do, my son, we do understand and love you." Sima kissed his brow and rocked him as she had when he was small.

"I am pleased I am having this dream. It means so much to me. I hope I remember it when I wake." His eyes were drooping, and his speech was slowing and barely audible.

"Sleep now, my boy. Sleep and sweet dreams. May the Ancestors protect you on your journey and may they have mercy on your soul," Sima said as his breathing became laboured and rattling in his chest. "We love you, our son. Da and Ma love you."

Tears trickled down Carling's face as she watched Onnist take his last breath. He let it out and took no more. The fire died down beside them and she called out to the Ancestors.

"He is gone. Onnist, son of Sima and Drest, brother to Brietta and Una has left this world. Take charge of his soul and have mercy and pity on him. Welcome him into your realm and take care of him. Forgive the actions of this life and reward him with another."

The seven Ancestors answered her call and stood around them, their hands raised over the mother and child. A soft murmuring emitted from them, and a shade of Onnist stood before them. Sima carefully laid his body back onto the ground and stood to meet her son one last time. Carling came to her side and took her hand.

"Thank you, Carling, for bringing Ma to me. Thank you for not letting me die on my own." She nodded her acknowledgement to him, and he then turned to his mother. "I am sorry for causing you such heartache, Ma. I see the error of my ways now clearly in hindsight. You tried to warn me that the way I was thinking was wrong, but I had a voice telling me another."

"I know, my son. There is nothing that can change the past now. Rest well, and go with your father and mother's love," Sima said, her voice trembling at the words.

Onnist walked towards the circle of Ancestors and through a gap they had made. As he passed through, he faded from their sight, and Sima gave a great wail. Carling held her in her arms and comforted her as much as she could, weeping tears of her own at the passing of Onnist. Looking through her tears, she could see the Ancestors slowly winking out one by one until only two remained.

"You know what must be done, Carling, and you have the abilities to see it through," the hooded man said.

"It will hurt her to see it," Carling said with sadness in her heart.

"It must be done. As Marcus was consumed, so must Onnist. The evil will remain for as long as their bones are whole. If he should return too soon, then it would become impossible for you to stop him," he told her.

Carling nodded and moved Sima away from her son's body. She stood over him and raised her hands. The fire flared once more and illuminated the ground around them. The heat was intense, and Sima stepped back from it, fearing being burnt. The light changed from a soft orange glow of flames to an intense white-golden light, and it was dazzling to look at.

At her feet, the body caught alight and burned just as brightly. Carling held her ground and gritted her teeth against both the brightness and the smell. His body was consumed by the fire, reduced to ashes, and she lowered her arms when the flames winked out. Carling stumbled at the effort she had expended, and Sima was at her side.

"It is done," the woman said from under her cloak. "His ashes will spread throughout the land, and he will walk this earth once more. It cannot be guaranteed that he will be a help to the two, or he will become an enemy."

The two Ancestors came to stand beside her, and each reached out a hand to her. She took them in her own and felt how warm their touch was.

"You need to travel to the sacred stones once more, our child. There is something important that needs to happen there. The one who guards the stones is impatient to meet you," the woman said.

"Our blessings go with you and your little family, Carling. We will watch over you."

"Thank you, my ultimate mother and father. Thank you for your gifts and your love." She bowed her head and closed her eyes. Carling felt their hands slip from hers and their presence leave them to the night. When she opened them again, Sima was at her side.

"I think we had best get back, Carling. Drest will want to know." Tears still tracked down her wrinkled face, and Carling kissed her cheek.

"I think we had." She took her hand, and the world shifted under them once more.

"Thank you, Granddaughter, for taking me to his side. Thank you for forgiving him." She held on to her hand for a moment before letting it go and walking away, back to the fire and her husband.

Carling watched as Sima approached the old man and laid a hand on his shoulder. She bent and whispered into his ear, then took a hand and led him away to tell him the news. Carling walked back slowly to the fire and to Galen's side. Marc opened his eyes and watched his mother come towards him and started to squirm in Galen's arms.

Galen caught her expression—which she quickly covered—and knew something important had happened, but at that moment Carling was not willing to say what it was. He handed Marc to her and watched with great delight as she began to feed him, his arm around her protectively once more.

"We need to go visit your mother," Carling said as she raised her son to her shoulder to tap the wind from him. "Before the summer is out."

"We will leave in a couple of days." He smiled at her. "Are you sure you are ready to meet her?"

"Yes, I am. I know she grows impatient that we are taking so long."

"So long? How does she know about you? About us?" he asked very confused.

"I think she was visited by the Ancestors." A small grin played on her lips.

"Also, we have only just been betrothed," he whispered in her ear.

"That ceremony was no betrothal," Carling said, her grin broadening. "It was a bonding of the highest degree. We are not betrothed, we are married," she corrected him.

"But wait…there was the knot ceremony that is only at the betrothal. There is a whole other ceremony for becoming married," he said, his voice rising a little.

"The ceremony was performed by an Ancestor of mine and yours. That beats the druid's betrothal. The marriage will be acknowledged down through the ages, forevermore. In our lives to come, we will find each other and be together."

"I thought that was just…you know, just…" He stumbled over his thoughts.

Carling suppressed a laugh and hid it by changing shoulders with Marc.

"If you wish to consider it just a betrothal, then we can have the wedding ceremony when the betrothal time is finished," she told him seriously.

"Bound for eternity," he whispered softly. His eyes met hers and held them fast. "So, I pledged, and so it shall be. For eternity my heart shall be yours."

"And mine shall belong to you. I will know you, Galen. I will recognise you. How could I not with those beautiful blue eyes of yours?" She leaned in to kiss him, and Marc wriggled between them, letting out a loud and long burp.

They waited a few days before setting off to see Galen's mother. They travelled slowly in the cart, with Bear bringing up the rear. The farewells had all been said, and they were long and sad. Carling went to each and said her goodbyes, imprinting their faces and energy into her mind so she could find them easily. When she came to Talorgan, he pulled her aside for a moment.

"When you come back, Cousin, try to convince Galen to become chief. Da is all well and good, but he is not suited for it. He only wanted to be chief because of your da; he wanted to carry out Carvorst's wishes."

"I don't think Galen will want to," she told him gently.

"Well, then, it will be forced on him. The other men are thinking the same as I am. There is no better man to follow than him. He is fair and honest. My father would be much happier handing it over to him—once I convince him, of course," Talorgan said as he smiled through his ginger whiskers.

"I will let him know what you are all thinking," she told him. "But I am not promising anything."

"Good. Oh, and there is a broch already being built on the other side of the hill for you to use." He grinned at her.

"No. I would really rather stay on this side, Talorgan, within site of the loch," she objected.

"Too bad; your things will be moved before you get back." He laughed at her reaction and went to stand by his father.

Carling shook her head at his stubbornness and went to take Marc from Brietta's arms. As she hugged the mother of her heart, she whispered in her ear. "This time next year, you will have one of your own and not someone else's to raise." When she pulled away, Brietta's eyes were wide, and she blushed when she looked at the man who had been courting her.

The track was bumpy as they travelled, and the going was hard through the woods. Eventually they left the cart where it stood, blocked in by the trees, and carried on by foot. They passed over the river at the shallowest point and carried on up the track until they came to a large, old oak.

Carling moved towards it and placed a hand on the great trunk. The energy was there. The awareness in the tree welcomed her, and she felt the love coming from it. In his sling, Marc started to fuss and wriggle. She could sense he was not happy near the tree, and with some regret, she left its side and returned to Galen, who was waiting patiently.

"There are seven great trees in the lands," she told him as they carried on up the track. "Each one very special, each containing the presence of an Ancestor. I have found two, a great yew and that oak."

"Do you know where the others are?" Galen asked her.

"No, but I fear for them. One day there will be less forest and woods in the land. I can only hope that they survive."

"They are the Ancestors. I am sure they can look after themselves," he said, and they walked in silence for the rest of the way.

Finally, they made it and found the little house in the valley. It was tucked up against the joining of two hills to one side of the brook that tumbled down and out into the valley.

A woman stood in the door, waiting for them to come closer, then she walked out to greet them.

"Galen, my son, it is about time you came back to see me." Her laughter was light and sounded sweet to Carling.

"Hello, Ma. I have brought my family to meet you," he said and placed an arm around Carling.

"The One True Child," Rowena said, stopping in front of Carling. "You are as beautiful as the Ancestors say. And the little boy, Marcus. He will grow to be so unlike his father. He will be happy and not a touch of evil in him." She smiled at Carling.

"Thank you, Rowena," she said to Galen's mother.

"Call me Ma. And you could have seen it, if you would only allow yourself to do so." She ushered them inside, and they were soon settled.

Carling liked Galen's mother from the moment she saw her. There was no artifice, no mystery. They talked easily together, and Galen was happy to see them get on. The next few months were peaceful and relaxing for Carling, with the domestic duties she shared with her mother-in-law. They worked well together while Galen worked on the maintenance of the house.

Late one night, Rowena woke both Carling and Galen up with an urgent shake.

"Wake, you two. They are waiting for you."

"What are you talking about, Ma?" Galen said sleepily.

"You are wanted up at the stones, son. The Ancestors need you both," she said as she threw their tunics at them and told them to dress. "Now up and go. You can't keep them waiting. It needs to be done by the middle of the night. It is a special night, a special moon."

The couple was soon dressed and heading out the door. Carling looked up above them and saw only stars twinkling in the night sky. There was no moon. Rowena hurried them away, and Galen led her up the path that ascended the hill.

When they came to the first switch, awaiting them was an Ancestor who started to walk before them. At each turning, another joined them until they were being led by all seven. Walking on silent feet, they passed the large up thrust of rock and the spring that sent out its tinkling waters to the valley below. They entered the stones and stepped into place between each rock, while Carling and Galen stayed by the entrance watching.

They raised their arms into the air and began to chant. The words she understood and could see Galen did not.

"They are asking the highest one for favour, the light that they came from. They are bringing down their blessing and ask to be made one for a moment," she told him, and figures began to walk towards the center.

A flash of light blazed from the point where the seven merged, and when it diminished, only one stood. She beckoned them into the circle, and they entered; hand in hand, walking together to meet her.

"Our children, my blessing on you both. In this circle shall the spark of the two be created." She raised her hand, and the knot was once more binding their hands together with the brightly hued ribbon. "This union between our children is sacred, and none shall sunder it. It is blessed by the light, the one from whom all come." The Being rested her hand on their joined ones.

"Though they may be separated after their lives, they shall come together as sisters once more to drive the evil from the land with the help from their brother. These three will find love and happiness of their own, and from the brother shall come the one, the Ultimate. The one who will once more join those of the north and those of the south, who have been parted too long. The one whom the world awaits as a teacher, a leader, a healer, and more."

The hooded figure removed her hand from theirs and moved to the entrance of the circle. She turned to face them and then disappeared. Galen and Carling stood in the center, still staring at where she had been. Galen went to move from the standing stones, but Carling held him back.

"I think we are supposed to stay here," she said quietly to him, looking up at him from under her lashes a small smile playing on her lips.

"And do what? Wait for the moon to rise?" he asked, not realising what she was saying.

"I can think of something we could do while we wait." Carling pulled him to her and reached up and kissed him gently. Finally understanding took him, and he reached around her and held her tightly.

"Here?" he asked, looking around, expecting to see figures still in the spaces between the stones.

"Yes, here. It is important that it is here, in the sacred spot, with the blessing of the Ancestors still on us." She turned his face back to her and whispered to him, "Make love to me, Galen. Here and now, let us share our love with the world."

Epilogue

Marc toddled around outside the door on unsteady feet, squealing with delight as Galen chased him. His chubby little face was glowing red, and his little hands were balled into fists as they waved around. Galen caught him up and lifted him high into the air, then put him back down to the ground on his sturdy little legs.

"Da, again! Da, again," he called out with great enthusiasm. Galen lifted Marc onto his shoulders and galloped around like a horse, making the noise of thundering hooves. Marc hung on to his long hair and laughed heartily.

A great scream rent the air and Galen stopped, looking up at the stone house that the clans had built them before they came back from his mother's home at the sacred stones. Again, another cry rang out, and he lifted Marc from his shoulders and held the little boy's hand.

"Ma?" Marc asked, looking up at his tall father.

"Yes, Son. That is Ma, but there is nothing to fear. She is having your sisters," he told him, still looking at the broch. A baby cried out, a loud, healthy cry. "That is one. The other shouldn't be far away."

Galen walked over to the stone seat by the door and sat down. Marc climbed up on his knee and leaned against him. Again, they could hear Carling cry out in pain as the second child began to be born. They waited and waited until the sound he had been wanting to hear came to him. Another healthy cry.

"Baby?" Marc asked his father.

"Yes, that is the second. Shall we go see if we can meet your sisters?" Galen asked the boy.

Marc nodded his head very solemnly, and Galen stood up and held him on his hip. They entered the stone entrance and walked further into the house. Very carefully, they climbed the steps set into the wall and headed to the upper level. Lying on the bed was Carling, her hair damp from her labour, and in each arm a tiny baby. They had come a month early, and Brietta, Keelie, Bron, and Sima were all worried about how small they were.

Looking at them, Galen knew that they would survive. These were the two they had waited for. Their daughters. He put Marc down on the bed and went to Carling's side, looking at the tiny girls. One with dark hair, the same shade as his own, and the other with gold, like her mother. He leaned down and kissed Carling and sat down on the bed at her side.

"I have something for you, my love," he said and gently held out a stone attached to a length of leather thong. The light-coloured stone was round and polished. The engraving he had placed on it was a boar. Gently he placed it over her head and kissed her again.

"Thank you, Galen. It is beautiful. I shall wear it always," she told him.

"Babies," Marc said as he stood on the bed at Galen's shoulder.

"Your sisters," Carling said, smiling up at her son.

"What are we to name them?" Galen asked her.

"The names that they are to be known by when the time comes. This one is Claire." She handed the dark-haired girl to

Galen to hold. "And this one Carling." She passed the second child into the arms of their father.

Galen looked at the pair, so different, but so perfect. He kissed each little head. "Claire and Carling," he whispered their names. "Perfect."

"Care, Carl," Marc said as he looked down at the pair, his little tongue having trouble with their names. "Sissers."

"Come here, my boy." Carling held out her arms to her son and he toddled over to her and fell into them. "You are their big brother and must look after them, care for them, and love them. That is the duty of a big brother."

The little boy nodded and gave his mother a kiss. At that moment Claire began to cry, the cry of a hungry child. Galen passed the little bundle back to her mother, and Marc moved out of the way and watched as the child fed. He sat beside his father and the baby Carling, reaching out to take her hand in his.

"Sisser," he said again.

To be continued far into the future...

The One True Child saga continues…

Many generations have passed since Carling first faced Chaos' rage. With each incarnation, his desire to find and claim her gifts grows. In modern times, Claire is like any other 17-year-old, until the ancient evil reaches out awakening her abilities.

AWAKENINGS

Book 3 of the One True Child Series

The first few stars of the evening were just starting to twinkle into existence as the last of the sunset's ruddy glow disappeared in the windows of the surrounding buildings. The bright reflections were soon replaced with the illumination of fluorescent lighting from within. Traffic below snaked through the narrow streets, honking and revving as people tried to get home from their daily lives while the city started to wind up into its own nightlife. From somewhere in the distance Christmas music blared from a shop, competing with the *thump, thump, thump* beat coming from a nearby bar along with the noise of its patrons. It was the heartbeat and rhythm of the city, which brought out the best in some but the worst in others, reflecting the often gritty and grimy streets that surrounded them.

Above these streets and noise stood two teens looking down at the alley, which—from their perspective—looked like the Grand Canyon dividing two identical buildings. Claire leaned out over the abyss. Her hands rested on the low wall, the only barrier to a five-floor drop to the hard, dark pavement below. The large hand of Adam pulled her back to safety, and she shook him off.

"Come on, Claire; you're never going to be able to jump that!" he said to her. Adam pointed the camera that seemed to be permanently adhered to his hands at the gap before them, filming the distance between buildings, and then pointed it back at Claire. "You're crazy! I think you have gone bloody mental on this one." Adam's face was knitted into a worried frown.

"Watch me," Claire said determinedly, plugging her earbuds in and cranking up the music to drown out the surrounding noise. She jogged to the opposite side of the roof and turned back to face Adam. A look of concentration set on her face, she let out a couple of deep breaths and waited until a certain part of the song came up. Drums beat suddenly in her ears, loud and fast, and Claire started her run-up. Determination exuded from her while her long blonde hair, caught up in a ponytail, flew behind; her large blue eyes fixed on the spot she knew she must leap from. Her heart thumped in time with her footsteps, and the heavy beat pounded away in her ears while her arms pumped at her sides. It was only a matter of seconds until she reached the point of no return, but to her, time stretched out and slowed.

Her foot reached for the invisible mark on the low wall, and she pushed off with all her strength. This was what she lived for, the feeling of flying, of nothing underneath her. The freedom of open air and not being tied to the ground always made her wish she was a bird and could continue to the horizon. Adrenalin pumped through her veins and heightened her senses. She could see her landing spot; she visualised it, and all too soon it came rushing up to meet her. First her right foot, then her left contacted the roof, and she went into a tumble to slow herself down. She came back up on her feet and raised both fists into the air in triumph.

"Suck that, Adam! Told you I could do it!" she yelled at him and then danced around in a circle.

"You're a freak, Claire Brown!" He laughed and continued to film her.

"Well, are you going to try it?" she called out to him.

"Nuh-uh, not me! I'm not stupid enough to try that stunt. This one is all yours." He bowed to her with an exaggerated flourish. "Meet you down on the street and we can go over the footage from tonight."

Claire nodded and then went looking for the fire escape at the back of the building.

Once back on the street, Claire waited at the entrance to the alley. She was only seventeen and was fast gaining a reputation as being the best freerunner in the city. Her best friend since childhood, Adam Ryder, was always her cameraman. He enjoyed freerunning as much as Claire but was the first to admit that he was nothing compared to her. He was her voice of reason in most of the stunts, making her stop and think about whether she could make a leap, what obstacles there could be in her way, and generally if it was a stupid idea. He was also the one who posted the clips online to share with the world. But most of all, he was her confidant.

A noise made her turn, and from behind a large bin a dark figure came running towards her. Adam soon reached her side, breathing heavily. His dark hair was plastered to his face with the early summer heat and the exercise; his green eyes were bright and shining, and they always made Claire smile.

"There's some amazing stuff here," Adam told her between breaths while they walked down the street together.

"You know, you need to exercise more. You're getting a bit out of shape. I know—next time *I'll* hold the camera and *you* can do the amazing, dangerous stunts!" Claire hit him in the stomach lightly and laughed at him.

"No way! You're mental, you are," he said as he held open the door to a coffee bar and waited for her to enter.

"Thank you, kind sir," she said mockingly. They ordered some food and drink, found a booth in the back, and sat down. "So, come on; let's see," Claire demanded, holding out her hand for the camera.

Adam passed it over and watched her face as she reviewed her performance. This was always the best part of the night, just the two of them together, laughing and enjoying each other's company. They would sit and enjoy a meal, talk, and sometimes when things were tough at school or at home, they would vent as well.

The waitress arrived with their food, a grilled sandwich and water for Adam and a large cheeseburger with fries and a large milkshake for Claire. "Where do you put it all, Claire?" He shook his head.

"I dunno! I'm a growing girl," she protested, taking a bite from the burger.

"Growing? Huh! The only growing you are going to be doing from now on is *out* if you keep this up," he said, indicating the food in front of her.

"Who are you, my own personal fun police?"

"You keep eating like this and there will be no more jumps like that last one. I don't know how you do it; it's almost like you're flying." He grinned at her, and she blushed, feeling all fluttery inside.

"Oh my God! Are you blushing? Have to mark this date in the diary. The day I finally made Claire Brown blush."

"Stop it, you dick! I'm not blushing; it is only the exercise making the capillaries in my cheeks flush," Claire said as she put on a posh accent.

"Yeah, right! And pull the other one; it's got bells on!"

"Does it? Can I see?" She ducked under the table jokingly.

"Get up, you fool." He gave her a gentle swipe and pinched one of her chips.

They fell into a companionable silence as they ate their food, Claire occasionally slapping Adam's hand whenever he tried to take one of her fries. They talked of school and the teachers they hated. Claire complained of the girls who were so catty that they needed to be declawed, and Adam sympathised and told her that they would be all clambering to be her friend when she was famous. The conversation turned to talk of their plans for the rest of the weekend.

"Hey, Jordan was talking about going to the skate park. Is that still happening?" Claire asked him, popping the last chip into her mouth.

"Nah; he's been dragged away for the weekend by his olds. But I have something in mind."

"Do tell, please, Mr Ryder; what is this big announcement you have to make?" She held a pretend microphone under his nose and looked very seriously at him until she started to crack up.

"Can't you take anything seriously?" Adam shook his head at her, but the grin that spread across his face betrayed his true feelings.

"Yes, when I need to. Now what is it you have in mind, Adam?" She put her head in her hands and looked at him with a vapid smile on her face.

"I'm going to ignore that for now. Well, you know how you are always looking for a challenge?" She nodded and he went on, "I think I have found a good one. I've been talking to Dad about you and showing him the videos, and he wondered if you would be up for a bit of a game."

"What type of game?" she asked hesitantly, becoming serious. On the occasions that she had met Adam's father, she had not liked him. Marcus Ryder always came across as a bit standoffish and uninterested in whatever his son and his friends were doing, but his eyes had always followed her.

"Well, he's got this new building and it's just about finished. They've just put in a new state-of-the-art alarm system, and he was wondering if we would like to test it out. Dad said we could have full run of the place and he will pay us for each alarm we don't trip. It's so he can see if it needs to be beefed up or not. He wants to make sure he isn't being ripped off." He looked at her and smiled. "Come on, Claire; it'll be cool."

"So what you're saying is, he's going to let us into this building so that we can run around, trying not to get caught on camera or by sensors?"

"Yeah, but no. Sorry, I know that didn't help. No, we have to break into the building first and then try to get to the top floor, where he will be waiting for us with the money." He waited for her reply.

"We have to break in?" she asked, and he nodded his response. "I'm not sure about this, Adam. I've got a bad feeling about it."

"What's to feel bad about? He's giving us permission to break in, and Dad will be waiting for us when we have finished, and he'll pay us money for having fun. There is nothing to worry about." He smiled at her and reached across the table and laid his hand over hers. "It's all legit; I promise."

At that moment a group of their friends joined them noisily at the table, and Claire didn't have a chance to give Adam an answer. She couldn't even say to herself why she was uneasy about the plan; it just didn't sit right with her. While trying to enjoy the rest of the evening, Claire mulled over the problem until it was time to leave.

Adam walked her home—or at least he walked while she jumped, tumbled, flipped, leapt, and scaled objects along the way. At times he would ask her to do a move again so that he could try a different camera angle, or he would suggest adding a twist or two. They kept this up until they finally reached her door.

"You didn't answer me in the café," Adam said while she fumbled with her keys.

"Can I give you an answer tomorrow? I want to sleep on it for now." She found her key and slipped it into the door.

Adam reached up as if to touch her hair and then dropped his hand down again. "Sorry," he apologised, looking slightly embarrassed.

"I promise I'll give you an answer in the morning, Adam. See ya." Claire pushed the door open, waved goodbye, then closed it, leaving him standing on the doorstep. She watched through the frosted glass as his shape moved down the steps and out of sight, then turned to enter the living room.

It was a large, comfortable room with a masculine suite of green leather chairs and a couch with matching darker green cushions. Sitting in his favourite chair was a very long-legged man reading a book. He looked up at her over his glasses as she entered the room and rested the book on his knee.

"Good night?" he asked as he looked at his watch.

"Yes, thanks, and I am in well before curfew. It's not even nine thirty yet." She launched herself onto the couch and put her feet up.

"Claire, how many times have I got to tell you not to throw yourself onto the furniture or put your shoes on it?"

"Yes, Uncle Geoff." She swung her legs and kicked her shoes off onto the rug, then returned her feet to the couch.

Geoff Brown was Claire's guardian and great-uncle. She had come to live with him after a car accident claimed her parents' lives when she was ten. Her parents had named him her godparent and guardian when she was born. She had been a timid girl at that age, and it took a while for her to warm to the uncle she had not seen very much.

"Uncle Geoff, you work for Marcus Ryder, don't you?" she asked as she played with the zip on her jacket.

"Yes, I do some legal work for him. Why do you ask?"

"What sort of company does he run?"

"It's really a bit of this and a bit of that. Everything from developing projects such as buildings to making boxes. Why the sudden interest in Mr Ryder's empire? Are you thinking of trying to wed his son for his inheritance?"

"Oh, God, no; Adam and I are just good mates."

"Methinks the lady doth protest too much," he told her. "Come on, Kid; there is something you want to ask me, so out with it."

For as long as Claire could remember, he had always called her Kid; it never failed to make her feel secure when he did. "It's just...Adam told me his father wants to test a new security system in a building that is just about finished. The idea is to break into this building, make our way up to the top floor, and meet his father up there. He said that Mr Ryder is willing to pay us for every sensor and camera that we don't trip."

"Is that so? I am pleased that you have come to me about it. He hasn't mentioned anything to me; I take it you are a bit hesitant about doing it."

"I am. For a start, breaking in doesn't seem right to me; why not just let us in and take it from there? I wouldn't have a clue how to break in to a place like that."

"I am very glad to hear that, Kid. When do you have to let him know if you will or won't do it?"

"I told Adam that I would let him know tomorrow. We're meeting up at the park after lunch; I have to finish that English assignment for Miss Pollard in the morning," Claire said, making a face. "I swear she just gives us these assignments to torture us."

"Miss Pollard is a very nice woman; you should be happy to have such a caring teacher."

"It's only because she has the hots for you!" She giggled at the face he pulled.

"Let me make a phone call in the morning to check if this is all aboveboard and you can have your answer by the time you leave for the park."

"Thanks, Uncle Geoff." She slid off the couch and bent down to kiss him on the forehead. "I'm going for a shower and then bed. Good night."

"Night, Kid; have a good sleep." He watched her leave the room and picked his book up again, but he did not resume reading. A worried frown creased his face as he considered what Claire had told him.

The following morning Claire was finishing up her assignment, tapping away quickly at her keyboard, when Geoff walked in. He leaned up against the door frame and watched her work for a while. Concentration etched her face as she moved from laptop to paper and back again. It always surprised him how much she could retain from just a glance at a book. When she was younger, shortly after coming to live with him, he had made a game of it as a way of distracting her. He would give her a book and ask her to skim through it, then he would take it back and open it up to a random page and ask her what was on it.

Geoff entered the room and started to straighten up her bed and pick clothes up off the floor. "When are you going to clean this pig sty?"

"Yeah, I'll do it in a minute," Claire told him absently. "Busy now." Geoff sat on the bed and watched her work some more.

When she finally sat back after a single keystroke to print the assignment, she let out a sigh. "Thank God that's over." She turned in her seat and jumped when she saw Geoff sitting there. "When did you come in?"

"You don't remember? I talked to you about cleaning your room."

"Did you? Sorry." She stood and started to gather up her books and papers, pushing them into her backpack. "Was there something you wanted to talk to me about?"

"Yes; you came to me last night and asked me about Marcus Ryder."

"Oh, yeah; you said you would make a phone call to check it out."

"And I have done that. Marcus was a bit cagy, but he confirmed that he had asked Adam if you two would like the challenge. Claire, if you are not comfortable with doing it, then don't. You never have to do anything you don't want to do; please remember that."

Geoff grabbed Claire's hand and pulled her down to sit beside him. "The choices we make today affect our lives in the future. If by doing this you have fun and make a little money on the side, it is all well and good. But if you have reservations of even beginning this, then I say stick to your gut feeling. The choice is yours, Kid."

Claire kissed her uncle on the cheek. "I still haven't made up my mind, but thank you for caring and for always helping me." She hugged him briefly and then stood again. "Now can I please get you to leave so I can get dressed? I can't go out in my pj's."

Geoff did as he was asked, but he turned back just before she shut the door. "Can you at least put your dirty washing out? Your room is starting to stink worse than a teenage boy's." In answer, Claire shut the door in his face.

Within twenty minutes she was walking out the door, calling her good-byes to Geoff and running down the road to meet Adam. Along the way she ducked and dived around people on the footpath, jumping over rubbish bins and generally enjoying herself. She waited at the lights to cross the road to the park and spied Adam sitting on a swing; his head was down, looking at the camera screen in his hands. He looked up, spotted her straight away, and came to meet her as she crossed.

"Hey, Claire! How's it going?" He already had the camera up in her face.

"Will you put that thing away? I'm fine; finally finished that assignment for Pollard this morning. Agh! I hate her. *'So, Miss Brown, when are we going to see that handsome uncle of yours?'*" Claire imitated her teacher and then shuddered at the thought.

"You're free now; let's not think about her. What do you want to do today—leap a tall building in a single bound? Climb up the side of the tallest tower downtown? Or we could break into Dad's new building?"

"About that...yeah, I'm still not sure. I just have this really bad feeling something's going to happen."

"What can happen? It's an empty building, we have permission to be there, and Dad's going to pay us money for doing it. You know how tight he is."

"Yeah, says the guy whose allowance is ten times more than mine!" She laughed.

"Hey, let's at least go look at it. You can make up your mind then." He smiled at her. For some reason she could not see any harm in just looking, and she agreed. "Sweet. You won't be disappointed; I promise."

They walked out of the park and headed downtown. The air was electric with sounds, smells, and sights; their senses were so used to the noise and pollution of the large city, they didn't register any of it. But that afternoon Claire was on edge. A large truck blasted its horn as it sped past them and she jumped at the sound. Adam noticed and laughed at her reaction; she smiled back, trying to make light of the moment, but she felt uneasy.

"There it is," Adam told her as they stopped on a street corner. He pointed at a new and shiny building across the road on the opposite corner. The walls were still white and had none of the grey grime that seemed to cling to its neighbours. The bottom-floor windows were covered up with signs announcing the shops that would soon be moving in.

"It's huge! How many floors is it?" she asked, looking up at its silhouette against the sky, the many panes of glass reflecting the moving clouds that marred the day.

"Dad said there are twenty floors with a penthouse up on top. The top three floors are going to be apartments and the rest are all offices." He looked at her and could see the curiosity starting to affect her. "Do you want to go in for a closer look?"

"It couldn't hurt to just look, I suppose." She glanced both ways and ran across the road. Adam had to dodge a few cars before he caught up with her.

"There's an alley that runs up the side and to the back of the building to a parking garage underneath," he told her. "See, he even told me the best way to get in."

"What about the alarms? Are you sure we'll not get in trouble with the cops?"

"No, we won't. Dad told me that the alarm system is in, but it's not hooked up properly to any monitoring place yet. He has a computer set up in the penthouse that he has hooked into the system, so he can see if we trip the sensors and which cameras pick us up. It's all good."

"Look, Adam, I had Uncle Geoff ring your dad and ask about it. I hope you don't mind."

"He told me this morning. This is going to be some serious fun, Claire. Can you imagine the hits we will get off this one? It will be off the charts!" he said, referring to their internet channel.

His enthusiasm was infectious, and she began to be swayed to his side. Claire put up her hands in surrender. "Okay. All right. I give in. We'll do it. What time is this all supposed to happen?"

Adam started punching the air in his excitement. "Awesome! Claire, you will not regret this; I promise."

"Okay, Adam; calm the hell down!" she said, looking around her to see if anyone was watching.

"Sorry; I guess I am just a bit excited. When does it go down? About eight tonight. He said to stay away until then 'cos there may still be workers inside, and he has to get into place, so he can track our progress." He was talking fast and when he finally ran out of puff, he took a deep breath. "Sorry," he said sheepishly.

"No more coffee for you today," Claire admonished him. "Come on, I'm hungry; I haven't had lunch yet."

Claire dragged him down the street to a fast-food restaurant and pushed him inside when he started protesting about unhealthy food. They spent a good hour in the restaurant making a plan of attack. The rest of the afternoon they spent in a similar way, planning, talking, and generally joking around.

Eight o'clock on the dot found the pair standing at the entrance of the alleyway attached to the building that towered above them. The streets were ablaze with light and bustling with people intent on having a good Saturday night. Neon signs competed with LCD ones, and music spilled out from bars and clubs further up the road. Cars drove up and down looking for nonexistent parking bays, honking their horns at other drivers and pedestrians in frustration. The wind whipped lazily around the buildings, bringing with it the smell of exhaust fumes, overflowing rubbish bins, and the salty hint of the harbour nearby. It was a thriving city, full of life, and it was the city Claire loved.

She had been born in this city, and it was her home. She knew every street, back alley, and abandoned building where a person who was obsessed with free running could get a thrill. Regardless of what she had said to her uncle, this was not the first time she had broken into a building, but this was the first new building and for her it still felt wrong.

Both Adam and Claire watched the shadowy alley. Bins full of discarded construction materials lined one side of it, and a light further in indicated the entrance to the underground car park. They looked at each other and started towards the beacon. Claire was slightly behind Adam when they reached the pool of light, and she stopped before truly entering it. Adam made his way to the security door and turned back to her.

"Are you coming, or are you gonna pike out on me?" He beckoned her over to him.

"Yeah, yeah; calm the farm," she told him with a bit of bite to her voice that was not like her.

"It's okay. Everything is all squared up." He placed a hand on the door and then punched a number sequence on the keypad. They both heard the loud click of the lock opening; Adam pushed on the door, and it gave. He held it open for her, and as she brushed past him, he smiled down at her.

The lights in the corridor flickered on when the door was opened. The buzzing from the fluorescent lighting above seemed loud to her in the sudden quiet as the door shut behind them. She looked about her surroundings and took in the stairs leading up and down, and the white walls, bare except for the green exit signs and lock-release button beside the door. She did not see alarm sensors or cameras up on the ceilings or walls.

"Right; shall we get started?" Adam asked her as he made his way to the steps.

"Can you tell me how we are breaking in if you have got the code for the door in the first place?" She followed him up the steps, always keeping an eye out for the alarm traps he had told her about.

"I told you it was all squared up," Adam said, his voice hushed in the quiet of the building.

"Then why are we whispering?"

"I don't know; you started it." He carried on up the steps till they reached the first floor. He stood at the access door and waited for her to catch up.

"You don't really seem that worried about alarms, Adam; why?"

Just then his phone started to buzz in his pocket, and Adam rushed to answer it. Holding it to his ear, he listened to the person on the other end.

"It's Dad," he told her, holding the phone so his father couldn't hear. "He caught me snooping around earlier with the security guy, trying to get inside information. He wants you to do your tricks to see if the cameras can pick up any dead spots."

"What does he want me to do?" Claire was looking around her at the large staircase. She leaned out over the rail and looked upwards as it snaked around and around, climbing higher.

"He says he can see us now. Try moving about a bit," Adam instructed her.

Claire moved to the wall and placed her back to it. Following it around, she kept an eye on Adam, who shook his head. "He can still see you."

Taking another look at the staircase, Claire climbed the railing and jumped up to the next level. Hauling herself over the metal balustrade with ease, she leaned on it to see his reaction.

"He couldn't see what you were doing," Adam called up to her with a grin.

With that in mind, Claire tried again and again, working her way up as Adam raced up the steps, trying to keep aligned with her, phone still pressed with one hand against an ear and camera in the other to capture her moves.

Working their way up the flights of stairs, Adam was puffing by the time they reached the third floor and Claire stopped so he could catch his breath. She did make a suggestion of taking the elevator, but he waved it away, saying that it was not part of the fun of the evening. So they continued until they reached the tenth floor.

Claire stopped, and as she waited for him to catch up and gain control of his breathing once more, she pushed on the fire door to level ten. Her curiosity had once more got the better of her, and she wanted to have a look at what was behind these doors that they had passed on the way up. She stuck her head through the small gap; the hallway beyond it was lit up with wall lights that sent beams both towards the white ceiling and down to the grey tiled floor.

"What're you doing?" Adam whispered breathlessly in her ear, so close that it made her jump. The phone was back in his pocket, but the camera was still focused on her.

"Just looking. You said that these were going to be apartments?"

"Not on this floor; higher up," he indicated with his finger. "These are offices. You want to have a look? Some of them are just about finished." She nodded, and he pushed past her into the hallway. The door closed with a soft thud behind them, and they made their way down the short corridor.

A large, glossy black door stood out against the stark white of the walls at the end, and Adam pushed it open. The carpet under their feet masked their footsteps. Claire looked about her in wonder at the huge, open space. Along one wall stood glass cubicles all waiting for office furniture to fill them, and the expanse of ceiling-to-floor glass on the opposite opened up to the world outside. Claire walked over to the window and looked down at the street below, watching the cars drive past. She smiled when she started to compare it to her uncle's small, pokey office, which looked like something out of the 1930s.

"Dad said you did a good job; he couldn't see you at all climbing the railings." He was still following her around, filming her every move and reaction. "This is nothing. The best part is the penthouse—wait till you see that one. It's got gold-plated taps in the bathroom," Adam told her, and he looked at his watch. "Are you finished looking around? Just we've got to go meet Dad."

He seemed nervous to Claire, but then again, she knew his relationship with his father was not a very good one and chalked it up to that. She followed him back out of the office, and they had just reached the fire escape door leading back to the stairs when the black door opened behind them and a figure appeared. He was a large man in a dark suit, and he stopped dead in his tracks when he saw them.

"What are you kids doing in here?" he demanded and started to walk towards them.

Startled, Claire quickly reached for the door and pushed hard, sending it crashing against the wall, and sped through the opening with Adam on her heels. As she skipped stairs on her way down, she heard the man yell at her to stop, and a loud bang echoed down the concrete walls, making her ears ring.

"Don't shoot!" yelled someone else from farther up. To Claire's ringing ears, it almost sounded like Marcus, Adam's father.

"Run, Claire; get out of here!" Adam urged her from somewhere behind, and she didn't need telling twice.

Taking the stairs two at a time seemed to be taking too long. Soon she was leaping over the railings to the level below her, making good use of every skill she had learned freerunning. By doing this, she outran not only the men pursuing her, but also Adam. She took a moment to look up and see if she could see him somewhere above her only to see his head being pulled back from the railing by a disembodied hand.

"Run!" he called to her in a desperate voice, and she did.

She kept up the pace until she reached the exit door and saw two men entering as she landed at the foot of the stairs. Without thinking, she turned and headed down the stairs that led to the garage, both of them hot on her heels.

Once inside the dark, open space, she realised she had nowhere to go. She ran as fast as she could to put a bit of distance between her and the men, then hid behind one of the large pillars that held the ceiling up. She waited for the two men to pass her so she could double back and get out of there, but she could not hear them running. Slowly she calmed her breathing, and soon her heartbeat was no longer beating so hard in her ears. From her left came the soft scuff of a shoe on the ground; they were close and had split up.

Claire crouched down where she was and pulled herself into a ball, praying that they would not spot her in the darkness. Her head was on her knees, and she could hear their footfalls come closer and closer. She prayed harder, embracing her legs tightly in her arms, trying to make herself smaller. The seconds dragged on and on as she promised every god she could think of and even her parents that if she got out of there, she would never do such a thing again.

Footsteps farther away from her brought her head up; the two men had passed her. Thanking her luck, she stood up and carefully made her way back to the door. From behind her, she heard one of the men swear.

"She has to be here somewhere; go back and look."

It was at this point that Claire knew she had to get out of there quickly, and she started to run. Unfortunately, her pounding feet gave her away, and she could hear them call out and begin chasing her again. She made the door and slammed it behind her, leaping up the stairs two by two until she reached the entrance foyer and rushed to the door. She slammed her hand on the lock release and yanked the door open. Once outside in the back alley, she did not give the building a second look but continued to run.

If she thought she was home free, she was wrong. From behind her another shout came ripping through the air; she cast a quick look behind her and saw two figures giving chase. Claire did not know or even care if they were the same ones from the garage. She hit the end of the alley and turned right, running down the street and dodging the late-night revellers. She could hear the men behind her pushing people out of their way trying to get to her.

Up ahead and across the road, a building she knew well came into view. It was the old Regent Theatre. It had been abandoned for decades but was under the protection of the Historical Places. That did not stop the likes of Claire and her friends exploring the interior for themselves. She had found a network of walkways above the stage that had thrilled her, not to mention all the other good hiding spots.

Cutting in front of a car that came to a screeching halt with the blast of a horn, Claire crossed the road and made her way to the rear of the theatre. Behind her, more cars could be heard sounding their horns in protest as the two men followed. With a running leap, Claire launched herself at the chain-link fence, making the climb to the top with ease. She pushed off the other side and landed in a crouch, taking the opportunity to look for her pursuers. They were fast, but not as agile as she was, and she felt sure they did not know the place as well as she did.

Back up on her feet once more, she circled the large building until she came to the loading bay. Hauling herself up onto the large platform, she ran to the huge double doors that once accepted magnificent scenery for performances gone by. A smaller door was cut into the left-hand side, and she pulled on the handle. It opened easily with a creak that made her wince, and she slipped inside. Claire stood in the darkness, making her way unerringly to her right toward the back of the stage.

At first, the building seemed to be in total darkness, but as her eyes adjusted she could see small shafts of light coming through the walls from the streetlights outside. The building was crumbling and in a bad state of repair, but it was quiet except for the soft cooing of the pigeons above that now made this once magnificent theatre home. Claire came out onto the stage and made her way down the side steps to the right. She had already decided to hide in the many rows of rotting seating that still remained in the main auditorium; the boxes and the higher balconies had all been stripped bare years ago. She had considered hiding in the orchestra pit, but she knew what was down there.

Claire chose a row and slipped into it on her hands and knees with time to spare. A light shone out over the auditorium, and two voices were calling to each other. She did not want to risk looking up and made herself small again, trying with all her might to squeeze under the seat at her back.

"I swear she came in here," one said with a very deep, booming voice.

"I know; I saw, too," another answered, softer and gentler.

There was silence as the light moved around the stage and over the seats, its beam visible with the dust motes that it caught.

"You had better call him. Mr Ryder is not going to be happy about this."

"You're telling me; we are going to be in some shit for letting her get away," said Deep Voice.

"You might as well come out, girl. We know you are in there, and there are men all around the building now waiting for you," the other called out. Claire stayed where she was. If she could just hold out, maybe she could get away.

"Hey, Tony, Mr Ryder is sending someone. He said that this guy can find a needle in a haystack," Deep Voice called.

"Good luck to him. Keep your eyes peeled; we don't want her getting away again," Tony told his companion.

The minutes ticked by, but Claire didn't dare move even an inch to look at her watch. She wondered what had happened to Adam and why Mr Ryder and his men had been there with guns. Questions went around and around in her head— questions she had no answers to, but when she got hold of Adam again, she was going to beat them out of him. She could feel herself start to shake with the cold that was seeping in under her clothing, and she hugged herself tighter.

The theatre fell quiet, and she could hear the wind whistling through the holes in the roof. Wings flapped somewhere above, and she wondered if one of the men had risked the walkways that crossed above the stage and auditorium. She risked a peek upwards, but it was lost in the darkness, so she remained as still as possible.

She could hear more footsteps coming from the stage area. Some were slow and measured, but others were hurried.

"She is out there somewhere," Tony spoke to the newcomer, and in her mind she imagined him pointing out to the auditorium. A softer voice replied, but it was hard for Claire to pick out; she did not even know if it was a man or a woman. She tried to make herself smaller and creep closer to the chairs.

Going up both aisles, they threaded their way through the block of seats Claire was hiding in; she could hear their footsteps. The torchlights shone up and down the rows of seats, and she prayed they would not see her. Her heart was thumping in her ears and her mouth had gone dry.

The footsteps had stopped. Claire tried to swallow; she had never known fear like this, not even when she had been told her parents had died and she wondered what was going to happen to her. Thoughts of her Uncle Geoff came into her head, and she wished she were home with him. It was at that moment she became aware of someone standing over her. When she pried her eyes open and took a look, a dark figure loomed large, and she almost gave a cry of alarm.

The figure bent down, and a beam of light caught his features; Claire did not know what to make of what she saw. It was her uncle. He held out his hand to her, telling her to get up. She froze for a moment, her head spinning as she tried to make sense of it.

"Uncle Geoff?" Claire asked in a soft and confused voice.

"Come on, Kid; we don't have all night." He reached down and pulled her up into a standing position.

"We were told you were to take her to Mr Ryder immediately, Mr Brown," Deep Voice said, shining his light on the girl.

"I am aware of that," Geoff told him curtly. Then to Claire in a softer voice, he said, "I'm sorry, Kid."

Awakenings available May 2022
PREORDER NOW FROM ALL MAJOR
BOOKSELLERS

Loraine Conn grew up on the outskirts of Upper Hutt, New Zealand. Her backyard encompassed the surrounding farmland, river, hills, and mountains which she wandered with her brothers and fed her imagination. After discovering a love for writing in English class at the age of eight, she continued to write in secret. It was not until much later in life that Loraine turned what she thought was a hobby, and something fun to do, into her first completed novel. Now married, Loraine moved from New Zealand to Perth, Western Australia in 2008, and became a stay-at-home mum. While caring for her family and after battling breast cancer, a series was born from a kernel of a dream. Loraine has now published the seven book fantasy series, The One True Child Series, and Realm of Dragons, Fight for the Crown. Both the series and book have been released with the American based indie publishing company Between the Lines Publishing, under their Liminal Books branch, using the pen name L.C. Conn. She continues her career with many more stories waiting in the wings to be released, and even more ideas to be written.

CONNECT WITH L.C. CONN

Email: raindropc1970@gmail.com

Facebook: http://www.facebook.com/LCConn

Twitter: https://twitter.com/ConnLoraine

Instagram: https//www.instagram.com/l.c.conn

Web Page: https//lcconnwriter.wordpress.com/

9 781950 502783